BEYOND RUBIES

BEVERLEY OAKLEY

AUTHOR'S NOTE

Beyond Rubies is Book#4 in the *Daughters of Sin* series. It introduces Lord Partington's younger illegitimate daughter, Kitty, and follows the dastardly doings of Kitty's nobly-born half-sister Araminta, and the noble pursuits of her natural born sister, Lissa, the heroine in Book #3, **The Mysterious Governess.**

Each of the four sisters in the series—two nobly born and two ille-gitimate—have quite different reasons for pursuing villainous Lord Debenham, a suspected traitor to his country.

When their very different worlds collide, the consequences become the talk of the London gossip sheets and a greater rivalry ensues between the sisters to restore or bolster their respective repu-tations.

The first three books in the *Daughters of Sin* series can be read as stand-alone stories but **Beyond Rubies** should, ideally, be read after **The Mysterious Governess (Book 3)** and before the concluding book #5, **Lady Unveiled: the Cuckold's Conspiracy** which reveals the consequences of each sister's actions and decisions throughout the series and culminates in divine justice for all.

I hope you enjoy the trials and tribulations of Lord Partington's very differently deserving daughters in this Regency-era *'Dynasty'* that was so fun to write!

Beverley Oakley

PRAISE FOR THE DAUGHTERS OF SIN SERIES

"…lies, misdeeds, treachery, and romance. What an impressive story! Ms. Oakley has a unique way of telling her stories, bringing unknown heroes/ heroines into the spotlight, as they navigate a world of espionage, and intrigue, all while trying to survive and find their HEA. Magnificent and mesmerizing!" ~ **Amazon reader**

"Full of secrets, murders, intrigues and you feel you know the characters and want to strangle some of them, especially Araminta!!! I have since read all in the series and can't wait for Book 5… This is a series I will read again and again." ~ **Amazon reader**

Below is the order of the books:

PROLOGUE

"*A*nd he vil be as reech and handsome as a preence vis ink-black hair! His eyes vil smolder vis passion like...varm trea-cle, his mouth vil be soft as butter yet firm as zee mouth of zee greatest lover in zee vorld!"

Kitty stretched out the palm of her hand even wider. *Passionate, yet kind?* At last, Kitty was being told what she'd wanted to know for as long as she could remember—how her future would unfold.

"But how will I know him?" she whispered, her eyes watering from the smoke of the cheap tallow candle and strange, cloying perfume of the gypsy fortune-teller hunched over the table in the cramped, oddly-smelling caravan.

"How vil you know him?" The noisy revelry of St Bartholomew's fair drifted through a chink in the dirty curtains as the gypsy brushed back a hank of oily black hair and made a moue of her brightly-painted mouth. "You have much fire and energy, girl." She puffed out her bosom. "You vil know him by the surge of fire and energy in your breast."

Kitty nodded slowly. The gypsy woman seemed to understand what she was talking about. She'd identified Kitty and Lissa, not just as sisters, but had differentiated their personalities, despite Lissa declining the palm reading because she'd promised their mother she'd return home before dusk.

Lissa, according to the gypsy, was an obedient creature, while Kitty was drawn to a life full of wonder and adventure. Kitty couldn't get over just how on the money that had been.

"But what if I feel that…that special feeling in a crowd of people and I don't recognize who, exactly, is causing it?"

"Ppphtt!"

Kitty stared at the droplets on the scratched table surface resulting from the gypsy's explosive sound of derision. She wasn't quite sure how to respond.

"How old you are, girl?

"Almost sixteen."

"A leetle girl, to be sure," the gypsy sneered as she stabbed a grubby finger in Kitty's face. "When you become woman, you feel zees thing here." She poked Kitty in the chest. "Ees no doubt in your heart what you feel when you grown woman. Understand?" She stood up to the sound of jangling metal beads and coins as she shook out her skirts and tossed her scarf about her head.

"Will he marry me?" Kitty rose and hurried after the gypsy. It was the question she'd been angling to ask throughout the entire interview. In fact, it was the main reason she'd paid to have her palm read for she needed to be reassured that she would not suffer her mother's fate—jilted at the altar then suffering the shame and ignominy of living in sin for the next twenty years. That's what Kitty's father had done to her poor mother though by the time he'd said 'I do' to the suitably chosen earl's daughter, he'd already regretted it.

"Yes, yes, he will marry you."

"Are you sure?"

The gypsy sent Kitty an impatient look over her shoulder as she reached for the heavy curtain. The sound of restless foot shuffling— her next customer—could be heard on the caravan steps.

"I'm sure."

"What sort of man will he be?"

"Reech, reech nobleman."

"So I have only this to go by?" Kitty tapped her heart and tried not to let her disappointment show. The gypsy seemed a trifle oversensitive. "There's no other way I can properly identify him? Only by what I feel when I meet a rich nobleman with dark hair and eyes?"

The gypsy turned and made a slicing motion through the air with her hand. "And zee scar beneath his right eye from a brave and daring piece of swordplay," she muttered. Hesitating as she gripped the curtain, she added in a more considered tone, "My girl, I should charge you more but I tell you zis for free. You vil be great actress. Like famous and beautiful actress what became Lady Emma Hamilton you vil marry nobleman. Now, next! Come in, come in! You very handsome boy. You have great life, already, I can tell. Come and let me tell your fortune."

Kitty left with mixed feelings. She was thrilled to learn her destiny included becoming a famous actress, though her family had made it clear such an occupation was out of the question. She was also thrilled that true love would lead to marriage. That was what she wanted, more than anything.

She just wished she had a little more information to help guide her.

CHAPTER 1

hree years later.

Kitty enjoyed breaking the rules. Often she'd creep into the grounds of The Grange, dressed as a servant girl or peasant, to look through windows and admire the beautiful gowns worn by its nobly-born and far more fortunate occupants—her half-sisters. Sometimes she overheard snippets of gossip, which she relayed to her mother who pretended she wasn't interested, although she never stopped Kitty from describing every detail. With the flamboyance of the true artiste, Kitty knew how to create just the right drama and color to transfix her audience.

The days were growing colder and shorter, now, so Kitty's free and easy ramblings would soon be coming to a close. Lissa had gone to London to be a governess after her dearly-held plans for running a village school had come to nothing. Meanwhile, Kitty was left at home to help her mother who needed her more than ever with yet another baby to look after—another bastard, as she was used to hearing the villagers whisper in her hearing.

And although it might highlight the drudgery of her own life, Kitty took great pleasure in keeping abreast of the antics of the young ladies at the Grange—beautiful Miss Araminta and her plain but much nicer sister, Hettty.

The previous season, both girls had been vying for the same man, their bacon-brained cousin Edgar. Araminta had wanted to marry him because he was her father's heir and she'd always been determined to be mistress of The Grange. Hetty, however, had simply always loved her cousin whom everyone had believed had died in battle but who had appeared unexpectedly one night.

Kitty was as adept at ferreting out gossip as she was at adopting a persona as different as possible from plain Miss Kitty Hazlett, the illegitimate village girl.

Now, as Kitty navigated the pathway in the fast gathering dusk, she realised with growing concern that she should have been at home long since. Her mother would no doubt greet her at the door with a clip over the ear.

She hastened her footsteps, careful not to slip on the damp, leafy laneway, then squealed as a pheasant burst clumsily out of the bushes in front of her. Kitty was not born for the country. No, give her the gaiety of London any day. And yet, the tragedy was that she was destined to molder away in this forgotten corner of England, with no new clothes except her more fortunately-born half-sister's castoffs which her father had purloined, though he always protested that wasn't the case. Kitty had, however, seen with her own eyes the lavish creations, like fur-trimmed pelisses, satins and crepes, opera gowns and morning gowns, the young Misses Partington took for granted. Several dressmakers had toiled for weeks to ensure Miss Araminta shone for her second season out.

Well, if last season's attire was not good enough for Miss Araminta, Kitty was happy enough to take advantage of beautiful designs and fabrics, though Lissa had turned her nose up at their father's offerings. A governess, she maintained, needed serviceable gowns in drab, dreary colors. It was as if she wanted to highlight her lowly status, Kitty thought, whereas Kitty wanted to shine.

She was disappointed she'd never be given the opportunity to wear something in the first stare. Why should her father favor so greatly the two legitimate daughters born to the wife he did not love, while those he'd so carelessly foisted on the solicitor's daughter he'd abandoned at the altar in order to please his parents, should get nothing but the castoffs?

But Kitty was strategic. She'd shown her father the gratitude he'd expected, then stowed the lovely garments in her wardrobe, ready for the moment she'd run away from home and burst onto the London stage.

On this particular evening, Kitty was returning from a visit to old Widow Nuffley to whom she'd fed a bowl of her mother's famous calf's-foot jelly. Her return home now included a detour through the woods, although she knew she had no time to venture across the emerald-green stretch of lawn to peer through the windows of her father's grand old manor house, The Grange.

She was therefore about to take the most direct route home when she heard voices issuing from a copse of trees a few yards away.

"And so it is the scandal of all London town," she heard her father say with great energy. "Araminta has defied me and brought ridicule on herself and her family. As if it were not bad enough that her sister should elope—*elope*—with that traitor and rascal Sir Aubrey. Now Araminta, who has always harbored such lofty marital ambitions has done the very same, within twenty-four hours of accepting Mr. Rockerick Woking's proposal."

"Mr. Roderick Woking? That chinless, spineless cipher of his uncle Lord Debenham? I can scarcely believe it," came the answer.

Kitty stared, panic-stricken, at the curving path in front of her. Her father's voice was coming closer, and she had nowhere to run, for the path behind her was blocked by a large fallen tree trunk too difficult to negotiate in a hurry. She'd be discovered before she'd managed to clamber over it. Frantically she whipped her head around, looking for escape. But the only place was...up.

Tucking her skirts out of the way, she found a foothold on the lowest tree branch beside the path and hoisted herself into the fork of the tree. She wasn't used to climbing trees, caring too much for her clothes and any unsightly scratches that might result, but desperate times called for desperate measures.

By the time she'd climbed out of sight into the oak's dense foliage, she thought she was safe. Her father and the man in whose company he walked would turn back once they reached the fallen log.

To her dismay, they settled themselves upon it to continue their conversation.

"I will admit," came her father's voice, "that I am surprised at Araminta. I thought I knew my daughter better than that."

The other man spoke in laconic tones. "I cautioned her strenuously against courting Lord Debenham's interest, and she evinced a sincere abomination of the villainous viscount, as he is known. That she has eloped with him defies all I know of her."

"And *that* is saying something." Her father sounded highly cynical. "I was aware of the way she threw herself at you, and would that you had found her to your liking, Stephen, it would have been entirely to my satisfaction. Yet you are still my heir, and despite everything, I am glad of it. I would prefer to hand the reins to a fellow such as yourself, whom I have the measure of, than a knucklehead like Edgar, or worse, an infant."

Aha, so her father was talking to his heir, Stephen Cranborne, the young man who had been summoned from obscurity the previous season to take up the reins after it was believed that Lord Partington's nephew, bacon-brained Edgar, had been killed. The young man whom everybody had expected would marry Araminta. Araminta, though, had switched her interest from Stephen to Edgar in the brief time before he had been Lord Partington's prospective heir.

There was a long pause, and from her perch, Kitty watched with interest as Cousin Stephen colored up in the face of her father's fierce stare. At least, fierce was how Kitty interpreted it since she'd often been on the receiving end of it. Her father seemed to relax upon a sigh. "One's children are so wearying."

Kitty drew herself up in indignation. It was all very well for her father to say such a thing when he was responsible for them all. Responsible for making her mother so unhappy for not marrying her as he'd promised, and condemning Lissa and herself and Ned and the new baby to living half-lives—not accepted by the society to which Kitty longed to be a part; not accepted by the villagers who dropped their eyes when she passed as if she did not exist. Or worse, who whispered the word 'bastard' in her hearing.

Well, her father might have spent many nights in her mother's small cottage by the bridge. Kitty suspected this must mean his wife, Lady Partington, was even more unhappy than Kitty's mother though she'd heard whispers that suggested Lady Partington had found other avenues to console herself. A lover? Kitty had only a vague idea of what having a lover entailed beyond kissing and was surprised that a matron of Lady Partington's age would indulge in such behavior.

Most of what Kitty had learned about such matters came from Millie, the kitchenmaid, who had a very romantic turn of mind though she buttoned her lips at some of the questions Kitty asked.

Asking Lissa was pointless. Her older sister refused to indulge in such talk. Lissa was quite the proper miss, but Kitty had been dying to find out for months now what it was they'd seen when she and Lissa had been walking home one evening and, fearing a sick cow needed assistance in their neighbor's cowshed due to the low moaning sounds, had rushed in to find the milkmaid lying underneath the baker's boy whose breeches were around his ankles. Lissa had dragged her younger sister away and refused to say a word about it, other than that if she ever caught Kitty in such a situation or heard she'd done anything like it, she'd have nothing more to do with her.

When Kitty had taken up the matter with Millie, she'd been told that she would understand when she was visited by the romantic stirrings of her body.

So Kitty remained essentially ignorant, and had to come to her own conclusions as to how kissing while pressing one's body against another might be a sin, and that if only Lord Partington and her mother hadn't done it, then she, Lissa, Ned, and the new baby, would not be bastards.

Stephen Cranborne, Lord Partington's handsome heir, was speaking now. "I'm sorry, my Lord, but you must know that my concerns are greater than they were when I counseled Araminta against furthering her unwise acquaintanceship with Lord Debenham, and, in fact, the reason I suggested this walk was to avoid any possibility of being overheard by the servants."

Kitty pricked up her ears. At this stage of life, she regarded herself as a dispossessed child with no future prospects other than the unremitting hard work that was already fast ruining her soft hands; but now her father was talking scandal with his heir and Kitty needed to arm herself with every bit of possible information that might give her an edge so that her future was not one of complete drudgery. She wasn't sure exactly how she was going to achieve the lofty heights the gypsy had foretold three years before but she felt she was on the precipice of change, though she'd not breathed a word to anyone, not even Lissa. Soon she would leave this sleepy village where everyone looked down at her, and make her name in the world.

The men were now talking of the scandal that had consumed those above and below stairs for the past few months: the "Castlereagh Affair" involving the two dangerous gentlemen—Lord Debenham and Sir Aubrey Banks—whom Araminta and Hetty had now married, respectively.

"As you know, it's long been believed Sir Aubrey was the key player in the failed attempt on Lord Castlereagh's life, but we have credible information that in fact Debenham attempted to make Sir Aubrey his scapegoat." Kitty heard the tremor in her father's voice as he added, "My own daughter has married a suspected traitor."

"I'm sorry, my Lord." Stephen Cranborne sounded truly regretful. "Although I must be careful what information I impart, I can tell you this: Debenham is being watched, together with a number of his close companions, Lord Silverton, Lord Smythe, and a lowly shoemaker known as Buzby."

"And how am I to receive Debenham? With suspicion or with the due regard it is only right I show my new son-in-law?" Kitty's father clicked his tongue, and she craned her neck through the leaves in an attempt to glimpse his face. How exciting to be witnessing this moment.

"We have no evidence against Debenham at this stage. At least that will make your task easier," Stephen Cranborne said. "And the three men under suspicion—Debenham, Smythe and Buzby—deny knowing one another. Nevertheless, a skilful sketcher in our employ has provided irrefutable evidence of a meeting between the three several weeks ago."

"Indeed? And they could be recognized?"

"The artist rendered likenesses that are truly remarkable." Cousin Stephen—for if he was Araminta and Hetty's cousin, he was also Kitty's—exhaled on a sigh. "I sympathise with your dilemma, my Lord. The fact Araminta is now married to Lord Debenham is a grave matter indeed."

Kitty heard her father groan, and peeked through the branches once more. She wanted very much to see Cousin Stephen up close. He was, she thought, very handsome, and she'd also heard he was engaged in a secret liaison. A very unsuitable and dangerous liaison, it was rumored, though Kitty did not know with whom.

Leaning perilously low to improve her view, Kitty was gratified by what she saw. Up close, he was even more handsome than she'd thought. His thick, dark-blond hair framed a striking face with a strong nose and sensitive mouth. Kitty always took an extra interest in men's mouths. It was not something they were usually commended for. Square jaws and well-built physiques—which Cousin Stephen also had—yes, but the descriptions Kitty most often heard never mentioned mouths. Since Kitty had secretly observed the kiss between the milkmaid and her lover, and heard the woman remark upon the man's ability to do such "magic" with his mouth, she'd been fascinated. The man she would take as her husband must have a mouth that could do magic, too.

Gripping the branch even more tightly in order to risk an even closer look, Kitty had to dislodge herself slightly from the safety of her perch. But to observe better the man at whom Araminta had thrown herself and who would one day succeed her father at The Grange, was too much to resist.

Unfortunately, so was the tree branch's ability to hold her weight.

With an earsplitting noise, the branch gave way, disgorging Kitty into the air and sending her tumbling into a heap onto the soft earth right at the feet of her father and Cousin Stephen.

"Dear God, what is this!" Her father's horror rather matched Kitty's own as she straightened, dusting down her dirt-soiled skirts.

"I'm sorry, Papa!" She knew he'd not forgive her easily. "I know I'm forbidden to come onto the grounds, and that you're justifiably angry but I was only going for a walk and then I felt I had to hide when I heard your voice."

His expression was apoplectic. For a moment, he seemed lost for words until he thundered, "How dare you eavesdrop on your elders' conversations? You will be severely punished for this. You understand?"

Kitty felt the tears threaten. She was always so bold in her own imaginings, and yet her father could reduce her to a trembling wreck. He held absolute sway in the small household by the village bridge where he was like a towering colossus, yet here, master of these magnificent grounds, he was like a demi-god.

Cousin Stephen, beside him, seemed more curious than outraged. He had a kind face, she decided. She was definitely bolstered by the fact that he seemed far less concerned by having a trespassing eavesdropper tumble into his midst than her father.

"You will return home this instant, and you will not be allowed outside for a week unless it's to do the errands demanded of you, do you understand?" Her father, still purple with rage, spoke with difficulty. An image of Hetty and Araminta, his natural-born, cosseted daughters, both of whom had scandalized society and brought shame upon the family by eloping with dangerous, unsuitable men, appeared before Kitty. They were much the same age as she, and yet they did not suffer the myriad ignominies Kitty did every day. They had fine clothes paid for by their father, while Kitty got their castoffs. They got to dance the night away at London's grand balls and rub shoulders with dukes and duchesses every night of the week, while Kitty rubbed her mother's chilblains.

All the painful indignities of her eighteen years rose up to give her the courage to say, "I will not, Papa, for I am going to London. Yes, I'm going to London to become an actress, and even if you lock me in my room for a week you cannot keep me there forever. I am weary of this life where I'm nothing, looked down upon by all the villagers. I won't do it any longer! When you next hear of me, it shall be as the celebrated actress, Kitty La Bijou, and all London will be talking of me as the most beautiful, talented woman in the country. Yes, you might be scandalized, but at least I will be appreciated by *somebody*."

CHAPTER 2

wo months later

Kitty glanced up at the flaking wooden door in the laneway and then down at her fashionable fuller skirts—well, they were fashionable last year, and she was not, after all, trying to compete with any society miss but, rather, with the other hopeful actresses who sought to land the lead role in this production of *Romeo and Juliet*. Unlike her mother or Lissa, Kitty wasn't good with a needle and thread, otherwise she'd have worked magic and turned her gown into the height of fashion.

She'd been delighted when Lissa had proudly spurned it with the lofty claim that serviceable serge and cotton would do well enough for her while she was a governess in the Lamont household; proving to the world that she was a more worthwhile creature than the cosseted Araminta and Hetty, and, by inference, living by a higher moral code than Kitty. At least, that's how Kitty interpreted it.

Kitty, by contrast, was more than happy to wear Araminta's castoffs which would serve her well in the theater where she was confident she'd meet her heart's desire—the gentleman whom she'd know with the exchange of a single smoldering, impassioned look.

This scion of the nobility would pluck her from her lowly status, recognize her worth, brand her his, and ultimately make her his wife. It had all been prophesied, and Kitty was looking forward to lording her newfound status over her half-sister, Miss Araminta Partington, whom she was determined would not only notice her, but desire above all to swap places.

For now, Araminta did not even know Kitty existed.

But she soon would.

And when Miss Kitty La Bijou was a name on everyone's lips, she'd visit Lissa, who'd been so unhappy in her London job, and who'd loathed lazy Mrs. Lamont who believed herself so much grander than she was, and spoiled Miss Maria Lamont, who was embarking upon her first season with all the airs of a duchess, and offer to take her sister away from her awful life. Kitty, for once, would be her older sister's savior.

The slight difficulty was that although Kitty was now in London, she had no idea how to find Lissa. Her sister had unexpectedly left the Lamont household to live with a dressmaker, where she continued doing her sketches, from what Kitty could gather, though how she could keep body and soul together in such employment was a mystery.

And Lissa had left no forwarding address.

Not that Kitty intended staying with Lissa. She'd soon be in her own grand lodgings.

At least, she hoped that would be the case. Several months earlier, a troupe of actors had been performing *The Taming of the Shrew* in their little village before it went to the next county and Kitty had made herself known to the director, Mr. Lazarus. He'd looked her up and down in a very appraising way, then invited her to sit down and offered her biscuits and Madeira, something she'd never tried before and which made her feel quite lightheaded, and at the end of a very heartening conversation, he'd given her a very stylish London address where she could find lodging when she came to London to audition after his company returned to Covent Garden. Kitty knew the address must be stylish because Mr. Lazarus was a very smart gentleman, if a touch flamboyant with his green felt hat and loudly-patterned waist-coat. But he was the man in charge, and he decided who would act in his plays and which actresses would take a lead role, their ticket to fame and glory. So when he smiled his very white smile, and smoothed his sideburns in evident satisfaction at the well-put-together package Kitty had tried to present to him, she knew she'd surmounted the first obstacle.

Of course, her plan to become an actress in London was a huge secret she'd had to keep from her mother. She'd worked very hard at home, helping with the baby and household chores since she'd made up her mind, hoping to compensate in some small measure for the subsequent loss of her services, which her mother could not know about beforehand.

Kitty and her mother were not close, and the baby was docile. Besides, why should Lissa be allowed to escape to a life far more exciting than village life—even if she hated being a governess—while Kitty, only a year younger and who dreamed of the excitement of the metropolis, was denied such opportunities?

Now, as Kitty waited on the doorstep of this strange London abode for the response to her knock she felt a twinge of uneasiness, for the neighborhood didn't look respectable at all; though just because one was poor didn't mean one wasn't respectable, she knew that very well.

From behind the door, came a shuffling and a loud and repeated clearing of the throat before a sharp nose emerged between the small crack that opened and a reedy voice demanded, "What's yer bizness for I ain't in the market for moldy taties, last week's fish or anythin' else, missie?"

Surprised, Kitty replied, "Mr. Lazarus gave me your address, ma'am. I beg your pardon, but I thought you were expecting me."

"Ah, Miss La Bijou, is it? Why, I bin expectin' yer two days 'n more. Come in, lovey. Come in."

The warmth of her welcome made up for the former sharpness, and gratefully Kitty entered the dim, narrow passage along which she was led. She was only able to see the woman properly when they entered a tiny parlor where a sliver of light penetrated the dirty windows.

Crossing her arms upon her ample breasts, the woman turned to inspect her from the rag rug in the center of the room. "My but ain't yer a beauty? The eye o' Mr. Lazarus is a discernin' 'un 'n the toast o' London is what 'e predicted yer'd be. Ain't that the truth?"

Kitty's glow of pleasure helped to dissipate, slightly, the distaste she felt at the evidence of neglect. Mrs. Mobbs was clearly not a particularly assiduous housekeeper, for dust coated the windowsills and spider webs festooned the low ceiling between the beams. Kitty's mother was fastidious about such matters, which brought a pang for what she'd done. Her mother would be frantic with worry. Kitty only hoped the letter she'd left would be sufficiently reassuring. She'd told her she was going to visit Lissa, who would look after her and introduce her to some respectable families where she might find some work, and she'd promised to send home a portion of her wages every month.

"So dearie, Mr. Lazarus is very pleased indeed that yer 'ave 'onored 'im wiv yer desire ter grace 'is illustrious theater wiv yer talent 'n beauty." Mrs. Mobbs sat on a dusty chair by the unlit fire and indicated a rickety piece of furniture beside her. As Kitty lowered herself gingerly, Mrs. Mobbs leaned across and picked up her hand. This made Kitty highly uncomfortable, but not wishing to offend, as she presumed this was how London people showed their hospitality, she allowed the woman to stroke her fingers. Mrs. Mobbs looked her up and down. "Well-nourished yer are, wiv a very sought-after beauty, indeed," she said approvingly, replacing Kitty's hand in her lap. "Mr. Lazarus ain't keen on these half-starved waifs who faint on stage. But 'e's seen yer fer 'imself 'n don't need me ter do 'is assessin' fer 'im, ain't that so?"

Kitty nodded, not sure how to respond.

"So yer've left yer family wiv their blessin' no doubt, 'n now yer goin' ter take all London by storm? That's the idea, eh, dearie?"

Kitty blushed. "I ran away," she admitted. The walls were very thin, and she hated the idea of her shame being transmitted to the neighbors whom she could hear arguing in the adjoining dwelling.

"Ran away, did yer?" To Kitty's surprise, Mrs. Mobbs sounded approving. "That shows courage. Yes, a love o' adventure makes yer jest right fer the stage. Me uvver young miss stayin' wiv me 'ere 'asn't quite yer spark o' adventure. She's destined fer uvver work. I'll call 'er now so yer can meet the lass. A real country miss, yer'll find. Can 'ardly make out a word she says, but she'll learn London ways soon enough. Dorcas! Come 'n join us, dearie. I've found a friend fer yer."

Within a moment or two, a buxom brown-haired lass with a round, rosy-cheeked face and a welcoming smile entered the room and, after bobbing a curtsey, took a seat on a faded green and gold settee by the window.

"I arrived in London on the stage early this mornin' an' Mrs. Mobbs 'as bin ever so kind," she told Kitty in her soft Welsh accent when their landlady encouraged her to give an account of her travels and the reason she'd come to London. "I'm the seventh girl in a family o' fourteen, 'n I came ter the city ter find work as a servant. The vicar in me village wrote me a character. I *were* goin' ter stay wiv Mrs. Fairfax, a good woman 'the vicar's wife knew who lived in the big town nearby, but then on top o' the stagecoach, I met a woman, ever so kindly she was, 'n she told me she knew jest the place I could find work, where they'd pay me good wages 'n feed me good 'n proper, so I changed me mind 'n came 'ere ter Mrs. Mobbs where I can rest, 'n where I'm ter wait 'til my new employer comes ter fetch me. The woman I met on the coach said she'd see me note were delivered ter Mrs. Fairfax so the good woman don't worry. I bin ever so fortunate." Dorcas beamed. "Yer goin' ter be an actress, are yer, Miss Hazlett?"

"We don't need airs here. It's Kitty 'n Dorcas, fer yer lasses are already great friends, I can see. And yer can stay up late as a treat, 'n I'll ask nuthin of yer 'cept ter 'elp tidy away after we've 'ad our victuals. The sun is low, and yer'll need ter rest 'n look yer best fer the mornin' when Mr. Lazarus 'n Mrs. Montgomery come ter look yer both over fer ter employ yer." She leaned back with a smile of satisfaction. "What a fine, comely pair of misses yer both are. A fine day indeed fer Mrs. Mobbs. But now, answer Dorcas's question, Kitty. Tell 'er yer grand plans. My, my, but I think Mr. Lazarus will indeed give yer the role o' leadin' lady. With yer fine bright hair yer'll steal the performance. 'N I reckon I'll jest be there meself on openin' night."

A great sense of belonging surged through Kitty. It had been a long time since she'd felt so happy and among people who understood her aspirations. "I know I can be a fine actress. Papa disapproved when my sister and brother and I liked to put on our Christmas performances. He was afraid it would give us ideas, but it's impossible to turn off the wanting if something is so important here." She tapped her chest as excitement bubbled up inside her. Tomorrow she'd see Mr. Lazarus again. She'd gained the distinct impression he'd been impressed by her rendition of Desdemona when he'd asked her to give him a short display of her talent. Now that he was returning from touring the provinces and was to be auditioning for his new play at Covent Garden, Kitty felt her timing was auspicious indeed.

Daringly, she whispered, "I'm going to be London's most famous actress, you wait and see. Miss Kitty La Bijou will be a name on everyone's lips by the end of the season."

"Ah now, a girlie with ambition. Reminds me o' meself when I were a young 'un," murmured Mrs. Mobbs, dabbing at her eyes with a grubby piece of linen. "Jest yer remember old Mrs. Mobbs when London's fine gennulmen can't get enough of yer, mind?"

Kitty lowered her eyes. She wasn't used to compliments. "I shan't be courting the attention of London's fine gentlemen. That's not why I want to be an actress," she protested. "I want everyone to watch me and believe I am Desdemona, or Juliet or Portia. I want them to weep and laugh. I want to entertain them, and I want them to think I am *good*. Everyone else in my family has always been praised for being good, or at least good at something. Now is my chance to make them proud, even if they disapprove of me treading the boards. I can still be a fine actress and a woman of virtue, can't I, Mrs. Mobbs?"

"Course yer can!" Dorcas interrupted, and Kitty was too busy smiling back at her that she didn't think to look at Mrs. Mobbs.

Despite the chance to stay up late, both girls were exhausted, and the moment they'd finished eating a satisfying dinner of chops, they collapsed into the bed in the 'guest' room which Mrs. Mobbs said she always made sure she had ready for girls just like themselves.

After a deep sleep, Kitty and Dorcas were woken by Mrs. Mobbs who tapped on the door, before sailing in with a pot of hot chocolate. Dorcas was wide-eyed at such luxury.

"I neva thought I could imagine 'ow a fine lady lived in 'em grand 'ouses with all them servants ter dress 'em in their fancy laces, but now I can," she confided to Kitty when Mrs. Mobbs had gone, and they both sat propped up against pillows sipping from chipped teacups. "Though from t'morra, I'll be back ter doin' the servin' again. Oh, but I do 'ope I can get a job some day as a lady's maid. Course I got ter start at the bottom, I know that, but one day." She raised her face to the low, soot-stained ceiling while a beatific smile lit up her face, and Kitty thought what an artless and appealing young girl she was.

"Well, when I am a fine actress who needs help being dressed in my laces, ermine-trimmed capes, and ballgowns, I shall come looking for you, Dorcas," she promised. "So do make sure and let me know where you're employed."

Another knock on the door heralded Mrs. Mobbs once again, who now began chivvying them to get themselves ready as Mrs. Montgomery would be arriving shortly. She seemed flustered.

"It ain't her usual style to be 'bout at sparrows but there yer are, there's no accountin' fer any old body, is there now?" She pulled back the covers then clapped her hands, saying to Dorcas, "'Ere's a jug o' water for washin' an mind yer put yer best foot forward. Yer want ter impress the good lady, now don't yer?"

Kitty also readied herself in her finest ensemble, though it evinced violently mixed feelings. The gown was a very flattering shade of rouge, which gave warmth to her pale coloring and looked very fine with her fair hair. Naturally, it had belonged to Araminta, who'd discarded it at the end of her first season. In fact, Kitty had heard that it had been the very dress Araminta had worn when she'd rejected the suitor she'd initially accepted; the suitor who then went off and blew out his brains. Kitty had been greatly affected by this tragic declaration of a young man's love, and wondered if any suitor would ever be similarly impassioned about her. Araminta's reputation, however, had not fared so well, and her first season had ended under a cloud. No wonder she'd been keen to make a good match with the wealthy and well-connected Lord Debenham, even if he was a fair bit older than she was and had this dangerous reputation she'd heard her father and Cousin Stephen discussing.

Dorcas was wide-eyed with admiration after she'd helped Kitty into the creation and put her hair up into a flattering topknot with natural ringlets curling about her ears.

"Oh my, but in all me life I neva seen a more beautiful lady," she murmured. "Yer *will* be a famous actress, an' soon as I get me first wages I'm buyin' a ticket ter Covent Garden."

Bolstered by this praise, Kitty accompanied Dorcas into the tiny parlor which felt full to overflowing as a very large, grandly dressed woman with fiery red hair piled on top of her head, topped with a lavishly adorned bonnet to match her frilled and furbelowed visiting gown, rose to greet them with a great show of appreciation.

"My, but what a fine pair! Indeed, just as Mrs. Mobbs promised!" she cried, circling the two of them as she cast her appraising eye over their feet, ankles and upwards. Kitty thought it was most odd, but was pleased that they seemed to give such satisfaction.

"What a refreshingly healthy and buxom country lass you are," she added, looking at Dorcas. "Not one of these pinch-faced London girls, sallow and stick-thin. Oh yes, you will do very well." The feather in her bonnet waved back and forth as she swung her head around to appraise Kitty. "And what a beauty! Oh, my dear, *do* come and work for me. I can offer you twice as much as Mr. Lazarus. Truly, I can."

Startled, Kitty looked from Mrs. Montgomery to Mrs. Mobbs, who grinned her uneven smile and said, "Now there's an offer yer can't refuse. My, but Mr. Lazarus will be put out, but a girl's got ter think o' 'erself. And money talks, indeed it does."

"But...I want to be an actress," said Kitty, confused by the turn of conversation. "Not a servant."

"My dear girl, I offer ever so many opportunities for girls of bearing and beauty like you. If you come along with Dorcas and me, we can discuss *all* the possibilities. I can have a contract drawn up, and before you know it, you'll be living the high life. Mrs. Mobbs can come after me with her frying pan if I'm lying."

They all laughed at her little joke, though before anyone had a chance to respond further, a loud booming voice cut the air and the curtain to the parlor was thrust aside and the doorway filled with the colorful figure of Mr. Lazarus.

He stood in the center of the room with his thumbs in his waist-coat pockets, assessing the scene. "Trying to steal my star actress, are you, Maggie Montgomery?" he demanded. "Looks like I got here just in time. You're never up before midafternoon, with the hours you keep, but you heard whispers about what was in the offing, didn't you then? Now, Miss Hazlett, allow me to welcome you to London." Beaming, he executed a flourishing bow before fastidiously patting his cravat above his garishly-colored waistcoat. "Ain't you just blooming? Why, I have thought of nothing else than casting you for the role of Juliet in my next play since you introduced yourself to me. Wondrous day it was indeed when you stepped into my humble abode to offer your services. Of course, I will require that you audition properly, so as not to offend any of my fine potential leading ladies who toil with such assiduity to their craft. Can't set the cat among the pigeons for showing favoritism so early in the piece, though to be sure I've not laid eyes on such a rare prize specimen as yourself, and to that Mrs. Montgomery will surely attest, else she'd not have dragged her wondrous form from her bed so early in the morning. Now, do you have your things? That is your bag, yes? Allow me to play your knight errant, and we shall quit these lodgings to find you a place worthy of so astonishingly lovely a creature as yourself. Pray take my arm, so I might convey you to a future more dazzling than any of which you ever could have dreamed."

It was almost more than Kitty could take in. Her last sight was of

Dorcas, staring wide-eyed with wonder and admiration, and Mrs. Montgomery looking mightily put out while Mrs. Mobbs patted her ruby velvet shoulder.

And here she was, clinging to a gentleman's arm with the world suddenly at her feet, just as she'd always dreamed.

CHAPTER 3

*I*t was all really too marvelous. The theater was a bustling hive of activity, heavy with the smell of paint and turpentine and filled, it seemed, with scurrying women in various stages of undress. Kitty was at first shocked to see chemises and petticoats on full display, and sometimes even a bare ankle with one woman being so bold as to reveal her knees in clear sight of Mr. Lazarus as she rested her foot on a stage lamp to adjust her garter. The sly look she sent the stage director didn't escape Kitty, and when he chuckled and told her in quite a conspicuous tone that some of his girls would resort to anything to get the lead role, the fiery young redhead flounced off stage and behind the curtain.

It was clear that Kitty was a figure of great interest. A number of women had been lined up since early morning to audition for the role of Juliet, but Mr. Lazarus seemed quite happy to keep them waiting as he strolled about with Kitty at his side, pointing out various locations on stage with instructions on how she'd interpret certain positioning instructions. Kitty felt very important, and knew indeed that she was destined for a long and illustrious career if the singular time and attention her director was devoting to her instruction was any indication.

"But can you really act when put to the test?" Mr. Lazarus suddenly demanded, hands on hips and putting his forefinger beneath her chin to tilt up her head. He pointed to the lineup of hopefuls.

"You there, Jennie; recite for me Juliet's part when she's speaking to Romeo," he called, ushering the redhead with the errant garter onto the stage. "You're an old hand at this. Three seasons, and always the support actress awaiting your moment. Well, perhaps your time has come. Demonstrate for Miss Hazlett the dizzying talent she will have to match if she is to snatch the plum role away from your fair fingers."

Jennie smiled prettily for her director and, with a sideways look at Kitty, flounced across stage, throwing her head back and whisking her skirts above her knees as she recited two verses of her own choice with great passion.

Mr. Lazarus applauded loudly. "Done with great feeling. Ah yes, you know how to please your director, but I must take our fair newcomer upstairs where Mrs. Lazarus can give her opinion. The great but eminently obliging Mr. Lazarus does nothing without the full endorsement of Mrs. L." He proffered his arm with his trademark flourishing bow, and bore Kitty across the stage in front of the goggle-eyed lineup and was about to exit behind the curtain when a loud voice cried, "Ahoy there, and what loveliness have you discovered from the provinces? Word has got out, oh sly one, and here I am, the first to bear witness."

Embarrassed, Kitty turned. The voice was well bred and full of confidence, but the man himself was unlike any she'd ever seen. He must have been about six feet with broad, well-formed shoulders, an athletic physique, and the handsomest face she'd ever seen.

"Oh, but I like what I see!" he said with even greater interest, advancing a few steps and putting his head on one side to observe Kitty from the ankles upward, while Kitty's blushes blazed in her cheeks and her heart beat a raging tumult in her chest.

"You'll have to be satisfied with seeing her on stage, my Lord, for Miss Hazlett is too busy auditioning and then learning her lines to be cajoled by you into any dubious adventuring."

The young man grinned, doffed his hat and bowed. He was now

only several feet away, looking up, and self-consciously Kitty tugged at her skirts in case too much ankle might be on view, yet at the same time her skin glowed with happy warmth to be the object of his obvious admiration.

"Lord Nash at your service, divine goddess," he said, tossing back a head of inky-black curls as he rose from his bow.

Breathlessly Kitty nodded, her heart racing as she saw the tiny scar beneath his right eye. The observation was mind-shattering. Did this mark him out as the man she was destined to meet? "A pleasure, my Lord." She could barely get the words out before Mr. Lazarus swept her backstage, through the curtains and up a narrow staircase.

"Are we going to see Mrs. Lazarus now?" she asked, her mind occupied with images of the wickedly handsome young man who'd just introduced himself. It seemed fate was playing its hand the moment she arrived in the metropolis to grasp her future.

"Not only that, but you are going to impress the good lady with your abundant talent. We have, I feel almost certain, our next Juliet, however a good director needs to be certain he has made the right choice of leading lady." At the top of the stairs, he led Kitty into the center of a small, cluttered room with a change curtain draped with various pieces of flamboyant clothing, and a chaise lounge pushed against one wall beside which was positioned a deep green upholstered chair in which sat a large effigy of a grotesquely featured, enormously fat woman. She seemed to be constructed of material, stuffed and elegantly dressed.

Kitty put her hands to her cheeks and gasped. "What is that?" she cried, turning to find Mr. Lazarus suddenly rigid, his stern eyes upon her.

"What do you mean, Miss Hazlett? You speak of the very image of my late good wife. I wouldn't dream of failing to consult her on every important decision to ensure the continued success of this eminently successful theater."

"That is Mrs. Lazarus?"

"Indeed it is. Now, my dear Miss Hazlett. Let me see how much *feeling* you can inject into my favorite, most tender scene between

Romeo and Juliet. I shall stand here as Romeo and you, my dear, are my fair Juliet." He handed her a dog-eared script and pointed to a line halfway done the page. "Proceed from here, if you please. You indicated a familiarity with the play so you will understand that I, as your lovelorn swain, must hold you in my arms, thus."

Kitty squeaked as Mr. Lazarus's arms went about her so tightly that her legs buckled.

"Juliet, my Juliet," he intoned passionately, his mouth going to Kitty's before she knew what was happening.

"Mr. Lazarus!"

"How fair art thou." His right hand cupped her bottom causing her to shriek even more loudly.

"I say, what's all this!"

At the intrusion, Mr. Lazarus dropped his hands, and Kitty stumbled backward, staring wildly between her red-faced director and the curious gaze of a young man lounging in the doorway. "Pardon me for interrupting. I was downstairs paying my respects to one of your chorus girls when I heard a loud shrieking. I did not realize you were rehearsing."

"Oh Mr. Lazarus, I'm sorry; I didn't realize we'd get quite so quickly to the...love scene. I didn't mean to cause offense." Kitty tried to keep the trembling from her voice. She could see Mr. Lazarus was very angry, but she didn't know how else she might have responded to such unexpected overtures. Nervously she fingered her skirts and looked at the floor.

"That will be all for today, Miss Hazlett." His voice was cold. "Lord Silverton, a pleasure to see you, as always."

Kitty stared, panicked, between the two men, uncertain what to do. "So...I am to return to Mrs. Mobbs while I await your decision?" She felt close to tears. Everything had gone so differently, and now she felt belittled yet also as if she were in the wrong. When he did not answer immediately, she said boldly, "Perhaps we can try that scene again."

Mr. Lazarus shook his head and ran both hands dramatically up over his face and through his hair. "I am unable to summon the feeling required. You have drained me, Miss Hazlett. Disappointed me. I had hoped for better than that from you."

"Please, Mr. Lazarus...please give me one more chance. What am I to do if I can't work for you? It's the reason I came to London?"

"You came to London hoping to prove yourself, but you have a lot to learn, Miss Hazlett."

"Please, Mr. Lazarus, I...need work. I want to be an actress. Please let me audition once more."

"Oh, I'll find something for you while we work on improving your technique, but I'm too weary now for any more of your simpering nonsense. Return to Mrs. Mobbs until I summon you again."

Kitty took an uncertain step toward the top of the stairs. Mr. Lazarus had barely looked at her. She wasn't sure if she was dismissed properly yet, or whether he had more of a tongue-lashing in store. If only she'd not been so foolishly prim and proper. She realized he'd put her to some enormous test, and she'd failed miserably, but she had not known of London ways and how quickly one was expected to reach certain points that in the country were advanced toward at a far more leisurely pace.

As she started to descend the stairs, the handsome, light-haired young man whom Mr. Lazarus had addressed as Lord Silverton stepped forward to block her path. He executed a flourishing bow. "Allow me to convey you to wherever you're going. I fear you might lose your way if you are new to the city."

Kitty didn't respond with more than a nod as she stumbled past him and the young ladies eagerly awaiting their turn. She heard a few titters and speculative whispers, which only increased the weight of the world already resting on her shoulders. Her one opportunity to prove herself as a consummate actress had ended in disaster.

Blinking in the sunlight, she regained her senses when Lord Silverton, now at her heels, asked for an address. She thought his name sounded familiar, but she felt too burdened by other matters to try and sift through her memory. Her father often spoke of Lord this and that, as he mixed with so many of them. Kitty had always longed to mix with this other illustrious world. Unlike Lissa, she had no intention of doing so from the subservient position of governess. No, Kitty wanted to entertain them, be feted by them, orbit within their hallowed ranks, but that now looked highly unlikely.

Still too downcast to pay much attention to his Lordship, she nevertheless told him Mrs. Mobbs's address while her thoughts were occupied by the blaze of connection she'd felt between handsome Lord Nash and herself. Those few seconds had seemed part of her life's pre-ordained plan, for wasn't he the handsome nobleman with the scar beneath his right eye who would sweep her off her feet while she was London's most feted actress?

"I hope you don't mind traveling in a phaeton. That will certainly give you a bit of fresh air and show you the sights." She realized on vaguely that Lord Silverton was talking as he leaped up first into the equipage before reaching for her hand, and before she knew what was happening, was swinging her up beside him.

She let out a squeal. She'd never seen such a strange conveyance, yet it certainly looked smart and exciting. As she settled beside him, she smiled with sudden appreciation of her new and lofty situation as he picked up the ribbons, saying, "So you live in Black Cat Alley, eh? That's a salubrious part of town. Do you enjoy living there?"

Kitty shrugged, not prepared to voice her reservations for Mrs. Mobbs had been good to her. "I've only just arrived, but now I fear I'll have to return home if I can't find work."

"Come now; you're far too pretty to look so glum." His brows knitted together, as if he were considering something. "Let me show you some of London. You're dressed for it, and I suddenly find myself at a loose end due to a canceled engagement."

The thought flashed through Kitty's mind that she ought not to be consorting with young men without a chaperone, but as she'd already run away to London, she supposed there was little worse she could do. No one from her village knew she was here, and neither did her family, and the offer was very tempting.

"Do you like animals? I could take you to the Tower?" he suggested, signaling to his two fine bays with a flick of the reins to move on. "Yes, the Tower of London and the British Museum. What say you to that? I've nothing better to do."

The suggestion sounded much more thrilling than returning to Mrs. Mobbs, and Kitty responded with a smile and a clap of her hands as she straightened, determined now to make the most of every opportunity. "Splendid. I want to see London and learn London ways, and tomorrow I'll do whatever Mr. Lazarus wants me to do if I'm to please him enough to be part of his new play. What did you say your name was?"

He looked a little startled. "Lord Silverton, at your service. And I'm happy to show you London ways and prepare you for your audition tomorrow. We shall have lots of fun, Miss Hazlett; I promise you. I'm sure being new to London can be quite daunting, but it would be a pleasure to help you feel... less unworldly."

"That is very kind of you, Lord Silverton," Kitty said, liking his face, and deciding that being less unworldly would certainly be an advantage having failed to impress the one man who held the key to the future she desired—Mr. Lazarus. "Proceed to show me London, my Lord!" It was exciting she thought, though she'd have to prod him a little so she might recall where she'd heard his name. She was a little disappointed he wasn't the raven-haired Lord Nash who'd shown such interest in her earlier, who clearly was the man for whom she was destined, but she certainly liked Lord Silverton's disarming manner. He seemed delightfully unselfconscious and at ease with himself.

And Kitty was always ready for an adventure.

The ride in Lord Silverton's phaeton was an excitement in itself, and Kitty felt very grown-up and flamboyant as she held onto her bonnet and, at one point, Lord Silverton's knee when rounding a particularly sharp corner.

"Got you, Miss Hazlett!" he cried over the sound of clopping hooves on cobblestones, as he threw his arm about her shoulders and literally saved her from being bounced onto the cobbles to a certain death.

By the time they drew to a halt outside the Tower of London Kitty was visibly shaking: from excitement, cold, and fearful exertion. Lord Silverton lifted her down from his sporting vehicle with a wry smile. "I fear I nearly frightened you to death, but it's preparation for the amazing sights and myriad extraordinary animals you are about to behold if this is your first time in London." With a flourish, he signaled the great White Tower before them. "My favorite is Old Martin, gifted to King George from far across the sea, a place called Hudson Bay. And who is Old Martin, you ask? Why, a grizzly bear. And what is a grizzly bear? Take my arm, Miss Hazlett, and, with the same flamboyance your erstwhile director would have adopted, allow me to show you." He caged her hand on his arm and his lopsided smile and the general effervescence he exuded filled Kitty with warmth. He seemed a very *nice* man and she felt quite safe.

It wasn't long before any residual misery Kitty felt over her audition with Mr. Lazarus was swept away by wonder and amazement at seeing so many exotic creatures, some of which she'd never even heard about, much less seen.

Lord Silverton was a charming companion, allowing her plenty of time to marvel, if she chose. By late afternoon, Kitty had forgotten all her cares, and only felt a pang of her earlier dismay when she stopped to exclaim at how low the sun was in the sky.

"Time to move on to other entertainments, eh, Miss Hazlett?"

Kitty smiled at him. He really was rather charming, the way he quirked his mouth in that humorous manner of his while above a very Patrician nose, his blue eyes twinkled with merriment. And he did indeed cut a very dashing figure in his buckskin breeches, Hessians, and superbly cut blue superfine coat, which stretched across a well-built chest. His hair was fashionably cut, his brown curls slightly longer on top and brushed forward framing a high brow above his strong nose, high cheekbones delineated by a thin line of sideburn, and a very sensitive-looking mouth, though Kitty quickly looked away—quite surprised at herself—when that thought popped into her head.

"I really should be getting back to Mrs. Mobbs." She glanced down at her lovely delicate rouge walking dress with its two rows of flounces, worried it might have become soiled when she needed to get further wearings out of it before it was laundered. She doubted Mrs. Mobbs would be as assiduous as she was when it came to ensuring it received the care it required. With another pang, she thought of practical Lissa who didn't worry about such things and who was no doubt industriously toiling away in some dark and dingy attic.

But just as she was starting to feel quite sentimental about the sister who was so different from her, they rounded a corner and almost collided with a couple, strolling arm in arm, the lady occasioning more astonishment and indeed fright in Kitty's breast than any of the animals. For, lo and behold, it was the young woman she'd viewed so enviously from afar, or through the window panes of The Grange on so many occasions, her half-sister, Araminta.

Silverton nodded at the pair. "Lady Debenham, what a pleasant surprise. You look blooming." He raised an eyebrow as he turned to her escort. "Debenham, it's been a week you since you had the devil's own luck playing Hazard at Lady Renton's."

Kitty was too busy to pay attention to how Lord Debenham responded. She was transfixed by the very large belly sported by the beautiful Araminta, at the same time as she suddenly realized where she'd heard Lord Silverton's name. Good lord, he was the man she'd overheard Stephen Cranborne denounce as a suspected collaborator of Lord Debenham's who, together with another man, Smythe, were regarded by the Government as potential plotters. Traitors. She put her hand to her mouth to stifle her gasp as Lord Silverton patted Kitty's hand, still clinging to his arm, saying, "Allow me to introduce a young friend, Miss—"

"Bijou," Kitty blurted out hurriedly. "La Bijou. It's my first visit to London, and his Lordship has kindly undertaken the task of showing me the sights." She railed inwardly at the faintly derisive look Araminta sent her, though it appeared her sister did not recognize her which was one of the reasons Kitty despised her. Araminta was so self-absorbed, she'd never have noticed Kitty sitting every Sunday in a pew behind the district's first family, Lord Partington, his wife and two daughters.

Lord Silverton sent a faintly amused glance at Kitty before corroborating her new identity. "You will see much of Miss La Bijou in the future for she arrived yesterday with the sole purpose of taking London by storm."

Kitty was unsure how to respond, but decided to stay silent in the face of Lord Debenham's snide laugh and Araminta's raised eyebrow, accompanied by only the hint of a smile.

"So you are an actress, Miss La Bijou," she said in tones of the greatest condescension. "Indeed, I shall look forward to seeing you *on stage*." The way she said it, tugging at her husband's sleeve as if it were now imperative to move away from the contamination of such a lowborn creature, sent the blood rushing to Kitty's head together with a renewed determination that she would do whatever was required to secure the lead role in Romeo and Juliet—save compromising her virtue—if that meant the start of her intended rise to a position where she received more adulation than Araminta. Her next thought, that perhaps charming Lord Silverton would champion her, was dented by the worry that she should stay well away from such a dastardly traitor to his country. The idea was horrifying and thrilling in equal measure. Kitty ought to despise a man who would compromise his own people however he exuded enormous charm. Yet, she determined with a burst of patriotic fervor, she would not be swayed from doing her duty, no matter how charming he was. If she stumbled upon evidence he was a traitor, she would immediately alert Mr. Cranborne, even if that did mean Lords Silverton and Debenham would rot in an English cell.

Though she'd much rather see that fate befall the latter. Kitty did not like Lord Debenham one bit. His eyes were cold, his mouth thin indicating a cruel character, and he appeared as vain and arrogant as his wife.

No, Kitty decided, the less she had to do with Araminta and her new husband, the better. However, she couldn't help remarking, just to see what Lord Silverton would say, when they'd passed on, "Lady Debenham is very beautiful." She picked up her skirts to step over a channel of dirty water that washed over the cobblestones from the rain earlier that day. To her relief, Araminta hadn't recognized the gown as having once belonged to her. Kitty had obviously done a fine job trimming it with contrasting ruffles and was wearing a pelisse and a bonnet festooned with flowers, making the ensemble appear very different to anything Araminta would have worn.

Kitty reflected, also, that Lady Debenham had looked a trifle care-worn, despite her beauty, and wondered how Araminta was coping during the latter stages of her pregnancy. She did not look the kind who would bear it very well at all.

"Lady Debenham is, I am afraid, rather too much hard work for a man of my tastes, though I'm sure she and Lord Debenham do very well together. I far prefer golden-haired beauties such as yourself."

Kitty was interested by Lord Silverton's ironic tone with regard to Lady Debenham and a little put out at his somewhat careless manner towards her, though she supposed that's how gentlemen spoke to unchaperoned young ladies they took on afternoon jaunts. No doubt he didn't expect ever to see her again unless he came to throw flowers at her on stage.

This reminded her of the urgent need to repeat her audition for Mr. Lazarus, and she gripped Lord Silverton's arm to draw his attention back from the pig that could apparently spell, though Kitty hadn't seen evidence during the three minutes they'd been observing it.

"Please, Lord Silverton, what do you think Mr. Lazarus is looking for to cast me in the role of Juliet?" she asked. "When I met him at the theater in my village during their tour of the provinces, he said he felt in his bones I would be his next leading lady. He even said I looked perfect for the role of Juliet."

Lord Silverton transferred his attention from the pig that could spell to Kitty's no-doubt anxious face. "Did you flatter him?"

"Flatter him?"

"Of course, every man loves to be flattered. Especially a man like Mr. Lazarus. You need to show enormous admiration for his theater skills and then add a hefty dose of personal flattery. He's not getting any younger, but he wants to believe he is as handsome as he was when a young buck of thirty."

"Is that what you like to hear, Lord Silverton?" Kitty asked with a flash of a smile.

"Oh, I don't need your flattery, Kitty, and if you start now, I shall know not to believe it after this little lesson I've given you." He patted her shoulder. "Besides, I'm only just past thirty, very handsome and athletic, so, in fact, in my prime. I fancy I'm also too intelligent not to recognize false flattery, but Mr. Lazarus is an altogether different beast. I suggest you return to see him at the theater, looking suitably tragic and contrite. Ask if you can audition again because you're heartbroken to have been so green as to have flubbed your first chance at what you've always desired…to be directed by the incomparable Mr. Lazarus, a theater director greater even than David Garrick."

Kitty considered this as they left the spelling pig and wandered off to visit the tiger where she shrieked when it lunged at her, though it was of course repulsed by the bars of its cage.

"Do you think Mr. Lazarus will want to kiss me again?" she asked after a while, thinking that the majestic tiger was as frightening a proposition as submitting herself to Mr. Lazarus's unpredictable overtures.

"I expect so. That's why he chose that passage from Romeo and Juliet." Lord Silverton gave her a considered look as they were about to move on. "No doubt he wants to see if you are able to pretend to like being kissed by someone you hardly know. You will need to be very convincing if the audience is to believe you'd rather take your own life than be parted from your Romeo. Perhaps you'd like to practice with me later this evening."

Kitty jerked her head up, shocked, to find he was grinning at her. He pinched her cheek. "I am joking, but I'm also quite happy to help you perfect this difficult role you must master if you are to secure Juliet from Mr. Lazarus."

Kitty put her hand in the crook of the arm he offered as they turned away from the tiger and started towards the stairs of the tower. "I don't know if I can do this…if I'm not in love," she said doubtfully. She thought of the dashing young buck—Lord Nash—

with his inky curls and blazing eyes who'd so flattered her earlier that morning and added softly, "Or, what if I am in love with another?" Surely he was supposed to be the man with whom she'd foster a romantic liaison and ultimately marry? Just the sight of him had made her heart pound while the scar beneath his eye had proclaimed him as 'the one'.

Lord Silverton shrugged. "Well, *I* am in love with another, but sometimes kissing a stranger can be quite the antidote." Almost distracted, he added as he assisted her over another channel of dirty water, "Well, that's what one tries to believe."

"You are in love with another? Oh, Lord Silverton, she would be so jealous if she saw you squiring me around."

"Not at all. She'd be delighted since she was so very sorry to have hurt my feelings last night when she rejected my marriage proposal in favor of someone far inferior."

Kitty saw he was trying to inject humor into his tone for she did not miss the bleak flare of his eyes. Despite knowing she must remain highly suspicious of him in view of what Mr. Cranborne had said, she felt a surge of sympathy. "I'm very sorry for it, Lord Silverton."

"It's an episode relegated to the past, and now you are here to help take my mind off my pain. What do you say to a night of dancing?" Suddenly, he was all exuberance as he glanced at the darkening sky and hurried her back toward the Tower entrance.

"But what about my landlady?"

"When I take you back, I'll have a more than adequate excuse and a few pennies to take the edge off her anger. But first, we must have some dinner. Come, Miss La Bijou. If we are both bearing broken hearts, then we must console one another, and tomorrow you will prove your worth to Mr. Lazarus. What do you say to such a proposal?"

CHAPTER 4

*K*itty had never been dancing before. Not even to the Assembly balls held in the village. Her mother had kept her daughters close, perhaps wanting to shield them from the whispers. Kitty realized the plan had always been for Lissa to find a post as a governess, Ned to be apprenticed to some worthy occupation—boys were not so damaged by the stain of bastardy—but Kitty, despite her love of adventure, was expected to stay at home to help her mother.

Clasped in Lord Silverton's arms, she once again felt pangs about abandoning her mother as she skirted the dance floor of the insalubrious salon above a row of unprepossessing shopfronts. This was a place, she supposed, where young bucks could take their fancy pieces without demur. As for herself, Kitty didn't expect to be recognized by anyone, and she assuaged her conscience with the knowledge she wasn't doing anything wrong and besides, she'd never been accorded the label of respectable.

Above all, though, it was a night of revelations, one being that despite knowing Lord Silverton was a dangerous man, she liked him very much, if the warm, liquidy feeling that pooled through her heart and belly when he clasped her in his arms during the gavotte, or guided her towards the supper table, was anything to go by.

"Well, Kitty, how have you enjoyed your first night of London revels?" Lord Silverton asked as he drove her back in his phaeton. It was a perfect evening with the air fresh and clean and the moon high and bright. Kitty couldn't remember having ever enjoyed herself so much.

"You've shown me such wonderful things," she whispered, raising her eyes to the few fluffy white clouds in an inky sky. "I never imagined having so much fun!"

"And more to be had." They'd drawn up in front of a smart townhouse, and now he was jumping down before reaching up for her hand.

"But I need to go to Mrs. Mobbs's. It's late." Suddenly, she felt nervous. "Where have you taken me?"

He tilted his head and frowned slightly. "For a snifter of brandy at my townhouse before I return you to your landlady's premises. Didn't I promise you I'd help you practice your lines?"

Despite Kitty's immediate delight at the prospect, she was aware of how compromising it would be to accept. Reluctantly, she drew back from his extended hand. "Lord Silverton, I don't want you to think that I...that I would do something unladylike."

"Well, I certainly shan't force you into doing anything unladylike." He regarded her a moment then jumped back up beside her. "You're right, though. You are an innocent, and I might turn into a rogue. I'll take you home."

But as he picked up the ribbons, Kitty saw the value in his proposal to help her and put her hand on his. "Stop. I shall come inside and we shall practice, yes indeed, but very quickly because I need a good night's sleep." She smoothed her skirts as she stood up, feeling very decided as she added, "Only certain adventuring women or ladies of the night go alone to gentlemen's premises, and I am by no means one of them. Though I suppose, who would know that since it's a secret I'm in London?"

"Indeed," he agreed with a quirk of a brow as he helped her down, occasioning a quick clarification from Kitty.

"Not that I intend doing anything I ought not."

"Of course not, as you have already made clear, Miss La Bijou. Now, isn't it much warmer inside? Thank you, Garvey," he added to the butler who was on hand to help divest them of their outerwear once they were indoors. "Two brandies in the drawing room, if you please."

Kitty had never had more than a sip of medicinal brandy in her life, and after two snifters, she was feeling quite lightheaded and more than ready to step into her assigned role. Lord Silverton, with his handsome face and friendly, easy manner, was a much more welcome proposition than Mr. Lazarus to practice her lines. As he sat opposite her, chatting with ease and making her laugh, it occurred to her that she'd never spent such a pleasant and relaxed evening.

When the clock chimed eleven, Lord Silverton eyed the second empty glass she put down upon the low table beside her and announced as he stood before her with his arm extended to help her to her feet, "Fair Juliet, the time has come."

With a nervous smile, Kitty rose, full of expectation, and went to stand in the middle of the elegant Aubusson rug, surrounded by delicate Louis XIV chairs and handsome gold and purple curtains. The sumptuous luxury reminded her of The Grange, so different from the simply furnished home she shared with Ned and Lissa.

These were the comforts Araminta took for granted and which Kitty was determined to similarly enjoy, though as Lord Silverton looked down at her with a very warm gaze making Kitty felt quite warm and strange inside, she had to remind herself that not only was she supposed to fall in love with another man, it was in fact rather necessary to do so since Lord Silverton was, more than likely, a villain.

But, of course, he wasn't about to fall in love with her and offer her all this, she knew that. Especially when he'd just told her he was in love with a young lady who'd rejected him the night before. She was surprised at the niggle of disappointment she felt at the reflection, preferring instead to take at face value the way he looked at her as if she were the most heavenly creature he'd ever set eyes upon. And when he took her into his arms and lowered his mouth, thrilling her with the softest brush of his lips against hers before deepening the pressure, she gasped in a quick, short breath but did not draw back, even though in the dim recesses of her mind she questioned how she could possibly trust a man who'd just told her his heart belonged to another yet who filled her head with wicked ideas totally foreign to her. Ideas which she knew could never be indulged by a young lady of even tenuous respectability. This, she had to remind herself, was playacting.

His cheek was warm against hers as he paused, his right hand gently stroking her hair and twisting a tendril of it around his finger as they paused in the aftermath of that heavenly kiss, Kitty to gather her wits and he to…think of the young lady who'd spurned him?

It did not matter. She stepped back as he nodded approvingly. To her disapointement his voice was matter-of-fact. "For someone who is in love with another lucky gentleman you've proved yourself a convincing actress. Well done, Miss La Bijou; even the most critical audience would believe you were ready to end your wretched existence if your father discovered what we'd been up to." He tapped his forefinger gently upon her cheek, his smile fond. "Hmmm. What *would* your father have done if he could see you now, Miss La Bijou?"

Kitty considered the question, enjoying the continued contact, for his hand was now resting gently upon her shoulder as if he were very invested in her reply. "He'd be furious. Now, no more questions, please, Lord Silverton. I do not wish to speak of my father or my past. It's the future that counts."

"Such wise words for such a babe in the woods." Lord Silverton led her to a chair, but instead of respectfully lowering her into it, he sat down first and drew her onto his lap.

Though Kitty liked the feeling very much, she tensed when he put his arm about her. "I must go home now, my Lord," she murmured, wriggling but not going so far as to actually get to her feet. "I must get *some* sleep."

"Why not here, Kitty, my love?" He tickled her cheek with his fingertips. "Our little kissing session has left me quite ready for more." His tone was more like a honeyed growl which made Kitty's nerves skitter. She didn't like the fact she wavered inside when he added, more serious now, "I like you, Kitty. And you surely don't intend staying with Mrs. Mobbs for long." He made an expansive sweep of his arm. "I could set you up in quite a charming bower where I could visit you after your performances."

She frowned. "But…that would not be respectable."

"Respectable?" He laughed. "You are worried about that *now*? Of course it would not be respectable but nor is becoming an actress, nor is spending the day unchaperoned with a gentleman. Or rather, the entire evening, and kissing him in his drawing room."

While his hands lightly caressed her, trailing up to her throat and sending sensation coursing wildly through her, Kitty worried at his words. "But what if I fall in love?" she asked. "What if *you* fall in love, Lord Silverton? In fact, we've already admitted that we have."

"We have?" He looked confused. "Of course we shan't fall in love, but we must like each other very much. *Love* is not a prerequisite for what I'm proposing."

"I don't mean with each other, for you've just told me you're in love with a lady who refused your suit. And I've already told you that I think I'm in love with another. In fact, I met him earlier today."

"*Today*?" He quirked a brow. "And who is this lucky gentleman?"

"A fortune-teller once told me to look out for a gentleman with raven-black locks and a scar across his left cheek. She said I would feel a jolt of sensation which would confirm—" She broke off when she saw he was laughing at her, and added defensively, "You think it nonsense but I believe in love at first sight."

"Love at first sight? No, I can't say I believe in that at all."

"Well, my parents fell in love at first sight."

He looked more interested at this. "How singular. My parents didn't. They married because they were told to. Bad business all round." He glowered but then brightened suddenly. "How delightful for you to have had the benefit of well-matched parents basking in the glow of mutual happiness. Love at first sight, marriage, children." To Kitty's surprise he actually looked wistful. But then Kitty had to confess, "They never married though they're still in love."

"Good Lord!"

"Yes, but I don't want to talk about it. It's the reason I'm an actress, I suppose. Nevertheless, it is also the reason I'm determined to find the right man and marry him. The one the fortune-teller prophesised I'd meet. I do not intend living the kind of life my mother's been forced to live."

"So you believe in love at first sight and marriage *and* the whole happy ever after, Miss La Bijou."

"I do," Kitty said, even more defensively than before. "And I shall make no compromises to get it. Which is why I must decline your very generous offer to...to offer me a place to live. Besides, suppose your lady-love changes her mind and agrees to marry you after all? I think my presence may complicate matters, don't you?"

He shook his head, and a slow smile grew as he settled her more comfortably on his lap. "My dear, you *really* are the innocent. Do you know, exactly, what it is I'm proposing?"

"What *are* you proposing, Lord Silverton? To keeping me in lodgings so you may visit me and we may do what we've been doing this evening? But instead of it being practice, it would be real?" She shook her head and added firmly, "But this evening was in the name of practice, and what you are proposing is something I'd only consider doing every evening with someone I loved very much and who wanted to marry me."

He put his finger under her chin and raised her face to him. In the dim light, his expression was interested. Earnest and assessing. She felt a strange tug somewhere in the lower reaches of her belly. A tugging that made her want to melt into him, which was quite absurd since he was most definitely not her destiny, and quite clearly was looking to spend the respectable portion of his life with a respectable wife. He lowered his head to murmur near her ear, "What I am proposing would require more than kissing, Miss La Bijou." His hand slid into hers, and he gave it a gentle squeeze.

"Lord Silverton!" Outraged, Kitty whipped her hand out of his. "What kind of young lady do you think I am? We are no longer practicing!"

He looked sheepish. "My apologies if I've offended you, Miss La Bijou. I thought if you were so agreeable as to spend the entire day with me, without someone in attendance, then you had no regard for your reputation. That perhaps you," he shrugged and looked even more shamefaced, "had none. I'm sorry, Miss Bijou ..." He stood up so that she slid from his lap and stood before him, her hands on her hips, as she looked at him enquiringly, waiting for him to finish, "I had no idea you were *so* fresh. And now I feel a complete cad for compromising you, much less proposing what I did. Tell me, have you run away from home? *Am* I to expect some furious papa on my doorstep with a pistol pointed in my direction, demanding that I marry you? Who are you really and what exactly are you trying to do?" He looked suspiciously at her.

Kitty smiled as she started to walk towards the door. "I've run away from home because since birth I've been treated as an outcast in my village. My father and my mother are not married, which makes me a bastard. Yes, a horrible word! But it means I have no name that needs protecting. And no reputation to speak of."

"My poor Miss Bijou." A look of sympathy replaced his suspicion as he matched his steps with hers, opening the drawing room door for her and leading her along the passage. "I understand very well now. You have decided to turn adventuress, even though you have no idea of the perils of this big bad city." The cool night air was like a blast of frightening reality as the butler opened the double doors and they stepped outside, just as Lord Silverton's carriage was brought around. "I've chosen something a little warmer, more comfortable and discreet for me to convey you home," he said as he helped her inside, then joined her after giving orders to the coachman. With a gentle lurch, the horses set off at a clip while Lord Silverton looked down at her with a curious expression on his face. "I hope you find the destiny you're looking for and are not disappointed, for you are quite enchanting and I have enjoyed our time together enormously."

Impulsively, Kitty reached out her hand and gave his a brief squeeze. "And I can't remember having enjoyed myself as much, Lord Silverton. Thank you for introducing me to London."

Once they'd reached Mrs. Mobbs's, and the coach had come to a stop in the narrow cobbled lane, he leaned forward to give her a chaste kiss on the cheek. "Beware, Miss Bijou, for the theater is a dangerous place. And the theater in London is very different from the provinces. I would hate to see one so sweet and innocent as you become spoiled or jaded."

"You are very kind, Lord Silverton." Kitty touched her cheek where she could still feel his kiss and wondered how such a nice gentleman could be embroiled in the villainous affairs of Lord Debenham. She took the hand of the postilion who was holding open the door, waiting to assist her to the ground. It was a shame she wouldn't be seeing Lord Silverton again, but the dangerous feelings he inspired in her suggested that wasn't such a bad thing.

For a gentleman who had no intention of providing her with the destiny she knew was hers if she made the right choices, it would be safer to keep her distance.

CHAPTER 5

*A*raminta looked down at her protruding belly where, it seemed, the last of the sun's rays through the window were coalescing. She wished they were somehow magic fingers of gold, or wands, that would remove the hateful creature that lodged within her. She was not enjoying pregnancy and she would not—she knew—enjoy motherhood.

"Tighter, Jane." The baby had grown larger and faster than she could ever have imagined and defied the constrictions of the stays she was now exhorting her maid to lace as firmly as she could.

If she allowed herself to dwell on the potential disaster of a full-term child arriving six weeks earlier than it should, she would terrify herself. All she could do was trust to the fact rescue would come in some form or another.

These days, Araminta loathed going out in public. When she was alone, she wore loose stays designed for a woman in the later stages of pregnancy. She could relax, eat chocolates and, in the absence of any other company, talk to Jane.

However, Debenham liked to promote the fiction they were devoted newlyweds, if one could call themselves that after being married only five months. Of course, when she was required to accompany him anywhere, she had to employ multiple artful means of hiding her seven-month belly. Thus far, Debenham suspected nothing. Araminta knew she was not being complacent in this belief. If Debenham had for one moment thought she was not the virgin he believed he'd married, he'd have made her suffer in every imaginable way. Debenham liked to show her he was master in all things.

With a grunt, Jane managed to generate an extra inch of slack in the laces. She then came to stand in front of Araminta and, with a frown, put her hand on her mistress's belly. Her censorious look made Araminta want to give her a sharp kick in the shins, except Jane was the one person who could bring her down and also the one person able to protect her.

Araminta smiled. "Another one of your lectures, Jane? You know what will happen if I keep Debenham waiting and make him late for the theater."

"'E will make 'is displeasure known, m'lady, but then yer knew what kind o' man yer were marryin'."

"If there had been *any* other man who'd have married me when I needed it—" Araminta drew her hand across her face as she took a shuddering breath. "Now, no more of this talk for it makes my head want to burst. Oh...Hetty, what are you doing here? You didn't knock!"

Araminta put her hands over her belly as her younger sister waltzed into the room wearing her characteristically beaming smile. But then Hetty had a lot to beam about whereas Araminta's life was full of woe. And Hetty was the reason.

"Goodness, Araminta, why, you're as big as I am and you're months behind me. Perhaps you're carrying two?"

The thought hadn't occurred to Araminta, but Hetty's artless comment gave her pause. That could be a useful proposition. It wouldn't help when the babe came early and there was only one, but she could, for the moment at any rate, plead two. Yes, she'd plant the seed in the physician's mind. And her husband's.

Araminta patted her belly thoughtfully, crooking her finger at Jane to bring her the evening gown she intended to wear. "Yes, that's what Dr. Horne believes, isn't it, Jane? Debenham will be so pleased."

Hetty stepped back as her sister raised her arms and Jane drew the handsome, dark red confection of embroidered netting over Araminta's head. "How are you, Jane?" Hetty asked. "I missed having you to attend to me during our wedding tour, but I thought Araminta needed you more than me. She was so upset when I left, and while I know that eloping was the wickedest thing we were so in love and I'm sure even my sister can forgive such scandalous behavior."

Araminta glared. How did Hetty have the nerve to refer to *that* evening evening when Hetty had run off with Sir Aubrey—the gentleman Araminta had in her sights and who'd given her every indication that he'd make her his bride. But there was Hetty, smiling as if she were making perfectly normal conversation. Had the girl lost her mind?

Jane bobbed a curtsy. "I'm well, ma'am, thank yer fer askin'. An' Miss Araminta 'as bin very kind, as is 'er way."

Araminta narrowed her eyes. Was she imagining the look she intercepted between the women? The secretive, colluding smile. She wished she could bang both their heads together, dismiss Jane, and scream at Hetty that she was a thief, and Araminta wanted nothing to do with her ever again.

Instead, she said, sweetly, "Jane knows how cherished she is. Debenham can be an exacting husband. Unlike you, Hetty, I didn't make the match of my heart."

"But you made it quite plain that expediency was more important. And Lord Debenham has all the attributes you were looking for, Araminta." Suddenly, Hetty looked concerned. "He is kind to you, isn't he, Araminta? I mean, he wasn't very kind to me but then..."

Hetty broke off, for she must surely be thinking of that terrible night at Vauxhall Gardens when Hetty had stolen the letter from Lord Debenham with which she intended to win Sir Aubrey's heart, and had found herself with a broken bottle at her throat. Araminta thought it was best to clear the air. It was a night neither of them would ever forget but neither had ever discussed. "Debenham was bosky when he treated you with such disrespect, Hetty. You knew you were playing with fire when you confronted him about the letter, threatening to ruin his reputation. Of course he was going to behave in a most aggressive fashion. You're so thoughtless, Hetty. Always rushing into things you know nothing about."

"I can forgive him only if I know he is good to you, Araminta."

Araminta brushed off her sister's concern. "Do stop prying into the secrets of my marriage, Hetty. And please go downstairs so I can finish dressing." She put her hand to her forehead. She didn't want to put Hetty offside. She might need her one day, too, and even though she despised her sister for being such a peagoose, as well as a husband-thief, she thought a more ameliorating tone was in order. "Forgive me for being a cross patch."

"Oh, I've always forgiven you that, Araminta. But tell me, dearest —and I'm not prying, you must believe—but you are happy, aren't you? I mean, you're going to have a *baby*!" And she hugged herself with joy.

"I don't know 'ow yer can look yer sister in the face," Jane muttered when Hetty had left the room.

Araminta, now sitting at her dressing table and putting on the ruby and diamond earrings her husband had given her upon their marriage, raised her eyebrows. "I don't understand you, Jane."

Jane bent to pick up a discarded shoe. "I don't know 'ow yer can face yer sister after what yer done. Whose babe is it yer carryin'?" Her voice was so soft Araminta could barely hear her. Perhaps Jane hadn't intended her to, but Araminta was riled, nevertheless.

"How dare you even suggest it's any other than whose it should be," she returned on a venomous hiss. "Don't ever say such things aloud. Who knows who might be listening?"

Jane's expression became sorrowful as she cradled the lone embroidered slipper. "What are yer goin' ter do, m'lady, when yer time comes an' the babe is full growed but..." she heaved in an outraged breath, "...two months early?"

"My jeweled comb, if you please!" Araminta clapped her hands imperiously, then muttered as she stared into her hand-held looking glass, "And it's only six weeks if I have my calculations right. However…I will make a plan."

"Like the plan yer made when yer was determined ter make Sir Aubrey wed yer—'cept 'e'd already wed yer sister leavin' yer in a right old mess? Yes, yer can dismiss me if yer like fer speakin' so plain, m'lady, but you 'ave jest got ter find a way out o' this conundrum else yer'll suffer fer it most sorely, and then I really will 'ave to find meself another job."

Araminta put down her looking glass and closed her eyes. Jane spoke only the truth. Her child could be born at any time within the next four weeks, and when it was discovered to be at full term, she was utterly terrified that Debenham would kill her. It was no exaggeration, either.

All the fears she'd tried to keep at bay surged up her throat. She sent her maid a beseeching look, very different from her usual careless hauteur. "You have to help me, Jane." The situation was indeed as dire as Jane had painted it, and she'd been a fool to pretend the problem would simply go away. When Jane said nothing, she swung around and gripped her maid's wrist until the girl cried out in pain. "Promise you'll help me. I'll think of something, but to do whatever I may need you to do, you must promise me your utter loyalty."

"Yer know yer've always 'ad that, m'lady."

Araminta dropped her hand and stared at her reflection. "You like Hetty more than you ever liked me."

"Yes, m'lady. I like 'er too much to tell 'er the truth 'bout yer and what I reckon yer tricked Sir Aubrey ter do wiv yer. But I'll no' destroy 'er 'appiness when she an' her new 'usband are smellin' o' April an' May. So yer can rest assured yer secret is safe with me, for it's over me dead body that I'll ever let poor Miss Hetty know that it's *Sir Aubrey's* babe in yer belly."

For a moment, rage blurred Araminta's vision as she swung round. She drew back her hand to strike the impertinent and challenging look from Jane's hateful face but managed, just, to master herself. She rose. "How do I look, Jane?" she asked with a regal smile. "Will my husband be pleased with me?"

"I reckon 'e's always pleased when yer look so beautiful and do what 'e says."

Araminta shuddered, her attempt at acting clouded by the reality of what her life had become. "I've learned to be very good at that. Now," she waved her hand toward the door, "I shall present myself downstairs. I shall probably carry on to supper after the play, so you may go to bed in the meantime if you arrange to be woken so can attend to me when I return."

"That's uncommonly thoughtful of yer, m'lady."

Araminta smiled. "I always look after those who have pledged me their loyalty."

So they were to present a united front: the newlyweds, recently following that new fashion of a love match. Tonight was one of those rare occasions Araminta preferred to be in company with her husband.

Hetty and Sir Aubrey had returned from their wedding tour in Italy a month ago and Araminta would have done a great deal never to have to face Sir Aubrey again. Patting her swollen belly as she lowered herself onto a velvet upholstered chair in her husband's box at the theater, she shivered afresh at her humiliation of seven months ago when she'd tricked Sir Aubrey into believing she was Hetty. How was she to have known Sir Aubrey had wed her sister in a secret ceremony not half an hour beforehand?

Of course, if Sir Aubrey hadn't given her to believe he was about to make her a marriage offer, she'd never have done what she had to in order to spur him on. The truth was, she'd been motivated by nothing other than the good of the family as a whole. With Papa on the verge of losing all his money, Araminta had thought to save innocent Hetty from having to earn her living as a governess. Everything Araminta had done had been motivated by concern for her family. But look what had happened?

She gasped with discomfort as the child kicked within her and

Debenham sent her an enquiring look, though he didn't actually ask if she were all right.

The child. Whose child? Of course, Sir Aubrey chose to pretend the whole ghastly business had never occurred. No, he simply offered Araminta a bland smile and inane pleasantries whenever they met—no agonized apologies for his brutishness whispered in private as he despaired over having chosen the wrong sister. Lord, it was as if it had never even occurred to him that *both* Hetty and Araminta were carrying his child, and likely to give birth within a few weeks of each other, if Araminta's calculations were correct.

So there the two couples sat in Debenham's box at the theater, pretending they all rubbed along so well.

It was a relief when some gentleman across the stalls beckoned Debenham over, and then Hetty and Sir Aubrey made their own excuses to leave just before the interval. Generally, Araminta didn't like being on her own but tonight was turning into a nightmare. Though she hated to touch it, she again put her hands to her belly as the wretched child refused to be still. Dear Lord, what was she going to do? It was one thing to tell Jane she had a plan or would make a plan, but what plan could she possibly make?

"Good evening, Lady Debenham. Should you flaunt yourself in public when you are so advanced?"

Shocked at the familiar tone uttered with uncharacteristic condemnation, Araminta jerked her head up and beheld in the gloom a tight-lipped Roderick Woking.

For a moment she thought she would faint clean away. Roderick Woking was the man she'd regarded as her salvation six months ago when she so desperately needed a father to the child in her belly after Sir Aubrey had made himself unavailable by eloping with Hetty.

Mr. Woking had been so bowled over by Araminta's overtures that he'd done exactly as required and begged her to marry him. Or rather, Araminta had told him while he was recovering from a drunken stupor that that's what he'd done.

Not that their betrothal had lasted very long.

Tonight, was the first time Araminta's erstwhile suitor had spoken to her since she'd eloped with his uncle, Lord Debenham who'd blackmailed Araminta into marriage because he needed her testimony that she'd spent all night with him during that fateful evening at Vauxhall Gardens.

Araminta supposed Mr. Woking had every reason to feel uncharitable toward her, but it was his uncle to whom he should direct his ire.

She tilted her chin and sent him a frosty look. "My husband is not far away, Mr. Woking, and I know you detest him very much. Perhaps you should leave." Yes, Araminta really didn't need Mr. Woking creating a scene to make her evening worse than it already was.

Usually, Mr. Woking did as she told him. It was the one reason she'd thought he'd make an acceptable husband when she was desperate to have any husband after her predicament with the wretched baby.

Instead, he advanced a couple of steps and, to her utter horror, put his hand out to touch the great protuberance beneath her high-waisted evening gown. Hidden from the rest of the audience in the theater by the red velvet curtain, his face loomed close, his lips a tight, angry line, his eyes stormy with recrimination. Even in such poor light, Araminta shuddered to think of what her desperation had led her to do with this ghastly creature. Indeed, had Debenham not forced her into marriage, she'd have been saddled with this inferior specimen with his weak chin and turkey neck, bad teeth and worse breath—for life. But then she wondered if that would that have been such a bad thing. After all, she'd have been able to wield more power over him than she managed in the case of his commandeering uncle. To make matters worse, not long after her hasty marriage to Debenham she'd learned the undeserving Mr. Woking had been elevated to the peerage upon the unexpected death of two relatives in quick succession. Yes, indeed, if Debenham hadn't all but kidnapped her and blackmailed her into marriage, Araminta would now have everything she could have wished for—a wedding ring on her finger and an indulgent, if spineless and unattractive, husband.

That didn't make her feel any more charitable toward the chinless peer looking at her with such condemnation.

To her horror, he now asked in a low voice, "Have you told Debenham that it's my child you're carrying? Or shall I tell him?"

"How dare you insult me?" Araminta tossed her head and turned in her chair so she presented him with her side view, holding up her fan so that her outrage would not be observed by anyone who chanced to glance up from the stalls. Her whole body trembled, and she felt in that moment like bursting into tears. "What if you are overheard telling such lies?"

"Lies?" He sounded aghast as he plunged forward, whisking up her hand and bringing it to his lips. His look was no longer censorious but tortured. "There you sit, like an exquisite Madonna, carrying my child whom you are now going to parade to all the world and to my hateful uncle as the new heir to his estate if it's a boy. Do you know how it makes me feel every time I lay eyes upon you," he choked on a sob, "and to know that you were nearly mine? That you could have been my duchess, making me the happiest, proudest man in the land, squiring you to every grand occasion you wished to attend while we awaited our happy event?"

"You're dreaming, Mr. Woking."

"Lord Myles, if you please."

"You will always be Mr. Woking to me, and what…happened that night did not result in this for your uncle kidnapped me, as you know, and did the very same thing you did to me." She pushed up her chin, proudly. "Tell me, which of the two of you is the bigger, stronger man?"

Mr. Woking seemed unable to speak for the surge of apoplexy that rendered him like a gesticulating lobster.

"*Kidnapped* you? That's not what my eyes saw when I followed the sounds that drew me from Miss Hosking's ballroom to that bed chamber where my hateful uncle had enticed you, and where the pair of you were—" He broke off on a strangled hiss of rage. "What I beheld did not give the appearance of Miss Araminta Partington being *kidnapped*."

Sulkily, Araminta dropped her fan and fiddled with the tassel of her pelisse. "Your uncle blackmailed me. He needed my testimony to save him from the noose. He needed me to tell the world that I was with him at Vauxhall all night, when really he was having a meeting with two other men whom the Government believes are plotters. What were their names? Smythe and Buzby, that's right. Radicals out to bring down Westminster, I understand. He said if I did not pretend to be enjoying his attentions, he would...he would..." She thought wildly for something that might elicit Mr. Woking's finer feelings, or at least his sympathy.

"He would what?" Mr. Woking didn't sound too affected.

"He would ruin Papa and destroy Hetty's happiness." Araminta looked up at him with tear-filled eyes. "You know how tenuous things are between Debenham and Sir Aubrey who of course is now married to my dear sister? I couldn't let the worst happen to Hetty and Papa. The two people I love more than any others in the world, except for Mama."

Mr. Woking was still. Thinking. "He really threatened you?"

"Of course he threatened me," Araminta snapped, her anger getting the better of the affected tragedy she'd striven so hard to achieve. "Do you think I wanted to marry your uncle when I was already betrothed to you, and knowing that you had such prospects? You know me sufficiently, I'd wager, Mr. Woking, to realize that I would have far preferred to have married you than Debenham had he not all but held a knife at my throat, ripped off my clothes, and told me to smile for the crowd that he intended to see witness his evil plan to have me ruined and thereby force me to marry him." She dropped her fan into her lap and put her hands to her face, and the tears in her voice were real. "I am so unhappy, but what can I do?" She heaved in a breath and took her hands away. "What could I have done? You didn't save me," she added accusingly. "You believed I was as bad as everyone painted me."

When Mr. Woking leaned closer in, she waved him away, dismissively. "Leave me, Lord Myles." Her voice was quietly dignified now. "Whatever you might want to say, it's too late. And I hear footsteps. I do not want Debenham to catch us together when he's already so wildly jealous of you."

When she turned, there was no sign of Mr. Woking, but to her astonishment, there in the curtained alcove, stood the man she really would have chosen to marry above all others in the world—if there had been time—she reflected, tragically, clasping her hands across her swollen belly.

"Lord Ludbridge." Her gasp was unfeigned, the roiling excitement between her hips on par with the desire in her wildly beating heart. "My dear Teddy!" She half rose, as if he might take her in his arms and hold her to him. Like the last time they'd been together. Oh Lord, why had he been such a gentleman, refusing to allow himself to be seduced before he rushed off to do some apparently noble deed on the Continent?

Araminta had had everything so beautifully planned. With the child in her belly needing a father, and knowing Teddy was so madly in love with her, she knew he'd make her an honorable offer. Of marriage.

Indeed he had, but with the caveat that he needed to take the next boat to France and that he'd wed her when he returned. If he'd only taken what Araminta had offered, they could have been enjoying wildly blissful days and nights together, and Araminta would have been the happiest newlywed in the entire world. She'd have been married to the handsomest, kindest, most honorable man to walk the earth.

Instead, she'd been entirely abandoned by Teddy. *Of course* she couldn't wait two months for him to marry her. That's why, not one hour after Teddy had proposed and departed, and she'd come upon Mr. Woking as she'd been returning home in her carriage, her only option had been to seduce *him* in order to get the marriage proposal she so desperately needed.

She gave a little sob, then looked up when Teddy did not come to her. To her horror, he met her gaze with a cold stare so unlike his so perennially good-natured expression she almost felt like giving up on life. "I saw you from my box and waited until you were alone." His voice was stony, full of recrimination. "I told myself I should not. That I would only torture myself, but in the end I could not stay away."

Araminta forced herself to retain her dignity rather than display the hot indignation that had followed her brief desire to end it all. She did not deserve this. "Yet you chose to remain on the Continent more than two months, my Lord."

His eyes bored into hers with the heaviest reproach. "What reason was there for me to return when I heard the news of your marriage? I had left England the most joyful man on earth, but within days, the news of your faithlessness had caught up with me."

Araminta bit her lip as she wondered how much detail had been contained in the news he'd received. She dropped her eyes and studied the embroidery on her slippers. Debenham was generous with her wardrobe. The pin money she received was more than sufficient. He also did not demur when she presented him with the increasingly exorbitant bills of her milliner and mantua maker. Around her neck, the rubies and diamonds of her exquisite wedding gift, were cold. However, Teddy's generosity would have cast Debenham's in the shade, she was sure, and he would not have made her do the things Debenham enjoyed doing. Her husband's pleasure seemed to be heightened the more reluctant she was. Searching Teddy's face with tear-filled eyes, she said in a strained voice, "I tried to go after you the very night you left. I was mad with grief that you would leave me behind, and after Lady Marks's Riverside Soiree, I took a hackney and went with my maid and my chaperone to your townhouse to entreat you to delay your journey or to beg you to take me with you. Perhaps your butler did not tell you? I thought I would die if I were parted from you for so long after what we'd shared. The fireworks. Do you remember?"

He remained in the curtained alcove and his breath left him in a soft sigh before he admitted sadly, "I cannot see fireworks without being reminded of the woman I once loved more than life itself...until she wed another within days of my departure, proving just how little she truly felt for me."

Araminta stared at him, unsure what she could say. The cold, measured tone of the last part of his remark was torture. Yet this man was her destiny. The vibrant rapture she'd felt in his arms was the most sincere experience she'd ever had.

"I was blackmailed," she whispered.

"By Mr. Roderick Woking or by Lord Debenham?" He sounded curt as he shifted his weight and for a moment she was afraid he would leave her like this. "If I recall, you declared your betrothal to the former within a day of my leaving the country, but then you reneged on *his* offer in order to elope with Woking's *uncle*. What kind of a woman does that make you, Lady Debenham?"

Araminta's mouth dropped open. She was *really* indignant this time. "Do you truly imagine I wished to marry *either* of them? After I could have enjoyed wedded bliss with *you*? I despise Mr. Woking and I fear Lord Debenham, but I was in their clutches. All because of your brother!"

"My brother?" Teddy looked shocked. "What on earth are you talking about?"

Araminta beckoned him closer so she could lower her voice. Meanwhile, her mind was running in circles. Lord Ludbridge was angry, but she'd seen cracks in his armor. He could be brought around if she only found the right words, the right argument. And here it was. She even had truth on her side. "Surely your brother has told you about the government's suspicions regarding Debenham's involvement in a certain matter pertaining to...to espionage?" She went on at the flare in his eye. "You know of course that your brother, Ralph Tunley, is both Debenham's secretary and also sweetheart is my half-sister? Yes, it's scandalous, and I'm ashamed to admit it. I learned the truth a few months ago when we were mistaken for one another. Apparently, we share an uncommon similarity. You do not think so? Well, in certain lights, if we adopt the same smile and mannerisms we could be mistaken for twins. I've heard it from many, and I heard it from Lord Debenham. Come closer, Lord Ludbridge, so I can tell you of the terrible fate that befell me no sooner than you'd abandoned me."

Warily, he advanced, his expression a mixture of uncertainty and desire. Araminta reached up and touched his cheek briefly, leaving him, she hoped, in no doubt about the sincerity of her feelings. At last she could reveal a little of what lay behind Debenham's successful blackmail ploy. "The fact is, I was tragically mistaken for my half-sister Larissa when she visited Sir Aubrey in his supper box—alone—in Vauxhall Gardens," she whispered, cupping his cheek to bring his head closer to her lips. How she longed to nibble that beautiful earlobe. And that would only be the beginning. Exhaling on a heartfelt sigh, she continued, "Lord knows what she was doing, but then, to make matters worse, she was observed visiting Debenham. He didn't know what to do; he was outraged, of course, and sent her away. But evil tongues began to wag, claiming it was *me*. But Debenham *had* been with men he knew would place him under suspicion, and that's the reason he kidnapped me when I was for a moment separated from Hetty, and he held me prisoner in his supper box as he all but forced me to agree to marry him." All right, there was a bit of artistic license with this latter part but to her relief Teddy seemed to accept her word.

"Dear God, he kidnapped you to try and force your hand? Did he...?" Lord Ludbridge broke off, his skin taking on a darker hue which Araminta could see even in this dim light.

"Did he force me into anything? No, he did not. Not on this night, anyway." Araminta was conscious of the wretched baby turning a summersault. She'd thought her difficulties would be over when she found a father for it; yet keeping up the fiction that it had been conceived two months later than, in fact, this particular night in question, was proving a nightmare.

"Why did you not tell me this? I'd have ensured your reputation was not besmirched. Why could you not have trusted me?"

"I *wanted* to tell you, and that's part of the reason I rushed after you in the middle of the night after I'd agreed to marry you...but you'd already left for France." She gulped. "I knew there could not be this terrible secret between us. On my return in the carriage, not two minutes after my maid had spoken to your butler, by chance we happened upon Mr. Woking who was in his cups and who stumbled in front of the carriage. Lord, we nearly rode right over him! We stopped to pick him up and take him home, and he told me that his uncle was about to tell the world that I'd...spent the *entire* night with him in his supper box, as he needed an alibi since my half-sister had sketched a drawing that showed Lord Debenham in company with the other two plotters whom the English Government are investigating for some nefarious dealings. You do realize your brother is working in secret for them? Yes, I discovered that through my maid, though I've not told Debenham. No, not even my own husband, for I never wished to marry the blackguard. Never! Mr. Woking said that his uncle was intent upon this ruthless plan, and that since you had left the country and could not protect me, he would do the honorable thing, and that we could *pretend* to be betrothed as it was the only way to keep me safe from his evil uncle's clutches. But even that wasn't enough." She put her hands to her face and shook her bowed head. "No, the night we announced our betrothal, Lord Debenham followed me to the lady's mending room at Miss Hosking's own betrothal ball, dragged me into an empty room, and ensured that my being compromised was thoroughly witnessed and documented. He forced me onto the bed so that I would have no choice but to marry him...and you were not there to protect me," she added with a little sob and in a suitably accusing tone as she dropped her hands.

Watching Teddy's mouth drop open and the flare of horror in his eyes was the only satisfying part of her entire evening.

And the fact that she had not lost the art of turning a bad situation to her advantage.

CHAPTER 6

*K*itty breathed in the now familiar smell of oil paint, rancid powder, and smoke with her usual delight as she sat at her dressing table and powdered her face with a well-dipped rabbit's paw. Around her a dozen chattering, bustling actresses prepared themselves while Kitty, as the jewel of the night, had her own attendant to comb her hair, two thick fair ropes adorned with ribbons in the first scene. By the end, it would be a lustrous, tangled mass of curls after a stricken Romeo knotted his grasping hands in it.

Shakespeare's *Romeo and Juliet* had been enjoying spectacular reviews since it had begun playing the week before after three weeks of rehearsals. Each night they'd played to a full house. Mr. Lazarus had forgiven Kitty after she'd pliantly kissed him during rehearsal and allowed him to fondle her rump. Fortunately, it seemed that was all he was after, so Kitty had been given the role with her virtue intact.

She was now enjoying a great deal of fawning admiration from a range of men. Bouquets of flowers were delivered nightly, notes declaring ardent love from complete strangers were regularly handed to her by glowering chorus girls, including one very sweet piece of parchment from Lord Silverton, in which he lauded her stage presence and beauty and wished her much happiness in her chosen career, evincing the deepest regret that another had stolen her heart and offering her a refuge should she need one.

Kitty had hugged the single yellow rose, signifying loyalty rather than love, while an odd feeling had roiled in her belly; but then, a mealy-mouthed Jennie had come into the dressing room carrying an enormous bouquet of red roses, and a message from Lord Nash that he looked forward to paying his respects to Kitty in person after the night's performance.

"Don't go losing your heart to this one, now," Jennie warned. "'E likes to break in all the new ones."

Kitty thought Jennie was just jealous, for she knew sincerity, and that's what had shone from her first shared gaze with the handsome viscount. Lord Nash, she was quite sure, was the handsome dark-haired swain the gypsy fortune-teller had prophesied as her destiny. If his inky-black curls and smoldering eyes did not make the argument sufficiently, how else could the small dueling scar beneath his right eye be explained? Not everyone believed in destiny, but Kitty didn't have a more compelling argument to guide her.

So, while generally Kitty relished every moment on stage, tonight she couldn't wait for the performance to be over so she could at last gaze upon the Adonis whose image had haunted her since he'd first swept his extravagant bow just before her first disastrous audition.

It had been love at first sight. She'd relived the scene so many times, pinpointing the moment they had seared each other's souls with that single, piercing look. She conceded that it had been very brief and that right on the heels of that piercing look she'd gone off to enjoy herself very much with Lord Silverton.

But Lord Silverton had declared quite roundly that he was offering only to set her up as his mistress and would not marry her.

Lord Nash, by contrast, was utterly besotted and, if the fortune-teller was correct, inclined to follow the lead of Lord Hamilton who'd plucked his true love from the gutter, making her the incomparable Lady Emma Hamilton, famed for her beauty—and her scandalous love affair with Admiral Nelson.

And then another performance was over and Lord Nash was here, exquisite in evening clothes that molded his well-built form, his dark, curling hair falling rakishly over his noble forehead.

"Miss Bijou, you were superb!" With a mixture of feline grace and almost uncontained exuberance, he crossed the room to offer her another of his extravagant bows. And Kitty, aware that Jennie was nearby and clearly furious, basked in the praise and attention from this scion of nobility, this creature from another planet, it seemed.

"I should like to take you to supper. Do, I beg you, accept." He went down on one knee and held his arms out in a gesture of supplication, causing Kitty to giggle while Jennie huffed just behind her shoulder.

"I should love to go to supper with you if you will allow me a few moments to change, my Lord." She knew she was blushing furiously, and that heat beaded her upper lip over the thick make-up she'd not yet removed. Yet still, he called her exquisite as if he could see beyond her failings. That was true love.

When he'd left the room after telling her he'd wait for as long as it took, Jennie sidled up to where she was sitting at her dressing table her and began to run her fingers over the cards and bouquets. "I used to get the same attention when I played Desdemona last season," she said. "Lord Nash used to invite me out to supper, too."

Kitty refused to allow her exuberance to be dampened. Jennie was pretty but in a common way. With her fiery red hair and pale skin she was striking, but already she was starting to look raddled. And her voice was coarse. Lord Nash might flatter and flirt with such a girl, but he would not, could not, marry her. But Kitty was the daughter of Viscount Partington. She had ambitions. One day, she *could* be like the beautiful but low-born Emma Hamilton who had married Lord Hamilton, the British Envoy to Naples. Lissa had told her such dreams rarely happened in life, but the gypsy had foretold it.

"Then you agree he is a charming gentleman," Kitty said sweetly. "I'm sure you won't begrudge me an evening out in his company, too."

"'E will expect more than supper." Jennie lounged against the dressing table, twisting one of her red curls about her finger.

Kitty felt herself blush even more. She turned, suddenly angry.

"What business of yours is it whether we go for some dancing? Or to play a game of faro?"

Jennie sniggered. "You think I'm jealous, and so I am. But I'm also giving you fair warning of the kind of rogue our fine and handsome Lord Nash really is. I would 'ate you to 'arbor grand illusions only to 'ave them shattered by the end of the evening. Or morning."

Kitty rose. "You think I am so easily seduced?"

"The mere fact you will be alone with 'im will 'ave others assume it. You are naturally not so naïve. You 'ave such airs and speak like a lady, but you must 'ave lived under a stone before you came 'ere if you don't know that all actresses are considered lightskirts. And most of us are, if only to pay the rent. Where do you live? With your respectable mama and papa? I think not. Do they even know that their daughter is an adventuress, about to fall from her lofty 'eights if she accepts 'is Lordship's invitation?"

Kitty felt like tossing the shoe she'd just removed from her right foot in Jennie's direction, but remembered that ladies didn't do such things—although she'd seen Araminta do just this when spying on her through the window once. Snatching up her evening gown from where it was folded among a pile of her other modest belongings, she shrugged herself out of her robe and began to dress for the most exciting night of her life.

"Thank you for offering me such pearls of wisdom and insights on your own life, Jennie," she said through gritted teeth. To her chagrin, Jennie was now helping do up the tiny pearl buttons at the back of her gold net evening gown.

When the girl had finished, she ran her hands over the beautiful fabric and murmured, "Where did you get this? Not from a second-hand barrow for it is barely worn? Did you steal it? Or were you once a loyal retainer given it by your mistress before you were dismissed without a character? That's what 'appened to me, you know. I wasn't always an actress. In fact, I were quite 'appy in service until the master of the 'ouse took a liking to me, causing 'is missus to take a definite *unliking* to me and throwing me out on my ear. If there's anyone who knows the fickle ways of men, it's me. So now I've warned you about 'is Lordship, you go out and enjoy yerself. Just don't come crying on my shoulder when 'e breaks yer foolish heart."

Kitty didn't respond. She bent down at the dressing table to secure her feathered headdress, pulled on her gloves, stood up to fasten her pelisse quickly down the front, and then hurried toward the door.

She could hear Jennie's light footsteps behind her, but ignored her parting words. "My, my, but ain't you the lady of quality? 'Eads will turn as 'is Lordship squires you to London's finest establishments, though I reckon 'e might take you to better places than 'e took me. I always wanted to dine at *Madame Mirabeau*, a most rarefied and elite establishment for dancing with a fine bit of supper served, but I never 'ad the rigout and I couldn't get me voice quite right. You'll do just fine."

Kitty refused to turn her head, but she could hear the sudden brightness in Jennie's voice as she added, "But 'e'll break your 'eart just the same."

KITTY WAS ABLE TO DISMISS THIS PREDICTION THE MOMENT SHE BEHELD his Lordship's beatific smile as he met her at the theater door.

"I thought we would dine at *Madame Mirabeau*," he told her. "If anyone asks who you are I shall tell them you are a runaway foreign princess. That'll keep them guessing." It seemed he was as caught up in the excitement of the evening's possibilities as she was. Beneath a gas lamp, she slanted a look up at him and was instantly reassured by his burning gaze and the tiny scar beneath his right eye. Yes, he was the man of her fantasies. She'd dreamed of him; she could almost persuade herself she'd known him from another lifetime, and she was sure he felt the same. They were as one. The future was thrilling. She imagined the gossip sheets gushing over the extraordinary Miss Bijou who'd taken London by storm and then stolen the heart of Lord Nash, a viscount who was in the marital sights of every designing debutante and her mama.

"Up here, my sweet." They'd taken Lord Nash's carriage several blocks to their destination and now, out on the pavement, he stood back for her to step through a low doorway from which swept a narrow staircase. Kitty could hear a rumble of noise from the hidden chamber above and excitement fizzled through her, but at the same time she felt nervous.

"*What* is this place you taking me?" she asked.

"*Madame Mirabeau's* salon, and if you have not heard of her, let me tell you she has the only salon in London worth attending." He paused and lowered his voice. "Only at *Madame Mirabeau's* salon will you see a duchess take tea with an actress, which is why it amused me to bring you tonight. *Madame Mirabeau* is a great admirer of the arts and will no doubt already have heard of you."

"Do you really think so?"

To her astonishment, he bent his head and gave her a quick kiss on the nose. "Who would not have heard of the astonishingly talented and completely delectable Miss Bijou? Ah, here is our hostess herself, the Countess of Orne. Comtesse, might I have the pleasure of introducing to you fair Juliet. I told you it was my intention to pluck her from the theater and bring her here to meet you."

Kitty stared wide-eyed at the stately woman who was regarding her critically through a pair of bright blue eyes that seemed to have been chosen to match her gown of royal blue satin. Behind her the company ebbed and flowed like a sea of richly garbed marine creatures.

The comtesse inclined her head and Kitty curtsied, suddenly afraid, for she did not seem to look kindly upon her at all. But then, her hostess smiled and held out her hand. "Child, for that is what you are, you have stolen the very role I coveted when I was your age, and might have played as well as you had such pursuits been permitted to one of my station. Alas, I was forced to follow a very sedate path, if you discount the upheavals that forced me to flee my old home in Paris."

"I'm sorry, Comtesse."

"Life is too short for regrets. I find enjoyment in meeting the artistic world here in my drawing room. Tell me a little of your life in the theater. Lord Nash knows how much I love to hear such stories, though he may choose to leave us alone for such a conversation. That's right, Lord Nash, you are dismissed."

To Kitty's astonishment, this woman of such rarefied grandeur seemed to hang on her every word as Kitty told her of the rehearsals and the mishaps, but the excitement and triumphs, too.

"If I could have had the choice when I was a child, it would have been to live daringly. To be someone exciting and different, like you. Make the most of what you have been given. Don't squander your gift and beauty." Kitty was enraptured. Lord Nash had obediently left her side to converse with various others, but every few minutes he'd return like the most attentive of lovers. Speaking to this grand old woman, Kitty felt reinforced by the rightness of the path she was taking. She had followed her dreams to become a celebrated actress and she had found the love of her life. The man who would marry her. It was all as the gypsy had foretold.

After an hour of riveting conversation, she looked up when Lord Nash touched her arm, indicating the exit with a smile. Kitty was fully aware that going out into the night, alone with Lord Nash, was the start of her greatest adventure and her heart skittered with excitement.

In the moonlight, he looked at her with such love and longing, she almost stamped her foot with impatience that he bundle her into his carriage and take her to their place of assignation. He would brand her his. She had learned much since she'd left her cloistered home. The stirrings of her body when Lord Silverton had kissed her had been the start, but she knew he was mixed up in dangerous activities, that he would not marry her and that he could not be the destiny that had been foretold.

Silently she settled herself in the carriage, enjoying Lord Nash's warmth as he joined her, sitting close and obediently raising her head so he could kiss her in the dark. The gentle motion over the cobblestones seemed to feed the kiss. There was something magical about being in a capsule, transported through time to some unknown but exciting and magical destination with the gentle, sensitive mouth of the man of her dreams making magic in her first real intimacy.

No word was uttered throughout the short journey. Nor did they speak when they stopped in front of what she presumed was his townhouse, and he led her down some stairs and through a back entrance. His concern was that she not be recognized, and so going through the servants' entrance bolstered her belief in his care for her. She was taking a dangerous path—one that would horrify every member of her family—but so assured was she that it would lead to the outcome she believed was her destiny, she was prepared to take such risks along the way. If she hadn't taken the risk of coming to London, she'd still be at home looking after Mama and the baby, and she'd be miserable. If she weren't taking this risk to prove to Lord Nash how much she trusted him, he'd lose faith in her.

He took her hand at the bottom of a staircase and gently led her, with only the light of a candle he'd plucked from a sconce in the scullery, up two flights of stairs and along a dark passage. Near the end, he stopped before a door and quietly turned the doorknob.

Kitty's heart was almost bursting by the time he'd opened it, led her inside, and put the candle down upon a chest of drawers. She needed no persuading, melting into his arms and raising her head for his kiss. Tenderly he touched his lips to hers, trailing sparks of fire along her décolletage as he moved his mouth lower, kissing the swell of her breasts, slowly moving up along her throat, kissing her ears, her eyes. She went limp in his arms, and he whisked her from the floor and placed her on the bed. The mattress was the softest she'd ever felt beneath her. She thought of Mrs. Mobbs's dreadful straw pallet and imagined her life with darling Lord Nash.

In two weeks, she'd already become the toast of Covent Garden, and Lord Nash had feted her after every performance in the most gentlemanly manner. He'd lauded her beauty and talent to the Comtesse, taking Kitty to mix with high society. Was that not proof of his ultimately honorable intentions? It did not occur to Kitty to play the coy maiden, even though it had been drummed into her since infancy that young ladies did not go alone—into bedchambers—with single men. But nor did they become actresses and have any kind of adventure. Kitty was taking charge of her life, one adventurous step at a time, to achieve the marvelous outcome, the dazzling future, she knew was her reward.

Lord Nash was respectful, thoughtful and kind, and she was going to win his heart. Being an actress and illegitimate would not prove the irrevocable impediments everyone said they would. Not in the face in true love.

She gave a little giggle when he caressed her ankle and tossed off her slipper. "A bed is not the place for that, is it?" she whispered, and he nuzzled her nose, his smile faintly discernible, and laughingly agreed. "Nor for these," he added, walking his fingers up her calf to her knee and playing with the laces that tied up her stockings. "Oh, and my goodness, is this a petticoat? We shall have to remove that also. Only we can't reach that until we remove your gown, can we, my love? Oh, but you are a goddess. I want to see you naked. Completely naked." And he rose onto his knees, turned her on her front and undid the five tiny buttons that secured the back of her gold net and silk evening gown.

Kitty would agree she didn't want to spoil her gown, but she wasn't entirely sure she liked the idea of being viewed with nothing on.

"Shy?" he asked when she resisted the removal of the next layer. "Well, if you've never done this before, as I suspect, we'll take it more slowly." With agonizing care, he inched his hand up her thigh, caressing her skin in slow circuits, which had the result of firing Kitty up to a ridiculous degree. But her breathing was a giveaway, and he chuckled again. "I'm taking it slowly, my angel, because it's your first time, but oh Lord, I'm in a fever to have you."

Kitty was in a fever to be had. She'd been warned by the girls at the theater that the first time would be painful, though she found that hard to imagine when her insides felt molten, and when her body cleaved with desire as his fingers breached the slick wetness and heat between her legs.

"Oh my, this will be delightfully easy and not at all uncomfortable for you," he said approvingly, but when he moved aside to hastily divest himself of his breeches, and she saw the huge appendage that apparently was supposed to force itself inside her, she gasped with fear.

Rejoining her on the bed, he guided her face around so he could smile at her. "It's very large, I know, but you will gain so much more pleasure for that." He licked his lips as he smiled lazily at her. "Take it in your hand and feel it. Get used to it first. Ah yes, that's very good, squeeze a little harder. And now it's time for it to find a new home. Are you ready?" With a soft murmur of endearment, he gently pushed her onto her back and rose over her. Cupping her cheek briefly, he positioned the tip of his manhood at her entrance and half entered her.

Kitty gasped with surprise, and he smiled reassuringly. "Nothing to fear. Take a deep breath." He pushed again, and this time Kitty felt a ripping, burning sensation and cried out with pain. But he didn't stop to accommodate her discomfort this time; and besides, the increasing rhythm of his plunging in and out soon caught her up in her own pleasure. The escalation of desire that had been put on hold suddenly burst free and was soon all that occupied her mind as she clung onto it like a drowning woman. Until finally it was as if the dam of pleasure within her burst and she was gripped by contractions of unadulterated delight, which seemed to launch Lord Nash into his own journey of satisfaction.

Breathing heavily, once he'd well and truly climaxed, he clutched her in his arms, while Kitty laughed for the sheer joy of it. "Oh my, that was mighty good," she gasped.

"I'm sure you're the first deflowered virgin who's ever put it in those terms," he said, stroking her head against his shoulder. "And you're all mine. The toast of Covent Garden. You are pure heaven, Miss La Bijou. I shall treat you as you deserve to be treated...like a princess."

What magic words. She'd followed her heart, and it had not let her down. Kitty felt the world a wondrous place as she drifted off to sleep beside her valiant viscount. The kindest, handsomest, most exciting man in the world. And when he woke her in the early hours of the night to repeat the exercise, she was more than ready, and with the knowledge that she would not be like her mother and conceive an unwanted child. Darling, incomparable Nash; she felt she could never get enough of him, a feeling she truly believed was mutual, and one backed up by his devotion the following morning when he helped her to dress, took her to a mantua maker for some articles to augment her wardrobe, and then escorted her to the theater for rehearsal. Kitty didn't mind that Jennie passed them on the stairs, turning to look over her shoulder and to raise an eyebrow that said so much that didn't need to be put into words.

Well, Jennie was going to have to eat her words. Lord Nash was going to break her heart, was he? No, he was going to make Kitty the happiest young woman in the entire world.

CHAPTER 7

*K*itty felt like purring as she opened her eyes to the morning light streaming through the window. She curled against Nash, who put his arms around her and kissed the top of her head.

For two weeks, they'd been inseparable. Finally, he was talking about securing her own accommodation though she'd much rather he talked about making her his wife. Her vague memories of what the fortune-teller had said all those years ago were that the true love she would find would be like a brilliant, brightly burning star that would obliterate all society's obstacles. And wasn't that turning out to be true?

Gallantly, Nash had escorted her to the theater each night, waiting for her after her performance with a lavish bouquet of flowers.

On one occasion, she'd seen Lord Silverton passing by in the street, a well-dressed young lady on his arm. Kitty had just issued out from the theater with Lord Nash, as it happened, and the two men had doffed their hats, Lord Silverton offering her a warm smile. She'd wished she could talk to him for he had been such pleasant company, but he was with a lady who must have been some relative or respectably married, for he did not stop. Kitty felt a stab of disappointment. One day, she would be deemed respectable company enough for Lord Silverton to happily introduce her to his escort. She would not be like her mama, always the subject of whispers and never able to appear in public with Kitty's father. Nor would Kitty keep producing infants to bear the moniker of bastard, a blight that had all but ruined Kitty's life. Thanks to the advice of the girls from the theater, she'd sought help from Mrs. Mobbs who, it transpired, regularly dispensed vials containing the seeds of the Queen Anne's Lace plant, supposed to prevent conception if taken immediately after the act.

Now Lord Nash put the tip of his tongue into her ear, chuckling as the action caused her to shiver with anticipation. "Alas, I have work to do today and you must take your leave, but when you have your own abode, I can visit you anytime I want to, and we'll not be forced apart like this."

"Newlyweds are forgiven for wanting to be together all the time."

"Indeed they are, but we are not newlyweds. Now Kitty, out or you'll be late for rehearsal."

She liked his commanding tone, while the fact she was working for London's busiest theater made her glow with pride. She was, however, slightly disappointed by his dismissal of her reference to newlyweds. Still, she had the knowledge to cling to that her future was carved in stone. So much of what had been foretold had come true. As for achieving the rest—the joyous legal union— she just had to be patient.

When she was dressed and ready to leave, she wondered how she had not died of boredom in her little country village. She tried to feel guilt over leaving Mama, then considered that her mother had willingly chosen to live in sin and break her own parents' hearts, so how could her mama condemn the life Kitty had chosen.

"Go forth and thrill the audience with another of your heart-stopping performances, my sweet." Darling Nash kissed her full on the lips as he prepared to leave her just inside the theater door that led off the side lane. Several actresses halfway up the stairs craned their necks, and Kitty felt a thrill at the spectacle they must make. Here she was, her dreams almost fulfilled. She was doing something with her life that made it extraordinary, and she was being rewarded with everything for which she could have hoped.

"And you'll be waiting for me?"

"Of course, my love."

Jennie swept in from the street, enveloped in a black cloak. She pushed back the hood and sent Lord Nash a coquettish smile as she bent and ostentatiously adjusted her garter on the top step, saying over her shoulder, "You're looking tired, my Lord. I 'ope you will relax long enough to see tonight's performance. It's never the same twice."

"Indeed, it's not, but tonight I have other business. I shall return to fetch Kitty at the usual time."

"Ah, Kitty, whom we all adore." Jennie rose and put an arm about Kitty's shoulders, saying with false camaraderie, "The audience loves 'er, everyone backstage loves 'er, and your love is the crowning glory, Lord Nash. I speak from experience."

Kitty stepped away at the look of feigned tragedy upon the other woman's face, adding when Lord Nash had left, "He's no longer yours, Jennie, and I'm sorry you feel dejected but life moves on and so must we."

"Aren't you the wellspring of all wisdom? Speaking from *such* experience, too. Just you wait, Miss La Bijou. One is never 'appiest than just before a fall."

They were in the busy changing rooms now amid the bustle of costume changes, urgent requests for assistance in the hair and corsetry departments, and general frenzy. As she seated herself before a mirror, Kitty sent Jennie a cold stare. "I'm sorry you resent me, but I didn't chase Lord Nash and force him to shower me with his attentions."

Jennie returned the stony stare. Then she shrugged and smiled brightly as she wriggled into a figure-hugging peasant's costume. "I don't resent you. Not too much, at any rate. I feel sorry for you with your eager innocence. You think 'e's in love with you, don't you?"

"He *is* in love with me," Kitty returned hotly before lowering her voice, for several girls who'd been giggling in the corner as they helped each other with their hair, had turned. "Tomorrow I move into a townhouse he has secured for me."

"With a six-month lease? Or perhaps twelve months? It really doesn't matter." Jennie shrugged, tying the laces at her bodice and smoothing her hands over her hips. "Unless 'e marries you—which 'e won't since you're just an actress 'e can 'ave you whenever 'e wants—then I cannot believe your claim. Love? All men have a wandering eye, and Lord Nash is one of the worst."

Kitty jumped up from her seat, drawing herself up to her full five feet four inches, and glared. "You think I can't keep him. That's what you're saying. Well, mark my words, Lord Nash will remain true and loyal. You only have to think of Lady Hamilton to know that there *are* men who make wives of girls like us."

Jennie waved a dismissive hand as she prepared to quit the dressing room amidst a gaggle of chorus girls. "We must continue this diverting conversation another time, Kitty darling, for Mr. Lazarus is shouting for us to get ready to go on stage in ten minutes."

Kitty found it hard to put away the anger she felt at her conversation with Jennie. Perhaps it was this, combined with the knowledge that she wasn't being observed tonight by Nash, that made her miss her lines several times. She knew her performance was less than glittering and so was hardly surprised, yet still rather chastened, to be called up to Mr. Lazarus's sitting room when the play was over and everyone had started filtering out into the night.

"Mrs. Lazarus and I wish to speak to you about tonight," he told her, drawing her to stand in front of the stuffed mannequin purported to be his late wife. "Three times you had to be prompted. That is not at all like you, Miss La Bijou. We have an understudy eager to step up if you continue such disappointing performances."

This was worse than Kitty had feared. Jennie had made it clear she was only too eager to knock her off her perch. She sent a panicked glance between Mrs. Lazarus who was leaning at a rather odd angle, and her director. "Please, no. I...was very upset when I went on stage. I know my performance left much to be desired, but I've not disappointed the audience on every other night. You've said so yourself, Mr. Lazarus."

He pursed his mouth as he nodded thoughtfully, his thumbs stuck in his waistcoat while he paced around her to stand before the mannequin. "What do you say, Mrs. Lazarus? Should this be a warning only, or is it indeed time to give Jennie an opportunity to play the fair and lovely Juliet?"

After a moment's silence, he returned to face Kitty. "Mrs. Lazarus believes in giving everyone a single chance. Her charitable nature was one of the reasons I married the good woman, and it is why I continue to seek her advice. So, Miss La Bijou, ensure you get a good night's sleep, put your worldly cares aside for they do not belong on stage, and we shall see you at the theater tomorrow when you thrill the audience with another of your exceptional performances."

Gulping her relief after gushing thanks to Mr. Lazarus, Kitty hurried down the staircase to the almost deserted theater. With the actors and actresses having left, it felt, and even smelled, strange. Not just empty, but abandoned. A few candles burned from sconces offering a little light, but Kitty had never seen it with such a cold and loveless feeling. Several girls—little more than children—were sweeping the stage, and one of them looked up when they heard Kitty ask into the darkness, "Nash?"

"If you's after Lord Nash 'e's got 'is carriage waitin' fer yer in the street."

Relieved, Kitty hurried across the slippery cobbles in the dark laneway toward his Lordship's handsome equipage, the footman jumping down from the running board to open the door for Kitty and help her inside. She closed her eyes as it rocked gently on its journey, and she imagined the comfort she'd feel from having his Lordship's arms about her as she poured out her distress. She hoped he wouldn't be too late home to join her. Tonight was the first time since he'd taken her into his bed that he'd been away from her, and she felt strangely bereft.

She'd performed each night for two weeks without a break, so it was little wonder she was exhausted and easily upset, she thought as the carriage drew to a halt. The coachman came around to open the carriage door and she stepped outside, shocked to find herself in front of Mrs. Mobbs's lowly residence.

"'Is Lordship says it's only fer t'night, Miss La Bijou. 'E says 'e will send a carriage 'round to fetch yer jest after noon.'"

To fetch her just after noon? She knew what that meant. Tomorrow he would take her to look at the sweet bower he intended to secure for her. She shivered with excitement, wishing she could curl into his side tonight and be woken by his usual lusty dawn love-making before another wonderful day began.

"Thank you, Jack," she said when he'd seen her safely to the door, for it was a neighborhood rife with rogues, and she was only too happy to see the last of it. Mrs. Mobbs was more slovenly and bad-tempered than she'd first thought.

She was certainly bad-tempered when she opened the door to Kitty's repeated knocking, pushing back the greasy strands of gray hair that had escaped from beneath her grubby nightcap, and pushing out her massive, equally grubbily upholstered bosom with a show of belligerence. "Wot yer doin' 'ere when yer said, quite certain-like, yer'd not be sleepin' 'ere agin. I got three in yer bed, so it's the floor fer yer, miss."

With awful certainty, Kitty knew that meant no blanket, either. Before she had come to live with Mrs. Mobbs, her only real experience of deprivation had been when visiting the cottagers with her mother on some of their 'do-gooding' expeditions. Not that there'd been too many of those. Kitty well remembered the disapproving responses that had made her mother blush, and Lissa cry, before Kitty was old enough to realize that poor people liked to be able to take the moral high ground when it made them feel superior.

"Well, are yer comin' in or wot?"

Kitty swung around and hailed John who was just climbing back onto the box. "I've changed my mind, Mrs. Mobbs," she said over her shoulder. "Sorry to have woken you."

She didn't wait to hear the inevitable grumbles, or worse, but instead climbed into Lord Nash's carriage, reassuring Jack that Lord

Nash would be delighted to be surprised. Hadn't she'd spent the past ten days all but having taken up residence with Lord Nash, and, in fact, a number of articles of her clothing were in his keeping. He'd been immensely generous, buying her gifts to supplement her wardrobe, or just to please her during every jaunt they'd taken together. Of course, he'd be delighted to find her in his bed when he returned from his night of gaming or drinking at his club.

Kitty understood it was too early for a marriage proposal, but was satisfied by the intensity of his Lordship's devotion and confident it would lead to the ring, the legal union her mother had failed to secure. But then, her mother had been weak. Kitty would never have forgiven a man who had betrayed her as Lord Partington had betrayed her mother. She'd never have consented to live with him in sin, and bear his bastards.

Bastards. The description never failed to make Kitty hot with shame, and deeply resentful toward her mother. Her whole life, Kitty had only ever known disapproval. It was only here in London that she felt accepted. She was good at her craft, and the exhilaration of being feted wherever she went, and admired—no, loved—by the handsomest, most eligible young buck in all the country was like an addiction.

"Thank you, John," she whispered to the coachman who had again tried to persuade her to return to Mrs. Mobbs. She stepped onto the pavement into the dark. It was only a few feet to the railing. Tonight she would take the servants' entrance.

Susan, the tweeny who slept on a pallet by the kitchen fire, let her in, rubbing her eyes and greeting her sleepily. With mounting excitement, Kitty crept along the corridor toward his Lordship's bedchamber.

She didn't knock as she quietly turned the doorknob. She was too excited at the prospect of sliding into bed beside him and surprising him, if he'd returned from his club. What would he do? He'd laugh his delight, kiss her nose and then make wild and passionate love to her. Oh, but he made her ridiculously happy. Kitty had never known such lighthearted joy in her whole life. She was young, beautiful, with the world at her feet, and soon she'd be slotted into the kind of life she ought to have had if her father had behaved as honor dictated.

Softly, she closed the door behind her, anticipation bubbling in her veins. Lissa had always painted herself as the sensible, older sister, but Kitty was the one who was going to distinguish herself in the family for having gone after her dreams and achieving what the rest of her family had not: wealth and respectability.

The room was in darkness, but the window was open, and a slight breeze rustled the curtains, bathing part of the capacious four-poster bed in light from the large, waxing moon outside.

With each step toward the bed, Kitty divested herself of one more article of clothing. She'd be completely naked by the time she slid in beside Nash, she decided. Darling Nash, who appeared to be murmuring in his sleep as he sometimes did. Occasionally, even, he'd thrash about, which he suddenly began to do now. Kitty always comforted him after these nightmares which he said he'd had for as long as he could remember, and somehow it endeared him to Kitty even more. She liked to think of herself as somewhere between his muse and the woman who brought him peace and, yes, comfort.

But then another odd noise jarred a discordant note in the stillness. A throaty purr of satisfaction. Feminine. Kitty stopped a couple of feet from the bed and strained to see in the darkness. She could make out Nash's handsome head upon the pillow, turned toward the window, and the mound of his body beneath the bedclothes. He gave a soft groan, and Kitty smiled. She'd make him moan even more throatily before long. She'd removed her gown. The four buttons at the back and her front-laced short stays meant she could dress and undress on her own, and relatively quickly, which was what she was doing now, her fingers eagerly loosening the ribbons of her corsetry so that she was only in her chemise when she climbed beneath the covers

Her arrival created more of a stir than she'd expected. Nash jerked upright with a cry, but it wasn't his surprise that jolted Kitty to the very core. No, it was the wriggling beneath Kitty of a second body followed by a sharp, feminine shriek as Jennie's head emerged from where, Kitty now realized, she'd been attending to pleasuring her darling Nash's nether regions.

The two women looked at each other with horror and loathing. Nash, meanwhile, was choking out some kind of excuse. Apology. Kitty didn't wait to hear it. Gathering her discarded clothes into her arms as she made her sobbing progress from the bed to the door, she dashed into the passageway, ignoring his shout of pain as she slammed the door and obviously caught some tender piece of his body in the process.

Barely able to breathe, she stumbled down the stairs and into the kitchen, crying even harder as she clumsily put on her stays over her chemise in front of the fire. Susan blinked at her owlishly, crawling up from her pallet to help Kitty slip first her petticoat over her head and then her evening gown.

Kitty had lost one shoe along the way, but she wasn't going back for it. Her complacency and confidence in Nash's love had been shattered, and she couldn't face him right now. She knew he'd come after her. Well, she was reasonably certain he would. He'd try and bluster his way through it. Maybe he'd say he'd mistaken Jennie for Kitty. All Kitty knew was that this was her greatest betrayal, and she had to get away immediately and gather her thoughts.

"I'll be all right," she told Susan as she flung herself out of the door and into the dark street, hobbling in only one shoe, and only realizing as the cool night air grazed her cheek that she had nowhere to go. Where did Lissa live? She had no idea. Walking alone in the darkness was madness. The only place she had to go was Mrs. Mobbs's. She fumbled in her reticule. Thank the lord she had just enough to pay for the journey. And hopefully standing on the cobbles in such a respectable area was not immediately perilous. At least, it wouldn't be as perilous as if she were standing in the street outside Mrs. Mobbs's where she felt she could not return to disturb her irascible landlady a second time in one night.

Still wracked with sobs, she waited, but no passing hackney offered salvation. Her mind was in a whirl with what she'd just witnessed. Her heart was breaking. She thought she'd go mad.

Would Nash follow and beg her forgiveness? What would she do then? He'd betrayed her. Just like her father had betrayed her mother. Kitty had thought she was cleverer than her mother. She'd thought she knew what to do once she'd snared her man, how to hold him and make her his—forever. She'd always condemned her mother for failing to hold her father. Maybe she was just like her mother after all. Easily persuaded. Stupid.

Maybe Nash would lurch out into the street, go down on bended knee and ask her to marry him. Would she say yes after he'd deceived her with another woman?

But, of course, he was not going to do that. The best she could hope for was to have him groveling before her. Of course, he must care. But did he care enough to—

"Kitty!"

She turned toward the townhouse, the voice issuing from the stairs from the basement. Nash.

"Kitty!"

But then her name was called from a quite different direction. She heard the jingle of harness; the creak of leather as the heavy equipage of a fine carriage came to a halt right in front of her.

On one side of her, Lord Nash, who'd appeared in breeches, his shirt flapping about his thighs, his dark curls flopping about his face, was begging her to come back.

Meanwhile, in the street, Lord Silverton was leaning out of the carriage window inquiring with concern if she was all right.

"Kitty! I'm sorry! It wasn't what you thought." That was Lord Nash. Distraught! Ashamed, but only because he'd been caught. And telling lies! Did he think she was stupid?

Then Lord Silverton was asking again, this time more urgently, "Kitty, has something happened?"

She hunched over, not wanting Lord Silverton to see her distress.

"Do you want me to take you home?"

Despite her grief, there was something familiar and comforting in Lord Silverton's voice. He had not deceived her. He was a good man, despite the fact he was caught up in some havey-cavey business that was beyond her knowledge. That didn't matter right now. All that did was that he was offering her a chance not to be caught up in the treachery and deception that mired a woman in misery for following her foolish heart. She couldn't go back, even as she heard Nash's voice draw nearer, louder with urgency and self-recrimination.

Oh, she wanted to go to him, but an image of her mother loomed large. She could not be like her mother.

Nash's voice cut through her thoughts with greater urgency. "Forgive me! It was a terrible mistake. I'll never do it again. Believe me."

She wavered. She could go back to him, of course. Probably he'd sent Jennie packing, and his bed would now be free to accommodate Kitty's warm and supposedly willing body.

But, not yet. Not so easily.

"Thank you, Lord Silverton!" she cried, hurrying toward the open carriage door, taking the hand he offered to help her in. She saw him raise his face and grin across at Nash, who was only semi dressed, with arms outstretched in entreaty, and who now cried, "Good God, Kitty, what do you think you're doing? You can't get into a strange man's carriage, no matter how upset you are!"

But Lord Silverton wasn't a strange man, and Kitty could do as she liked because she was beholden to no one. It was an unusual situation she'd come to value and, right now, the only advantage she had. No father could thunder at her for behavior which was no worse than he'd forced her mother into committing. No brother could take the moral high ground because Ned was not like that and she rarely saw him, besides. No husband could claim her earnings for his own, spend her money as he chose, and treat her like the property she was. No, Kitty could do as she pleased, and as Nash had betrayed her, she was going to punish him as much as he deserved.

She was crying again by the time she threw herself back against the squabs, dabbing at her face with the edge of her sleeve.

"Here, take this."

A large, snowy white handkerchief was put under her nose, and Kitty blew loudly.

"You found him in bed with another woman?"

She jerked her head up, and he laughed gently.

"I can't imagine any other scenario that would have you all but throwing yourself under my horse's hooves in your haste to get away from your erstwhile lover."

"I didn't nearly throw myself under your horse's hooves," Kitty objected. She slumped forward and put her face in her hands. "But you're right." She sniffed and added in a quavering voice, "Tomorrow he was taking me to the house he was going to be leasing for me."

"My, how you've gained in experience during the few short weeks since I met you, Miss La Bijou. Yet, how little you still know of the ways of men."

"He's not just any man. He's my destiny. I knew it when I saw him. You think it's nonsense, but I was so sure here—" she tapped her heart —"that I would never give myself to any other man but the one I knew would be true. Well, true as in who would marry me."

"Marry you?"

Kitty jerked her head up. "Do not make it sound beyond the realms of possibility or make me out to be a fool. I still believe what I said before. When I was sixteen, a gypsy told my fortune. She described Lord Nash right down to the small scar beneath his right eye. She even described the exact feelings that would tell me for certain that he would be the man who'd become my husband. She said I would follow in Lady Hamilton's footsteps, and I'm sorry to say it, but Lady Hamilton was born of much lowlier stock than I."

"I hope you kept your aspirations to yourself, Miss La Bijou. Perhaps that was what frightened him off."

"I didn't say anything, but I knew it would happen some day..." Kitty trailed off. She began to pleat the handkerchief with her fingers. "Where are you taking me, my Lord? I thought you lived on the street we've just passed."

"Very perceptive. I'm on my way to look in on an old friend. You could stay in the carriage, but I fear you might catch cold, or I'm perfectly happy to have you accompany me, though I can't say you are my cousin if the lady of the house is awake since I believe she knows you. What story shall we invent since we can hardly have her believing I'd insult her by parading my mistress before her."

"I hope no one will think that, my Lord, and that you don't get any ideas, yourself."

"Indeed, I know exactly the lowly position I occupy in your heart, Kitty, and offer my services merely out of friendship." With a smile, he held out his hand.

"I'm afraid I was after my handkerchief," he said when she offered him her hand. "It's far too big to try and stuff into your reticule. Now," he said, tucking it into his waistcoat pocket after she'd handed it over, "are you ready to put on a brave face? You can tell me how much your heart is breaking later over a medicinal brandy or two, and then I'll tuck you into a nice, warm feather bed with the promise I shan't even think about taking liberties. In the morning, we can put our heads together to work out how you can make Lord Nash dance to your tune, if you're prepared to forgive him." He squeezed her hand reassuringly as he helped her onto the cobblestones and there was a tinge of wistfulness to his tone as he added, "You're irresistible, Kitty. I believe you can make him do anything you wish."

CHAPTER 8

*A*raminta couldn't sleep. Her belly was too big to lie in any position except on her back, which she hated, and her fears over the child's impending birth had become like a hot poker jabbing into her brain.

When she heard the clock strike midnight, she struggled out of bed, lit a candle and began to pace, holding her hands to her lower back to ease the pressure. Her hateful, unwieldy body pulsed with the unwanted life inside it. These days she didn't walk, she waddled. Men, who used to look at her, eyes lit with that appreciative glow with which she was so familiar, now ignored her. To be so disregarded was almost more than she could bear.

Perhaps a medicinal brandy might help, she thought. She hadn't resorted to such remedies before, but her mind was spinning, and she needed to calm her nerves. She was very much afraid she was nearly at full term, and she still had not formulated a suitable plan. She'd tried to persuade Debenham to go on an extended hunting trip to Scotland with friends, but on the verge of him leaving, he'd been caught up with business in London. Nefarious dealings, no doubt. Debenham entertained some dubious friends at all hours from heavy-drinking Irish peers to radical shoemakers. He told Araminta he didn't distinguish between the classes, but Araminta knew there was more to it than that. Sir Aubrey and Cousin Stephen called him a *Spencean*. She still didn't quite know what that was, though she gathered it meant a political radical. Not that she really knew what that was, either. She did, however, understand blackmail, and she'd found clear evidence of that. As she wasn't averse to rummaging in Debenham's drawers when she got the chance, she had, a week earlier, found part of a draft letter of what looked like an extortion threat against a lesser member of the royal family whose secret mistress had apparently rather more of a high profile in society than the average mistress fare. Lady C. Oh, if only Araminta could have seen the rest of her name, she might have found a way to profit from the information herself. It was intriguing, though, that a certain Lady C. was linked with the Duke of Cumberland, so Araminta intended to keep her ears and eyes open.

Quite frankly, as long as Debenham didn't get caught, Araminta didn't care what he did.

Following a shaft of moonlight, Araminta paced the length and breadth of her bedchamber, and thought with longing about Teddy. The fact she was so huge with child was thankfully a deterrent to a repeat of the depraved sexual exploits Debenham had enjoyed in the earlier days of their marriage. She'd been seduced by the sense of danger he exuded, but she'd soon found he thought little of her pleasure.

But thinking of Teddy, instead, and how much he desired her and wanted to please her made Araminta—even now when she was so big with child—pulse with want. Teddy might be a little reticent about trying out some of the things Debenham enjoyed, but in Araminta's hands, he'd be like soft clay.

The more she thought about it, the more enticing a medicinal brandy sounded.

Wrapping a shawl about her shoulders, she picked up her candle and crept down the stairs. The house was in darkness. Debenham was no doubt at his club or some bawdy house; perhaps gaming. He was very fond of that, which Araminta could understand. She enjoyed gaming too, and would indulge in it a great deal more if she were able to go out in public.

She turned the doorknob and opened the library door, expecting to find it in darkness. Instead, she got a huge fright to find four pairs of eyes staring at her from the gloom— Debenham and his friend Lord Silverton, together with Silverton's fancy piece and another man she didn't recognize.

"You should be in bed, darling." Debenham did not look at all pleased to see her. Well, the feeling was mutual, and she was even less pleased that Lord Silverton had seen fit to invite a woman who was... definitely not the kind she should be associating with. Miss La Bijou.

"I can't sleep."

"Have a drink."

He was clearly bosky. He held the bottle up and waved it in the air. He'd only risen briefly at her entrance before collapsing back into his seat, unlike Lord Silverton and the balding shoemaker who paid her the deference she was due by jumping to their feet until she waved them back down.

"Maybe I will." She took a few steps forward, and then clutched at her side with another of those increasingly frequent cramps which were totally debilitating.

"Here, give her the bottle." It was her husband's bored, uncaring voice.

Araminta closed her eyes as she tried to breathe through the pain. Was it coming now? Surely not. No, she'd had this cramping before. And Debenham wasn't even coming to her assistance. Instead, that blonde creature who thought she was London's gift to the stage was hurrying forward with both the bottle and the offer of a shoulder.

"I'm perfectly all ri—" She went to push the girl away, but instead found herself gripping her shoulder simply so she wouldn't slither to the ground in a writhing heap. No, surely the baby wasn't coming now.

"I'll take you back to your room."

The woman's voice was soothing. Debenham clearly wasn't going to trouble himself. Araminta could hear him talking loudly to the other men. Wordlessly, resting heavily on the actress's shoulder, she allowed herself to be helped from the room. She wished she'd decided to go back to The Grange two months ago. That would have been sensible, but at the time, Debenham was still enjoying making the most of his conjugal rights so wouldn't let her leave and besides, she was supposedly little more than four months gone, then.

"Down this corridor?"

Araminta nodded, and the young woman supported her back to her bedchamber.

"I'll help you into bed. Take your time. My mother was brought to bed only a few months ago. She wasn't as big as you, though. We have met, you know. At the Tower."

"I remember. Miss La Bijou." She wasn't going to humor her. "Lord Silverton's mistress."

"His…friend, actually. I'm an actress."

"I know." Araminta accepted the girl's help to settle her, then downed in a single gulp the glass of brandy on her bedside table. She felt like a flounder, a great, ungainly fish that couldn't move anywhere but on its back. "So you consider yourself the toast of the town, do you? Move the pillow this way, will you?" She sighed as she closed her eyes. "That's better. Well, a great deal has happened since that day at the Tower," she murmured, raising herself a little on her elbows and regarding Miss La Bijou from beneath her lashes. "I believe you'd only just arrived in London."

Miss La Bijou nodded and Araminta, who had been about to send her away, thought she saw a tear glisten in the corner of her eye. Good! If the girl was miserable, it would be some diversion to find out why, considering no one could be more miserable than Araminta. Lord knew, she needed something to take her mind off her troubles.

"So much attention, yet not enough of the right kind?" Yes, apparently a perspicacious question. Araminta had known that would strike home for anyone with aspirations toward success. Hadn't she had her own dreams of wild success? They certainly hadn't included being vast, ungainly, no longer feted and admired by the general male population, and unappreciated by her husband. Lord, how she despised him, but she was bound to him for life. Her only avenue for success was completely dependent upon Debenham's ability not to become embroiled in some grubby scandal that would drag them both down. As soon as this wretched baby was born, she could concentrate on finding her own pleasure through different diversions.

Excitement. That's what she craved.

In a perspicacious flash, it occurred to her that this *demimondaine*, creature of the sordid underbelly of life with whom she should not be consorting, might indeed be the very one to provide a conduit to another more exciting world.

"I suppose you have lots of admirers." She peered at Miss La Bijou, then waved her to back into her seat as the girl obviously prepared to leave.

"A few."

"Well, tell me about them. Do they send you flowers?"

"I receive about a dozen bouquets at the end of each show. And notes and letters."

Araminta tried not to let the admission make her feel any worse. "So you could have any lover you choose, by the sounds of it." She smiled to herself at the girl's gasp. So coy. Covertly, she studied her in the dim light of the single candle. She was lovely, she'd have to grant her that, if one liked pale, insipid beauties who pretended they were so innocent, when they were the worst of all with their pretended lack of guile to disguise the fact they were plotting all the while. Araminta had once been regarded as London's most beautiful debutante, but it had been a few months since she'd received any accolades worth mentioning. She was bored and disgruntled, and talking to this creature was mildly amusing. She therefore decided she'd need to change tack when Miss La Bijou took offense to her words and stood up decisively.

"No, you're lovely, and I'm jealous. I want to know more," Araminta said before she could think of something more artful to say.

"Jealous? But you're married to..."

"A knave, though if that ever gets back to him, I'll have your hair shorn off because I'll know it was you." Araminta laughed to show she'd meant it as a little joke. "No, the fact is, I once regularly received notes and flowers, too. I was going to be married, in fact, to the man of my dreams—Lord Ludbridge—before Debenham forcefully compromised me and ensured I had no choice but to marry him."

The girl's gasp of shock jerked Araminta back to the present. She hadn't meant to be so forthcoming. A combination of brandy and boredom had made her lips a little loose. Still, maybe that wasn't such a bad thing. Miss La Bijou really did look a gullible little goose, for she'd taken Araminta's hand and was stroking it in a most sympathetic manner as she'd reseated herself.

"I had no idea," she was saying in that breathy innocent voice of hers that the men no doubt adored. "It was not a marriage you'd have *chosen*? But of course, no one can ever know and I would never tell." Her mouth turned down in sympathy. "Yet the two of you are bound in marriage. Forever."

Araminta nodded. "A prisoner. What opportunities for love will I ever have now?" To her surprise, she gave a little sob, which was actually quite real, then slanted her gaze across at the girl's large-eyed dismay. In those dark, dismal hours near midnight, a tiny sliver of hope had presented itself. Perhaps Miss La Bijou really could help Araminta achieve what she so desired. Desires that were so simple, really, and no more than any woman aspired to...to bask in the embrace of the man she loved, while not jeopardizing her place in society.

Since her brief encounter with Teddy at the theater, she'd constantly dreamed about him, thrilling at the remembered horror in his eyes when she'd told him of the responsibility he bore in her terrible plight.

At first he'd been so angry with her, but that was only an indication of how much he loved her. Once he'd heard the true story from Araminta's lips, he'd quickly changed his tune.

How wonderful and right it would be if she were adored and revered by a man over whom she exercised complete power. And wasn't Teddy just that man?

She returned the pressure of Miss La Bijou's hand. "Have you ever met Lord Ludbridge?" she asked.

She'd started off despising this creature but with each passing minute, Araminta was increasingly enjoying their exchange. Miss La Bijou was not judgemental.

She was quiet, attentive and surprisingly pliable.

"I haven't but I've heard he is a very nice man."

Araminta tried not to let her smile get the better of her. "He is," she agreed, squeezing Miss Bijou's hand once more. This innocent with her extensive connnections, she decided, may well be just the one who could help Araminta claw herself out of the mess she was in.

CHAPTER 9

*A*n hour later, in front of a banked-up fire and feeling far more comfortable than she had with Araminta, Kitty stretched her legs out and smiled tearily at Lord Silverton.

"You've been awfully good to me, rescuing me, and then offering me a bed for the night. I really would have been sleeping amid the vermin on Mrs. Mobbs's floor."

"I'm sure you have more options than you imagine, Kitty, if you think about it. And that's what we must do. Hit upon what to do with you, eh?"

"You really want to spend your time helping me when I'm completely responsible for my own disaster? I don't know anyone else who would." It was true. Her father had probably disowned her already; she had no intention of slinking back home to Mama, in any case, and she still had no address for Lissa. "I'm not going back to Nash yet. I can't. I need to make him realize how terribly he's betrayed me."

"Will you forgive him?"

Kitty nibbled the top of her brandy glass and stared into the fire. Quietly, she said, "I thought he was my destiny. Was I a fool? No, I have to believe in something. Everything the fortune-teller told me—"

Silverton chuckled. "Coincidence and smoke and mirrors, Kitty. A gypsy who's never laid eyes on you before cannot accurately foretell your future. You believed only what you wanted to believe. And yes, Nash may be your destiny, but only if you make him so. He is a philanderer, albeit a charming one who is, *perhaps*, madly in love with you. But that aside, he won't stay true, and he won't marry you."

Kitty put down her glass and sent Silverton a beseeching look. "He may and he may not. He wants me to forgive him, but you caution me against taking him back."

"Only to spare your poor heart. You *will* find happiness, but I don't believe it will be with him."

"Then what should I do?"

He stood up, crossed the room to sit down on the arm of her chair and stroked her hair. "I've told you what I think, but only you can make the final decision on how you act. Nor do I think that is a question that can be decided until you've had a refreshing long sleep, which you will need if you are to remember your lines for tomorrow. Now, come with me and I will personally show you to a chamber where the bed is made up, and you will be undisturbed until noon if you so wish."

Kitty took the hand he offered and, like a child, allowed herself to be led to bed. Lord Silverton even returned, as he'd promised, with a night-shift and some tooth powder, courtesy of another female guest he'd once had staying with him, he told her.

Kitty was too tired to wonder about Lord Silverton's female associations, though she did think him the nicest man she'd ever met. But this pleasant thought was soon superceded by memories of the ghastly scene she'd witnessed between Nash and Jennie before her despair was neatly wrapped up in a cloud of blue smoke, and she lost consciousness.

IN THE MORNING, SHE FELT A LITTLE BETTER, THOUGH STILL SUBDUED. Soon she'd have to leave for the theater, but as she arrived in the doorway of the breakfast parlor, Lord Silverton looked up from pouring her coffee and advised her immediately after wishing her good morning not to go rushing off to make up to Lord Nash as he needed to be taught a lesson.

"I had no intention of going back to him, just yet," she bridled. "I was going to ask Mrs. Mobbs for my old room back."

"Amid the vermin? You're welcome to be my houseguest for a few days." He raised an eyebrow. "Make Nash jealous, if you like."

She hadn't thought of that, but now she smiled her first real smile as she clasped her hands together. "How could I resist your kind offer? It answers everything."

A tumult of mixed feelings continued to beset Kitty after the following evening's performance when Nash arrived with six dozen red roses, an artfully delivered apology, and a tantalizing little velvet box, which he opened to reveal a ruby and diamond bracelet nestled on a bed of black velvet. There was some consolation to be had by the fact he raised the lid when they were still in public, by Kitty's dressing table, and Jennie happened to be passing by. Out of the corner of her eye, she saw the flare of feeling in the girl's eye and, briefly, Kitty exulted in her triumph. But despite the offer of such riches, she was not going to give in so easily. If Nash could do betray her once, he could do it again, as Lord Silverton had warned. She had to accept that. No, she could not let Nash assume she'd be so easily mollified each time he strayed.

Nevertheless, Lord Nash insisted she keep the bracelet as a reminder of what he offered her, before he sadly departed.

Dressing herself the following day in the comfortably furnished spare bedchamber Lord Silverton had offered her, Kitty acknowledged the truth of her host's bald statement that Nash was not her destiny, yet in the very next breath, while twisting her hair into a fetching cluster of curls, she qualified the unpalatable truth with the fact that he'd only strayed once. Surely, there was every chance he might have an epiphany and decide to make her his wife?

By the time she'd threaded a ribbon through her curls, Kitty had decided she would take him back. Despite what Silverton said, he was the man most in love with her and, right now, he was very sorry for what he'd done. Perhaps he'd be unusually eager to atone and would make her an offer she couldn't refuse. Kitty didn't like to think of herself as a superstitious green girl wanting to believe everything the gypsy woman had foretold, but she didn't have much else to cling to. As a child growing up, she'd believed in destiny; as an adult, it was becoming clear there was sometimes a rocky road to navigate to achieve it. Yes, she would take him back.

Only, not just yet. Her dewy-eyed look, which she caught sight of in the mirror as she reflecting on these possibilities with Nash, reminded her that she'd always been susceptible to letting her soft heart get in the way of sensible decisions. Lord Nash needed to suffer. He needed to know there were consequences to betraying her, and that jewels and roses and pleading words were not always going to gain him forgiveness.

As usual, Kitty had slept in past noon. When she appeared languidly at breakfast, she was dismayed to be greeted by Lord Silverton laughing at her. He'd just finished his repast and was rising, about to leave.

"You really do need a maid to ensure you are respectable when you venture out in public," he said, pointing to the mismatched buttons that fastened the front of her dress.

"A maid is a luxury I can't afford, although Nash promised me I'd have one to attend to me and one to attend to the house." Kitty sighed as she sat down. "He's been at the theater every evening for the past five days, on his knees. Begging."

"But you're not ready to forgive him?" Lord Silverton's tone was conversational, but he was at her side now, leaning to help her with the fastening of her gown, and Kitty was acutely aware of the faint whisper of his breath upon her cheek and the feel of his fingers deftly correcting her morning's oversight.

Her heart rate sped up and she swallowed. Hoping her voice didn't quaver, she replied, "I have nowhere else to go." She was glad when Silverton returned to his chair, enabling her temperature to return to normal. She slumped over the hot chocolate her host pushed in front of her. "Of course, I love him," she added hastily. "And of course, I must yield soon otherwise he'll slip through my fingers." She raised her head and tried to smile at Lord Silverton. "You've been so kind, my Lord." It was true. She'd enjoyed their evenings playing cribbage in front of the fire and chatting about all sorts of silly things more than she cared to say. "Besides, what would your prospective bride have to say about you having a female under your roof?"

"The servants have put it about that you're my father's ward, and we grew up together."

"Imaginative," Kitty agreed.

"As for my prospective wife, well, she's found herself another prospective groom. Miss Bunting would not care, either way."

"Do you love her very much?"

"I thought it was love at first sight when our eyes met across a crowded ballroom at the beginning of the season. I certainly didn't know she'd been contemplating several offers and that in the final analysis I didn't meet her lofty criteria."

Kitty suspected his forced irony covered up a broken heart. She reached across the table and patted his hand. "Well, she's not married yet. She could change her mind."

"She could."

"And then you'd have your wife, and you'd live happily ever after." She sighed again. "That's what I want. To live happily ever after." Glancing about the room to ensure no servants were listening, she confided, "I've told you that my parents were not married, though they've always lived together. Well, I should say that Papa prefers to live with us, but—"

"He has another family?" This time, Lord Silverton was the one bestowing the sympathy.

Kitty nodded sadly. "And an estate to manage, though his nephew helps him now."

"An estate, eh?"

Kitty wasn't surprised that he sounded skeptical though she was glad he'd obviously reconsidered his plans to leave the room and had taken a seat at the table once more. She speared a piece of delicious-looking bacon and put it on her plate. "He left my mother at the altar to marry the suitable bride chosen for him by his parents, and has regretted it ever since. It's why I set such store by following what I feel here." She tapped her heart.

"Very romantic, Miss La Bijou, but I believe it is wisest to follow one's head, if there is indeed a competition." He raised his eyebrows at her over the top of his cup. "That's why I'm so disappointed I failed to secure Miss Bunting as a bride. She had the credentials to please my family; the grace, breeding and sensibility required to become my hostess, and I liked her very much."

Kitty gave a relieved little laugh. "Well, if you only liked her very much, then your heart is not broken, and I am glad for it, Lord Silverton." She clasped her breast and said earnestly, "A broken heart is not to be recommended at all."

"My poor Kitty. You've done a fine job of being entertaining for my benefit, in that case. Tell me, what does your family think of you gallivanting down to London to take the stage?"

"Well, my half-sisters are in London." She thought of Araminta and wondered what either of them would think if they actually knew who Kitty was. Not that she had any intention of revealing the truth. Araminta would despise Kitty even more than she already did if she knew she was her half-sister. "They move in society circles. And my sister—who, like me, was born out of wedlock—is a governess."

"Good lord! You really are the tearaway of the family. I should have taken you back to your father myself at the outset. Why Kitty, you chose a very bold and dangerous path for a young lady brought up—"

"Respectably. Yes, but destined for what?" she asked, dejectedly. "The truth is that the stain on my birth makes it all but impossible for me to contract a decent match. I watch my half-sisters find ideal husbands, and I feel resentment. To tell you the truth, my father's position made me believe I might have a chance enticing Lord Nash to marry me if I could make him love me enough. I'm not sure about anything now." She sighed again. "Except that I will go back to him."

"You *will?*" She was surprised at the energy in his tone. "Why? You don't sound passionately committed."

"This is just a test." Kitty stared resolutely at him. "He'll change. Yes, I'm sure of it. I'll return to him in a few days, and then I'll move into the little house he's leased. Then I'll find my friend, Dorcas, who I met in London when we were both staying with Mrs. Mobbs, and I'll ask her to be my lady's maid. It'll be like the dreams we both talked about that night will have come true."

"Poor Kitty." Lord Silverton clicked his tongue. "I'm not used to having conversations like this with young ladies who've just disclosed their links to fashionable society. I may know your father. He could be after me with a pistol if he saw me alone with you."

"He never comes to London."

"Cheer up, Kitty; you have a day off from the theater. What are you going to do? Plot and plan or shall I take you somewhere?"

Kitty sat up straight as an idea hit her suddenly. "Actually, I'd like to find my friend Dorcas I told you about. She's a country girl and has secured a good job somewhere, having had the good fortune to meet on the coach to London a woman who arranged everything. Dorcas said she'd come and see me in Covent Garden, but she hasn't yet. If I am able to employ a lady's maid, I'd like to see if I can persuade her to leave Mrs. Montgomery's employ."

"Mrs. Montgomery, eh?"

'Yes, she has a grand establishment in Soho where she has lots of girls working for her, I believe. Dorcas had to sign a very complicated contract to get the position."

"Surely you're not talking about Maggie Montgomery's?"

Kitty was surprised at the explosive reaction her words caused, because before she'd even finished, Lord Silverton was all but spitting out his coffee as he repeated, "Maggie Montgomery of Soho? Your friend thought she was getting a job with her as a....*what*, may I ask?"

"Why, a household servant. Mrs. Montgomery came herself to Mrs. Mobbs's house, and said how pretty and fresh and healthy Dorcas and I looked. She tried to persuade me to sign a contract to work for her, but Mr. Lazarus came in just then and seemed most put out."

"Lord, a blessing in disguise." Silverton shook his head. "Kitty, do you know who Mrs. Montgomery is? What she does?"

"She places girls in work."

"Indeed she does." He stood up. "You say Dorcas is your friend, and you'd like her to work for you when you return to Nash?"

"Well, only if she wants to." Kitty wished he'd tell her what was making him so agitated. He clearly didn't think Mrs. Montgomery a suitable employer. "I fear she'll be terribly disapproving when she discovers what I am to Lord Nash."

"I don't think she'll mind a jot about that," Silverton said grimly.

Kitty rose also. "So Mrs. Montgomery has a reputation as a hard task-master? Then I definitely need to rescue Dorcas. Perhaps you can tell me where I can locate Mrs. Montgomery, then, otherwise I'll visit Mrs. Mobbs and ask her."

To her surprise, Lord Silverton came around the table and put a restraining hand on her shoulder. "I think you should leave that to me, Kitty."

"You'll find Dorcas?" The idea that he would concern himself with looking for a household servant on Kitty's behalf seemed extraordinary.

He nodded. "In good conscience, I would not dare let you loose in even the vicinity of Mrs. Montgomery's place of work. Give me a description of the girl andny other details you can tell me, and I shall find her myself."

Kitty smiled, warmed by his eagerness to put himself out on her account. Whatever else Lord Silverton might be, he certainly was a very kind and pleasing gentleman.

CHAPTER 10

The hours seemed to pass so slowly, Araminta thought as she stared at the furnishings of Debenham's London townhouse during one of her sister's regular visits. She was so bored she could barely attend to Hetty's prattle.

"So, Araminta dearest, aren't you looking forward to having a dear little baby to love?" Hetty seemed unable to comprehend the degree of horror and disgust Araminta felt at the entire prospect of anything associated with giving birth. She was now looking at Araminta with the usual dewy-eyed expression she adopted at such talk as she sprawled in a chair by the window, gently stroking her belly.

Araminta, similarly sprawled, but with her hands on the arms of her chair as she detested feeling the monstrous mound that was so much bigger than Hetty's, struggled to smile. She was glad Sir Aubrey had not returned from the library to join the ladies following the meal. He rarely did, as it was well known he and Debenham detested one another, and the truth was, his presence made Araminta highly uncomfortable.

Surely he must suspect the child she carried was his? Perhaps he was afraid she'd say something. Lord, if she did it would be all over for her, and he must know she wasn't that stupid.

"You've always been so much more maternal than I, Hetty darling. Just because I detest losing my figure doesn't mean I won't love the child just as much as you will love yours." She knew what to say, even if she knew she'd never love this child as Hetty would love hers. "As you've never been slender, you cannot know the pain I feel at becoming stout like you. It's not my natural way."

Hetty extended a hand and said sympathetically, "Poor Araminta; you've not been in very good spirits at all the last few weeks. I wish I knew what might cheer you up."

"I'd like to go to the country, but Debenham won't hear of it. That would make me happy."

"You want to go to the country? That's not like you."

"I want to have my baby in peace and quiet. I don't know why Debenham insists I remain here when he's forever at his club or some gambling den," she grumbled.

"I'll speak to him, shall I?"

"Yes, I'm sure he'll listen to you."

Hetty didn't appear to notice the sarcasm, for she said suddenly, "Oh! I met that very pleasant young woman, Miss Hazlett, who asked after you." She picked up her tatting and set to work, continuing animatedly, "She wanted to know that you and the baby were well, and asked if I'd attended your marriage to Debenham."

Araminta stared. Was Hetty so ignorant she had no idea of their father's other family? Did she not know of the brood of bastard offspring he'd sired who had no love for either Hetty or Araminta?

Or perhaps she was just testing Araminta.

"Good lord, Hetty, how can you speak so charitably about Miss Lissa Hazlett? That mousey little governess everyone says looks like me? Well, there's a reason for that: She's papa's daughter, don't you know. She's also the special friend of Debenham's secretary, Ralph Tunley. And Mr. Tunley is the brother of Lord Ludbridge." She lowered her voice as mention of that gentleman made her skin burn.

Hetty raised her eyebrows but to Araminta's surprise made no comment about anything Araminta had said as she got to her feet.

"Anyway, Miss Hazlett passes on her best wishes and now, as Debenham is returning soon, I must be off."

"Do stay, Hetty. I'm so bored, and I'm sure Debenham would be delighted to see you."

Hetty sent her a long look then finally said, "Lord Ludbridge is coming for dinner. I must oversee matters in the kitchen."

"Lord Ludbridge?" Araminta put out an arm to detain her sister. "He's having *dinner* with you?"

"Yes, I've no doubt it'll be a very congenial evening." Hetty looked uncomfortable, adding quickly as she detached Araminta's grip, "Now look after yourself, Araminta."

"Oh yes, and you go and enjoy your lovely dinner with Lord Ludbridge while I stay here, alone, and endure another tedious evening while Debenham drinks and gambles to his heart's content."

Hetty seemed torn, turning with her hand on the door knob. "You know you're always very welcome to come to dinner, Araminta, only I wasn't sure you really wanted to see Lord Ludbridge, and I've sensed you feel uncomfortable around Sir Aubrey." She dropped her eyes, adding, "Just as I do around Debenham."

"Well, since we have a lifetime with our respective spouses to look forward to, and we cannot change the fact we're sisters, I suggest we ought to put the past behind us." Araminta felt suddenly buoyed by her own advice. She could forget what had happened between herself and Sir Aubrey during that terrible night at Vauxhall Gardens. She needed to. Her heart gave a little hitch at the thought of Lord Ludbridge, her one *true* love. The one man who could have made her happy had life not been so unfair.

"Yes, that is good advice. And on any other night, I think it would be a wonderful idea, but Araminta, I truly thought you'd not wish to be in company with Lord Ludbridge after...." Hetty was unable to finish her sentence. Indeed, she looked greatly upset.

"After what?" Araminta answered her own question. "After I was supposed to marry him except that he rushed off to the Continent and instead I ended up being forced to marry Debenham? Hetty, are you trying to stop me from having *any* fun while my husband carouses to his heart's content?" Araminta hauled herself up, gasping at the pain and silently cursing the cargo she carried. This baby was not going to stand in the way of what she deserved. "Surely I have the right to be as happy as you, Hetty." She dashed away the sudden wetness on her cheeks, surprised by the force of her emotion. "Am I not as worthy? As for Lord Ludbridge, he knows the wicked, scandalous way Debenham behaved toward me, and that he gave me no choice but to be his wife and to forsake the man I truly loved."

"Mr. Woking?"

"Lord, Hetty, I'm talking about my darling Teddy. *Lord Ludbridge.* We were mad for each other. Do you truly imagine I'd have *chosen* to marry Lord Debenham if I could have had Lord Ludbridge for my husband?"

"Lord Ludbridge would have been easier to manage," Hetty agreed.

Araminta didn't like her doubtful look, and rushed to ensure that her sister knew the truth.

"You don't believe those awful rumors everyone was whispering, do you, dearest?" she asked, moving with ungainly haste across the soft carpet to detain Hetty. "I mean, what Debenham orchestrated was truly dastardly. You, of anyone, should know that. Especially after he...he threatened you. *With a broken bottle.* I didn't think I could ever forgive him after that, but when he used those awful threats that forced me to become his wife and to sacrifice my happiness in order to protect you and Papa—"

"What are you saying, Araminta? We agreed never to talk of that night again."

Araminta put her hand on her sister's shoulder and looked earnestly at her. She'd managed to convince darling Teddy of how things really were; now she needed to persuade Hetty. Taking a deep breath, she said, "You need to know the *real* truth, Hetty. Debenham was madly in love with me, but when I said I didn't want to marry him, he said he would ruin Papa and that...that he wasn't done with Sir Aubrey. So yes, of course I had to marry him." She swallowed. "To protect *you*. You see why I now wish to put my terrible, tragic past behind me and to find *some* happiness where I can? Even if it's only spending an evening talking to Lord Ludbridge, whom I wish with all my heart I could have married. Oh Hetty, all I want is to have a brief respite from my misery and to get rid of this baby!"

"Get rid of it!?"

"You know what I mean. Look at you, you're happy, you were made for breeding. I'm not. I despise the way it's ruined my shape. I detest the clumsy, awkward way it makes me feel. I won't pretend to be better than I am, but do afford me some sisterly sympathy. I'm trying to change...and...and be a better, nicer...sister," she added with sudden inspiration, "but I can't do it overnight, and I can't do it without a little understanding...and help...from you."

She was astonished at the transformation her words had upon Hetty. Immediately, her sister turned and swept Araminta into a fierce hug.

"Oh, Araminta, you truly mean that? Why, I think it's motherhood that's changing you. You say you hate breeding, but the truth is that it's making you a softer, better person, just as you say. Don't fight it. You *can* put the past behind you, but you can't do it without compromises, and you mustn't risk your health or Debenham's temper. Now that you see the error of your ways, I truly believe you can look forward to a much more rewarding future."

Araminta didn't like the reference to being guilty of any error. The only reason she was in such an unhappy predicament was because of Lord Ludbridge's error in leaving her at such an inconvenient time, and evil Debenham's calculated ploy to trick her into becoming his wife. Yet, it seemed best not to go over this once more since Hetty had gone from quite prickly to remarkably pliable in such a short time, and Araminta needed her sister's good offices if she were to get what she wanted, and to find the happiness she deserved. Well, tonight at any rate.

"So you'll set an extra place for me at dinner?"

Hetty glanced doubtfully at Araminta's mid region, her eyes

widening as Araminta doubled up once more at another painful spasm. "Dearest, I think you'd be best staying at home tonight. You need to rest. You're carrying two, and you're very big. Debenham would be cross to hear you'd sought gaiety when you should be looking after his baby."

"Debenham wouldn't even know. He'll return at dawn, totally in his cups, and collapse in his own apartments. I daresay he won't even ask Jem to check with Jane that I'm not dead in the middle of the carpet in one of the rooms which those lazy servants don't even bother to dust properly. I'll probably be a skeleton by the time he remembers he has a wife."

The thought of how poorly Debenham cared for her compared with the tender solicitude of passionate Lord Ludbridge, brought tears to her eyes and Hetty's immediate sympathy.

"Yes, of course I'll ensure an extra place is laid for you, but I'll quite understand if you decide at the last minute that you'd rather have an early night."

Ignoring the persistent tugs of pain that assailed her, Araminta farewelled her sister with a smile, mentally wondering which of her gowns would flatter her most in her hideous, bloated state. She might have shied away from seeing Lord Ludbridge if he'd given any sense of being disgusted when he'd sought her out in Debenham's opera box. Instead, she knew she'd won him over with the tragedy of her story. His love for her was pure, and he was no longer prepared to believe those wicked lies about her. Besides, once Araminta was seated opposite him at the table, he'd focus his attention on her lovely face. No doubt he'd struggle to keep his eyes straying from her rather tremendous bosom. At least, that was one small compensation for her pregnancy...her magnificently enhanced bust.

By the time she was back home and seated at her dressing table, she was so excited by the possibilities the evening had in store that she could barely wait for Jane to answer her summons.

"Jane! Quickly! Help me to decide what to wear for dinner. No, I do not intend staying in tonight and don't you start haranguing me, or I'll think you as bad as Hetty, who only cares about appearances. You should know that once I make up my mind, there's no way to change it."

And as Jane hurried to do her bidding, Araminta felt a glow of satisfaction at the thought that it was time she enjoyed herself for once.

CHAPTER 11

*L*ord Silverton did not make it his habit to frequent the lower
end of town, but he bolstered his reluctance with the knowledge that he had no choice if he was to be anyone's savior
tonight—and that's what he was determined to be. Miss Bunting's
preference for another had briefly dented his belief that he did not
need a woman to admire him in order to be perfectly content.

And nor did he.

However, Miss La Bijou's transparent joy, enthusiasm, sorrow—all
those emotions he'd recently witnessed in her company—were a
reminder that he derived more satisfaction from playing the gallant
knight and assisting a damsel in distress than he did in being admired
by one.

Miss La Bijou didn't admire him, though it was clear she liked him
well enough.

But in truth, he wanted more than that.

Pulling up the collar of his greatcoat, and pulling down the brim of
his low-crowned beaver, he now stood upon the front steps of the
house he sought.

He did not like the idea of being recognized, for the unsavory fact
that his mission to Maggie Montgomery's would likely be misunder-

stood. Silverton had never paid for sex. Never had to. He found his pleasures with willing women from various walks of life. He'd had liaisons with widows of his own class, forward misses from the serving classes and several times, an opera dancer. For some reason, women liked him.

Even pretty Miss Bunting, though not sufficiently, which was disappointing since she'd have made a very suitable wife, and he'd thought her sweet. But beyond his surprise that she had, in fact, chosen someone else when he'd made clear his intentions and had thought she returned his interest—and a day of feeling less than his usual ebullient self—he was not particularly downcast, though he didn't like the fact his mother had resumed her efforts to ally him with someone the family could embrace. Indeed, she was harking back to her favourite, Miss Octavia Mandelton, a shy, plain young lady of whom his mother was inordinately fond and whom the family had known since she'd been born on the neighboring estate two decades previously. Silverton tended to think of Octavia as akin to one of his mama's favorite pet Pekingese. Not potential wife material though she might be a last resort if he were to fulfill his promise to his increasingly impatient mama and find himself a wife within the next six months.

Now he was mounting the steps of Maggie Montgomery's establishment, feeling suddenly sheepish but relieved he'd met no one he knew. Without delay, the grated door was opened, and a young girl greeted him and ushered him into the heavily-perfumed interior.

"I say, Silverton!"

Silverton was already inside the dim drawing room, being led toward a cluster of red-velvet upholstered seats by Maggie Montgomery herself, when he was hailed by the familiar, gravelly voice.

Inwardly, he groaned as he perceived in the gloom, Lord Debenham. The viscount was lounging on a sofa with a girl on his lap, but he pushed her off when he struck up conversation with his erstwhile colleague. "Can't say I've seen you here before, Silverton. Drowning your sorrows after Miss Bunting's rejection, eh? So, what are you in the mood for? I can recommend the little dark-haired fairy over there. Daisy. A poppet, ain't she, except I don't like to share."

Silverton gave a considered nod as he lowered himself into a chair. Debenham must be half corked. He didn't usually talk like this, but Debenham was a strange man. He liked things on his terms, and was likely to become as prickly as a hedgehog if he felt he was being snubbed. It was one of the many odd characteristics Silverton had included in his reports to the Foreign Office over the past year. Not that matters had progressed as speedily as had been hoped. The man to whom Silverton had previously reported to, anonymously—had recently died under mysterious circumstances—and only very recently been replaced by a worthy seeming gentleman, Stephen Cranborne, Lord Partington's recently recognized heir. Silverton hoped that when he met Cranborne in person for the first time, he'd have at least something further on Debenham to report since the Sir Edward Keane, who had recuited him shortly before being posted to Constantinople, had supplied him with several excellent sketches depicting Debenham in apparent collusion with a number of known miscreants who were suspected of being involved in operations counter to the good of the country.

But there'd been nothing.

Silverton nodded at Debenham. "I don't like to share either." He felt reluctant to put his desires into words when Maggie sidled up to him with a large brandy and a simpering smile. "Welcome, Lord Silverton. Now, what takes your fancy? We have Brenda over in that corner. She's quite new and already very popular with the gentlemen."

Nash cast his gaze over a somewhat gaunt young woman with very pale hair and skin. She returned his look with a knowing gaze, and Silverton turned away. "I'm in the mood for a fresh country lass," he said, hating the way the words sounded.

"Not my taste," Debenham remarked, leaning over the girl who'd crawled back onto his thighs. "A bit of polish, I say, never goes astray."

Mrs. Montgomery flashed Silverton a smile. "A country lass? Well now, we have Susan. She arrived only last week. Barely broken in and, like Brenda, already so popular with the gentlemen—"

"Dorcas comes highly recommended. Is she available?"

"I'm afraid Dorcas is with a customer." Mrs. Montgomery looked regretful. "I do think you'll like Brenda, though."

Silverton appeared to consider this. "Perhaps I'll finish my drink and wait for Dorcas."

"She might be some time, my Lord. What about—"

"No, no, Lord Debenham and I have some catching up to do. I'll while away a little time and then see."

"As you wish."

With an inward sigh, Silverton raised his glass to Debenham. He could have thought of better companions, but perhaps this was fortuitous. He usually saw Debenham when he was in his cups with his fellow radicals though unfortunately never while they were hatching their plots to turn the country upside down. No, Silverton had heard nothing of a serious nature that he could report. Perhaps it was simply a case of too many agendas, wild ideas, and incompatible personalities. Debenham liked to bully; Buzby was easily offended and quick to anger, and Smythe had too many crazy ideas. The sketch Sir Edward had shown him, and which he learned had been executed by the accomplished young governess to the Lamont family whose identity had been supressed—had been astonishing in its detail but while it had shown Debenham in company with two suspected radicals and traitors, there was nothing concrete with which to charge any of them. Even the sketch, together with the letter that incriminated Debenham with regard to the failed attempt on Lord Castlereagh's life, was not sufficient to charge anyone with anything.

Silverton wondered if Debenham and his colleagues had lost focus when their dastardly attempted assassination had come to nought and insufficient evidence had been found to convict Debenham and his cronies. Nevertheless, the rumors persisted which was why Silverton was still on the case and still struggling to appear on friendly, familiar terms with Debenham whom he now believed was more interested in reversing his parlous fortunes than toppling the government.

Daisy sashayed over to Debenham's side and skimmed her fingertips the length of his arm. Their eyes met, and Silverton could feel the heat between them. Briefly, he wondered how Lady Debenham was spending her evening. She'd been large with child when he and Kitty had visited not long before. Debenham was a man of strong appetites and little tenderness. Silverton felt a touch sorry for the haughty beauty, who was no doubt used to being feted as a rarity and now was relegated to the shadows.

"My Lord, Dorcas is now available if you're still of a mind, though there are lots of other lovely girls who would be only too pleased to ensure you have a...memorable evening."

Silverton rose, ignoring her last comment. "Miss Dorcas? I'm most interested to meet the young lady," he murmured. He thought it best to sound salacious, and then wished he hadn't. It really didn't sound too good to his own ears.

Maggie Montgomery preceded him along a short corridor from the drawing room, and then up a flight of stairs. Rooms led off another long corridor, and he heard the sound of pleasure echoing from within. Much of it must be feigned, he decided.

When Mrs. Montgomery opened the door to a small bedroom, he was struck by the utter forlornness of the young girl who sat on the pink satin coverlet at the end of a large bed.

"Dorcas, Lord Silverton has a special desire to see you. Do treat him well."

Even Silverton heard the threat in the words, and was sensitive enough to discern the split second of utter weariness that weighed down the girl, before she turned with a forced bright smile upon her ruddy countenance.

"Wot a pleasure, m'Lord. Thank yer, Mrs. Montgomery. I'll make sure 'tis an evenin' 'e won't forget."

She rose from the bed, and again Silverton sensed the effort it cost her. He stood at the doorway and smiled back at her. She was a pretty girl with soft brown hair and large, soulful eyes. He had the impression she'd lost weight suddenly, and that it didn't suit her as much as the soft curves of the country lass Kitty described.

With a pang, he imagined Kitty and Dorcas sharing their excitement when they'd first met at Mrs. Mobbs's, and he shuddered at his little friend's feelings if, or when, she learned of the horrors Dorcas had endured since they'd parted.

"Wot's yer pleasure, m'Lord?" She was going through the motions, pushing up her breasts as if for his perusal as she half reclined on the bed.

"Don't."

She looked surprised, then crestfallen as she sat up. "Yer don't like 'em, m'Lord?"

"Sit up, Dorcas."

A flash of fear crossed her face at his serious tone, and Silverton realized she might interpret his lack of interest for something more sinister. A cruel streak.

"I'm not here for you to pleasure me."

Dorcas flashed a frightened look at the walls, as if they might have eyes. "Don't matter wot yer want o' me, or don't, m'Lord, yous goin' ter 'ave ter pay, all the same."

"I know that. Perhaps you'd care to accompany me on a walk."

"Can't do that, sir."

"If that's my pleasure, you're paid to serve me."

"Ain't allowed ter leave the premises, m'Lord."

"What, never? Surely you get a half day on a Sunday, Dorcas? Are you not free to meet whomever you choose on a Sunday?"

She toyed with the skirts of her gaudy primrose and lavender sarcenet gown, then rose and took a step forward as if she were curious or confused as to his motives. "Wot yer talkin' 'bout, m'Lord? I ain't neva leavin' 'ere 'cept in a coffin." She clapped her hand to her mouth and then said in a louder voice, "Let me give yer a good rub down, m'Lord. Take the tension from yer bones." As she drew closer, she put her mouth to his ear. "I don't know wot yer come 'ere fer, m'Lord, if it ain't ter get yer money's worth out o' wot I can give yer, but don't talk ter me o' leavin' this place cos it ain't neva goin' ter 'appen. 'As someone 'eard 'bout the depraved depths I sunk to? Are yer 'ere on their orders? If so, I won't an' can't live wiv the shame, an' I ain't neva goin' ter be redeemed. Hell is where I'm goin' ter, an' no mistake. 'Sides, I signed a contract. Ain't no way I'll pay me way out o' that afore I'm already in me grave." She thrust out her chest and drew in a shuddering sigh before adding in a more robust tone, tinged with resignation, "'Ere, m'Lord, yer must be ever so 'ot in yer coat."

Silverton gripped her wrists and she froze, staring into his face with sudden panic. "Please don't 'urt me, m'Lord."

"Hurt you? Good lord, I'm not going to hurt you," he responded, appalled. "Please, Dorcas, I want to *help* you. I'm here because a friend has asked me to help you."

"A friend? I ain't got no friends." Terror welled in her eyes. "Me family…? Oh lordy, do tell me they know nothin' 'bout wot I've sunk to?" She tore out of his grasp and almost staggered to the window, whispering over her shoulder, "If yer ain't here fer wot most gennulman want, then please let me be. I can't talk ter yer like this, m'Lord. Mrs. Montgomery an' 'er son, they won't like it. It'll be bad fer me."

Silverton advanced and put a hand on her shoulder. Gently, he turned her back to face him. "Please just come with me, Dorcas." He tried to inject the necessary reassurance into his tone, but she was like a trembling rabbit, staring between him and the door as if she feared she'd be set upon by either.

"Can't, m'Lord. Can't ever," she muttered. "Yer don't undastand what yer suggestin'."

"I want to help," he said, pushing down his frustration.

Dorcas seemed to relax at this, causing Silverton to drop his hands, and the smile she offered was full of sympathy. She patted his shoulder in an almost motherly fashion. "It ain't often a gennulman wants to 'elp me, so I feel bad throwin' yer kindness back in yer face. I don't know who has sent yer and I don't want to know fer I just told yer that I've made me bed." Almost distractedly, she leaned back a little to stroke the grubby pink counterpane. "An' 'ere's where I got no choice but to lie until the Lord sees fit to cast me into the fiery furnace of hell. Ain't no use thinkin' it'll be otherwise."

Silverton did his best to persuade her that girls who were tricked into wickedness were not destined for Hell but it soon becamse clear that Dorcas would not go willingly with him.

He thought of Kitty who had chosen her life of sin, and who shared none of Dorcas's qualms about the afterlife. Increasingly, he found himself thinking of Kitty, for it amused him to imagine what delight she might take in a particular sight or anecdote. Ridiculous, of course!

She'd certainly be utterly distraught to learn of poor Dorcas and her plight, but if Dorcas would not leave Maggie Montgomery's he could hardly drag her out, kicking and screaming.

Eventually, with a sigh, he put his money on the dressing table and left.

CHAPTER 12

*A*raminta had ignored the growing pains in her belly for as long as it took to get herself dressed, with Jane's help, occasioned by Jane's perpetual grumbling.

"Yer can't go, m'lady. It ain't right in yer condition," her stubborn maid kept saying.

"I'm a married woman who can do what I please, and I won't have a servant telling me what to do."

"An' all alone?" Jane went on, as if she hadn't heard Araminta. "Madness, that's wot 'tis! Wot if summat 'appens while yer in the carriage? Wot if the babe decides ter come, *then?*"

Araminta held up the exquisite diamond and ruby necklace Debenham had given her as a wedding gift. The ruby that formed the centerpiece was shaped like a love heart, making it the most unusual, and beautiful, piece of jewellery she'd ever seen. "What do you think of this, Jane?"

"Yer going ter wear that ter go ter yer sister's fer dinner? Ter impress Miss 'Etty? Or per'aps it's Sir Aubrey yer want ter impress?"

Araminta might have swung around in fury on any other occasion. But the wretched baby was so active, and she needed to take her mind off her misfortunes, so she managed to exercise a higher than usual degree of tolerance. "I can't imagine why you'd say such a thing, Jane. No, there is another guest who will be there. Someone far more interesting than Sir Aubrey."

"Well, I don't fink yer should go, m'lady. Not wiv Sir Aubrey there who'll be lookin' at yer belly an'—"

"And what, Jane?" This time, Araminta did round on her, her voice a low snarl, though not before deciding against the necklace and instead wearing only the matching dangling earrings in her lobes. It had been less than six months since Debenham had presented them to her, together with the matching necklace on her wedding night and, by god, Araminta felt she'd earned them. Let Lord Ludbridge admire the way they made her eyes sparkle. Perhaps the jewels might help fund a future together. Life wasn't all about money and riches, and if Araminta could escape her dreadful marriage to Debenham with a few small sacrifices, she'd do it.

As she gazed at her reflection, she imagined fleeing to France with handsome Teddy. How romantic if the jewels Debenham had given her could fund a few years of them living together in a charming chateau. Then, as soon as she'd heard that Debenham had drunk himself into an early grave, she could return to England and resume her rightful position in society. As Lady Ludbridge.

"I ain't goin' ter say it again, miss, in case the walls 'ave ears, but I reckon yer know wot I mean."

Araminta rose quickly, sweeping over to the bigger, rectangular looking glass that hung above the fireplace. She looked beautiful. Exquisite. As long as no one cast their gaze below her breasts, they'd think her the most stunning and desirable woman in the world. Lord Ludbridge certainly would.

"I heard the carriage pull up outside the front. Come, Jane. I may as well stay at Miss Hetty's tonight. Tell Jem to let Debenham know—if he ever returns—though I doubt he'd be remotely interested."

She didn't care about Debenham. As she labored down the stairs, excitement skittered up her spine. In a few more weeks, the wretched baby would be out, and she could start afresh and as she meant to go on. She'd be free. Free to have the life she deserved.

Ensconced inside the carriage, she wrapped her furs more closely about her. The journey was not long. She'd not confirmed with Hetty that she'd come, so she would be a delicious surprise for Lord Ludbridge. She thought with delight of the passionate light in his eye when he'd last regarded her. Poor man, he'd imagined her lost to him. Not that he hadn't deserved it. His shocking abandonment of her ought to be punished. But tonight, she'd find a way to communicate that his patience since would be rewarded. Her entire body shivered in anticipation at the thought. She would reward him in a way that would satisfy the desire of any lovelorn, red-blooded male.

"Go!" She rapped on the roof of the carriage she'd asked Jem to hire since Debenham had taken theirs. He'd recently sold the phaeton, pretending he was ordering a finer equipage, but Araminta knew it was to settle a gambling debt.

Closing her eyes, she gripped the leather seat as she lurched forward and the horses set off at a brisk trot. As soon as she reached Sir Aubrey's townhouse, Hetty would see to her comfort like the good sister she was. Lord Ludbridge could see to her amusement. She was looking forward to more fun than she'd had in months. Dreamily, she watched the tall houses pass by as they traveled through the cobbled streets and headed toward Covent Garden.

Lulled by the rhythmic motion of the carriage and the pleasant thoughts that were occupying her, she wasn't prepared for the ripping pain that seemed almost to wrench her in half. She'd been feeling uncomfortable stirrings and a tightness between her legs all afternoon but nothing like this.

"Dear God!" She dragged herself upright and took a deep breath. The pace was sedate, and the horses had not lurched or taken a corner too fast. Perhaps she'd imagined it.

Araminta sucked in a breath and tried to convince herself that the baby was simply turning over. "I'm quite alright—" she began to say aloud but she couldn't finish the word. There was the pain again. Unbearable. This time, she screamed, hunching into herself as she felt warm liquid oozing down her thighs. Panic-stricken, she put her hands to her belly and felt the movement within while another pain, more intense than the previous and worse than she'd ever experienced, convulsed through her again. What was happening?

She must have screamed like a banshee rather than a refined lady of quality for the carriage halted, and the coachman appeared now, his face in the doorway he'd opened a crack. "Did I hear yer wished to stop, m'lady? Is everyfink o'right?"

Araminta, in an undignified heap half on the bench and the floor, made an effort to get herself sitting upright and tidily. She was going to tell him to crack his whip and get moving, that she needed to reach Hetty's townhouse, but another contraction caused her to shriek once more and she couldn't reply.

"M'lady, wot d'yer want me to do?" The coachman sounded panicked, but Araminta was gasping like a fish, her pain too acute to answer him. Dear God, the baby was coming. The baby was coming early. No, perhaps not early. Just earlier than it should be coming, and she had not the remotest idea what to do about it. She'd buried her head in the sand, and now the nightmare was upon her.

"Lady Debenham, wot d'yer want me ter do? Fetch 'elp?" he shouted over her screaming. "Lady Debenham, please tell me what to do!"

Araminta was in no position to tell anyone what to do as the nightmare she was living seemed to envelop her like a suffocating black cloak.

"I say, did I hear the name Lady Debenham?" It was a young, female voice. Araminta didn't open her eyes, but she heard the breathy concern and wasn't sure whether to be relieved or dismayed. The child was early. But it could *not* come now. She had to get it back in. *Somehow.*

The door opened wider and a slight figure stood beside the coachman though in the gloom it was impossible for Araminta to know if she knew this person who now said more urgently, "I recognised your name being shouted and then I heard you scream. How can I help?"

Fortunately there seemed a hiatus between the agonizing contractions, and Araminta struggled to muster all her wits. "Get inside," she ordered, breathing hard. "I don't care who you are, just get inside and tell the coachman to keep moving."

She heard the creak and groan of the carriage door opening wider, then felt the equippage tilt as it was occupied by another, before a soft hand was placed on her forearm. "Lady Debenham. It's Miss La Bijou, if you recall."

Araminta opened her eyes which she'd squeezed shut. Once again she made an unsuccessful attempt to straighten and to push back her shoulders, though she managed to respond with dignity, if between clenched teeth, "Oh yes, Miss La Bijou. Well, Miss La Bijou, I do need some help, as it happens. I need to find somewhere I might...I might...lie down."

Miss La Bijou sent her a questioning look and Araminta realized the carriage was still stationary. "Shall I tell the coachman to take you home?"

Home? With Debenham due back at God knew what hour. "I do not want to go home. No, definitely not home. You don't understand. I need to go *anywhere* but home." Fear was coalescing, crawling up her throat and making her want to cry except that she couldn't succumb to weakness. She hadn't made a plan before, but now she could leave it no later.

"Where do you live, Miss La Bijou?" She had to make clear her wishes before she was wracked by another contraction, which might mean others decided for her what was best.

"*Me?*"

"Yes, I asked you where your lodgings are? I need to go there." But she couldn't explain why for she was forced to break off as another contraction gripped her. Unable to control the pain, she threw her body the length of the seat, her torso pressed against the unopened door.

"You're having a baby, Lady Debenham. You can't have it in my lodgings when your home is around the corner." The girl sounded panicked.

While she wiped her sweating forehead with a linen handkerchief, Araminta summoned the energy to speak. "Just take me to where you live! Or to someone you know who's delivered a baby before. A midwife!" she hissed. "And I will make it more than worth your while. The fewer who know I'm having this baby now, the better. Understand? No? I will explain when we get there. I simply cannot return to my townhouse, and if you tell the coachman to take me there, I'll make sure you regret it." She gasped at another spasm of pain. Heat and agony threatened to smother her like a blanket. "Just...do...as...I...tell you!"

She could feel the sweat dripping between her breasts. Her thighs were damp; her petticoats soaked. Already she was covered with the filth of this child who'd not yet made his entrance to the world; this child who had blighted her hopes of happiness. No, she would not have it at home, and she'd not let the world know what was happening. She'd not let this ill-begotten child ruin the rest of her life.

Vaguely, she heard Miss Bijou say something to the coachman before her voice sounded calmly in her ear. "What can I do to ease the pain?"

Araminta closed her eyes in relief as the vehicle began to move. "Nothing can ease the pain," she whimpered. "I just need to get the baby out."

For a while, the world seemed a haze of unreality. Araminta was barely conscious that they'd stopped in a dark laneway. She could hear Miss La Bijou's shoes clicking on the cobbles, her loud rapping upon a thin wooden door somewhere nearby, and the tension in her voice as she called out a name.

Then the carriage door was opened, a woman's voice commanded, "Coachman, lift 'er unda the arms and 'elp me take 'er inside. That's right. I'm the 'ealer she's requested. It's 'er ladyship's wish that I attend 'er and ya can go 'ome and say nuffink about wot yous seen or done tonight." This was followed by the chink of coins and the surprised grunt of the coachman.

Araminta didn't open her eyes until she was set down upon a very hard surface, and when she did take in her surroundings, she was horrified by the lowliness of the room. The damp was palpable; the thick dust on the windowsill immediately caused her to sneeze, and her scream in the midst of another contraction was extended when a large spider web drifted from the ceiling to brush her cheek.

When she'd recovered, she could only stare about her with horror. This was Miss La Bijou's dwelling? The roof seemed to bear down on her; the cold and damp rose up from the bare wooden boards, but then the horror was tinged with something else. The realization that, perhaps, this was the best that could have happened. Oblivion. Anonymity.

The woman, whom Araminta had heard Kitty address as Mrs. Mobbs, filled the doorway as she put her plump hands on her ample hips. Her gown was open at the throat, and Araminta could see her sweaty, blotchy skin, which at first made her recoil, until it occurred to her that this lower-class woman, who in all likelihood had little contact with society circles, might be the most valuable assistant she could wish for.

She certainly seemed capable. "Kitty! Fetch all the linen yer can find so we might assist 'er ladyship!" the woman shouted. "Water! I need water! Yer'll 'ave to go ter the pump. I've none left. I'll see ter the fire. Warm water is wot we need. 'Urry now!"

There was a moment of relief when Mrs. Mobbs covered Araminta with a blanket, but the wool was coarse and then the pain came again, and she screamed, instinctively drawing up her knees.

Pieces of sharp straw jabbed at her, pricking through the narrow, stuffed mattress though dimly she acknowledged that was the least of her problems. The force of the creature within threatened to breach her, rip her in two, and she couldn't bear it.

"Get it out! Get rid of it!" she muttered between clenched teeth, breathing short, shallow breaths, vaguely conscious of the woman returning to the room. "Get it out! By God, I hate it!"

Mrs. Mobbs dabbed at her forehead with a dirty piece of linen. "Now that's not charitable. 'Ate yer own babe?"

"Yes, I do! I hate it! It's come too early!" she sobbed before she realized the words were out, turning her head to add mutinously, "It'll ruin my life! It's already ruined my life!" She opened one eye defiantly, ready to repudiate whatever else Mrs. Mobbs might have to say about that; however, the woman merely smiled as she settled her large bulk on a stool and pushed a greasy strand of hair beneath her grubby mob cap.

Thank the lord she was in this hovel and not lying in state in Debenham's townhouse or country estate or, God forbid, at Hetty's with Lord Ludbridge in the next room listening to her birthing pangs and frowning as he calculated the months, just as Debenham would be doing.

"Me good lady, I am indeed troubled to 'ear this. Why, yer 'usband will be only too delighted when yer return 'ome an' present 'im with a fine bonny…well, whatever it is. There now, breathe 'ard. It's goin' ter come fast, this one."

"Not fast enough," Araminta muttered. "If I never have another it'll be too soon."

"Ah well, some of us are made fer pleasure and some made fer breeding."

"Breeding is not for me. It's ruined my figure but…" Araminta gave a sob, "I'm a married woman with a brutish husband, and I'm fated to do this…oh god, once a year."

"Course not, luvvey. Ah, Kitty, yer've brought us 'ot water. Wot a good girl. We'll need plenty more, now. 'Elp me sponge down our fine lady an' then go an' fetch another pail. That's a good girl."

Araminta felt the gravitational pull down in her lower regions, together with another desperate wave of pain. She truly didn't think she could bear it this time. She tried to draw in her breath, but couldn't. The sweat was pouring from every pore, it felt, and she was more a prisoner than she'd ever believed possible.

The woman sponged her forehead, the warm water small relief before another wave of pain swamped her. "Get…it…out!" she shrieked.

"Breathe in…an' out…bite on this." The woman stuffed a filthy strip of leather into Araminta's mouth which Araminta immediately spat out, glaring, before suddenly she felt a sucking, heaving, slithering motion.

"Push!" shouted the woman. "Push!"

Instinctively, Araminta did as she was bid. She felt as if she were expelling a monster, but the relief was almost instant, and the woman's satisfied cry bore out her success.

"Lordy, it's a boy! I've neva seen a babe come so quickly!"

The sound of a quick slap was followed by a lusty cry, and then the babe was placed on Araminta's chest.

Araminta looked down at the wrinkled, waxy, loathsome creature and turned her head away, curling her lip in disgust.

"I don't want it," she whispered, the words ending in a sob; the relief of pushing out the baby was followed by the catharsis of uttering the truth. "May God forgive me, but what can I do?"

The woman put her face close to Araminta's and pushed her hair back. "Yer is a grand lady and now a mother. Yer don't know what yer sayin', m'lady. Course yer want it. Yer 'usband wants a son, to be sure 'e does. A fine, lusty son. Yer've done yer duty and provided 'im wiv an 'eir fer I can tell this is yer first. Now, let's clean yer both up a bit. My, but wot a fine 'ead o' 'air 'e has. The devil's crown, eh? Black, wiv a streak of white. No doubt it runs in yer 'usband's family? 'Is Lordship will be proud."

Araminta, who'd been about to utter another moan of despair, felt the breath leave her in a rush. Horror deafened her to everything but the silent shrieking inside her head. Finally, she croaked, "What did you say?" She struggled up onto her elbows and stared, horrified at the bundle of...devil's spawn. The hair—thick and black cut through with a swathe of white at the right temple— was a trademark of Sir Aubrey's lineage and no mistake. Feverishly she ran her hands over the child's springy crown. A fine head of hair, indeed! A head of hair that would see her spend the rest of her days locked up, or paying in a myriad of other ways for her deceit. The baby's mouth was gaping like a fish. The woman pushed the child toward her nipple, and it latched on like an alien creature.

"Get it off me!" Araminta wept, pushing away the child. Immediately, it began to scream.

"Fine pair o' lungs. What a 'ealthy child! Oh m'lady, we need ter send a message ter yer 'usband 'lettin 'im know of the strange an' unexpected events t'night."

"No!" Panicked, Araminta's gaze roamed over the grubby walls, the dust-laden windowsill, the bloodied, filthy linen tangled up about her legs, the straw that was scratching her. "My husband must never know!"

The woman leaned closer. Her eyes darted to the door at the sound of footsteps in the corridor. She clapped her hand over the baby's mouth and called out, "Kitty, run next door fer...fer more linen. Quick! An' find a box, too, in case the poor babe don't survive."

She rose, stepping in front of Araminta and the baby as Kitty appeared in the doorway. Araminta gave a wail of grief—and it *was* grief for this was not how her life was supposed to be—which smothered the mewling of the child. She closed her eyes as she heard the woman repeat her command. "'Urry, Kitty! The baby is too early. We need ter stop it comin' an' we need more linen! Go!"

Araminta caught a glimpse of the confusion that crossed the face of the girl in the doorway but then, thankfully, Miss La Bijou obeyed, retreating into the passage; running to the front door and letting herself outside, and Araminta was left with the only confessor, the only assistant, she could in her present circumstances, rely upon.

"It's come too early. Two months too early. Or six weeks, at any rate. The babe is enormous. I can't...I can't take it home and claim it's my husband's. I have to get rid of it. Please, you must help me." The unfairness of her situation pressed down upon her like a thousand hands, kneading and pummeling. She began to sob. Her life was in tatters. She might as well throw herself into the river and be done with it.

A grubby, meaty hand cupped her cheek. "'Ush now, an' answer me, quick. Yer've jest given birth to a fine, lusty son, but yer tellin' me yer cannot claim 'tis yer 'usband's?"

Araminta rolled away, partly to deflect the woman's smelly, dirty hand. She saw the gleam in Mrs. Mobbs's eyes, and thought she didn't look nearly sympathetic enough. But then terror washed all but the truth away. Mrs. Mobbs could help her. Mrs. Mobbs was capable of tidying up her life. She'd organized everything else so far.

It was a relief, rather than a blight, and Araminta surrendered to her emotion. "I can't present him with…this!" she sobbed. "Why…his hair! My husband doesn't have hair like this run in the family, but he knows who does."

The woman stood above her, sucking on her gums as she pondered Araminta's situation. Then she gave a lusty sigh. "Ah, love, 'tis easy enough ter mend such inconveniences. We'll jes' find a comfy, cozy, lovin' 'ome fer the child." Mrs. Mobbs sounded remarkably equable, and Araminta searched her face, hopefully.

"Find another home for it?" she repeated. "One where it will receive the care it deserves, for it wouldn't if I delivered it to mine. Could you really do that?"

"Course, m'lady! Why, wot a coincidence yer should come ter me. That's a big part o' me bizness, don't yer know? Findin' 'omes fer babes wot need uvver parents ter love 'em. I've done it fer many a fine lady, jest like yer." She patted Araminta on the shoulder, then picked up the child. "See, 'e's sleepin' already afta a bit o' a feed. We'll jes' put it 'bout the babe's died, and I'll send it next door ter be wet-nursed. I'll find it a 'ome in a good family, and yer can return 'ome an' do the job 'Is Lordship married yer fer, an all. Yer can produce 'im a fine, lusty 'eir that e' can call 'is own. All's well, m'lady. Nuthin that Mrs. Mobbs can't fix."

But Araminta's hopeful attention had faded by the end. Have another child? Go through all this again? Dear God, no! "I don't want another. I don't want another. Ever!" she cried, prostrating herself on the bed and beating her fists. "Oh, Lord, what can I do? Give him an heir? I'm doomed."

Then she felt Mrs. Mobbs's hand on her shoulder, and the woman's insinuating voice in her ear. The hope and promise in her words overrode the rottenness of her breath. "Mrs. Mobbs can 'elp yer there, too, m'lady, if that's yer wish. With the 'elp of' 'em pretty earrings wot yer're wearin', I think I 'ave jest the solution to *all* yer problems."

CHAPTER 13

Kitty was unprepared for the warmth of her welcome from Lord Silverton.

"I thought you'd abandoned me," he said, jumping up when she was let into his library. His smile was broad and unfeigned, but immediately it disappeared when he saw her creased brow.

"What is it? Nash? Has he distressed you?"

Kitty shook her head and obediently sat down where he settled her so he could apparently look into her face. She gazed up at him, still in half a daze. "What an extraordinary evening. I rendered aid to Lady—" She stopped herself from mentioning names. There was something not right about everything that had happened and she needed to mull over the matter. Besides, Lord Silverton knew Lady Debenham as the wife of his dreadful compatriot, the unsavory Debenham, and Kitty certainly didn't want to cause trouble, even for the half-sister she'd always despised. "Well, a lady who was...in danger of having a child. Too early, I gather. I took her to Mrs. Mobbs for we were just around the corner, and she..." Kitty shrugged. She was so confused for she was sure she'd heard that baby cry. But she felt she could not speak of her half-sister's plight to anyone, not even to Silverton, much as she despised Araminta. Well, she *had* despised her and she probably ought to, still, but she'd been surprised at the sympathy she'd felt for her when Silverton had taken her to Lord Debenham's townhouse and she'd glimpsed an insight into the young woman's unhappiness. Araminta might be insufferably haughty and thoughtless but her entire marriage was a punishment. A lifelong punishment. It was a salutary reminder to Kitty that perhaps there was some compensation for being illegitimate and therefore worth less than nothing—well, not valuable enough to trade for a supposedly good marriage. In answer to Lord Silverton's interested look, she went on, "Well, apparently the panic was averted, and the child was prevented from making its appearance too early after all and..."

"And what?"

"The lady went home. So it all ended well."

"So you saved a life this evening, my precious one."

Kitty looked up at him suspiciously, and he laughed. "Does the endearment make you suspicious? Well, it ought to for my motives are indeed suspect in keeping you by my side. I would much rather you stayed here than returned to the undeserving Nash."

Kitty sighed, unconsciously leaning in against Lord Silverton's side then jerking straight to keep a little distance between them as she realized what she was doing. "I went to fetch something from the theater this evening and there were three bouquets of flowers for me. He delivers flowers and notes to me every day." She extended her arm to study the ruby-studded bracelet he'd gifted her to try and atone for his deplorable behavior. Strangely, she did not feel the leap of want and need she'd previously felt for him. Obviously, the trauma of his infidelity ran deeper than she thought. Or perhaps she was too caught up in what had happened tonight. It seemed incredible that her half-sister had passed by in a carriage, in the throes of labor, and Kitty, of all people, had rendered her assistance.

No, she couldn't tell Silverton—or anyone—that part. About what Lady Debenham really was to her. But, engaged on other topics it was certainly pleasant chatting to him while he sat on the arm of her chair stroking her hair. Indeed, he certainly wasn't shy about making it clear he liked her and that he'd happily set her up with as much generosity as Nash had.

But although Kitty liked Silverton very much, that could never happen. Aside from the fact that she still clung to the belief that her future was with Nash and tried to tell herself how this was borne up by the dangerous, desirous glint in his eye which never failed to communicate itself all the way to her lower belly in the most wickedly wanton way, Silverton was her friend. He'd been very good to her. And friendship was rare and precious, and something not to be risked for the transient pleasures of the flesh.

Sadly, too, he was not all he appeared, though she'd seen or heard nothing to suggest he was the villain Stephen Cranbourne had suggested.

She sighed, opening her mouth to broach the rumors she'd heard about Silverton being involved in Debenham's misdemeanors but then thought better of it. The rumors were too vague to even articulate. Besides, if wicked Debenham remained safe, unsullied and in full possession of his goods and chattels despite the myriad rumors that swirled about *him*, Silverton would be much safer even than that.

So she just smiled. No, she wouldn't hint that she knew Silverton was not all he presented to society; she'd just enjoy what he offered her. And that was safety and friendship in an increasingly turbulent world. "I was thinking about how I'll need a maid when I'm living in the little house Nash has leased for me, and that I wish I'd found Dorcas, the friend you might remember me telling you about. The one I met when I first arrived in London."

"Yes, of course I remember." He shifted in his seat, looking surprisingly uncomfortable before adding, "But you *really* plan to leave me so soon?"

She was surprised at the flash of genuine disappointment she thought she heard and hugged it close. She was not used to anyone evincing any form of real pleasure in her company.

"You are very sweet to sound like you'll miss me, Lord Silverton." She patted his shoulder feeling very fondly towards him. "Tonight, as I stood in the quiet of the theater and read Lord Nash's messages, I was touched by the growing desperation for forgiveness and the sweet words he wrote. He truly is so sorry and…of course men will stray when temptation is put in front of their noses. I've no doubt Jennie threw herself at him, and what man could resist? I think the time has come for me to go to him." She hugged herself, conscious of the swelling of excitement inside her as she conjured up an image of the burning desire in Nash's eyes. He'd learned his lesson. He'd not stray again.

Lord Silverton put his hand on her shoulder when she made a move to rise. He started to say something, but then apparently changed his mind. After a long pause, he took both her wrists, cleared his voice and said, "Kitty, I have something to tell you about Dorcas."

She darted her gaze back to Silverton's face. He looked and sounded surprisingly intent, considering Dorcas was just a maid he'd never met.

"I found Dorcas," he went on. "When you told me the name of her employer, I was horrified. You see, I know about Mrs. Montgomery; about her business, that is, and it's not something a young lady should have any dealings with. So I found Dorcas and tried to persuade her to come back with me, but she refused."

"She refused?" Kitty straightened as she met Lord Silverton's eye, suspicion at Dorcas's true situation warring with pique that she should not wish to work for Kitty. "Is she so well situated, then, she has forgotten her old friend?"

Lord Silverton shook his head, his look grim. "I only wish it were so, Kitty." Gently he chafed her hands as he proceeded to explain, as delicately as possible, the precise nature of Dorcas's predicament.

And Kitty listened with growing horror, while at the same time she tried to be immune to the lovely warm and cozy feeling that was sweeping through her body, and which made her want to climb onto Lord Silverton's lap and rest her head against his chest while he stroked her.

All over.

So now it was up to Kitty to save Dorcas. If the poor, ill-used girl wouldn't accept the assistance Lord Silverton offered, she surely couldn't refuse Kitty if Kitty begged her in person.

Standing on the pavement with her veil pulled down and wrapped up in a voluminous cape, Kitty felt safe from prying eyes as she watched the comings and goings to the large, four-square house in Soho.

Though it was dark, the gas lamp on the pavement just outside the front of the house illuminated each face clearly for one split second. What a variety of men were ushered in and out of that door. The majority appeared, by their clothing and the equipages that dropped them off, to be gentlemen of good social standing. But equally, there were soldiers, sailors, men of middling rank, even the occasional struggling clerk, casting a furtive glance over his shoulder before hurrying up the short flight of stairs and then, upon a hasty rap, being admitted through the imposing black front door.

Kitty made sure she kept to the shadows; her heart thumping with pained horror. It was as Lord Silverton had said. This was a house of ill repute, and her friend Dorcas was a prisoner there.

She knew she couldn't rescue Dorcas by brazenly bursting through the doors and dragging her out, but she'd needed to see for herself where Dorcas was housed, and the kind of clientele Mrs. Montgomery's abode attracted.

Fighting back tears, she turned away. What stroke of fate had favored Kitty, easing her path toward her achieving her long-held dream for fame, fortune, and love?

Poor Dorcas, whose dreams had been so much more modest, had become a pawn in a scheme that ruined young girls' lives to line the pockets of an evil few.

Did Mrs. Mobbs know what her friend, Maggie Montgomery, was up to? Kitty wiped her eyes with the back of her hand. She suddenly felt a great deal more grown up than she had such a short time ago, before Lord Silverton had pulled the wool from her eyes.

With her head bent, she shouldered her way through the evening crowds. If she were truthful with herself, she knew Lord Nash was not the smoldering-eyed Adonis ready to pledge her his heart and soul and everything he had to make her happy.

He was just a handsome, fallible young man with a straying eye who desired her, and whom she found attractive when she was ready to give her heart to the first likely contender.

No, that wasn't true! she rebuked herself, as she rounded a street corner and sidestepped a child selling matches. If she allowed herself to be so downcast at the first hurdle, then how could she make a success of her career? She had beauty; she knew that. But now she needed to be strong and firm and handle matters with conviction.

She *would* rescue Dorcas, and she *would* extricate herself from Lord Nash. It was the only way to retain the independence and control of her life that was the central tenet of her running away at all.

So she reached the theater entering through the side door, ready to perform with a lightness of spirit she didn't feel, for the tragedy that ended *Romeo and Juliet* better suited her mood right now.

Then it occurred to her that if Silverton had failed to persuade Dorcas to leave with him, Lord Nash would surely use every device to get Dorcas out of Maggie Montgomery's clutches; that is, if he loved Kitty. Lord Silverton was fond of Kitty and wanted to set her up as his mistress but he was not madly in love with Kitty as Lord Nash's daily imploring notes professed him to be. It was very kind of Lord Silverton to visit Maggie Montgomery's but he'd merely done what he could to help a friend.

However, if Lord Nash wanted to mend the damage he'd done between Kitty and himself, he could start by indulging her with the rescue of Kitty's own dear Dorcas.

By the time she sat down at her dressing table and read the notes that accompanied the three bouquets of roses Lord Nash had sent, Kitty was feeling a good deal more settled in her mind. Her natural pragmatism and romantic turn of mind were now of one accord.

Lord Nash may not be her destiny, exactly, but he was easy to be in love with, and the most hopeful prospect on the horizon right now for giving Kitty the long-term security that would enable a single girl in her situation to sleep at night.

THE PERFORMANCE WAS ONE OF HER BEST EVER, AND KITTY'S HEART felt full to bursting as applause and flowers rained upon her as she took her bow.

It really did almost burst with excitement and happiness when she hurried backstage and found herself face to face with Lord Nash, whose tragic look of sorrow melted the last of her reservations. Into her arms, he thrust a large bunch of red roses and a black velvet box to which was attached a small card.

"Forgive me," it read.

Kitty opened the box, then gasped as she held up the exquisite diamond and ruby earrings to the light.

Turning with a smile, she stepped into his open arms, while his cry of joy was truncated by his kiss.

"Come home with me, Kitty. Tonight and every night." His impassioned murmur vibrated against her lips.

Kitty's legs buckled. This was getting close to the proposal she longed for. Not quite, but she had him begging, realizing his need for her. Oh yes, she'd show him how much he needed her.

Nestling her head on his shoulder, she rocked happily in the carriage that took them back to his townhouse, and whimpered with pleasure as he undressed her.

Lord Nash needed her. She could feel it as he gently laid her upon the bed, trailing his fingertips delicately over her face and down her throat while he seemed to drink her in with his eyes. Lord Nash was her slave in love. It was clear with every soft breath that caressed her as he divested her of her clothes, gently massaging her breasts, kneading then suckling her nipples.

Lord Nash couldn't live without her. This he told her in anguished tones as he tossed off his shirt, pulled off his boots and breeches, then trailed kisses over her breasts, down her belly, burying his face between her legs and pleasuring her with tantalizing strokes of his tongue.

Kitty squirmed with pleasure, believing him. She'd never felt such happiness. Nash had learned his lesson. He was hers now.

She hardly got any sleep that night. Twice Nash woke her, eager to repeat their incendiary lovemaking. When a knock on the door heralded morning hot chocolate, Kitty was exhausted, still on a cloud. And as they dined opposite one another in the window embrasure, he spoke of his plans.

"Today, I shall sign the lease on your little house, and we shall go shopping for all the accoutrements a lady needs for her wardrobe, eh? That's once the mantua maker has come by to measure you."

Kitty couldn't believe his generosity. He loved her even more than she could have imagined.

"And I shall have my own maid to attend me?"

He nodded. "Indeed you shall. I've already made inquiries."

"But Nash, there is someone I expressly wish to wait upon me. A friend from past days."

He frowned. "I would rather I selected someone I could trust, my dear. You are young and may be taken advantage of."

For a second, Kitty thought he feared she may be taken advantage of by other men. Then she laughed. "Oh, don't worry about that. I know what to look for in a good servant. Mama always had me interview the maids we employed at home."

"What a curious past. You're very secretive. Servants? In your home? Who are you really, Kitty La Bijou?"

Kitty dropped her eyes. One day, she would tell him, just not yet. "I have reinvented myself since coming to London, and that is my secret. But there may be some difficulty in prizing away the lady's maid I wish to employ, for she has fallen into the clutches of a woman of ill repute. Oh Nash, please say you'll help me rescue her?"

She'd expected the same willingness to please as he'd shown last night. Instead, his mouth pursed with the indelicacy of the suggestion. "Rescue someone from a house of ill repute? Darling Kitty, I really can't imagine we'd have such a conversation the very morning after our wonderful reunion." He rose, smiling to soften his words perhaps. "Let's talk no more of such unpleasant matters. Are you ready to go forth with me and begin our frenzied round of purchases? I want to show you how much I've *really* missed you."

Kitty was prepared, for the moment, to allow Nash's wishes to eclipse her desires for finding Dorcas. Clearly, he needed careful managing, and she could not *force* him to do her bidding.

All she could hope for, now, was that Dorcas wasn't working in the capacity Silverton presumed. Kitty would bring Nash around soon enough, for she'd accepted she was helpless in aiding her friend, alone, but she'd need to be patient.

Nevertheless, anxiety sapped some of the thrill of promenading along the fashionable shopping streets on Nash's arm. After acquiring three pairs of Oxford tan gloves, a quantity of feathers, silk shawls, a pair each of dancing slippers and half-kid boots, they finished their expedition with ices at Gunthers before winding up at the sweet little bower Nash had secured for Kitty.

Kitty gasped and clasped her hands disbelievingly. Her own abode. She was equally thrilled when Nash turned her in his arms, kissed her nose and murmured, "Until it's properly furnished and decorated, and we've found you a lady's maid and a general cook and servant, you must let me look after you."

"And what might that entail, my Lord?" She sent him an arch look and with a wicked rumble of laughter, he swooped to kiss her before taking her hand and hurrying her up the steps. "I'm afraid it's not something I can explain to you for all the world to see."

Kitty allowed herself to be led, trying not to let the niggling disappointment and dismay she felt at his lack of response to her request tarnish her happiness.

She was happy, she told herself.

Well, as happy as a girl in her situation could be, she supposed.

CHAPTER 14

"M'lord, yer in all but darkness. Let me light the lamp."

Silverton barely attended as the maid bustled about, banking up the library fire before striking a flame to the the Argand lamp. He was not prone to moods of black despair, but today had started with the very real disappointment that Kitty was not around to share his breakfast with her bright chatter, and had ended with news of the horrifying circumstances surrounding his friend, Lord Calder's untimely death, not helped by Silverton's mama's latest reports on her efforts to find him a wife. To please her, he'd finally penned a letter to the young lady his mother had again put forward, whom he'd known for many years and, in fact, liked very much.

He just wasn't sure he liked her enough to want to make her his wife.

"Cook's made a fine dinna an' 'ere it is, untouched. Are yer poorly, m'lord?"

"Just not in the mood to eat, Mary." He waved her away. "Please don't fret. It's very good of you, but I wish to be left alone to think. And please, no visitors, do you understand?"

He therefore felt a frisson of anger when, an hour later as the snow fell outside and his gloomy mood was exacerbated by the whistling wind that rustled the embers in the fireplace, he heard footsteps in the passage and the door was unceremoniously thrust open.

"I said—" His cross words were arrested by the breathless greeting of his erstwhile houseguest, who hurried across the room and put out her hands in a gesture of entreaty, saying, "Oh Silverton, what a terrible day it's been! I know I shouldn't be asking favors of you when you've already been so good to me, but you just *have* to help me rescue Dorcas, even if you say she couldn't be persuaded by you the first time."

"And good evening to you, too, Kitty. What is this? You've left Nash?" He rose, gripping her fingertips as she was about to withdraw her hands, and was conscious of an unexpectedly strong wave of hopefulness that was immediately dashed by her response.

"Indeed not! Nash and I have never got along better." Extricating herself, Kitty stepped back. The damp air that caused her bright hair to curl about her temples, and her heightened color, made her look like the most exquisite china doll. It was hard to resist the impulse to hold her tight and soak up her warmth and kindness. But she was chattering excitedly, her words not at all what he wanted to hear as she went on, "It was quite the right thing to forgive him for he has been utterly darling to me, and my house is nearly decorated." She threw her arms wide and did a twirl before him, her face suffused with happiness. "Have you seen the gossip sheets? Lord Summerton is to wed the woman who was his mistress, Mrs. Pinkerton? Yes, indeed! Do you not think I should take heart from a real-life instance of exactly what you say cannot happen to me?"

Silverton took her hand and led her to a sofa, pulling on the bell rope to order tea after Kitty declined what he had to hand on the drinks tray. While he felt ridiculously pleased by her intrusion, he wasn't going to pander to her false hopes by pretending something other than he thought.

"Kitty dearest," he said gently, "Lord Summerton is in his dotage with grown children. He cares nothing for society's opinion—which will be condemnatory. He can afford to thumb his nose at society and do as he pleases." He took a seat beside her and stroked her hair to soften his words. "Lord Nash might prefer you above all others, but he will marry for expediency. He will marry for dynastic considerations. You cannot blind yourself to the truth."

Kitty's sigh tugged at his heartstrings. She'd not objected to the hair stroking which he'd ceased, for he found it created a whirlpool of raging desire which he was clearly never going to be able to act upon; but now she gripped his hand, holding it upon her knee as if unaware of the effect this had upon him and said, "You shan't dissuade me that it's possible, but that's not what I came here to talk about. I came here because I urgently need your help."

"To rescue Dorcas? Why, Kitty, I'm not saying I won't help you, but I've already tried once, and I can't *force* her to go with me." He knew he was resorting to low tactics to hear her say Nash wasn't prepared to help her, while she believed Silverton clearly would. And indeed, Silverton would. Yes, he would try again. Any opportunity to be surrounded by Kitty's cheerful chatter was worth an investment of his time.

"You see, Nash is terribly busy right now, besides which he's naturally wary of venturing near such a place in case it casts aspersions on his character."

Silverton chuckled. "That's what he told you?" Nash was more likely concerned at being recognized as one of Mrs. Montgomery's regular clientele.

"Yes, but you will help me, won't you?" She brushed aside his ironic chuckle, clearly pretending she did not understand. Or, turning a blind eye. Kitty, he noticed, had a charming way of seeing only the best in a person. She drew herself up. "I've been to Maggie Montgomery's house and watched the gentlemen go in and out."

Silverton raised an eyebrow. "Gentlemen?"

Kitty blushed. "If I wasn't so desperate, knowing that Dorcas was a prisoner inside such a...place, and that such shocking, terrible things may be happening to her, I don't think I could bring myself to even allude to Mrs. Montgomery's establishment for what it is. But the truth is, I am powerless to get her out of there alone. I've asked and asked Nash, and he won't do anything.

So now, between you and me, Lord Silverton, we must be her saviors."

The grim reality and desperation of her friend's plight aside, Silverton couldn't help smiling at Kitty's earnestness. No, not earnestness so much as faith in him. When he thought of it like that he was warmed by a wonderful glow of satisfaction.

"You know, Kitty, I think saving your friend from vice and iniquity is just the tonic I need. Yes, your arrival has bolstered my mood enormously."

She looked surprised, and instinctively put up her hand to cup his cheek. "Poor Lord Silverton, yes, I see now that you are tired and perhaps low in spirits. I'm sorry I didn't notice before. Is there anything I can do to help?"

As there was not—short of suggesting Kitty might like to switch camps and transfer her affections from Nash to Silverton—Silverton shook his head.

"But what has happened? Please tell me."

Her large, brilliantly blue eyes were so full of sympathy, he had to resist very strongly the urge to take her in his arms and place her head against his chest, just for the catharsis it would be to feel her womanly body pressed against his. Comfort. That's all he wanted, he told himself, knowing he wanted so much more.

"A very dear friend of mine took his own life last night." Silverton reached for a scrap of paper which lay upon the arm of his chair and waved it at her. "This is the reason."

Kitty took it, was quiet while she scanned its contents, then, with a gasp, handed it back to Silverton. "Poor Lord Calder. But…surely he could have denied it?"

Silverton sighed. "There are sufficient rumors involving his Lordship's…proclivities…and his association with pretty young men that he'd not be believed. This was the nail in his coffin."

Kitty shook her head. "Who wrote it?"

"I only wish I knew. A scurrilous, muckraking, pamphleteer. When I last saw Calder, he inferred he was being blackmailed. I told him to hold firm against emptying his pockets, believing the blackguard responsible would find more fertile valleys to plumb. So, you see, in light of what's happened, I feel responsible."

"You mustn't!" Again in that impulsive, familiar manner Kitty adopted toward him, she squeezed his hands. "But…"

"What?"

"I admit, I don't really understand the love of a man for a man. I mean, it's not possible to…"

"What?"

"Do more than just say words of love. So the fact that it should be punishable by death seems very extreme."

Silverton was not about to pursue a topic on which Kitty clearly knew nothing, so he said, "Lord Calder was a kind and gentle soul, and I failed him. But by God, I intend to find out who's behind the muckraking."

"Nash knows someone who's being blackmailed, so there's a lot of it going about. Quite the fashionable thing to do it would seem."

Silverton narrowed his eyes to discern if she were being ironic or naïve, and quickly decided it was the latter. With her innocent looks and ingenuous manner, it was hard to envisage her as the defiled and ruined creature society would regard her. She'd been born from sin, and had willingly pursued sin.

Ironically, Silverton thought she was a great deal more refreshingly guileless than many of the debutantes of spotless reputation with whom he was acquainted; Miss Bunting included.

He rose and began to pace. "So it would seem. Well, you let me know who it is Nash knows is being blackmailed and who he thinks is behind it, and we can get a little closer to apprehending the perpetrator…or perhaps I'll be next."

"Are you guilty of a terribly serious misdemeanor, Lord Silverton?" Kitty slipped her hand through the crook of his arm, matching her steps to his. "I thought you were the perfect gentleman in every respect. You certainly seem that way to me."

"Why, thank you, Kitty. I could kiss you for expressing such a beautiful and generous sentiment."

"But of course, you can't for that would make Nash terribly jealous."

He slanted a look at her. "Undoubtedly, it would make Nash jealous. Is that the greatest of your concerns?" He stopped and grinned.

He was expecting some lighthearted response, and was surprised at the way she colored up, turning her head away. Dear Lord, perhaps she truly did harbor feelings for him. The thought was more bolstering than he'd believed possible. Pressing his advantage, he went on, "And, of course, Nash could only be jealous if he knew, besides which, he hasn't exactly shown himself to be the faithful type."

Instantly, he realized he'd gone too far. She dropped her hand from his arm, and her voice was gruff. "I thought you were my friend, Lord Silverton."

Cross with himself, he tried to rectify the situation. "I'm sorry, Kitty. Please, forgive me. I shall be more careful in future."

"I shall forgive you, but it hurts me to think that you believe Nash a lesser man because he succumbed to Jennie's lures. Surely it's no different to your Miss Bunting succumbing to the offer of marriage from another gentleman after she'd given you reason to believe she favored you? Yet you'd forgive her if she changed her mind and begged you to marry her after all."

"There is more than a little difference in the two examples, Kitty." Silverton led her to the fireplace where she rested against the mantelpiece, staring at the decorative plaster ceiling while he lounged as close as he dared, pretending a more lighthearted demeanor than he felt. "Let us drop all talk of Nash, for I do not like to hear how wonderful he is when it only makes me want what he has."

Kitty laughed, immediately animated. "It's very nice to hear such flattery, but you're only saying it because you've not found someone to replace Miss Bunting, and you want to feel loved and manly. Just know that you can't win me from Nash if you're not about to make me a marriage offer. There," she challenged, "after what you've been telling me, that should make you turn tail and run."

"I could make you very happy notwithstanding." The trouble was, he would be very happy with a wife like Miss La Bijou.

"Hmmm…" She truly appeared to be considering the matter, and when she suddenly let out a gurgle of laughter, he was surprised at the degree of his disappointment. "I'm sorry, Lord Silverton, but I want a man who loves me enough to make me an *honest* offer."

"Lord Nash hasn't."

"I believe I can persuade Nash to see how very valuable a wife like me would be to him."

"Really, Kitty, holy matrimony is not a prerequisite for happiness."

This time, she didn't laugh. "It is when one's grown up, shamed and reviled, because of the lack of it. Now, are you going to help me rescue Dorcas or not?"

KITTY HAD BEEN ACUTELY CONSCIOUS ALL HER LIFE THAT THE LOCAL villagers reviled her as a lesser creature on account of her illegitimacy. Therefore, her decision to enter the *demimondaine* by becoming the mistress of a member of the aristocracy did not fill her with moral angst.

Lissa had chosen the virtuous path…hard work.

But Dorcas would view her own road to ruin in an entirely different way, Kitty realized…as entirely her fault, with earthly torment the only consequence to be followed by eternal damnation. Not just purgatory, but the eternal fire and brimstone meted out to true sinners.

But, however badly Dorcas was damaged, Kitty first had to get her out of Mrs. Montgomery's clutches.

"Stay quiet and obedient and do as I say," Lord Silverton ordered Kitty in a whisper as they stood opposite the brothel. "I'll not risk you entering that terrible house, where Mrs. Montgomery would snatch you up as if you were manna from Heaven, but I will want you here when, hopefully, I get Dorcas out."

"You're very commanding when you've embarked upon a matter of great urgency. Though if you were my mother speaking, I'd consider you insufferably bossy for telling me what to do like that."

Despite the gravity of the occasion and a certain nervousness—a *great deal* of nervousness—Kitty giggled. Or perhaps that's why she giggled. Nevertheless, she thought it true. Dressed in evening clothes with a very expertly tied stock of snowy linen, Lord Silverton cut a most impressive figure. A sartorial figure, the height of fashion, his lovely brown hair short at the sides with the natural wave allowed a little longer on top, he did not look like some of the dandies or fops who took fashion to ridiculous extremes. Nor did he look like the Corinthians who Kitty thought seemed more interested in themselves and their athletic physiques. Lord Silverton looked simply like a very handsome aristocrat who exuded confidence in a most commanding manner. Really, he was quite devastatingly affecting when the serious cast of his features relaxed into a smile. If she'd considered him a contender for her affections, he'd have quite made her legs turn to jelly.

Suddenly, his serious air was displaced by a disarming smile. "You have no idea how much pleasure it would give me to tell you exactly what I'd like you to do," he said with raised eyebrow. "Unfortunately, that's Lord Nash's prerogative. However, if I succeed in my mission, you might want to reconsider my earlier offer."

"To look after me, and enjoy me, but not to marry me? I think that's what you offered, if I'm not mistaken?" She tossed her head, smiling nevertheless. "No, thank you, Lord Silverton. However, I *do* believe that if we are to be successful, I should go indoors and speak to Dorcas myself, though we've argued it a hundred times." She pulled her hood up over her bright hair. "I can go in through the scullery. There would be strangers coming and going all the time, I'd wager, in a house that size."

Finally, she persuaded him. "Have faith in me, my Lord." She squeezed Lord Silverton's wrist. "Now, you go and request to see Dorcas, and I'll wait in the street until I get a sign of which room you're in before I head on around to the servant's entrance."

When, ten minutes later, Kitty saw the sash window go up on the second room on the east side, she hurried off to do her part.

Despite her cavalier words of earlier, she was afraid. However, that was nothing compared with her terror when the door to the kitchen was opened, and a young tweeny let her into its surprising warmth. An enormous fire was burning while two small boys sat on either end of a spit, turning it to ensure the even roasting of several chickens and a pig.

"Where is Mrs. Montgomery?" she asked. The girl, who looked to be only about twelve or thirteen, pointed upstairs. Her face was pinched and dirty, and she looked a cowed, overworked young thing. "In 'er room, restin'. Yer can't see 'er."

Kitty put her head close to her ear. "Can you keep a secret?" she whispered, slipping a coin into the child's hand.

With a gasp, the girl dropped the coin into the pocket of her hessian apron, nodding furiously.

"It's not really Mrs. Montgomery I want to see; it's Dorcas. I need to get a message to her that her ma is proper poorly. Mrs. Montgomery won't let her go, I understand that. I only want to tell Dorcas what she should know."

The girl bit her lip and didn't move, but Kitty was prepared for intractability. She suspected the tight rein Mrs. Montgomery would keep over her employees.

She patted the girl's shoulder. "Mrs. Montgomery would be very angry if she knew you'd let anyone inside, or told them that sort of information, wouldn't she?"

The girl nodded.

"But *you'd* want to know if your ma was poorly, wouldn't you? In fact, you'd be heartbroken if you heard the news after it was too late. That's all I want to do. Tell Dorcas. She can stay right where she is, and I'll leave, and no one will be the wiser. I tell you what." Kitty fished around in her reticule and pulled out her hand, brandishing another coin. "I'd give this to you when I return, only I'm afraid I might have to leave another way in order to avoid being seen by Mrs. Montgomery, so I'll give it to you now because I trust you. Now, where did you say Dorcas entertains?"

The girl confirmed the general direction from which Silverton had sent her a sign and within a minute, Kitty was hurrying up the back steps, armed with the necessary information. She had a good sense of direction, so it wasn't a difficulty locating the room.

Thrusting open the door, she gasped in horror as she found herself face-to-face with a couple in the throes of fornicating on a large four-poster bed.

"What the deuce!" came the angry cry of the black-haired gentleman, whose dark glower was enough to send Kitty back the way she'd come like a cannonball.

Her heart was hammering, but she could not lose courage. She was more circumspect the next time she quietly turned the doorknob. To her relief, when she put one eye to the crack, it was to see Silverton raising his eyebrows at Kitty as he faced a slender, brown-haired girl. Certainly too slender to be Dorcas, thought Kitty with disappointment. But then the girl spoke, her soft Welsh accent making it quite clear that her old friend had lost a great deal of weight —and much more besides —in the few weeks since Kitty had last seen her.

"Jest leave me be, m'lord," Dorcas was saying on a sob, hunched over with her hands over her face. She was being half supported by the dresser against the wall while Lord Silverton towered over her, his expression concerned and patient. "I told yer before and I'm tell yer now. I ain't goin' nowhere wiv yer or anyone else. Damned is wot I am."

Silverton began to speak softly, and Kitty was struck by his kindness as he tilted the girl's chin with his forefinger. "Please just agree to see Kitty once, at least, Dorcas. She's been so worried for you. She knows you're here, and she wants to help you."

"Ain't no one can 'elp me now," Dorcas said sadly. "I'm destined for 'ell, whereva I go. I've always bin the sort to land in trouble, but it don't get much worse than this. No, I won't bring shame ter Miss Kitty. Not now she's a famous actress, an all."

"It's not your shame; it's the shame of those who have ill-used you, Dorcas," Silverton tried to explain. "Mrs. Montgomery tricked you, and then you were ill-used by all the...men who frequent this place. You're not the one who is shamed. They are."

"It's true!" Kitty cried, rushing into the room and taking Dorcas into a hug. "Oh Dorcas, you must come with us."

Dorcas's eyes grew as wide as saucers, and she gasped, returning Kitty's hug with energy, before dropping her hands and shaking her head. "No, miss, ain't no way I can go. I jest told 'is Lordship why not. 'Sides, 'ow can I jest walk through that door? I'm always unda guard, ain't neva allowed ter leave this place."

"What if I said I needed you?" Kitty tried her most appealing voice. "You'd come if I needed you, wouldn't you?"

Dorcas looked uncertain, so Kitty pressed her advantage. "I'm all alone, Kitty, and the only person I consider my true friend is you."

"Oh miss, if only it were possible!" Dorcas wailed, close to tears. "But yer know it jest ain't."

"Do you never leave this place?"

"Never...'cept on Monday mornin's when I go ter the apothecary ter get the necessaries fer Mrs. Montgomery. An' then there's always someone wiv me."

"The apothecary around the corner? Since you will not come with me now, Dorcas, I shall try again. On Monday," Kitty said firmly, indicating to Lord Silverton that he should depart ahead of her, for what she had to say was between ladies only. "And if anyone was asking, I came here on the pretext of getting a message to you that your ma was poorly, but don't be concerned for it's not the truth."

"I'm dead to ma, or might as well be, so it makes no diff'rence, miss." Dorcas's voice was barely more than a whisper. "Now go. Please. I 'ave 'nuvver gennulman to see. Thankfully it ain't that awful Lord Debenham wot sparks terror in me chest. I 'eard Mrs. Montgomery singin' me praises to 'im, but he only likes ter see Daisy."

"Lord Debenham comes here?" Kitty gasped, as she was struck by memories of her recent encounter with his wife. Her half-sister, though she hated to acknowledge this, even to herself. "Why, he's married!"

Dorcas gave a lopsided smile. "If you's bin livin' the 'igh life in the theater an' 'bout town with yer gennulman wot were 'ere wiv yer, yer'd know that the married ones are worse than all the rest."

"Yes, I do." Kitty sighed, adding suddenly, "But Lord Silverton who was here just now and tried to persuade you, earlier also, to come away, is not my gentleman. He's my friend."

"Don't tell me a gennulman like that don't want more than bein' jest friends wiv a lady like yerself, Miss." Dorcas sent her a skeptical look. "They's all the same, wantin' only ter pleasure 'emselves, treatin' us like nuffink. I'll wager 'e's the same as all the rest, so beware, m'lady. 'E's only pretendin' ter 'elp yer so's 'e can get 'is way wiv yer in the end. Now that's all I have ter say on the subject. Yer got ter jest leave me be fer I've made me bed, an' I thank yer fer wantin' to 'elp but—"

"You're wrong!" Kitty gripped Dorcas's wrist. "Not all men are bad, like you've experienced. Lord Silverton has looked after me with care and kindness since my ..."

Dorcas's eyes widened expectantly, and Kitty swallowed and plunged on, trying a new tack. "Another very handsome gentleman, Lord Nash, has set me up very nicely in a little house and given me lots of presents." She extended her arm, and the ruby and diamond bracelet she always wore twinkled in the light of the candle on the dresser.

"Yer 'ave two...protectors, miss?"

"Well, only Lord Nash is my...official protector," Kitty explained, trying not to feel shame at putting it in these terms. "So, of course, I'm no better than you when it comes to sinning. Lord Nash and I are very much in love, and I'm quite determined he shall make me an offer of marriage before the year is out. We had a bit of a falling-out, so Lord Silverton put me up at his house, but he didn't try to take advantage of me," she added quickly to forestall the question it was obvious Dorcas was about to ask.

"But 'e's in love wiv yer, nevatheless."

"I don't know about that. But Dorcas, what about you? You say no man here has ever treated you with respect? Then you must come with me. You must let me help you escape."

Dorcas shrugged. "I s'pose they're not all bad, considerin' it's me life now an' no, I ain't goin' ter leave cos' I can't endure the shame, knowin' I'll 'ave ter pretend foreva afterwards I'm somfink I ain't when I'm in the real world." She raised her head, and appeared to concentrate on a water-stained strip of brown and gold wallpaper near the ceiling. "There were one gennulman wot treated me wiv respect. It were after I first come 'ere. Mr. Prism were his name, an 'e were a clerk in the gov'ment an' 'is father were payin' for 'is first time as it were 'is comin' o' age. 'E were ever so shamed by 'is father's coarseness, an' so we jest talked."

"Just talked? See, Dorcas."

Dorcas smiled her first smile, and her voice was dreamy. "We lied on the bed, side by side, an jest talked. 'E asked me 'bout me work, an' I told 'im 'ow I 'ated it, but that I were ruined so 'ad ter stay 'ere foreva. 'E was a very nice gennulman. 'Is father made 'is money doin' things ter coins ter make more money. Don't quite know 'ow that worked, but Mr. Prism were very snide 'bout 'is Papa wot weren't respectable but wanted 'im ter be respectable, yet also wanted 'im ter do wicked things like send 'im ter places like Maggie Montgomery's." Suddenly, she seemed to realize where she was and who she was talking to. Clasping both of Kitty's hands in hers, she smiled sadly. "Thank yer, miss, fer takin' the trouble. Yer 'ave a good 'eart. I saw it when I first met yer at Mrs. Mobbs's. There's few wot 'ave good 'earts 'ere. The girls get 'ard an' are mean a'cause o' the competition an' knowin' they's only got a few good years wiv their looks an' all."

"Oh Dorcas, you mean you have no friends here? But I'm your friend. Please come with me. I'll look after you."

"Truth is, I can't leave me friend, Sally, til I know she's goin' ter be o'right. She's more 'n seven months gone an' Mrs. Montgomery 'as been eva so fierce, tryin' first ter get rid o' the babe, but it *would* jest grow an' now Sally can't work anymore so Mrs. Montgomery said it was off ter the workhouse fer 'er an' the babe. That's when Mrs. Mobbs came ter the rescue wiv a plan ter save Sally an' the babe."

"Mrs. Mobbs! Why, did she offer to rescue *you*, Dorcas? She must know you were tricked and hate it here."

Dorcas shook her head. "She were very regretful an' said she 'ad no idea, but that a contract signed were bindin' fer life. But she said she liked ter 'elp where she could, an' she was goin' ter 'elp Sally by takin' 'er to Wiltshire where she'd be looked afta an' a nice family 'ad bin found fer the babe so Sally could come back an' continue workin' fer Mrs. Montgomery an' it would be like the babe 'ad neva 'appened." She shrugged. "So I s'pose Mrs. Mobbs 'as goodness in 'er 'eart, though I wish she'd a known 'bout Maggie Montgomery's plans afore she let me take a position wiv 'er. Now, we've talked much too much an' me next customer will be waitin'. Yer go an' enjoy yer life, miss, an' forget all 'bout me. I'm dead ter the world."

Kitty tried to persuade her once more, but finally she had no choice but to leave the way she'd come; her heart as full of woe as Dorcas's. Fortunately, there was no difficulty in slipping out of the house, dressed as a servant, and when she saw Lord Silverton waiting for her around the corner, she hurried over.

"She won't come, my Lord, and I must hurry back to Nash, but you have been ever so kind." She brushed his cheek with her fingertips and smiled, a warm inner glow suddenly permeating her.

Silverton found a hackney for her, and not long afterward Kitty returned to her little house where she found Nash waiting for her, reading the paper in an armchair in the breakfast parlor while he helped himself to grapes.

"Why such a sad face, my sweet?" he asked, but Kitty couldn't give him the truth. No, she felt she had to continue her playacting because that was the way to please Nash, who didn't like Friday-faced damsels cluttering up the place, as he'd told her when she'd been sad once before.

So she brightened up, changed into a night-rail of the sheerest lawn, which satisfied him no end, and did what a good mistress did to please her protector.

Then, in the morning she went to the theater, rehearsed for the show that evening, and felt that she'd not stopped acting for a full forty-eight hours.

CHAPTER 15

*D*ebenham glanced up from his newspaper and raked his enquiring gaze over Araminta's traveling attire. "And where do you suppose you're going?" The breakfast sideboard had been reset since Araminta had broken her fast three hours earlier.

"Home." Araminta raised her chin and prepared to do battle. This was one fight she could not afford to lose. With chilly recrimination, she added, "You've been nowhere to be found for two days and two nights, Debenham. I thought you'd had your throat sliced by footpads."

"Would you have shed tears, my dear?"

Araminta did not smile. "Of course. And will you shed tears if I am gone for but a week to see my mama, who can counsel me on how to be as good a mother as she is? Surely you'd not deny me a mother's care in my advanced state? After all, you cannot bear the sight of me, much less to touch me."

Debenham's lip curled, but he did not deny it. "And how do you propose getting there?"

"Why, I'll take the carriage and send it back. That was my intention since the carriage was to be at my disposal under the terms of our arrangement. You can come and fetch me. You know how Mama adores you."

Debenham laughed. "Oh, my dear. I did not think you possessed wit and irony as well as beauty."

"There's a lot more to me you've yet to find out, but the truth is, I'm weary of lumbering about London like this. I want some country air. The physician who attended Mama when she gave birth is highly recommended, and he can be with me in a trice, if necessary. However, Mama preferred the offices of the midwife who lives not far. I shall be in good hands." She was prepared for a fight over the location of where the baby should be born, but fortunately, Debenham merely shrugged and toyed with his coffee cup. His eyes looked more shadowed than usual, giving him a particularly piratical appearance. A pirate who'd been partaking of a ruinous amount of rum, and was all but dead on his feet. Araminta wondered, not for the first time, when he might drink himself into an early grave.

"You'd better be. You might no longer be the beauty I married, but it's my heir you're carrying." He drained his coffee and reached for a fig. "How many more weeks before your ripe and luscious body will again be mine for the taking?" He answered his own question. "Four weeks before the baby is due, and then another two to wait after that. I am all impatience, my dear."

"You are not the only one of us anxious for an end to this torture, Debenham," Araminta said over her shoulder as she turned into the passage, and she wasn't only referring to the baby. "Hurry along, Jane! At last, we can leave London."

To Araminta's relief, she didn't encounter further resistance. Debenham clearly found her repugnant when she was breeding, while her absence would give him greater rein to indulge in his other proclivities. Araminta had no doubt that he played fast and loose when he could. Well, two could play at that game. It was extraordinary that only a week after expelling the little creature who had blighted her life, she felt so well. Women were supposed to lie on their backs for a whole month, but she'd had no choice but to maintain the fiction she was still carrying...well, supposedly, Debenham's heir. Of course, she'd been a little weak and wobbly on her feet immediately afterward. She'd slept long into the next day at Mrs. Mobbs who'd then sent a message round to Jane who had then arranged transport. Jane had been horrified, naturally, but had told the household her ladyship had been staying with her sister. And at least padding her stomach with an enormous cushion meant Araminta could claim fatigue from her apparent advanced pregnancy, and lie down to rest frequently—and not have Debenham paw her constantly, like in the early days of their marriage.

Now she just had to bamboozle her mother.

WHAT A JOY IT WAS TO BE HOME. ARAMINTA WAS SO EXCITED AT HER newfound freedom, it took all her willpower not to run up the front steps, and into her waiting mother's arms. Instead, she made a show of laboring up each step, assisted by the postilion and Jane.

"Araminta, my dear! Why, you took us by surprise!" Her mother beamed. "We weren't expecting you for another hour at least. Come, let us get you into your bedchamber and comfortable. You must be exhausted after that long journey.

"Don't touch me...careful, I'll be quite all right. Jane can help me!" Araminta held her mother at arm's length, covering her large belly protectively as she offered her cheek for a kiss.

Then, slowly, they headed for Araminta's room, one of the parlormaids having rushed ahead to pull back the covers for her afternoon rest.

"Araminta!"

Araminta, who was being helped into bed by her mother, swung around at her sister's voice. "Hetty? What are you doing here?"

"Didn't you get my note? I left the day after my dinner with Lord Ludbridge." Hetty, who stood in the doorway looking as large as Araminta, smiled. Pregnancy obviously agreed with her, Araminta thought sourly as Hetty hurried forward, prattling away as usual. "It was on a bit of a whim, really, as the gentlemen got it into their heads to do some hunting on Lord Mowbray's estate north of here. It was decided to put me off at The Grange, en route, and they'll pick me up when they return in a week or two."

"Sir Aubrey and...and Lord Ludbridge? They'll be coming back here in a week?"

"Or two. Yes, won't that be nice? And...I take it Debenham isn't coming?" There was relief in Hetty's voice when she got the confirmation she was obviously hoping for.

Their mother settled herself in a chair by the bed and looked between the girls with a serene smile. "So, it'll be me and my beautiful daughters: Araminta and Hetty. Just like in the old days. Oh, and Celia, of course," she added with a smile at a loud, lusty cry issuing from upstairs. "How lovely that all the babies will be so similar in age. Oh dear, I think I should attend to her." She rose, excusing herself at the door before reminding the girls of the time their father would be home and expect to dine.

Araminta thought it quite shocking her mother should have a child in her dotage. And that she wasn't leaving all the work to the nursery-maid. Lord, *she* didn't intend breeding when she was forty. In fact, she didn't intend breeding ever again, and with the innocuous looking little seeds, the Queen Anne's Lace, Mrs. Mobbs had given her, she certainly hoped that would be the case.

But, one step at a time. Hetty reached out to pat her belly, but Araminta drew back. "Please don't!" she said sharply. "I do hate it!"

"Of course, dearest." Hetty sounded indulgent rather than put in her place, which was irritating, and, now safely in bed, Araminta drew the covers up to her neck. She hoped Hetty didn't intend staying too long.

To her dismay, Hetty lowered herself onto a seat by the window and gently patted her stomach. "I'm surprised you've left London with so much going on, but it'll be so much pleasanter, just the two of us, like in the old days. Sir Aubrey wants to have my portrait painted as soon as I'm back in town."

"Who will do that? The fine portraitist everyone is talking about? Mr. Lamont?" Araminta asked without thinking, and her sister gave an exclamation of horror. "He's a vagabond who did some sketches he most certainly should not have. I don't know the details, but he has a most unsavory reputation, and I don't know how he's still gallivanting about—though some think he's all the more intriguing because of it."

"He's a friend of Debenham's," Araminta said crisply.

Hetty rose and went to the window and looked out. "That doesn't surprise me. I heard Debenham was thick as thieves with a painter whose reputation had been blackened by some recent scandal. Goodness, but this baby makes it hard to settle sometimes."

"Lord, Hetty, where do you hear such things?" Araminta asked, ignoring her sister's reference to her discomfort. Hetty should try and live, for just five minutes, with the trials that afflicted Araminta every day and she'd never grumble again. "How do you think I like to hear criticisms against my husband?"

Hetty turned and regarded Araminta with no trace of her usual girlish levity. "Cousin Stephen told me," she said quietly. "And regardless of how a woman feels about her husband, she must know what the world is saying about him if she is to keep him—and just as importantly, herself—safe."

Araminta was about to dismiss this with a scoffing laugh, but the tightness about Hetty's mouth and the intensity of her look made her decide otherwise. There was an unfamiliar worldliness in her speech that made her take notice.

"Is there something behind your meaning you are trying to convey in words and tone far too subtle for my understanding, Hetty?" Araminta shifted her bulk beneath the coverlet, surreptitiously checking that the straps which held the padding in place against her body, were tight enough. She was going to have to be very careful to get through the next few weeks without detection. And just when she'd thought that was going to cause her the greatest challenge, Hetty had to add to her trials with talk of something even more unpleasant in which Debenham was involved.

Hetty rubbed her lip as she clearly pondered her words. "Debenham is being watched closely by...various important people. I know Mr. Lamont is one of his associates who is under deep suspicion."

"Yes, well, he's been commissioned to paint that flash-in-the-pan actress, Kitty La Bijou. I can't believe that green boy Miss Hazlett works for has come so far. Mr. Lamont is nothing more than a strutting popinjay. Anyway, the gossip sheets are full of it. I will concede that he is all hot air but fancies himself the cream of the crop and, yes, he is one of Debenham's friends, but Debenham laughs about him behind his back, don't you know?"

"I'm sure Debenham laughs behind the back of a lot of people to whom he is quite civil in person, because he finds them quite useful but, yes, although there does appear to be a cloud hanging over Mr. Cosmo Lamont; that sketch he did of Debenham that sits on your dressing table is an uncanny likeness and quite remarkable."

"The one where he looks so disreputable, and he's lounging with a cheroot in his mouth?"

"Don't you think it a very clever likeness? By the way, do you know that Miss Hazlett no longer works for the Lamont family? Something happened, and I don't believe they remain on good terms. Cousin Stephen hinted to me that Mr. Lamont was involved in something all but criminal, which is why he's being watched."

Araminta gave a gusty sigh and turned the topic. "Well, I'm sure I don't know what has happened to the girl. Miss Hazlett seems to have disappeared. No gratitude after all I did for her. Not that I want to be reminded of what harm she does to our reputation just by her mere existence. To think that Papa could...." She left the sentence unfinished, and shuddered instead to give meaning to her words.

"She's never to be mentioned in poor Mama's presence," Hetty said, lowering her voice. "Mama seems so happy these days. I don't want to see her cast into the dismals with talk of Papa's...other family." Hetty opened her mouth to continue, paused, then stared straight at Araminta as if deciding whether or not to speak until Araminta said irritably, "Do say whatever it is you're afraid is going to shock or outrage me, Hetty. It's something else that is less than flattering about

Debenham, isn't it? And clearly you'd enjoy revealing it, only you have to pretend otherwise." She huffed out a sigh. "Go on, then. Tell me."

Hetty looked taken aback, Araminta was glad to see. Always trying to play the good-hearted sister, she thought uncharitably.

"I'm sorry you think that, Araminta," Hetty said, a touch tartly. "Well then, I shall get to the point. Debenham is being watched due to the activities that have made him a person of interest to the Foreign Office. I think you must know that I speak of the letter you tried to burn. I overheard Stephen speaking about it at dinner to Papa a little while ago."

"Then they are trying to make more of this ridiculous claim by your husband's late wife about Debenham plotting with the Spenceans!" Araminta bridled. "Well, the letter's burned, and as far as I know, there's nothing else to suggest my husband is anything but as honest as the day is long."

Araminta was just relaxing back on the bed and closing her eyes in happy satisfaction that her actions in burning the letter had put the whole matter to rest when Hetty said, "Actually, Araminta, it would seem the letter you burned was a fake letter Jem supplied."

"What!?"

Hetty left the window and returned to her chair. She looked earnest and even a trifle scared. "It's true. I heard Cousin Stephen tell Papa that he'd been in discussion with a man investigating the matter who'd died in mysterious circumstances. This man had replaced Sir William Keane—I believe you met him at a ball. Anyway, Sir William had been investigating the matter before he was posted to Constantinople. Araminta, another thing…" She took a deep breath and Araminta felt her toes curl in confirmation that she really didn't want to hear any more but that she really ought to. "Dearest, this is a huge secret but I feel I ought to tell you because, as my sister, you might be in danger as a result. But Debenham's secretary, Mr. Ralph Tunley, produced the real letter. Indeed, it has been verified as the real letter in which Sir Aubrey's late wife declares Debenham guilty of treason, not Sir Aubrey, as Debenham had always claimed."

"Dear Lord!" Araminta whispered, covering her face with her

hands. "Treason? It can't be evidence, surely. I mean…it's just a letter by a madwoman. A woman who killed herself the moment she'd written it." The ramifications were terrifying; even she knew that.

"Yes, my poor predecessor," Hetty remarked drily. "You can imagine I am equally affected, both on account of the damage that was done to my darling husband's reputation when everyone assumed— thanks to Debenham continually casting aspersions—that Sir Aubrey was tainted." She drew in a deep breath. "I just wanted to warn you, that's all."

"You think you can just let the matter rest?" Araminta sat up. She was primed for action now. Angrily she went on, "You can't just tell me this, Hetty without realizing the need to avert what appears to be Cousin Stephen's objective—to accuse Lord Debenham of treason. Do you know where that leaves me if he's convicted?" She answered her own question. "With nothing! All his goods and chattels would be forfeited to the crown. I'd become a pauper. His baby and I would… we'd be destitute!" The more she explored the argument, the more Araminta realized how stark her position really was. "Destitute!" she repeated, this time more shrilly.

Hetty, clearly realizing she'd opened a veritable Pandora's box, strove to comfort her distraught sister. "Such a thing could never happen. And Debenham is too slippery to ever be caught. I just wanted you to know—"

"Too *slippery*? What's that supposed to mean? You clearly think he's a villain. What can I do, Hetty? I need to ensure that Debenham doesn't overstep the mark, yet I have no control. None! Every night he gambles, drinks, womanizes …I don't know what he does, into the early hours of the morning. He no longer listens to me. I'm an ungainly and disgusting creature in his eyes. I have no influence what-soever." She began to cry as the tragedy of her words hit home. Once, Araminta had been queen of her domain and confident of her ability to make men her slaves. Now, her life felt like it was in ruins about her ears.

She thought of Lord Ludbridge, and that immediately brought to mind what Hetty had said regarding his brother, Ralph Tunley who also happened to be Debenham's secretary and Lord Tunbridge's—Teddy's—brother. Her tears stopped abruptly as hope found a chink in her misery. Struggling onto her elbows, she asked, "Did you say Mr. Tunley is the man who purports to have the real letter which slanders Debenham? Then why has he not used it? And does my husband know?"

Hetty threw her hands up into the air, clearly upset already at having said too much. "I don't know, Araminta. I only thought to tell you—through sisterly loyalty—what I'd overheard so you'd be prepared for any eventuality."

"Meaning I'd be sure and have a trunk packed, ready for the workhouse?" Araminta began to chew her nails, agitation, but excitement, too, rising in her breast. "Mr. Tunley must be spoken to. Yes, that's what must happen. He has to be made to understand that he cannot use this letter against me and ruin my life. I won't speak to Debenham or he'll fly into the boughs but somehow this Mr. Tunley must be made the understand the gravity of the matter." She gasped. "Mr. Tunley is Lissa Hazlett's sweetheart! We shall have to find her and explain what's at stake. We'll tell her that...that Debenham will dismiss him if he refuses to hand over the letter and that she'll never be in a position to marry Mr. Tunley. That should make her take notice." Her thoughts were running away with her as she plumbed the depths of what this meant. "I'll have words when the men come back from their hunting in a week or two. Why, if Mr. Tunley's brother knew the injury he intended against me he'd never let him get away with it!"

"His brother?" Almost instantly, Hetty's brow unfurrowed. "Oh, you mean to ask Lord Ludbridge..." She trailed off as a look of greater understanding smoothed away her frown. "You mean to trade on your old...er...friendship with Lord Ludbridge."

"Of course I do! He'll make sure Mr. Tunley disposes of the letter so that no danger will possibly befall me. I know he'd do that for me."

"But Araminta, I know you like Lord Tunbridge very much, but it mightn't be so simple. In fact, if Debenham got wind of it, it might be dangerous."

"It's *for* Debenham I'd be doing it," Araminta objected. "Of course, I must trade on my associations, just like any man would do in order to gain the advantage. Lord Ludbridge has the highest regard for me. He'll do whatever I ask. You're sure they'll be coming back this way?"

"Yes, but Araminta, I wasn't supposed to reveal anything about—"

"What? You'd just see me cast to the lions?"

"Of course not. But what if the letter is only one part of a case of evidence against Debenham?"

"Don't be ridiculous. Debenham isn't so stupid as to involve himself in any other bad business when he's had this lucky reprieve regarding the letter. Well, to date, anyway. No, Mr. Tunley must be prevailed upon by his brother to withhold or destroy that letter. He must!" Her brain whirled over the many possibilities open to her. "I must see Lord Ludbridge when he comes back with Sir Aubrey after their shooting trip. Yes, that's the only way. Hetty, you must help me. If you don't want to see me and my babe cast to the wolves or breaking stones in the workhouse, that's what you must do!"

CHAPTER 16

*K*itty rearranged her skirts so that the tiniest suggestion of ankle showed below the rich ruby-velvet hem as she reclined upon the chaise longue. "Will that do, Mr. Lamont?" she asked.

The young painter observed her critically from the center of the room, sketchbook in hand, a frown furrowing his brow while he fingered the sharp cut of his side-whiskers.

"Indeed, Miss La Bijou, but perhaps the décolletage needs attention. May I?"

"Er...yes, of course."

He leaned forward, and the touch of his fingertips against her bare skin made Kitty wince. Immediately, she thought of Dorcas. What a nightmare to have to suffer the intimacies of men when it was against one's inclination. The pleasure in the fact Nash had commissioned a full-length portrait of her was diluted by these reflections. It had been ten days since Kitty's failed attempt to persuade Dorcas to flee. She wondered if she would ever see her friend now, for indeed Dorcas seemed to have been well and truly consumed by a fate she considered no one was able to change.

"Ah, but it is indeed a great honor to be allowed to render the exquisite beauty of London's most feted actress." Mr. Lamont smiled appraisingly as he settled himself on a chair in the middle of the room and began to sketch. "Your benefactor...he must be a generous man, yes?"

Kitty thought it an odd question.

Mr. Lamont quickly clarified. "His Lordship is known for his discerning taste and, indeed, his generosity toward the...women in his life. If you would tilt your head a little to the right? Perfect."

The women in his life? Kitty didn't like the insinuating way Mr. Lamont phrased that. Yes, Nash had a sister and a mother, but she was sure they were not the women to whom the painter referred.

"How so, Mr. Lamont?" Kitty asked bluntly.

He was clearly surprised at being called upon to elaborate, for he could not at first find the words. "The diamond choker he bought for Miss Beatrice Orlando was spoken of for months, and established his reputation as a man of ...great largesse."

"And who is Miss Orlando?" Kitty saw no point in pretending to know more than she did, even if she suspected she was not going to like the answer. Let Mr. Lamont describe her competition in his own words. At least watching his embarrassment was some compensation. Since Nash had strayed, Kitty found she was sensitive to any mention of other women in Nash's life.

"You've not heard of Miss Orlando?" Again, he looked like a gaping fish.

"I'm from the counties. I don't profess to have acquired London airs and knowledge in so short a time." She smiled and repeated her question. "Who is Miss Orlando? Or must I tell Lord Nash you mentioned how generous he was to this Miss Orlando, but could not tell me who she is?" Kitty was rarely rude but in the very short time she'd been in Mr. Lamont's company she'd formed a very strong dislike for him.

"No, indeed, I spoke out of turn, Miss La Bijou. I fear Lord Nash would not happy to know that I've discussed those with whom he was on intimate terms."

"Intimate terms? Lord Nash was on intimate terms with Miss

Orlando? You insult me, Mr. Lamont. I'm not sure I wish to be painted by a gentleman who shows me such little respect." Kitty felt the tears prick her eyelids as she sat up.

"Please, Miss La Bijou, I meant no disrespect, truly!" Mr. Lamont jumped up from his seat and hurried toward Kitty, an unruly curl flopping from its restraining hair pomade; his exquisite cravat looking in danger of unraveling. Kitty knew it must be an important commission for him. Perhaps his reputation had been unfairly tarnished and hes trying to prove himself. She decided she should not allow high dudgeon to cloud common sense. Nash was a young blade who obviously would have kept a mistress in the past, though he'd been careful to keep any mention of such matters from Kitty's ears. Well, other than when he'd been caught straying with Jennie. No, Kitty must not think of that. Kitty would be the last of the line.

She was confident she'd won Nash back. Certainly, the gratitude he'd shown her proved the power she had over him.

"Here, you dropped your sketchbook, Mr. Lamont." She reached down to pick it up from where it had landed amid the skirts arranged about her, and was about to relinquish it when she gasped at the name she saw penciled on the back. "Lissa Hazlett! Good Lord, what do you know of this young woman? Why is her name on your sketchbook?"

Mr. Lamont's eyes bulged. "Why, I really don't know. She's just a charming young woman I once danced with at a ball."

"At a ball? Which ball?" Kitty abandoned the languid pose she'd adopted for the sketch as she leaned forward eagerly. Her heart raced. "Miss Hazlett was *dancing*? At a society event? Please, Mr. Lamont! You must tell me. I've been desperate to find her, but she's left no forwarding address."

"What can I tell you?" Mr. Lamont shrugged, looking relieved to be once again in possession of his sketchbook. He walked backward, sat down on his stool, then picked up his pencil with a furtive glance at Kitty. "If I see her again, who shall I say was asking after her?"

Kitty's heart felt full to bursting as she realized how much she'd missed Lissa. Yes, they'd grown apart as Lissa had adopted the dutiful approach of earning a living as a governess, while Kitty had been ever more vociferous in her desire to tread the boards and abandon her duty to her mother, but there'd always be a closeness. Sensible Lissa had been more of a mother to Kitty in their childhood, as she'd schooled Kitty in the duties and skills and obligations required to make the best of their precarious situation. As Lissa had so often pointed out, if something happened to their papa, there was every possibility they and their mother would be left destitute, for Lissa had heard whispers that Lord Partington's financial situation was precarious. Those rumors had been the reason Lissa had found a position as a governess.

Now, Kitty suddenly felt deeply neglectful. Her pleasure-loving character had taken over to the detriment of everything else important in life—especially her family. Part of her reason for not making a greater attempt to find Lissa had been because she knew how much her sister would condemn her for leaving poor Mama. And with her career rewarding her more than she could have imagined, she had no desire to be made to feel guilty.

Suddenly, more than anything else, she wanted to find Lissa. And this gentleman had seen her, danced with her. "Her *sister*, Mr. Lamont. Her dear sister. Oh, I know it's just as much my fault that we've lost contact, but it's been three months since I heard from her. Yes, of course! Lamont was the name of the family she went to work for. *Your family?*"

"There are Lamonts all over London, Miss La Bijou. Possibly, it was my...artist cousin at whose ball I met her. Yes, that is more than probable." Nervously he played with the pencil. "I shall endeavor to discover what I can. Would that please you?"

Kitty nodded energetically. "My friend Silverton mentioned that his friend, Sir William Keane had dealings with Lissa, but Sir William has gone to Constantinople, so *he* cannot be quizzed. I feel at quite a loss." Kitty was now feeling far more charitable toward the young artist who might, in fact, provide the information for which she'd searched. "If you could keep your ears open and report back to me, I'd be most grateful."

Mr. Lamont sent her level look. Quite a searching look, she

thought. But then, he must be deciding how he would go about this sketch that would form the basis of the grand piece of artwork that would grace the walls of Nash's bedchamber. His eyes traveled the length of her crimson gown, over her rippling golden hair that he'd arranged over the pillow, and finally settled upon the parchment in front of him. "You look nothing like your sister, I must say, Miss La Bijou," he murmured. "I own, I am more than a little astonished, but rest assured that I shall be assiduous in tracking down Miss Hazlett. I think you will not be the only one who would like to know what she is doing." He began to sketch, his pencil strokes gaining rapidity as he added, "In fact, I would be vastly grateful if you could get a note to *me* if you, in fact, discover her whereabouts before I do. For I have just recalled that it was my second cousin's family for whom she worked, and that my aunt was distressed that Miss Hazlett left before she was paid some wages she was owed."

ARAMINTA GRIPPED THE WINDOWSILL AND SCANNED THE DISTANT HILLS for signs of the visitors arriving on horseback. She couldn't remember feeling so fidgety. And it wasn't because of the baby, of course! She sometimes felt guilty at having given it away, but she never allowed remorse to trouble her too much since what she'd done was as much to ensure the safety and future of the child as her own safety and future. Lord! What else could she have done?

So, now she just had to wait for the right moment to supposedly deliver the child who would be reared as Debenham's heir. She hoped it would be a boy and thus end the pressure for going through another ghastly confinement, but who knew what the girl Mrs. Mobbs had found would produce. All Araminta knew was that the prospective mother was the daughter of an earl; that her name could not be divulged—though she was sure she'd heard her referred to as Sally though that must be a code name since Sally was not a very refined name—but that, as an unmarried debutante, she'd had no choice but to give up her child.

That was fine with Araminta. She didn't need to know the woman's identity; in fact, she didn't want to. The less either of them knew about the other, the better. Araminta certainly didn't want to meet her at some ball or soiree only to have the young woman demand her child back.

No, Mrs. Mobbs had covered all eventualities. The prospective mother had apparently been accommodated at the home of a respectable farmer and his wife, who lived nearby, and her child would be delivered to Araminta when it was born. A wet nurse had been secured, and all Araminta had to do was contrive to conduct her labor at a convenient moment. No detail had been overlooked by the efficient Mrs. Mobbs.

Jane, seated in the corner, looked up from removing the dust from one of Araminta's walking dresses with a small brush. "Miss 'Etty reckons the gennulmen ain't s'pected fer anuvver 'our at least, m'lady, an' that's afta yer in bed, now that yer've taken ter turnin' in so early. Reckon yer'll 'ave ter wait til t'morra to see Lord Ludbridge."

"I only turn in early because it's so tedious in the country. If we're having company tonight, then of course I shall see Lord Ludbridge this evening," Araminta declared, walking over to her dressing table and bending to examine herself in the looking glass. Thoughtfully, she twirled a ringlet around her finger. "I'm glad to see the contours have returned to my face. I really did look quite puffy toward the end. I'd not have liked Lord Ludbridge to see me as I was a few weeks ago."

"No, m'lady, ' e'd ' ave bin right put off."

"He thought me as beautiful as ever when he visited me at the opera," Araminta pointed out quickly.

"Lord Ludbridge will be lookin' fer a wife. I reckon ' e's too good a gennulman fer dalliances an' I don't know why yer think it's wise ter be danglin' after 'im. Specially when yer know 'ow jealous yer 'usband can get."

Araminta sighed. "You say that as if you think I'm stupid, Jane." She sat down and stared at her maid with a sorrowful expression. "Apart from the fact that Lord Ludbridge is the kindest, sincerest gentleman I've ever met, I need him to avert a tricky situation that could cause the direst state of affairs, not just for me, but for you too, Jane. If you value your position, then you'll ensure that good Lord Ludbridge finds a way to speak to me in private, whether that's outside behind the bushes, but preferably inside."

"Don't know where yer could be private indoors wiv everyone 'bout 'cept in yer bedchamber, miss, an' that certainly can't happen."

"Oh, Jane! You are a marvel!" Araminta's eyes lit up. "Of course! I shall faint! I fainted at a musical afternoon not so long ago, and Lord Ludbridge carried me out of the busy drawing room to somewhere quite private. Well, I'll just do it again tonight. Mama will, of course, accompany him when he brings me back here, but you'll know what to do. You always do, Jane." At the sound of dogs barking and horses galloping up the drive, Araminta leaped up so fast she nearly dislodged the ridiculously cumbersome false belly. "You were wrong as usual, Jane, for here they are!" she cried, opening the casement and waving with due decorum to the group of horsemen who were passing beneath. They doffed their hats, and Araminta turned back to her maid, hugging herself.

"At last, something enjoyable is happening after two dreary weeks in this forgotten neck of the woods."

Of course, the worst would have to be survived. Araminta decided she'd greet Sir Aubrey when the rest of the family were milling about, so as to make her interest less conspicuous. With Lord Ludbridge standing beside Sir Aubrey, smiling his warm, disarming smile, she realized once and for all that the passion she'd once felt for Hetty's husband had now definitely shifted to the more deserving Ludbridge, despite his abandonment of her in her hour of need.

Now she faced another hour of need. But first, she had to find an opportunity to be alone with him. Fainting, she now realized, was not practical since it would be impossible to fool him into believing she was enceinte if he carried her to her room. Not even her mother or Hetty had physically touched her. For two weeks, she'd kept her distance or to her bed.

No, she would have to find a means to entice him into the conservatory when the others were gathered in the drawing room listening to Hetty play the piano.

The moment the men had dismounted and run up the steps and into the grand lobby, Araminta was conscious of Lord Ludbridge's eyes upon her. She pretended not to notice as she greeted the other gentlemen in the party, which included two friends of Sir Aubrey, up from London. Araminta recalled having seen them on the dance floor at various London balls the previous season. While they'd solicited her to partner them, they showed little interest in her now. Sir Aubrey inclined his head with cool civility; her father barely acknowledged his wife or daughters as he tended to the needs of his visitors. It was enough to make Araminta weep. Doing her best to appear to advantage in her great, bloated body, she was totally disregarded by the men who'd once feted her.

Only Lord Ludbridge showed the same adoration as previously, and her heart went out to him even more. Sir Aubrey had betrayed her. He'd led her to believe he would make her an offer, and then had secretly wed Hetty. Debenham treated her abominably. He'd tricked her into marriage then shown callous disregard for her comfort and desires the moment she'd begun to lose the outward attractions that had been his principal interest.

But Lord Ludbridge was pure of heart. Of all the handsome, eligible men she'd encountered, he deserved her the most.

Later, as she sat quietly embroidering in the drawing room, pretending her chief concern was embellishing the infant's cap Jane had sewn, her thoughts drifted to the life she should have had. A life at Lord Ludbridge's side, as his hostess, the adored angel he would have put on a pedestal if he hadn't left her vulnerable to wicked, wicked Debenham.

"Lady Debenham, are you all right?"

She hadn't realized she'd sobbed aloud, but here he was, bending low at her side, his voice an intimate murmur. The soft caress of his breath against her exposed neck sent a charge of desire right through her groin, piercing her heart along the way, and as she gazed at him, she could feel his answering need for her as though it were a tangible thing.

She flicked a glance past him. The men were discussing their ride in a cluster at the sideboard as Lord Partington refilled glasses. Hetty and her mother were quietly occupied in their twin armchairs on either side of the fireplace. The curtains were drawn for it was dark outside and the room was bathed in a soft, rosy glow that reflected off the red, patterned wallpaper and the rich cream and red Aubusson rug. Araminta knew she would be seen to her best advantage with such soft lighting. It would be a good time to press her advantage.

"I find it difficult to sit for so long when that's all Mama and Hetty wish to do. Perhaps you would accompany me for a walk to the conservatory, Lord Ludbridge." She smiled, hoping he'd appreciate the graceful curve of her neck after she'd angled herself slightly to the right. His hesitation was swept away when she surreptitiously brushed his coat sleeve, then the back of his hand, with her fingertips before picking up her needlework once more, pretending she'd never made a gesture that appealed to him so artfully. "My Cousin Stephen is a keen horticulturist and very proud of his pineapple, but perhaps I might show you, myself." She sent him an impish smile. "You can impress him with your superior knowledge of cultivation, later, when he no doubt collars you and the rest of the gentlemen and takes you all off to admire his latest achievements."

"I would be delighted, Lady Debenham. That is if you are sure it would not be too taxing."

Araminta rose, careful to do so with less eagerness than she was feeling. "No, no, the physician, in fact, recommends a little gentle exercise. Come." As she looked over her shoulder when she reached the door, her heart hitched a little to see him staring after her as if he truly were entranced.

And when she took his arm in the passage after the door was shut behind them, she was aware of the frisson of feeling that charged up her arm, and knew he felt it too, by the flare in his eye.

Leisurely, they made their progress along the passage to the conservatory at the rear of the house, passing through the pinery and into a separate structure, more private, where Araminta said, with a flourish of her arm, "Cousin Stephen is experimenting with oak bark in water to create the temperatures needed, for the pineapple does not grow as easily as his oranges." She turned, suddenly, for now they were in the center of the cavernous structure, the air noticeably warmer and moister. Araminta was feeling warmer and moister, too. With a heartfelt look at Lord Ludbridge, she whispered in equally impassioned tones, "You cannot know how I have missed you, Teddy."

Over his shoulder, the star-studded sky twinkled through the many panes of glass, but it was his face, pained and full of answering love, that drew her attention as he gave rein to the full force of his feelings.

"Dear God, Araminta, what are you saying? Why tell me this when you know it is torture to me?"

She was rather gratified by his lack of constraint. Lord Ludbridge was the most proper of men, and his response was even better than she could have hoped for, making it easy to swoon into his arms and twine her arms behind his neck, raising her head for his kiss.

His lips came down upon hers, hard and passionately, and she was about to surrender herself completely when she remembered the odd cushioned bulk about her middle that he would assuredly realize was a ruse if his hands were to wander. With a cry of real anguish, she broke free, stepping back and shaking her head.

"This is torment, Lord Ludbridge. I don't know how you can bear to look at me. I must be disgusting to you. Why, this would have been your child had you not left me vulnerable to the cruel clutches of that hated devil, Debenham." She clasped her hands over her belly. "How I wish it were *your* child, but how wrong of me to utter such blasphemies and to give in to my desires." Her shoulders shook with unfeigned passion. "Debenham is a tyrant, yet I am completely at his mercy."

"Araminta. Miss Partington. I mean, Lady Debenham..." Lord Ludbridge took a step forward, and would have taken Araminta once more into his arms had she not stepped backward.

She shook her head, and said in a small voice, "You are too good for me, Lord Ludbridge, and I must beware my wayward heart." Plucking a small white flower that sprouted beside her, she held it to her breast, beneath which her heart truly was beating painfully. How she longed to throw herself—her everything—to the wind and surrender to what he was prepared to offer her now, yet had not been able to bring himself to offer when she'd so *needed* him to succumb to his desires. The night he proposed. The night before he abandoned her to leave for France on that ridiculous journey to rescue some childhood sweetheart who'd apparently had such a claim on his conscience and sense of honor.

"Araminta, I don't know what to say."

"Oh Lord Ludbridge...Teddy? I can still call you that, can't I? You cannot know how your friendship sustains me when I think of the perversities Debenham will subject me to when I am back within his orbit and...no longer with child. Right now, in my current situation... breeding...he wished me out of his sight. I disgust him, just as I must disgust you."

"You would never disgust me, Araminta! My angel, my pearl, you are divine." Towering over her, he lowered his handsome, anguished face to gaze rapturously at her as he grasped her hands and kissed each knuckle. "You are my Madonna. Yes, Madonna; that worthy, blameless goddess who comes to mind whenever I gaze at your serene, maternal beauty." His voice broke. "I could refuse you nothing."

Araminta brought her hands up to her face, and felt her shoulders shake as she sobbed softly.

"My dearest, what is it? Tell me!"

Pacing, she shook her head as her sobbing intensified. "Oh, Teddy, I don't know what to do. I'm in danger. I fear for my life and the life of my child, and I don't know what to do!"

"Your life? Not..." His tone became ominous. "Not Debenham. He hasn't hurt you? Threatened you? Dear God!"

Araminta stopped and raised her tear-filled gaze to look at Lord Ludbridge, whose outrage was just what she'd hoped for. "He's not exactly kind but no, he hasn't hurt me," she said brokenly. "It's just that I heard a terrible story not long ago. About…"

When she couldn't go on, Lord Ludbridge strode forward and cupped her face. "Araminta, you must tell me. Perhaps I can help you. You know I'd do anything."

She gripped his hands and looked searchingly at him. "Would you, Teddy? Would you really help me? Can I truly believe that?"

"You must know it's true, dear heart. Whatever it is that I can do to stop your tears, I would do it gladly, if it were only within my power."

"But it *is* within your power, Teddy, it is!" She took another hiccupping sob. "It's about a letter. A terrible letter currently in possession of your brother. A letter that has the power to destroy me and send me to the workhouse. If you can show me that I have your heart and your loyalty and deliver that letter into my hands, I would do *anything* to show my gratitude."

CHAPTER 17

*K*itty felt ebullient as she returned to her charming new lodgings that evening. Minna, who was both parlor-maid and her personal maid, had turned back the bedcovers and arranged flowers in all the rooms, according to Kitty's instructions, and was now belowstairs, assisted by a young girl who did the heavy work.

Knowing how Nash liked to find her always ready to welcome him, Kitty changed into a white, sprigged muslin gown, and let down her hair before taking an apple and a good book to her bed.

It wasn't late, but this was where Nash enjoyed spending the most time.

Half an hour later, she was disappointed when he arrived in the midst of the most exciting love scene she was reading in her Sir Walter Scott novel, but her smile of pleasure came readily as she put the book down, stretching wide her arms as he strode across the room.

"Kitty, my darling, you are a picture! Talking of which, I want to hear all about your sitting. But later." With his usual enthusiasm, he was divesting himself of sundry pieces of clothing as he approached, discarding his coat, which fell into a heap upon the Aubusson carpet, to be followed by his waistcoat. Grunting as he fumbled to unwind his cravat, he finally tossed the length of snowy linen to the floor, desire radiating from the depths of his eyes.

"Oh Nash, I learned something that made me so happy—"

"You can tell me later, my sweet." He shrugged off his shirt, then set to work on the buttons of his trousers after kicking off his Hessians. Nash was an early adopter of the latest fashions, and for a moment Kitty was reminded of Mr. Lamont. Except that Mr. Lamont was clearly a popinjay who took fashion to extreme, whereas Nash had consummate style and finesse—like Silverton— which he immediately displayed as, naked, he slid into the bed beside her and began to stroke her flanks, his hand stealing up beneath her skirts while his other worked at the buttons at the back of her gown so he could remove her gown and then her petticoat and stays.

Kitty wriggled happily into his embrace and kissed him on the mouth, sighing as he cupped her mound and gently traced circles around her nipples. "Ah, but you make me so happy."

And it was true. While she felt he loved her, going to such constant lengths over the past weeks to prove it, she felt secure and safe. And very much loved. She'd never felt any of these things at home. Now she was mistress of her destiny and right now, wrapped in the arms of the most handsome and adoring gentleman any girl could wish to have for her lover.

"And you satisfy me on every level, *ma petite choux*."

Kitty knew the reason he sounded so strangled was because his erection was hard and pressing into her thigh, and he couldn't wait to enter her. Yet he was always assiduous in pleasuring her first. She had no other experience of men, but she'd heard whispers in the theater and knew that lovers who thought only of their own gratification, abounded. It was further proof of the fact Nash was the ideal mate. A man who was thoughtful and who respected her and her right to a happiness equal to his own.

"I hope I always will," she whispered, as he slid a finger inside her wetness then began to stroke the slick nub at her core. Her excitement notched up a level and she closed her eyes, reveling in the attention.

"Just stay as beautiful and willing as you are now, and you'll not have to worry about anything, my sweet."

Kitty's eyes fluttered open, for she wasn't sure if he'd said the words in jest. But his eyes were closed, and now he was rolling on top of her, positioning himself at her entrance before plunging in with a groan of satisfaction.

And Kitty, who hadn't quite reached the zenith of her own of excitement, felt it incumbent to gasp and enter into the act with equal enthusiasm, wishing he'd spent just a little longer pleasuring her. But she was not dissatisfied when it was all over, for Nash was gazing down at her with pure rapture in his face, and she surely must have misunderstood his meaning when he'd insinuated her security lay in retaining her looks.

When it appeared he would go straight to sleep, Kitty gave him a little nudge.

"Don't you want to hear how my sitting went? How I found Mr. Lamont?"

"Surely I'd be more interested in how he found *you*, my darling." Nash gave a little laugh at his own joke, reaching up one arm to lazily brush aside a tendril of her hair. "Delightfully en dishabille, no doubt, but respectable enough. I hope he will convey you as I see you…three-quarters the innocent virgin and one-quarter femme fatale." He curled his arm about her neck and brought her face down to his to murmur against her lips before he kissed her, "All in all, a delightful little enigma."

Kitty sighed with pleasure. "I learned something that pleased me very much." When he didn't ask her to elaborate, she went on anyway. "He told me he'd seen my sister."

"I didn't know you had a sister. Is she as beautiful as you?"

"She's considered beautiful, though she hides it. She's a governess. I'm trying to find her as we've lost touch."

"I'd have thought she'd have already found you if she wanted to. Your name is in all the gossip columns; your description bandied about."

He obviously didn't realize what a dismal reflection this was for

Kitty, for while Nash drifted off into almost immediate slumber, Kitty found herself staring at the ceiling with the chill fear that Lissa was so shocked and ashamed of Kitty, she wanted nothing more to do with her.

Suddenly she was gripped by the fear that she really was as bad as some might think her. She pretended she was immune to public opinion but the truth was that she'd left her village—run away from her poor Mama when she needed her most, in fact—because she could no longer bear public opinion.

So who, *really* was Kitty La Bijou?

She gazed down at the face of the handsome young man fast asleep beside her. She was his mistress. He said he loved her but would he continue to love her when her looks had faded?

And when that happened, what sort of roles would she be getting in the theater?

Meanwhile, Lissa was living by the high standards she'd always insisted for herself. No matter what happened to her sister, Lissa would be judged a good and worthy woman. Unlike Kitty.

Tentatively, Kitty put out her hand and touched Nash's cheek. He stirred and smiled in his sleep but instead of feeling warmed by his reaction, Kitty felt a wintry sensation permeate her bones.

This moment was transitory and brief. She'd traded everything on the wild and unfounded belief that Nash would indulge her and love her enough to make her his wife.

But if that never happened, what would she have? A few trinkets that would sustain her but her reputation would be in tatters. She'd be the bastard who ran away from home to prove that, after all, she was no better than everyone had believed.

And when Kitty awoke to find the bed empty beside her and that Nash had gone, she felt even more frightened and alone.

She might be a good actress and a good mistress but she was not *good*.

And in the world she lived in, perhaps *being* good was, really, all that counted.

It was still in this mood of somber reflection that she was nudged while gazing at the wares of her favorite jewelers in Bond Street.

"What a look of woe. That's not the carefree Miss La Bijou I know. You're not looking at betrothal rings, I trust?"

The goldsmith had just pulled out a tray of ruby and sapphire rings for Kitty's perusal, and Kitty had been studying an intricately crafted affair with great interest.

"Oh, Lord Silverton, I do feel full of woe," said Kitty, glancing up and adding quickly at his quirked eyebrow, "and it has nothing to do with Lord Nash. He's been charming and attentive—"

"So you *are* looking at betrothal rings."

"Not yet," she dropped her voice, "though it is my sincerest wish to be respectably placed in life, as you know. Lord Nash has showered me with gifts. His generosity is extraordinary—"

"Meaning you can set yourself up for life if you are wise with your investments and do not squander what you are given."

His mood was full of levity so despite her own heavy heart, Kitty forced away the blue devils and, with a smile, waved a finger at him. "A salutary warning, Lord Silverton. I might have high hopes you think cannot be fulfilled, but I am not stupid. My brother is apprenticed to a goldsmith for a career in finance, and he will advise me."

"You are indeed a woman of mystery. A brother who inhabits the world of investment. A father who is a nobleman. What do they think of you, Miss La Bijou?"

Kitty nodded to the goldsmith to put away his wares. "What do they think of me?" She repeated his question, sadly. "My sister, a governess, is ashamed. She has not contacted me, though she must know where to find me."

"And that is why you're in the dismals?"

"And, as you know, my friend, Dorcas, is trapped in a horrible situation and won't allow herself to be saved."

"So that compounds your mood, of course."

"And Nash is going away for a few days, and I shall miss him." She sighed and glanced up at the sun which was getting low. Soon she would have to make her way to the theater.

"You're welcome to visit me anytime you are feeling in need of company, Miss La Bijou."

Kitty gave him an ironic smile. "Nash didn't like it one little bit when he learned I'd been staying with you. I had a difficult time persuading him that he had nothing to be jealous about."

Silverton pretended he'd just received a blow to the solar plexus. "That is not something I like to hear."

Kitty giggled. "You're vastly entertaining, my Lord, and I enjoyed our cribbage evenings enormously, but, in case I haven't said so before, I'm not going to allow myself to fall in love with you."

"So you think that could be possible?" He tilted his head and looked interested.

Kitty shrugged then relaxed with a smile. "Not when I know Lord Nash is going to realize he needs a viscountess with all the attributes I possess. *That*—you say—is not possible, Lord Silverton, but I shall prove you wrong. And now I really must go."

"Well, Miss La Bijou, just remember my door is always open to you, and should you find the ennui overwhelming while Nash is gone, I'll ensure the cribbage table is ready in front of the fire so we can take up where we left off. How's that for a hospitable offer?"

"Thank you, Lord Silverton. It is indeed."

Kitty gave him a little wave as she said farewell, her mood well and truly brighter since their encounter. If there was one thing for which Lord Silverton could be relied upon, it was to make feel her happier.

SILVERTON'S MOOD, TOO, WAS VASTLY BRIGHTER FOR THE ENCOUNTER when he left the jewelers and returned home to change.

Kitty did strange things to him. She filled him with frustration with her stubborn insistence that she knew how to get what she wanted out of life, but with enormous admiration for the fact she refused to allow herself to be downcast for long after any setback.

Most of all, she unleashed a tremendous feeling of protectiveness, which left him being the one frustrated for, as her friend only—and one whose advice she, more often than not, chose to ignore—he was no position to keep watch over her and safeguard her concerns as he would like.

He was certain he could offer her everything, and more, that Lord Nash purported to offer her. If she became his mistress, Silverton would not put her out to pasture when her youth and beauty faded, as he was sure Nash would. No, Silverton could see himself enjoying her company through all the trials and tribulations of life. He would be as loyal and attentive as any husband. He just couldn't marry her.

After dinner with some friends at a chop house in Soho, he carried on alone to No. 10 St James Square, a snug gaming hall humorously known as the Pigeon Hole where he was to meet Debenham and Smythe.

Debenham, who was in the midst of casting the dice in a game of Hazard, hailed Silverton when he happened to glance up and see his colleague framed in the doorway.

Silverton found little enjoyment in the social encounters with Debenham he was forced to endure. Too often, Debenman lived up to his moniker, the 'villainous viscount'. Women, cockfighting, and other forms of gaming were his popular pastimes which had made it easy for Silverton to take advantage of an early opportunity some months before to save Debenham from pecuniary embarrassment and thus earn his gratitude, if not regard. ThoughDebenham had eventually settled, Silverton gained the impression that contrary to appearances, Debenham was in more dire financial difficulties than was suspected.

Now, as Silverton advanced toward Debenham, who was clad entirely in black relieved only by his snowy white cravat, he thought wistfully of a comfortable feather bed with crisp white linen, occupied by Miss Kitty La Bijou. Perhaps if he'd pressed his advantage when she was more vulnerable and thus susceptible to his overtures, that's what he could have looked forward to tonight. But then he berated himself with the knowledge that this was the way Debenham worked. It was certainly widely circulated that Debenham had seduced and tricked his viscountess, the lovely and lively Miss Partington that was—into marriage when she was particularly vulnerable.

Though that wasn't to say Miss Partington had an unblemished reputation.

"Feeling lucky?" Debenham stepped aside to let Silverton play, and Silverton sensed the tension in the man. He could smell the brandy on his breath, and suspected Debenham had already lost a great deal tonight. Clearly, he was in his cups, which might make him less cautious than he usually was.

"After you. One more throw. A lucky one."

Obediently, Debenham rolled the dice, and his fortune turned.

Silverton knew there were advantages to seeing Debenham get in deeper, bailing him out, and thus perhaps being in a position to see the man compromised, or, in fact, being the recipient of Debenham's drunken confidences, but he felt sorry for his wife.

As he watched Debenham rake in his winnings, he said to him over his shoulder, "Why not go home while you're ahead? Lady Debenham will be pleased to see your pockets lined with gold tonight."

Debenham waved him away. "Lady Debenham is in the country dutifully delivering my heir. There's no one to rein in my good fortune. Methinks I'll throw again."

So the tone was set, and another two hours at the Pigeon Hole saw Debenham win a small fortune only to lose it again before a bottle of Madeira had him suggesting Silverton accompany him to Maggie Montgomery's.

Silverton shook his head. "Not tonight. I've business to attend to in the morning and, like you, I've already lost quite enough. I'm sure Smythe will go with you."

It had been an unsatisfactory evening, he thought. If Debenham had invited him to a tavern where they might have talked, he'd have gone. But the last thing he felt like was a nunnery where there was every chance he might be recognized, or even greeted by young Dorcas.

No, Maggie Montgomery's and, in fact, brothels in general made him feel ill.

But Debenham was not to be denied. "An hour's bedroom sport at

Maggie's, and then a chop house to round off the evening. Surely you couldn't think of anything better, Silverton? Come! I won't take no for an answer."

Silverton went, but not to take advantage of the bedroom sport.

As he and Debenham were ushered into the reception room at Maggie's, which was lined with crimson paper upon the walls, gold trimmings, and tasseled ruby velvet curtains, he was discomposed to discover Lord Anstey sipping port with a buxom blonde in a dimly-lit corner.

As Anstey was the husband of the discontented Lady Anstey, with whom Silverton had enjoyed an initially torrid but ultimately lack-luster affair the previous year, he had no appetite to converse with the gentleman whose failings Lady Anstey had outlined to him in such minute detail.

Hoping to slip away unnoticed once he saw Debenham engaged by a red-headed beauty, Silverton decided on impulse to seek an inter-view with the venerable Madame Abbess, and was soon sipping absinthe in her private parlor, and wondering why he hadn't chosen this path before.

A large painting of the Prince Regent hung on the wall behind her, flanked by various heroes, including the late Vice Admiral Horatio Lord Nelson. He'd achieved legendary status among the populace during his final victory at the Battle of Trafalgar, but he was a hero in Kitty's eyes, he recalled, for other reasons. Silverton did not share Kitty's gilded image of the situation. The low-born Emma Hamilton might have achieved fame and notoriety for her affair with Nelson, cuckolding him after her marriage to Lord Hamilton had elevated her to the peerage. However, by the time Lady Hamilton had died just a few years previously, she was destitute.

He sighed to think that Kitty's dream of similar elevation or as she termed it, simple respectability through marriage, to Lord Nash, was only a pipe dream. Nash would tire of her, and then Silverton would be waiting to restore her faith in men. It was the best he could hope for, he thought dismally, as the over-nourished, beady-eyed Maggie Montgomery thrust out her ample bosom and simpered above her raised glass. "What a great pleasure to enjoy your patronage, Lord Silverton. You are not a regular, and I'm wondering if you are perhaps here to suggest a certain entertainment we fail to provide you." She patted what he was certain was a red, squirrel hairpiece above her right temple, and Silverton felt a nudge of disgust at her suggestive smile.

The girls at Maggie's were known for their broad repertoire. Debenham had told him of the enjoyment he had had with blindfolds and leather whips in the soundproof basement, and immediately Silverton's thoughts had turned to innocent Dorcas. He was relieved when Debenham said it was only the bolder girls who were paid more.

"No, Mrs. Montgomery, it is, in fact, my desire to know the price of breaking a girl's contract. There is one in particular I should take away from here and to set up."

"Oh my, Lord Silverton, you are full of surprises. We hardly see you here, and next thing you want the full package. Which girl do you want?"

"Dorcas."

"Dorcas!" Clearly, she was much astonished. She clasped her jeweled-ring-encrusted fingers, her expression suggesting surprise had got the better of her.

"Yes, you surely must have a figure to hand you can name?" Silverton prodded.

Mrs. Montgomery smiled unctuously. "I shall be delighted to come up with one, my Lord, once I've ascertained from Dorcas her eagerness in being set up by you." Her smile became playful. "After all, my girls' happiness is my chief concern."

Disappointed by the lack of progress, Silverton finally rose. He felt it best not to press her, and bowed from the doorway. "In that case, I look forward to hearing back from you, Mrs. Montgomery. Perhaps you'd be good enough to communicate your response by messenger tomorrow."

"Oh, I am sure we can find a price that is quite acceptable to all parties," she assured him.

"I do hope so, Madam." He'd not wanted to appear too eager, having no doubt Mrs. Montgomery knew how to exact her pound of flesh. While Silverton was prepared to pay a good deal to secure the happiness of the lovely Kitty, if it aided his chances of winning more than just her gratitude some day, he also didn't want to be taken for a mug.

He did not see Lord Debenham pause at the end of the corridor, and the man's thoughtful look as Silverton disappeared before he, too, rapped softly upon Mrs. Montgomery's door.

And he was greatly dismayed—and, quite frankly, astonished—to receive a missive from Mrs. Montgomery the next morning expressing regret that Dorcas was too happy in her current situation to wish to avail herself of Lord Silverton's kind offer.

CHAPTER 18

*A*raminta was only too glad to remain at her childhood home and not to return to London, and Debenham.

She farewelled Teddy with real tears in her eyes, but with a heart full of hope that everything she could ever desire would be attained through his good offices. Only he held the key to her happiness. She knew this now, just as she knew it was too dangerous to allow him to prolong his stay, even if it was balm to her soul to feel his adoring gaze upon her.

The temptation to let him hold her, in passionate despair that he had lost her to Debenham, might result in his discovery of her ruse, but denial now might augment her rewards later. Araminta fully intended to milk his ardor when the time was right.

But the time was not yet right, and Araminta, left alone at The Grange, chafed with frustration at having to continue her pretence instead of embarking upon the affair she desired so passionately.

At least Teddy seemed to have understood the seriousness of her claims that damage to Debenham's reputation would greatly impact her own safety and happiness.

Just before Teddy had left, Araminta had received a note from Mrs. Mobbs that she and her 'young lady' had taken up residence with a nearby kindly farmer and his wife, and that the midwife had given a good report on the health of the mother-to-be. Araminta simply had to orchestrate a means of leaving the house at the right time on some worthy mission, attended by Jane in the carriage.

Any day, she was told. "Any minute," Jane said now, coming into the room and adding with a cheery, "Not much longa ter 'ave ter wait, starin' at sunrises and sunsets an' waitin' for summat to 'appen." Araminta, with her elbows on the windowsill, was gazing sadly at the last of the riders as they disappeared over the hill. "Reckon poor Lord Ludbridge will miss yer. Pity yer didn't marry 'im. 'E'd a bin a good 'usband."

"I *would* have married him if he hadn't had such a lofty sense of right and wrong." Araminta dragged her gaze from the window and looked at her maid. "Well, he can put that to good use now and do what's right by me, finally." She dabbed at her eyes. "Consider yourself lucky, for you'd not have had Jem working in the same household if I'd married Lord Ludbridge."

"True, m'lady."

Araminta raised an eyebrow. "That was a forlorn response. Things not going so well between you and Jem?" It didn't surprise her. Jane was as plain as a pikestaff, while Jem was a dashing and extremely handsome valet not to mention an extraordinarily good kisser, as Araminta had been forced to find out in order to lay claim to the letter that had incriminated Debenham before she'd burned it that fateful night at Vauxhall Gardens. Well, she'd been so *sure* she'd burned it, but at least Teddy was on the case to return it to her.

"I ' ardly seen ' im, m'lady since I bin wiv yer an', o'course, 'e's bin wiv Lord Debenham, an' yer two ain't seen one anuvver fer an awful long time."

"Well, that's not my fault." Araminta ran her hand over her detested bulge. "When will Mrs. Mobbs tell me my time has come?" she asked, longingly. "Honestly, I can't bear another day of this. I will simply go quite stark raving mad." Then she clapped her hands, pleasure wiping away her discontent. "Lord Ludbridge will be back in

London in a fortnight after he's visited his mother up north. Isn't that wonderful timing, Jane?"

"Fer wot, m'lady?" Jane raised her head from tidying the various items of clothing Araminta had left around the room and tucked a strand of hair behind her ear. Araminta found the sight of her rough nails nibbled to the quick suddenly irritating.

"Wipe that miserable expression off your face, Jane, and be happy for me for a change. You have to admit, I've suffered terribly from the day Hetty eloped with Sir Aubrey, and you don't see me inflicting my misery on all those around me. You'll see Jem soon enough. As for me, I *make* plans to improve my lot and don't just wait for events to happen. Now, please lay out my jonquil walking dress and pelisse. I think I shall go for a gentle stroll. That may help to 'bring on' this detested child."

As it turned out, within minutes of this declaration Araminta was flying to her wardrobe to choose a Pomona green traveling gown, while thinking of how she might find an excuse for a hasty carriage ride instead of a walk. For word had just arrived from Mrs. Mobbs that her child had been born.

Hurrying into the drawing room, she tried to hide her excitement as her mother and sister looked up from their embroidery.

"Mama, I wish to take the carriage to visit the poor."

Lady Partington looked startled, while Hetty gasped, "When have you ever visited the poor, Araminta? And why now? It's nearly dinner."

"It's hours until dinner, and I've no reason to change since I can barely fit into anything, so I hope Papa understands that."

"My dear Araminta, you are overset. This is not a moment to go dashing out upon a wild whim." Her mama rose and came toward her, smiling her characteristic serene smile which set Araminta's teeth on edge, since it was a sign her mama intended to thwart her.

"Yes, the *poor*? That's the wildest whim I ever heard." Hetty looked like she was struggling not to laugh, which made Araminta angrier and more determined than ever.

She stood her ground, clenching her fists as she tried not to clench her teeth. "There happens to be a family I have befriended. A very... worthy farmer whose child ran beneath my carriage wheels just before I arrived here. I was..." she struggled for inspiration "...shocked I had nearly killed the child, and have checked several times to ensure his injured leg is mending. And now I am so restless and feel my time so near, I simply have to get out of the house and make this short visit."

"All the more reason to stay comfortably here." Her mother was relying on very clearly underhanded soothing methods to try and thwart her. "You are far too advanced to be taking such chances, Araminta. Now do sit down and join Hetty and me. We were having such a lovely coze. You've kept far too much to yourself, lately. We miss your company, darling."

Araminta shook her head stubbornly. "Jane will come with me. I'll be gone under an hour. I just need a little fresh air and to get out of the house. Surely you can understand that?"

Her mother gave a little sigh. "You are so determined sometimes, Araminta, and I do worry about you. What if Hetty and I accompanied you? Wouldn't that be nice? Just the three of us going for a gentle carriage ride?"

Araminta glanced, panicked, from her mother's gently urging smile to Hetty's more speculative one. "You and Hetty are not dressed for it. *I* am. See! In my traveling gown, and far too impatient to wait for you to change. I've asked John to bring the carriage around. I'll take Jane with me and...if you are so insistent, I'll return to collect you in half an hour if you still wish to accompany me, though I'll probably be wanting to come back by then, anyway."

Her mother glanced at her youngest daughter. "Would you like to go for a ride, Hetty?"

"Lord, no. I'm far too uncomfortable to want to do anything, and I wonder that you're so...sprightly, Araminta."

Araminta turned back toward the corridor. "I'll be gone such a little while," she said, ignoring Hetty. "Don't trouble yourself, Mama. Come along, Jane. I just need to breathe in a little fresh air, and then I'll be back to my usual easy self."

"That will be nice!" Hetty called after her. "You've been as fluttery as Lady Zena trying to get out of her cage these last weeks."

Araminta was glad to hear her mother admonishing her sister, but Hetty was right in that Araminta *had* felt like a canary trying to escape its cage.

Fortunately, there was not too long to wait, she reflected as the footman helped her into the carriage and slammed the door behind Jane. In the confined space, as the vehicle rolled down the gravel drive and picked up pace as it turned onto the road, Araminta could talk without fear of being overheard. Another reason the house had felt so confining, with her mother or Hetty likely to throw open the door with complete lack of regard at any given moment.

"Not long, Jane, until his Lordship has his heir. Oh Lord, I don't even know if it will be an heir, and I don't know if I'll be pleased it's only a girl, or pleased if it's a boy and I won't have to go through all this desperate agony again."

"Yer babe came inta the world a mite quicker an' easier than any of me mam's," Jane observed.

"I hope you're not inferring that I'm complaining, Jane." Araminta regarded her coolly. "Oh, look, is this the place?"

A drystone wall, crumbling in places, surrounded the ramshackle collection of buildings that made up what was apparently the Home Farm. As the carriage slowed to turn into the rutted road, a pack of barking dogs tore across the grass. From the main house, a middle-aged woman in a dirty apron and cap emerged, raising her hand, before trudging wearily across the grass to where the carriage had stopped.

"Afternoon, m'lady." She curtsied as Araminta was helped to the ground. "Mighty 'onored, we are, ter 'ave yer stop by an' favor us like this. I'm Mrs. Goodwin, Farmer Goodwin's wife. 'E's gone to town to sell some sheep, but if yer'd like to step inta the parlor, I'll make yer a nice cup o' tea. Mrs. Mobbs says as 'ow yer was worrit yer'd hurt our boy fer runnin' in front of yer carriage. Well, don't mind 'bout that. 'E got a good clip over the ear fer bein' so careless not but that our 'earts are gladdened yous shown such goodness. Now, up the stairs, there yer go."

In the kitchen, where Mrs. Goodwin paused to give the bootboy a jab of her foot in passing for clumsily dropping the leather belt he was polishing, Jane handed over the basket of victuals Araminta had hastily ordered from the scullery for the purpose at Mrs. Mobbs' behest.

"My, my, ain't yer the kindest soul," gushed Mrs. Goodwin. "An' thinkin' so much o' others when yer should be thinkin' o' yer an' yer young 'un. Must be nearly due now. Any minute, I'd say."

It was only at that moment that Araminta saw the sly smile the farmer's wife gave her. She must have revealed her shock, for Mrs. Goodwin clicked her tongue and her lips parted to reveal her browning teeth.

Self-consciously she patted her mob cap and dropped her voice as she led them into the cool interior of the house. "Don't mind what yer say to me. I knows all about it and it's safe here. Bin here more'n ten years." She nodded her head, still talking as she led the way. "I were a looker in me day, an' a good friend o' Millie Mobbs. We worked together, 'er and I, 'til I got inta the family way an' Mr. Goodwin made an 'onest woman o' me. Worth 'is while it were, jest like yer doin' what's worth yer while, m'lady. And don't fink anyone'll be the wiser. I got it all arranged. Now, 'ere we go then. Inta the guest bedroom wot I made all cozy-like, jest for yer."

She threw open the door to the homely, sparsely decorated room containing a bed, wash stand, and two chairs beneath a window hung with blue and white printed curtains, with a view out over the paddocks.

"No neighbors round fer miles 'bout, an' Farmer Goodwin won't be back from market fer anuvver day an' a bit. I sent 'im on 'is way, I did, when the uvver young lady arrived."

Jane pulled back the coverlet on the bed as she stared dubiously between Araminta and Mrs. Goodwin, obviously thinking what Araminta was thinking. Mistaking their concern over the lack of clean sheets for something else, the farmer's wife reassured them, "I always 'ave visitors 'ere from me London days so ladies in all manner o' finery don't faze anyone 'ere, let me tell yer. Now, let's get yer shoes off, eh, m'lady. Then ya can do a bit o' moanin' an wotnot after I tells yer to. Up yer get, there now, jest get yerself comfortable an' I'll fetch yer a mug o' porter to give yer strength."

Araminta prepared to climb into bed, while Jane put down the small bag she was carrying, which contained a few necessities. She hoped she'd not have to remain long, but she'd have to send someone to The Grange in an hour or so with the message that she'd been accommodated by farmer Goodwin and his wife after the first labor pains had come on rapidly.

Perhaps in another three hours she could be holding the baby, or rather handing it to the midwife she knew Mrs. Mobbs was organizing and then, in the morning, she could return home.

Home without that ridiculous padding. Home to the comforts she could finally enjoy once more.

Home to the anticipation of seeing Lord Ludbridge again.

Mrs. Goodwin returned when Jane was holding up Araminta's fine lawn night-rail.

"Got yer one o' mine, dearie, cos 'er ladyship, yer mama, will think it mighty odd yer came with yer own, don't yer think?"

Araminta shuddered when she felt the coarse linen against her delicate skin, but she suffered the indignity without complaining. At least the hateful cushion was finally a thing of the past. And soon she would be out of this dreadful place with her new babe. Mrs. Goodwin would obviously expect to be paid well for having provided this necessary service, and Araminta understood the need for keeping her onside.

Jane tucked the blankets comfortably around her, and Mrs. Goodwin was just telling her the message the boy would deliver to The Grange explaining Araminta's predicament, when she looked up at the sound of wailing.

As the sound grew louder, Mrs. Goodwin's smile broadened and she put her hands to her cheeks. "It's the babe, the newborn babe; a lusty boy not an 'our old," she said, misty-eyed. "Soon ter be delivered inta yer arms, m'lady."

"Indeed it is." Mrs. Mobbs appeared in the doorway, a smile of satisfaction lighting up her sallow face. "Yer'll want to 'old yer new son, o' course, m'lady."

Shocked, Araminta stared between the child and the women. "Not really. I can see him quite well from here," she said, waving Mrs. Mobbs away and trying to bolster her own trembling smile, for the babe was the ugliest she'd ever beheld. She tried to recall if the child to which she'd given birth had been quite so unprepossessing. It certainly hadn't been pretty. Perhaps it was just the way of newborns.

Frowning, she remarked, "It has no hair," though that was a good thing. Her own child's hair had been so thick and black—she shuddered, as she tried to put out of her mind the white streak that so branded its lineage. How lucky, though, that its hair had come early, giving her the chance to ensure the baby was removed.

"Many babes are bald, m'lady," Jane said, taking the child when Araminta refused, and looking doe-eyed before she began to croon to it. Immediately it ceased its wailing and stared blankly, as if mesmerized by Jane's plain visage.

"Well, I hope it improves in looks," Araminta observed, worried. "Jane, you keep it. I don't want to hold it."

"But yer must, m'lady."

"Don't tell me what I must do," Araminta snapped, closing her eyes briefly, then opening them to offer Mrs. Mobbs a beatific smile. "You've done your work very well, Mrs. Mobbs, and I thank you. Jane, will you give her payment, as agreed?"

Jane thrust the child into Araminta's arms and, not looking happy at all, rummaged in the bag at the foot of the bed, withdrawing a small velvet pouch which she handed to Mrs. Mobbs.

"Most kind, m'lady," replied the other woman, curtseying, before tipping the contents into the palm of her hand. The rubies and diamonds of Araminta's wedding necklace with its unusual heart-shaped centerpiece glittered in the shafts of late evening sunlight, and both older women could be heard to sigh audibly.

"As this matter has been discussed already, I trust neither of you will feel the necessity to revisit the events of this evening at some later date." Araminta forced herself to smile, but hoped they heard the warning in her tone. "I have been more than generous, but this will help pay for the necessities I expect for my child, such as clothing and education. Please don't expect me to offer more. My husband is not an easy man, and if he is ever made a party to this, it will not only be me who suffers. Do you understand?"

Mrs. Mobbs nodded. "Indeed, no one profits from quibblin' ova matters like this, m'lady, to be sure. An 'is Lordship's temper 'as bin remarked upon by me friend, Maggie Montgomery's girls many a time. We undastand completely what yer are sayin'." Her eyes glittered, reflecting the sharp-cut crystals from which she seemed unable to tear her gaze away. "Yer secret is safe, but there is still more we must do ter prepare the room fer yer mama's arrival. Mrs. Goodwin, 'ave yer the bowl of chicken blood? Oh Lordy, is that rain I 'ear a-thunderin' down?" She sent a gleeful look in Araminta's direction. "Well, well, ain't that the Good Lord smilin' on yer, m'lady. On such a dark night as this wiv our roads so poor an' prone to floodin', I can't see yer poor mama makin' it 'ere amid the pourin' rain. I'll 'ave me boy send a note ter that effect, shall I, m'lady? Reckon we might jest mention the tree wot's fallen ova the road that leads to the 'ouse."

Araminta nodded. Suddenly, she felt more overwhelmed than she ever had, lying in that uncomfortable bed with Mrs. Mobbs and Mrs. Goodwin and Jane all looking at her but, worst of all, the baby grizzling in her arms, which did not smell at all nice.

A boy, was it? Well, that should please his Lordship. And surely it would improve in looks. After all, it had blue blood in its veins, both parents nobly born. She exhaled on a deep sigh. Her own child would be well looked after with a small fortune to rear it well, and it would never suffer at the hands of Debenham should he have discovered he was rearing Sir Aubrey's cuckoo. Really, Araminta should congratulate herself for managing the situation to everyone's satisfaction.

She was about to hand the child back to Jane, complaining that the noise it was making was hurting her ears, when a loud crack of thunder seemed almost to split the humble dwelling in two.

Jane shrieked and covered her ears, and then to everyone's obvious shock, a loud female wailing could be heard, even above the din, growing nearer and accompanied by the sound of footsteps running down the passage. Upon a loud shriek, the door was thrust open, and a wild-eyed creature in a bloodstained night-rail hurled herself into the room and snatched the child from Araminta's arms.

Admittedly, Araminta was quite glad to be relieved of it, but realizing this must be the young woman who'd just given birth to it, and who had surrendered it through need and for more than a tidy sum, she cried indignantly, "Get away! What do you think you're doing? This is *my* baby!"

The young woman opened her mouth to protest, but Mrs. Mobbs clapped her hands over her face while Mrs. Goodwin tackled her and wrested the child from her arms. The young woman put up an admirable fight. In the minute or so Araminta observed her, kicking and scratching and biting for all she was worth, she had to admire her determination, even if she was not at all the beauty she'd hoped the babe's mother would be—though no one looked their best after giving birth, she supposed.

She, too, was wearing one of Mrs. Goodwin's coarse linen night-rails, and greasy strands of black hair fell across her tear-streaked face. Araminta turned her head away. It would be far better if neither recognized each other when a chance encounter on the dance floor at some worthy's 'drawing-room' might throw them into one another's orbit.

Jane obviously had realized the same thing, for she was quick to step in front of Araminta and to assist with some judicious shoving of the flailing creature back toward the door and into the passage. Soon, however, it was clear that it was going to require three of them to subdue her, and once again Araminta was in possession of the squalling child while Jane, Mrs. Mobbs, and Mrs. Goodwin hurled themselves into the fray. The din was disturbing and horrible to listen to as they bore the woman away, and Araminta hunkered under the covers and tried to wish away time so that it would be tomorrow, and she could be back in her own comfortable bed with the baby in the care of the village wet nurse who had been arranged.

She tried to close her eyes and rest, but the child was having none of it. Its lusty cries were on par with its birth mother's, and it was tempting to try and smother the horrible sound with the blankets, just to give Araminta the time she needed to order her mind.

But she was scared of doing anything to harm it. Knowing what to do with a baby was not in her experience, and she felt awkward and frightened as well as resentful toward it, as if it were the reason she was in her hateful predicament.

But then she realized that it had been her savior, and she must guard it well. She'd wanted a healthy son to present to Debenham so he would gloat that she'd done her duty in a very timely fashion. Now she had one.

So Araminta smiled at the baby and found she could, after all, block her mind to the noise and transport it to more satisfying planes...such as the knowledge that having satisfactorily executed her most pressing obligation regarding the family line, she could finally start to enjoy herself.

CHAPTER 19

*A*nother standing ovation. Roses littered the stage, raining down about her as Kitty curtsied yet again to the sounds of the orchestra in the background nearly drowned out by the cheers of the audience. Her heart threatened to burst with joy. Tonight, her performance was being witnessed by a gathering of the Royal Family; the newspapers and gossip sheets had been equally flattering about her singing voice, her lithe dancing, the heartfelt acting, and Nash was forever showering her with gifts, telling her how much he adored her.

She had everything, and more, than she'd ever dreamed possible when she'd run away to London.

Except her family's good wishes. Her mother had written one terse letter saying how deeply disappointed she and Lord Partington were at her defection, adding, pointedly, that the new baby was thriving.

Her brother, Ned, had visited her after a performance the previous week, and gravely told her that while he, personally, was proud of her achievements, he couldn't reconcile her desertion of their mother at this difficult time in her life. He'd added that Kitty's selfish desires had always trumped her concern for anyone or anything else.

From Lissa, she'd heard nothing.

Which meant that Kitty's sadness at her family's lack of support—

downright disapproval—was completely stripping the luster from what should be the most wonderful phase of her life.

She was just straightening up from her final curtsy when a figure, rising out of a seat in the stalls to leave, caught her eye. The particularly erect bearing and sheen of dark hair was familiar, and for a moment she thought it was Lady Debenham. Shocked, she realized it was her sister. Lissa. Lissa was here tonight in company with a gentleman. Perhaps she was going to meet Kitty backstage.

Excited, Kitty hurried from her final bow, accepting the well-wishes thrown her way from all quarters with much nodding and smiling, arriving in the crowded backstage area, breathless and full of hope.

She swung around, her gaze roaming over every face, familiar or not, trying to pick the dark-haired beauty she'd seen earlier. A cluster of giggling chorus girls were changing out of their village-girl costumes, while a throng of admirers waited impatiently to thrust their own tokens of love and other sentiments at Kitty.

But of Lissa there was no sign.

Nash had not come to the theater that evening. He had a dinner to attend. Kitty spoke with a few gentlemen who pressed forward, but after the disappointment of not seeing her sister, she now hoped Silverton might have chosen that night to come along.

He was not there either, so after changing into evening clothes, Kitty trudged through the busy streets toward her own home feeling unaccountably lonely. She knew she should take a hackney, and that Nash would be angry if he discovered she had not. Too often Kitty was mistaken for a lady of the night due to the fact she walked alone, but she never felt afraid. There were too many people about, and she had only a few blocks to cover.

As she passed the apothecary, she remembered she needed to replenish her supply of Queen Anne's Lace seeds. The memory of her half-sister, Lady Debenham, whom she'd last encountered the night she'd nearly lost her child—a child she'd clearly become encumbered with too soon—was a stark reminder of the risks Kitty took of having her own child out of wedlock.

But she was careful. It would break her heart to bring into the world a tiny being who, like her, would be branded a bastard from the moment it took its first breath.

Inside, she gazed at the dark wooden shelves full of their glass jars and phials of powders and potions, and nervously awaited her turn to be served. She knew the stooped and balding apothecary would peer at her through his wire-framed glasses with great opprobrium, which is why she preferred to shop for such necessaries from Mrs. Mobbs.

"Kitty!"

Kitty swung around at the sound of her name, then rushed forward when she saw Dorcas in the shadows, turning away from the counter having just been served.

She was about to embrace her but Dorcas stepped back, and Kitty noticed the lumpish fellow who stood close, towering over her with a distinctly proprietorial air.

"It's so lovely to see you," Kitty said, lamely. "I hoped you'd visit."

"Nah, miss, I told yer 'ow it is." Dorcas flicked a glance up at the giant beside her and looked as if she were about to nod farewell, but Kitty reached forward and pressed a coin in the fellow's hand. "Just two minutes to chat about old times?" she entreated. "I shan't entice her away."

To her surprise, the hulk nodded and stepped back.

Immediately, Dorcas beamed. "Oh miss, I bin thinkin' o' yer such a lot, I 'ave, but didn't know whetha I should say nuffink an' didn't know 'ow to get a message to yer."

"You want to come back with me?" Kitty dropped her voice and gripped Dorcas's arm with pleasure. "We can make a plan. Lord Silverton will help me, I know it!"

"It's 'bout Lord Silverton I wanted ter talk ter yer 'bout, miss." Dorcas glanced nervously toward her minder, but since he was ogling several pretty servants entering the shop, she clearly decided to take a chance. "I 'eard summat 'bout 'im an' Lord Debenham that got me right worrit, knowin' yer 'ad a fondness fer the gennulman, an all, since 'e 'elped yer, and since yer clearly like 'im."

"Lord Nash is the most important man in my life, but Lord

Silverton is a good friend," Kitty said firmly, feeling a sense of great disquiet and wishing her heart didn't lurch so greatly whenever Silverton's name was mentioned. Was this the moment she'd learn the full extent of his crimes? Yes, he was a colleague of Debenham's but Silverton was kind and charming and utterly dependable. Surely there was some explanation for why Stephen Cranbourne had said he was under suspicion. She decided that the less she knew about Lord Silverton's proclivities, the better.

"Perhaps you shouldn't tell me, Dorcas," she said, smiling. "I think I like him too well to know the depths of which he's capable, being such · a friend of villainous Viscount Debenham."

Dorcas's eyes widened. "Oh miss, then all the more reason fer me ter say summat an' I surely shoulda before only, like I said, I didn't know 'ow to get a message to yer. We don't get a moment ter ourselves, nor paper nor nuffink." She took a deep breath. "Which is why me friend, Daisy, goes through the gennulman's pockets, mostly so she can find scraps o' paper or summat she can write notes on the gennulmen she really likes, an ter 'er family. That's 'ow she come across the note 'bout Lord Silverton. Isn't that true, Sally?"

It was only then that Kitty noticed the slump-shouldered girl who stood slightly behind Dorcas. She'd assumed she was a customer, but as Kitty peered more closely into the gloom, she saw that girl was definitely under the protection of the great hulk whom Dorcas had indicated earlier.

When Sally didn't respond, Dorcas exhaled on a loud and sympathetic sigh. "Poor Sally ain't bin the same since 'er baby got taken off her. Mrs. Montgomery thought a bit of fresh air might do 'er a mite o' good, and I 'ope it does, fer if Sally don't pull 'erself together, she'll be on 'er own an' sellin' 'erself in the 'Aymarket." She reached for the girl's hand and pulled her into their conversational circle, saying kindly, "Yer used to be the prettiest 'o all 'o us, eh, Sally? An' yer will be again, when yer done wiv yer grievin'."

"I'm so sorry to hear of the loss of your child," Kitty said, gently addressing the girl.

"Loss?" The girl repeated the word as if in a daze, and when she raised her chin to stare at Kitty with a pair of intense violet eyes, Kitty realized that beneath the lank dark hair and lusterless skin, she really was a beauty. "I didn't lose the baby." Sally gritted her teeth, balled her fists and hissed, "It were *stolen*."

Dorcas smiled sadly and patted Sally's hand. "I know yer wanted ter keep it, Sally, but girls like us aren't s'posed to get inta trouble like that, which is why we're 'ere." She indicated the apothecary's with a sweep of her hand. "An' when we do get inta trouble, we're forced ter get rid o' it."

She put her head close to Kitty's and whispered, "Mrs. Montgomery tried all sorts ter kill Sally's babe afore it be born, but it were a real determined 'un." She turned to Sally and said in a bolstering voice, "An' now yer babe's got a 'ome in the country wot Mrs. Mobbs organized with that nice farmer's wife oo's settlin' it with a right grand family. Imagine it, Sally! Youse gived birth to a babe wot's goin' to want fer nothin'. 'E'll live in a fine 'ouse an' maybe 'ave a 'orse an' he'll neva go 'ungry like he woulda if yer'd a kept 'im. Such good fortune don't usually 'appen ter the bastard child born from 'un o' the likes o' us an' a Spanish sailor."

Sally looked unimpressed. "Coulda' bin Lord Heckleston's, too. Both o' 'em were customers the same night me womb quickened. If it were Lord Heckleston's, then the babe shoulda 'ad all that by rights."

Kitty bit her lip. "Oh, poor Sally, it's true! Bastards are rarely recognized by their noble parents. My father is a nobleman who never recognized us. I grew up in shame and I wouldn't wish it on anyone. If your babe has gone to a good home you should be overjoyed. Truly."

She had to try and revive the girl's spirits, for Dorcas spoke the truth when she made it clear Sally could not have kept the baby out of poverty. "But, I've changed my mind. Tell me what you were about to say regarding Lord Silverton." She was anxious now, afraid of what she might hear, but realizing she needed to hear it. Besides, it might help extirpate the residual fondness she had for him, which she increasingly found quite disconcerting.

"Well, miss, I'm 'opin' I'm rememberin' right, but the note Daisy

told me 'bout was ter Lord Debenham from a gennulman who signed
'iself Mr. Cosmo Lamont an'—"

"Mr. Lamont?" Kitty started. "He painted my portrait. Go on,
Dorcas."

"Well, 'e said summat along the lines o' a traitor in their midst an'
Lord Debenham must keep an eye out on Lord Silverton fer as 'e'd
'eard a rumor or two 'bout 'im. That's all, miss."

Kitty frowned and repeated, "Mr. Lamont was telling Lord
Debenham not to trust Lord *Silverton* because Lord *Silverton* was a
traitor? Is that right, Dorcas?"

"Summat like that." Dorcas shrugged. "Anyways, I reckoned yer
might want ter know, since I guessed yer were fond o' Lord Silverton
an' I don't think anyone wants ter be on the wrong side o' Lord
Debenham." She shuddered. "I don't know 'ow Daisy can stand it,
bein' 'is favorite, an all. Mind, but that she earns a bit extra fer the
secrets wot she tells 'im 'bout the other secrets wot uvver gennelmen
tell her."

"Goodness! Daisy trades secrets to Lord Debenham?" Kitty's
mouth dropped open. She could just imagine the damage that could
cause.

Sally nodded gloomily. "Reckon it were Lord Calder's secret wot
Daisy found out from 'is bruvver and told Lord Debenham wot did
'im in." She tapped her ear. "We knows a lot more than you might
think."

"Lord Calder? Why, he was Lord Silverton's friend, too. How terrible!" She felt a lurch of fear on Silverton's behalf. "When did Daisy tell
you about the note she found about Silverton?"

Dorcas frowned. "Were a couple o' weeks ago, maybe. Silverton an'
Debenham both came ter Maggie's—"

Kitty gasped, unprepared for the disappointment she felt that her
charming Lord Silverton visited Maggie's, but Dorcas added quickly,
"Oh no, miss, 'e neva comes ter visit the girls. It's 'cause 'e's thick as
thieves with Debenham, an' Debenham is a regular. Lord Silverton
drank absinthe with me mistress; that's all. But that were the night

Daisy found the note in Lord Debenham's coat." She shrugged. "I jest thought yer should know."

Kitty was about to respond with gratitude when the girls' minder stepped forward, impatient now to be gone, and Dorcas forced a smile that was twinged with sadness. "So nice ter catch up wiv the gossip, Miss Hazlett. I do 'ope we meet again."

***

For the rest of the way home, Kitty was consumed by the fear that Silverton might be in danger and that she had possibly, inadvertently, had a hand in the terrible business.

What could she do? Could she warn him? She had nothing substantial other than Dorcas's claims about the letter, but at least she could tell him about *that* so he would be on his guard.

In front of her small townhouse, she stopped and gazed at it in the moonlight. It seemed incredible that it was hers. Well, as much as it ever could be since she had no security beyond the attraction she held for Nash.

She shook her head, as if that might dispel Lord Silverton's warning that Lord Nash would never offer Kitty what she truly wanted, and that he could offer her more and her heart cleaved at the thought of being in Silverton's arms in a scenario that wasn't acting. That was real.

Immediately, she berated herself. She was Nash's mistress and she would be forever loyal to him. More loyal than he was, in truth, but Nash was a man and men did stray; she had to allow for that.

Dreamily, she thought of Silverton's gentle smile and his willingness to help her, even when it did not benefit himself. And of his willingness to offer her exactly what Nash offered her.

Not marriage, though.

A gentle breeze stirred the embroidered net overskirt of her lovely gown. Not Araminta's castoff, but another reminder of Lord Nash's generosity. This time, she forced herself to revisit her previous happiness by dwelling on the way Nash would rake his smoldering gaze over her naked body and lavish her with murmured endearments. She shivered, reminding herself yet again of how fortunate she was.

But by the time she opened her front door, her thoughts had returned to Lord Silverton and how he might be in danger.

Until everything was swept away by the astonishing vision before her. A trail of rose petals led from the front door and up the stairs. Kitty followed, her heart growing fuller with every footstep, until she reached the bedroom, throwing open the door and gasping even louder at the sight of Nash reclining, naked, upon the counterpane.

"I thought you were at an important engagement!" Delighted, she ran forward and threw herself into his arms. He curled his body around her, and she rested her head upon his shoulder, spooned against him, shivering with anticipation as he stroked her cheek.

"This was my important engagement." He made a sweeping motion with his arm, indicating the rose petals.

"Really?" She squeaked at the feel of his tongue tickling her ear and squeezed his knee convulsively, causing him to yelp and throw her onto her back.

"Yes, you irresistible siren!" His face, smiling above her, filled her with delight and warmed her to her toes. "But you have on far too many clothes."

Kitty was more than ready to divest herself of the impediments. With Nash's help, she was soon just as he desired her, naked but for her stockings, which he took in his teeth and pulled off her legs before returning north once more, tickling her flesh with his tongue and beginning a concerted onslaught upon her inner thighs. Soon her sighs of pleasure were moans as she writhed in growing ecstasy beneath him.

"Come inside me!" she gasped when she was nearly at the height of her pleasure, and he flipped her onto her stomach and entered her from behind, fondling her as he plunged into her depths with ever deeper, more intense thrusts.

"You are magnificent!" he gasped as he climaxed inside her, kissing her neck, her shoulders, and then when he'd turned her over, her breasts, as he lay panting on top of her. "The most magnificent woman I've ever met."

Kitty, gasping, breathless, laughed with unadulterated delight. "And you are the most magnificent lover I've ever met."

"And the only one." He raised himself on one elbow and regarded her with loving intensity. "A virgin, and the most beautiful woman in London. I can't believe my good fortune. You are mine. All mine. Why, to think that when you'd just arrived in London, you took one look at me, and lost your heart. And I was your first," he repeated. He trailed his forefinger tenderly over her chest, circling her right nipple as he added almost thoughtfully, "And I want to marry you."

For a moment, Kitty wasn't sure she'd heard correctly. She barely dared to breathe as she stared at him. "Marry me?" she whispered, sitting up, her face breaking out into a smile she thought would split her cheeks. "A real marriage?"

Nash nodded, curling her against his side. "A real marriage," he confirmed.

"But...what of your family? They'll never consent."

"I don't need their consent. I'm over twenty-one, and unlike our poor Royal Family, there is no Royal Marriages Act for peers which would prevent me from marrying whom I wish." Still holding her with one arm, he reached across the bed to the side table and picked up an oblong velvet box. "Here. I've bought you a gift. A betrothal gift."

Kitty's hands were shaking as she opened the lid. First a marriage proposal, and now....

This. Her breath left her in a whoosh, leaving her, for a moment, speechless. "Oh Nash, I don't know what to say," she whispered, staring with wonder at his handsome, loving face.

"Go on, hold it. It's real. Real diamonds and rubies."

"Oh Nash, I can't believe your generosity." It was true. As she gazed upon the exquisite ruby and diamond necklace with its highly unusual heart-shaped centrepiece, his marriage proposal reverberating in her ears, she felt as if the gates to Heaven had opened early to admit her.

He rose onto his haunches, saying eagerly, "I thought it would complement your lovely golden and cream coloring. Here, let me." He took the necklace from her and carefully fastened the catch, turning her in his arms to plant a kiss on her nose. "My family will love you. They will not be able to help themselves. But you've not answered me. Will you be my wife, Kitty La Bijou—whose name alone justifies such a glittering confection of jewels?"

"I will!" Kitty breathed, throwing her arms about his neck. "Oh yes, I will!"

He held her at arm's length. "There is one caveat. We must marry in secret. I promise you, I am not trying to trick you into a sham marriage. You may have whomever you like as a witness to satisfy you that all is in good order, but the fact is that my grandfather is very ill, and I can't risk hastening his end with a marriage that I know he will find difficult to countenance."

Kitty put her head on one side as she took in what he was saying.

"Of course, we could have a proper ceremony with all the pomp and circumstance if you wanted to wait another two or three years. I am offering you that, too, my sweet." He squeezed her hands. "I, personally, would prefer to marry you right this moment. Well, Kitty, it's your decision. What do you say?"

Kitty raised her hand to trace the configuration of jewels that now graced her throat. She couldn't believe how exquisitely cut the centre ruby was: in the perfect shape of a heart. It was the most unusual, and beautiful, arrangement, she'd ever seen. Gazing into his face, she whispered, "Did you choose the love heart just for me? Oh Nash, where did you get it?"

"I...had it made specially for you, my love. But I'm still awaiting your decision."

Kitty sighed once more. "You just tell me what to do and how it shall proceed, and I will be very happy to comply. Oh, Nash!" Again, she hurled herself into his arms. "I can't believe it! The rose petals, the ruby necklace you had made just for me, and now marriage. Truly, you have made me the happiest woman in the entire kingdom."

"IS IT NOT A LITTLE EARLY TO BE GOING OUT IN PUBLIC, MY DEAR?"

Debenham raised one eyebrow as he fixed his gaze upon Araminta's waistline. "It has been only two weeks since William's birth. Apparently, too early to resume intimate relations, yet not too early to rejoin the hectic social whirl."

Araminta glanced up from attaching her earrings and offered a beguiling smile as a defense against the thickening of his tone, which never augured well. "Soon you will be amply rewarded for your patience, darling husband." She smoothed her hair and contoured her lithe body with her hands. "You were not so anxious to court my interest when my body thickened, as it surely will again if you cannot show a little restraint," she teased. It was hard not to sing to the tree-tops as she reveled in the freedom of her newfound curves. Debenham would claim her, inevitably, but as long as she ingested the Queen Anne's Lace seeds immediately he'd claimed his conjugal rights, she could be assured, Mrs. Mobbs had told her, that she would not conceive. Mrs. Mobbs had apparently been dishing out Queen Anne's Lace seeds to young women for decades, and declared it almost one hundred percent effective, when used correctly.

Debenham skimmed the top of her dressing table, then leaned against it as he watched her pluck at her gown.

"William will need a sibling. No need to look so horrified. I'm well aware you are not maternal by nature, and I don't mean immediately." He sent her a critical look. "I believe I visit our son a good deal more frequently than you do. Have you even been up to the nursery today?"

Araminta avoided looking at him while she pulled on her gloves, and tried to remember the last time she had looked in on the boy. "Millicent tells me he's thriving." She offered her husband a bright smile, then took several leisurely steps toward him, pressing her body against him and skimming her hand up the length of his arm. She felt safe being so flirtatious, knowing the carriage had already been called around. "Haven't I been a clever wife, presenting you with an heir then getting my figure back so quickly? Aren't you going to reward me?"

She wished she hadn't spoken in such an unguarded fashion for immediately he said, "Reward you? My dear, if I had the funds, I would. I told you some time ago that I needed to have back the diamond and ruby necklace I gave you on our wedding day. Send Jane to The Grange to fetch it, if you must. If you've hidden it under the floorboard, as you told me, she surely knows exactly where it is. I've had some cursed luck lately, and I need it—as security only, I assure you. You shall have it back but I do need it by next Saturday."

All the happiness drained out of Araminta, but she bolstered her spirits with the knowledge that Teddy would help her. If she'd had the courage, she'd tell Debenham she was already being most assiduous in her wifely duties by having obtained Teddy's promise that he'd retrieve the note they'd all thought burned and that so badly incriminated Debenham. Regrettably, Teddy had reported only last week that he was finding his task more challenging than expected but when she'd tearfully begged him to use whatever means possible he'd finally agreed to resume his efforts.

Trying not to show her fear, she took a deep breath and exhaled on outrage. "I feared you intended selling my beautiful wedding present! That's why I prevaricated in fetching it, Debenham. I thought you were funning me, truly I did. Surely it is mine to do with what I wish." It occurred to her this might be a good moment for tears, but she hardly wished to venture out with a blotched face and besides, Debenham was notoriously unresponsive to such emotion.

"What is yours is mine, legally, Araminta. However, I'll buy you something lovely when next you deserve it and if I'm feeling particularly charitable and plump in the pocket. Besides, I only need the necklace for a short time. A week at most."

Without warning, he twisted her in his arms and crushed her to him, kissing her hard on the lips while he contoured her curves with his hands, ending with a squeeze of her breasts. "God, you are a vixen without a heart, but I'll have you crying for more when I'm finally allowed to have my way with you."

Araminta masked her sigh as she anticipated the sweaty pleasuring with which she'd have to involve herself. In the early days, she'd enjoyed herself, but the only time Debenham hadn't been a completely selfish lover was the night he seduced her at Miss Hosking's betrothal ball. What a fiasco that time in her life had been, when she'd felt overjoyed at being saved from marriage to plain and unprepossessing Mr. Woking, which is all he had been then. But Debenham's trickery and seduction had led to life sentence. All she had to look forward to was his careless cruelty, his cold contempt, and his gambling and womanizing. The only bright side about *that* was that thus occupied, he left her alone.

"You'll ruin my hair!" Araminta cried, furiously, when he started to run his fingers through her coiffure. She flew to the mirror and tried to rectify the damage while Debenham chuckled.

"You know, Araminta; you really are at your most entertaining when you are fired up. All right, I'll leave you to sort yourself out, but don't be late. Dobson is here to tell us the carriage is waiting, I believe."

Araminta sank onto the stool in front of her dressing table and covered her face with her hands, allowing herself a shuddering sigh as she heard his footsteps disappearing down the stairs.

Oh Teddy, please help me. Fear twisted her gut and she truly thought she might be ill. But then she remembered how much Teddy loved her and that he'd promised with such fervor to do what she wanted, before, that he'd help her in this regard.

And when she spied her darling Teddy, Lord Ludbridge among the throng, her spirits soared. As she'd seen him only once, and briefly, since before William's birth, he was quick to marvel at her stunning looks. "Is it right and healthy that you are here?" he asked with a consideration for her well-being that made Araminta want to cry again, only this time from happiness.

She tapped his shoulder playfully with her fan. "You are the kindest and most honorable gentleman I know, Lord Ludbridge. Debenham simply thought it was wrong to court scandal by returning to public life so soon, and was quite violent in the way he crushed me to him as we were about to step out." She dropped her voice making him bend his head to hear her. "Debenham can be a brute, and I fear returning to what we married women must endure when we are wed to insensitive men."

The shocked widening of his eyes made her feel quite gleeful inside. "Why, Lord Ludbridge, I fear I've embarrassed you," she gasped. "I must seem quite shameless, not to mention, jaded, when I speak of the realities of what you know nothing about."

Awkwardly, he shuffled his feet and cleared his voice, but daringly he gripped her wrist as he moved her into the shadows where they were shaded from view by a plinth bearing a voluminous plant. "I wouldn't say that is an entirely correct way of putting things." He drew in a labored breath. "Dear God, Araminta, if only I could save you from this horror in which you find yourself."

Araminta sent him a searching look at the same time as she softly, secretly, stroked the inside of his wrist. "But you can, Lord Ludbridge. You've already promised to secure that important letter from your brother and I just have one tiny other little problem which you can easily expedite and which will ensure that Debenham doesn't beat me most cruelly. It's my ruby necklace. You see, Debenham keeps me so short of funds and I had to use it as security for some pin money to pay a small debt. But I can't possibly fetch the necklace back myself." She moved closer and, fleetingly, cupped his cheek, her eyes dewy with very real affection for he truly was her darling slave. She could see it in his eyes.

She stared meaningfully at him to ensure he understood her, before dropping her voice to a whisper. "If you don't, I can't answer for what Debenham will do to me. But if you *can* do as I ask, then I am yours."

Teddy dipped his head to put his lips close to her ear, his voice a passionate growl. "I would never presume to take such advantage when I want only to help you, my angel."

"It wouldn't be taking advantage, Teddy, you must surely know that!" Placing her gloved hand to her eyes, she whispered, "Darling Teddy, I know it is so wrong of me to say it, but..." She took her hand away to reveal her eyes blazing with passion— certainly, she was sure the expression she strove for could not be mistaken for anything else — "you cannot know how I have longed to feel your arms about me. The night you asked me to marry you, I was the happiest girl in all of

England. No, this *planet*, Teddy. This universe. And then with Papa in danger of losing all his money, and me being pressured into this marriage with Debenham—"

"You were to marry his nephew," he corrected her.

"Yes, yes, but remember I told you that he was only pretending so as to help me." Her brain raced to remember what, in fact, she had told Teddy, and was pleased she could embellish her story when she added, "And Papa was pressuring me to marry Mr. Woking, or rather Lord Myles, since he was certain that both of the doddery relatives who stood in the way of him were on their last legs, meaning he'd be inheriting more than Lord Debenham and that, of course, made him the catch of the season. Of course, all that turned out to be true, but I held out, and held out, explaining that you *would* come back, but you sent no word, Teddy. I was distraught!"

"My darling Araminta, we've been over all this. I wrote every day, I promise you, but my letters must not have got to you in a timely fashion. Oh God, that I have ruined the love that we could have known."

"But we can still know that love, Teddy." She strove for tenderness now. "If I get my ruby necklace back, then I will be physically safe from Debenham whose roving eye means I am so often left to my own devices." Again, she touched his cheek. "You, Teddy, are all I've ever wanted. Please! Once, you let your scruples get in the way of us finding love." Her voice trailed off. "Don't let them stand in the way a second time."

The anguished look he sent her left her in no doubt that her latest request had landed on fertile ground. If there were any way on earth that Teddy could manage to get her ruby necklace back, he would do it.

CHAPTER 20

Kitty stretched her arms and rolled over in the bed, patting the empty space left by Nash, before sighing with pleasure as she opened her eyes to a repeat of the light tapping on her bedchamber door.

"Mornin', miss." Her maid brought in a tray bearing a pot of hot chocolate and dainty teacup and saucer, and set it on the table beside her. "There's someone downstairs ter see yer, miss. Bin 'ere a while only I said yer was asleep."

"You let him wait downstairs?" Kitty knew Nash wouldn't like an admirer gaining entry to the house, but the maid disabused her of this with a quick, "It's a young female person wot says she's a friend o' yers."

"A friend? Goodness!" Kitty couldn't imagine who would fit into that category, and excitedly she wondered if it could be her sister. But Lissa wouldn't call herself a friend.

"Says 'er name is Dorcas, an' she'd wait as long as needed 'til yer was woken, miss."

"Dorcas!" Kitty leaped out of bed and threw her shawl about her shoulders. "Tell her to come straight up. And bring another cup and saucer, Minnie. Dorcas!" she cried, even more excitedly when her old friend appeared in the doorway. "What are you doing here? Do tell me you're here to stay!"

Dorcas lowered her eyes, obviously nervous at the enthusiasm of her greeting. "I wills if yer'll 'ave me," she said softly. "Me bein' wot I am."

"What are you talking about?" Kitty put her arm about her friend's shoulders. "You're a far purer soul than I am. You were tricked into a life of sin. I chose it willingly."

Dorcas gave a little sob. "Yer look so pure an' beautiful wiv that golden 'air. People don't see yer as a sinner like they do me. It's true, though. I don't reckon I coulda come if yer'd been a proper married lady. Yer could no' be thinkin' o' 'irin' me if yer were that."

"But I am to be, Dorcas!" Kitty clapped her hands together and did a twirl. "Lord Nash asked me a week ago to be his wife. Can you believe it? I certainly couldn't, but it's true."

"Lawks, miss, yer don't mean it! An' there was I thinkin' yer was in love with Lord Silverton."

"Lord Silverton?" Kitty shook her head, while an uncomfortable lurch of her heart belied her response at Kitty's surprise. "Why would you imagine that?"

"Cos he's the one wot always 'elps yer an' tried ter 'elp me. Yer talk 'bout 'im with a special kind o' voice wot made me think yer were in love wiv 'im."

"He's my friend, Dorcas." Kitty forced a laugh as she poured the hot chocolate. "I'm certainly not in love with him."

"But yer like 'im well enough that yer'll come wiv me to 'is 'ouse to say thank yer ter 'im fer tryin' all them times ter get me away from Mrs. Montgomery's?"

Kitty raised her eyebrows in surprise. "I will if you want me to."

Dorcas nodded. "I want ter say thank yer, Miss Kitty. I do, that."

"Then we shall call on him sometime in the coming week, and I can tell him also about my wedding."

"Won't 'e already 'ave heard? Ain't 'e invited?"

"It's just a quiet wedding. Just Lord Nash, me and a couple of witnesses."

Dorcas narrowed her eyes as she settled herself on the edge of the bed where Kitty had waved her to sit down. "Reckon that don't sound right fer a viscount ter be marryin' in such a fashion. Mighty havey-cavey ter me, Miss, if yer don't mind me sayin' so."

"It's not a pretend wedding if that's what you think," Kitty said sharply, handing her a cup. "In fact, his sister will be one of the witnesses, and Nash said to me quite plainly that he hoped I wouldn't think it a sham, either. You see, his parents will not be happy, and his grandfather's ailing and he doesn't want to distress the old man and hasten him to his grave. So the idea is that we'll get married, and as soon as the right time comes, we'll announce it to the world."

"I don't want yer ter be tricked like I were, miss."

"I don't either, Kitty. But I have made inquiries." Kitty twisted in her chair to face her. "All I've ever wanted is to be properly married. I'm madly in love with Lord Nash, and now my dreams are about to come true."

"Wot if Lord Silverton asked yer ter be 'is wife."

"He's already said that could never be possible."

Dorcas gaped. "But if 'e did ask, would yer rather marry Lord Silverton?"

"Dorcas, is this the Inquisition? I love Lord Nash. He's the man I am destined to wed."

"Destined? I reckon yer told me that afore yer even met 'im. That yer were destined ter marry a 'andsome lord wiv a scar below 'is right eye. But I don't believe in 'em fortune-tellers. I reckon it's Lord Silverton yer wanna marry."

"Well, Lord Silverton isn't asking and Lord Nash is, and I've been sinning with Lord Nash for all the time I've been in London, so there's really no choice for me, Dorcas. Now stop all this silly talk and... " Kitty leaped up, determined to be happy, for Dorcas had dented her pleasure somewhat. "...come with me to see how my wedding dress is progressing. Oh, but I'm so delighted you're here to stay! You shall be my lady's maid, but we'll be the best of friends, and you'll come and live with me when Lord Nash can acknowledge our wedding, won't you?"

Dorcas smiled. "Course I will, miss. I'll go with yer whereva yer want me ter. I shan't forget what I owes yer."

"You don't owe me anything. And I'm dying to hear how you got out but you can tell me over ices at Gunthers. Now, call Minnie for me, will you, while I get dressed, and then she can organize a room for you to sleep. And it's too marvelous that I don't, in fact, have to be at the theater tonight."

"Could I see yer at the theater like I one day said I would?"

"Of course, you can! But I'll want to be the best I can be for the night you grace our performance with your presence." Kitty smiled, feeling happier by the minute. It was so lovely to have a friend, and she often felt lonely when Nash was out for the evening. "In fact, you can help me with my lines. I have a new part, and I'm struggling to remember the words of the scene that comes after the lovers make up. I'm not so fond of my leading man, and although that shouldn't matter to a professional, it's certainly much easier when you like the person you're pretending to make up to."

Dorcas giggled. "Yer want me to play the part o' yer leadin' man?"

"Yes, I want you to say his lines. I'm not going to kiss you, if that's what you're afraid of."

Dorcas clapped her hands and laughed. "Oh, lawks, Miss Kitty, I should 'ope not. But now yer've made me remember what it is ter feel 'appy!"

"And I'm so happy you are here, too," Kitty responded as she reached beneath her bed, then handed Dorcas a dog-eared script. "I didn't think I'd ever see you again. Lord Silverton tried so hard to get you away from Maggie Montgomery's, but it seems you worked out your contractual obligations to Mrs. Montgomery without our help."

A shadow crossed Dorcas's face and she dropped her head, prompting Kitty to say quickly, "We won't talk about it just yet if you don't want to. Now you have to forget about everything that happened in that dreadful place." She came to stand beside Dorcas and pointed over her shoulder to a place halfway down the first page. "You can read, can't you? We'll just practice a scene, and then I won't feel guilty about going out on the town with you."

But there was too much giggling and reminiscing for any worth-while practice to come out of the exercise, and soon Kitty gave up the idea in favor of ice at Gunther's followed by showing Dorcas the sights.

Her greatest pleasure, however, was taking her to see the exquisite wedding gown that was being made at a dressmaker's above a shop in Regent Street.

"What do you think?" she asked, as she stepped out in a confection of silver embroidered netting over a cream underdress with a long train, held up by the dressmaker and three assistants.

"Oh, Miss Kitty, but ain't yer a sight fer sore eyes. 'Is Lordship will think he's marryin' a fairy sprite. Ain't yer jest the most exquisite creature what ever walked the earth."

"You'll quite turn my head if you keep on in that vein. Not that my head isn't already turned the way Nash is forever complimenting me."

"So 'e's not ever done the dirty on yer again like...like when yer was so upset that time yer saw me."

Kitty couldn't meet Dorcas's eye. Remembering how he'd strayed had been the most painful experience of her young life, but not only must she forget it, she must make sure everyone else did, too. "Lord Nash made one lapse, and he says he would have sliced his wrists if he could only turn the clock back," Kitty said determinedly, her thoughts dwelling uncomfortably on his passionate avowals after she'd found him in bed with Jennie. "Since then, he has been the most true and faithful of men, and perhaps it was even a good thing for him to realize how nearly he lost me. Goodness, it's getting late. I'd better change."

"Yer was one to look on the bright side, miss, an' I'd 'ate to see yer disappointed so I'll offer me blessin', that I will." Dorcas followed her to the screen where she helped Kitty out of her gown after the dress-maker had made a few tiny adjustments. "Maybe we could stop by Lord Silverton's on our way 'ome an' let 'im know me own good news," she added hopefully.

Kitty bit her lip. Dorcas seemed very intent that they visit Lord Silverton at the earliest but Kitty wasn't at all sure that seeing him was a good idea. She knew he'd make her feel things she ought not feel and that he'd be disappointed she was marrying.

A memory of his tender, lopsided smile, the gentle pressure of his hands upon her shoulders as he enquired after her health and happiness on countless occasions, swept away all other thoughts. Silverton more than liked her. He *loved* her. A great sense of utter devastation settled upon her as she stared at her lovely wedding dress, now neatly folded by the changing screen. She didn't want to put into thoughts what she felt about him but she acknowledged that the great churning of want and need mixed a hefty dose of shame was because she was making the decision to marry Nash because marriage represented the pinnacle of her life's desires.

Not love.

Turning to Dorcas, she said in a tone of great determination, "We have a little time before we must return home. Yes, let's go and visit Lord Silverton, shall we?"

Since it was not possible to have Silverton putting her on a pedestal above all others, she'd have some pleasure in proving him wrong; reinforcing the fact that while *he* might not be prepared to marry her, Lord Nash was.

With this determining her, she and Dorcas made their way to Lord Silverton's townhouse and found him surveying the plants on his balcony. He looked up, startled, as they were announced, before hurrying across to take Kitty's hands in his, offering Dorcas a warm smile before evincing astonishment to see that she'd gained her freedom.

"My afternoon is complete," he said. "I pinked Lord Ludbridge at fencing this afternoon, and now my two favorite ladies have come to pay me a visit. When I heard Kitty announced I was going to ask to what do I owe this pleasure but seeing you, Dorcas, makes it clear that question is redundant."

He was clearly in buoyant spirits as a result of their visit, and when Kitty anxiously inquired if they were holding him up, he said he'd far rather spend the evening in their company than carousing with Lord Debenham.

"Are you and he truly such friends?" Kitty asked, screwing up her nose as they sat in a cluster of comfortable armchairs about the drawing room fire. She'd earlier gathered the courage to tell him what Dorcas had warned her about—that Debenham mistrusted Silverton —but he'd waved away her concerns, telling her all gambling men experienced ebbs and flows in their feelings toward those whom fortune favored one week, then abandoned the next.

At mention of Debenham, she now asked anxiously, "Are you certain there was nothing more sinister than that in the note Daisy found? Is it wise to continue to associate with him? Are you not afraid he'll implicate you in something dangerous or at the very least, unsavory?"

Silverton smiled warmly. "Your concern is touching, Kitty, but rest assured, we've known one another a long time, and our carousing has become habit more than anything else. Especially since Lady Debenham has been...indisposed, leaving him more than unusually to his own devices."

Tensely, Kitty said, "I hear Lady Debenham gave birth recently to a lovely baby boy. Lord Debenham must be vastly pleased." She remembered her half-sister's pain and terror the night Kitty had taken her to Mrs. Mobbs and knew how much Araminta had not wanted to go through the whole birthing process. She was glad to think that Lord Debenham might be kinder to her for giving him his heir.

But now the time had come to divulge her most important news to Silverton. She took a breath and said in a rush, "And did you know I am to marry Lord Nash?" This was the part she was afraid of. Lord Silverton would no doubt be disappointed—as she was that Lord Silverton was not prepared to back up his feelings in the way Lord Nash had.

She was correct in her assumptions. He stopped short in the middle of his sentence and stared at her. "Lord Nash has made you an offer of matrimony?" He sounded incredulous.

"He has, and before you make assumptions as to whether it is an honest offer, let me tell you that I'm not a babe in the woods, Lord Silverton. I have ensured he is true to his word. And I have verified that it is indeed to be according to the rule of law and the church, exactly a week from now."

A clock chimed in the silence somewhere far away. Kitty smoothed her skirts over her knees and wished her heart beat would return to normal.

"In that case, we will have to celebrate? Perhaps a glass of my best Madeira for you ladies?" But Silverton said it after a pause and with forced gaiety, rising with his long-legged grace to go to the sideboard.

"Wot, me too?" squeaked Dorcas in surprise as he handed her a glass.

Kitty looked at her over the top. "Of course, Dorcas. You might be my maid but you are also my friend, and I am hardly a conventional friend of Lord Silverton's. If I were a proper, respectable young lady like the one Lord Silverton was courting when we first came to London, we'd certainly not be alone with him and drinking Madeira in his drawing room." Kitty grinned at Lord Silverton. "I might not be the kind of young lady a gentleman like you can marry, but there are advantages to not being respectable if it means we can enjoy pleasant cozes like this." She turned to Dorcas. "Aren't I the luckiest girl, Dorcas? I have you, my dearest female friend in all the world back with me, and I'm drinking Madeira with Lord Silverton, my dearest male friend in all the world, and in five days' time I will be marrying Lord Nash who, like Lord Hamilton, loves me so much he is prepared to marry beneath him."

It was a small victory when Lord Silverton reacted with mild indignation. "You phrase it as if Lord Nash is somehow a better man for flouting convention, whereas I am too concerned with my own position. Kitty..." He shook his head. "If I were not so concerned for the inevitable pain it would cause so many around me, not least the children who might be born from a marriage to—"

"An illegitimate and common actress?"

"To someone not in the same social class, Kitty, that's what I meant to say, and I don't espouse such snobbery lightly. There are dynastic considerations, the well-being of my aged mother, and prospects that our children would be shunned—"

"Our children, Lord Silverton?" Kitty looked at him askance.

"For goodness' sake, Kitty, you know that if you were the daughter of…." He waved his hands in the air as he clearly sought inspiration, "Lord Partington, for example, there would be no impediment to my marrying you. But ladies like Miss Araminta Partington marry men like Lord Debenham. I am of that closely prescribed world where it is not possible to follow my heart if it will cause family disruptions, and threaten the viability of a family estate that has taken centuries and generations to build up."

Kitty's heart was still beating wildly as she answered softly, "No, you'd have stepped into Lord Nash's shoes and made me your mistress instead. But Lord Nash *is* marrying me. He's thumbing his nose at convention, and is prepared to take on the wrath of his parents and the potential opprobrium of society—"

"Please, Kitty!" Lord Silverton rose abruptly. "I'm sorry for my failings, and I'm also very happy for your good fortune, provided you are entirely sure Nash is playing an honest hand."

Kitty rose also, tears threatening and with the desire to tell him who her father was but Dorcas leaped up, intervening with, "Lord Silverton, please would yer practice a few lines with me mistress. We bin tryin' ter get it right this mornin' an' it jest won't come easy ter Miss Kitty fer she don't like her leadin' man."

Her eager entreaty defused the situation, and Lord Silverton chuckled. "I should like that very much," he agreed, adding when Dorcas thrust the script under his nose, "Well, Kitty, it looks like Dorcas has come prepared. All right, just a few lines, eh? Like in the old days." He scanned the several pages quickly, glanced at Dorcas, and said with quirked mouth, "Dorcas, perhaps you'd like to go into the kitchens, and Cook can find you something to eat."

Indignantly, Kitty put her hands on her hips and declared, "You just saw there was a…a kissing scene, my Lord, and you seek to take advantage—"

Lord Silverton raised one eyebrow. "Are you not a professional, Miss La Bijou? Surely you would not envisage me as anyone other than your counterpart in this production?"

Kitty sighed with frustration. "I told Dorcas we shouldn't come here."

He looked hurt. "You did? So it wasn't your idea to come here? Do you know how crushing that is? In that case, I insist that I oblige. You seem less than pleased with the turn the conversation has taken so I must render an honest service." His look gentled as he took a step forward and reached for her hands. In the shadows cast by the argand lamp, he looked mysterious, adoring and highly desirable. "Truly, Kitty, I am immensely pleased for you, and look forward to meeting you in fashionable drawing rooms and to dancing with you in London's finest ballrooms. I won't deny I'm mighty jealous of your Lord Nash."

"It might be a little time before we can officially announce the marriage," Kitty mumbled, awkwardly stepping back but finding her way blocked by a large potted plant. "Lord Nash's grandfather is unwell. But it will be a completely legal union," she added hastily. "You might consider me foolish and naïve, but I've made very sure it will be legal."

Silverton squeezed her hands. "I don't consider you either foolish or naïve. I'm exceedingly impressed by your determination to forge your own way in life. And I'm very happy that you and Dorcas were able to orchestrate her leaving that dreadful place when I could not, though I went to visit the old Abbess for that precise purpose, and even offered a sizeable inducement."

Kitty gasped. "*That* was the reason you were there?"

Silverton chuckled. "I do not choose to *buy* my pleasure, Kitty. No, I asked Mrs. Montgomery to name a sum to release Dorcas and she promised she would. However, I then received a letter from her, which, to my great surprise, declined my offer. She told me Dorcas was too happy in her present situation."

"Really?" She blinked. "I haven't asked her, properly, why she *was* allowed to leave. She said something about doing a favor for Mrs. Montgomery. When I pressed for more, she added that as the favor also ensured the wellbeing of someone Kitty loved very much, she agreed." Kitty raised a shoulder. "It sounded very cryptic but Dorcas refused to say more so I left it, though I do intend to discovery exactly what the favor was. We both know Mrs. Montgomery is not someone to trust."

"Indeed not! If I could, I would see her house shut down, not that it would do a jot of good. The sexual urge is a powerful one and perhaps it's better for men to take their pleasure in an establishment that offers girls some safety rather than in a lonely alley way."

Kitty's mouth dropped open.

"There, I've shocked you, and indeed that pleases me for I wanted to see what made you blush. Take it as a measure of my regard for you that I do not censor what I say to you as I would when conversing with the average debutante fare."

"But you'd never say such a thing in front of a lady?"

"You're an actress, Kitty. You've made your bed."

She nodded sadly before thrusting the script back in his face. She felt unaccountably upset and cross with the world. "I can't tarry so if you'd be so kind as to go through the next two pages, I'd be most grateful." Her curtness masked the growing pain she felt just by being in his company.

The part Lord Silverton was to play was a besotted swain who resorts to all manner of humorous and devious means to win the heart of his true love. The scene they were to re-enact placed the two of them in confrontational attitudes in the middle of a drawing room.

Lord Silverton stepped back and looked down at his script. "I believe you begin, Miss La Bijou."

Kitty, who was trying to do this without a script, threw her arms wide. "You have wounded me mortally, my Lord. Do you consider me so beneath you that you'd cast my heart to the wind?"

"Delilah, you could only make such a claim if you *had* a heart!"

"I have a heart that is full of feeling, my Lord. Feeling that you do not have, and yes, my heart has been trampled as I watch you cavort with other women."

"Cavort? That's just to make you jealous, my one true love." Silverton glanced at Kitty from above his script, took a step forward and whisked her up from the floor and into his arms. "Let me show you what love is."

Kitty protested, both as required by the script, but also because she was feeling highly self-conscious in Lord Silverton's arms, and her heart was beating far too wildly. It never did this when she was playing the role opposite Mr. Diglish.

"Put me down, cruel sir. You have no right to handle me so when you have played so unkind with me thus far."

"Only when I've kissed you, my fair Delilah. Only when you've felt the depth of my passion and can decide whether you would really cast me off, as you claim is your desire."

Kitty was about to protest that she felt it unseemly, after all, to continue, but as she opened her mouth Lord Silverton's came down swiftly, and her protest was a muffled squeak almost immediately extinguished by a sudden rush of pleasure.

This was only acting, she qualified in the brief moment she had any conscious thought as to the rights and wrongs. The woody, masculine smell of the man holding her filled her with remembered want. Just like the last time he'd held her so close, she was conscious of her mind spinning into a realm of pure pleasure, of the sense of her body going completely limp, as if she were drugged. She clasped her arms more tightly around his neck and kissed him back, while her breath ratcheted up a dozen knots, and then suddenly she was on the settee and he was over her, kissing her lips, his tongue plunging into her mouth, heightening her desire. She felt lost when he moved to kiss her jawline and throat, then exultant as he kissed her décolletage. Mindlessly, she hooked a leg over the back of his knees and arched into him just as his hand found her bare breast. She was no longer thinking. Acting her lines had turned into acting on instinct and she wanted him, needed him more than she'd ever wanted anything.

"I'm sorry, Kitty!" He stood up abruptly and stared down at her with deep contrition, his breath coming in shallow gasps as he raked his hands through his hair. "That wasn't in the script. Forgive me! I don't know what came over me."

Kitty sat up feeling dazed as she smoothed her skirts. "Nor me," she said, unable to look at him. Her heartrate was not abating and nor was her sense of distress and that terrible feeling of being out of control. She struggled for some sense of normality but there was nothing normal about the way her mind was reeling and heart felt like breaking. For no good reason she suddenly wanted to cry. "That was wrong of me, Lord Silverton. Please, pretend it never happened."

"No, No!" He shook his head and began to pace. "It was wrong of me to take such advantage. You're about to be married, and the last thing I would want is to get in the way of your life's ambition." Reaching the fireplace, he leaned against the mantelpiece where, hanging his head, he said in a low voice, "I envy Nash for having you, Kitty. I don't deny it. I've never felt what I do here—" he tapped his heart and looked her in the eye— "with any other woman. Your bright eagerness and your charming sweetness will never be dimmed, I suspect, and that is a wonderful trait." He looked so sad as he added, "I wish I was to be in Lord Nash's shoes on Saturday."

Kitty's heart felt torn in two. But this was not an offer, she realized. Lord Silverton was quite safe in saying such things.

She rose. "Don't berate yourself, my Lord. I showed my wanton nature, and that should disgust you. The trouble is, I do like you exceedingly." She smiled, still feeling tearful. "I don't think I've met a nicer man than you, but Nash loves me more. He's giving me what I want and I love him deeply, despite everything. It will be a good match, I think. And I shall enjoy dancing with you in respectable ballrooms, too. I shall enjoy gloating and will continue to hope, even, that you will come to feel you missed an opportunity for happiness when you put up all those important social considerations which are, of course, what prevented my father from marrying my mother and thus making me what I am. *Beneath* you, Lord Silverton, even if you never said it in quite those words."

She turned and took a step toward the door, but he quickly crossed the room and gripped her hand, turning her back to face him, his expression contorted with pain. "Would you really see me trade places with Nash if I had made a similar offer?"

Kitty forced herself to be insouciant. "I cannot say, my Lord, for I have not experienced the two offers to know how I would feel. But I am destined to marry Lord Nash, the dashing nobleman with the scar beneath his eye, and I love him and he loves me. I will not allow other considerations to cloud my happiness."

"Despite harboring such inconvenient feelings for me?"

"Now you are putting tickets on yourself, my Lord, for you do not know what my feelings are."

"I felt the way you responded to me." His voice sounded strangled. "I didn't have to be possessed of magical powers to know your feelings for me are very...warm."

Kitty turned with a tinkling laugh she hoped would put an end to what was becoming an uncomfortable conversation. Besides, there would be no changing the outcome. "Immaterial when you are not a contender for my affections, my Lord. No, you have made that very clear. You are very safe in espousing all that you have, for you are in no danger of ever having to act upon any of the sentiments you profess to have for me. Now, please will you pull the bell and summon Dorcas for me."

SILVERTON'S LAST IMAGE WAS FIXED IN HIS BRAIN. HER SMILE HAD BEEN bright as she'd waved to him before she and Dorcas left his townhouse to return to Kitty's abode. But her words had been loaded with portent as she'd told him, with a meaningful stare, that she must hurry if she were dress in order to receive Nash, whom she must duly honor forever more since he was prepared to defy society in order to fulfill Kitty's dreams.

Long after she'd left Silverton alone, sipping another glass of Madeira, he stared soulfully into the fireplace and wondered why he suddenly had no inclination to venture out, either in company with Debenham or to seek more preferable company at his club. He wished he could erase that image of Kitty staring hopefully into his eyes. She'd spoken defiantly of waiting to receive Nash, almost as if she were daring him to make her a better offer.

A better offer. Lord, if he only could...

Silverton shook his head and stared into his unfinished drink, touching a finger to his lips where he could still feel the sensation of her kiss; a kiss she'd tumbled into as if it had been an abyss and she'd had not been able to resist the plummet to its depths.

It had been a surprising experience for him, too. Although he'd long envied Nash and often spoke flippantly to Kitty of being prepared to offer himself up for trade with the man he regarded his rival, he'd not realized until that kiss quite how much she affected him. The more, in fact, that he dwelt on the physical reactions unleashed within him by their kiss, the more bereft he felt, knowing that the kiss would be their last.

Silverton shook his head. In just a few days, she'd be entirely another man's. The faint idea that, one day, either she or Nash might tire of the other was just a dream. Kitty was ever-faithful. She'd never leave Nash. Certainly not once she was his wife.

So now Kitty was out of reach forever and Silverton had never felt more alone. In fact, a sea of emptiness seemed to stretch before him for eternity.

Heaviness weighed down his shoulders as he opened the lid of his writing desk.

Reaching for the letter he'd received that afternoon, he scanned its few lines and wished he felt more excitement about what he had willingly pledged, if only for the sake of his ailing and insistent mama.

Dear Silverton,

Your offer was an expected surprise, if I can put it in those terms.

We have been comfortable with one another for so many years that I cannot imagine not having you in my life. Yet as your wife?

It's true that I have found myself placed in difficult circumstances suddenly, and that your marriage offer provides a multitude of conveniences for your family, for mine, and certainly for me.

But what of love? Do you love me? I would wish that you had assured me that you harbored some spark of feeling that transcended mere friendship if we were to become bound together for life.

I thank you for sounding me out on my feelings before you made a formal offer. My relatives would naturally be overjoyed at a union between our two families, and indeed it is eminently good sense.

But before I speak to them of your marriage proposal, I would ask for an avowal of the state of your heart, dear Silverton...

MISS OCTAVIA MANDELTON. HE DROPPED THE LETTER AND REFLECTED on her kind, homely face. She had a good skin; very pale, though. He did not remember the color of her eyes, and indeed would be pressed to find a complimentary name for the shade of her hair.

But she would make a good wife. Steady, loyal, and kind. Living on the neighboring estate, she was like a second daughter to Silverton's mother.

And her father had just suffered a ruinous financial setback, leaving his only child entirely vulnerable, just when Silverton was in need of a wife. Her godmother had offered her a decent-sized portion, provided she marry appropriately—meaning, of course, Silverton—and Miss Mandelton had long been suggested as a prospective bride in more than enthusiastic tones by both his parents.

Wearily, he returned the letter to his writing desk. There seemed little reason to delay with his answer. Kitty was soon to marry Nash, and he needed an antidote to the pain and disappointment he felt as a result.

Reassuring Miss Mandelton of the sincerest love he'd harbored but failed to show would be as much carrying out his duty to his family as—importantly— denying the love he felt for Kitty.

Some time later when the room was in utter darkness, he was disturbed by the noise of his butler entering with a candle, startling him when he turned in his chair.

"My Lord? Have you been waiting for a light all evening? I beg your pardon for I'd thought you'd left without telling the household."

"I've been thinking, Briggs."

"Pleasant thoughts, I hope, my Lord." His butler crossed the room to draw the curtains.

"Not at all, Briggs. The woman I love is to be married in five days' time."

"Miss Bunting."

"No, not Miss Bunting. A rather unsuitable young lady. An actress, in fact, who is to marry, rather incredibly, into the aristocracy."

"A second marriage, then?"

"No, not that, even. I think the gentleman in question must be quite mad for courting such scandal."

"You sound as if you envy him, nevertheless, my Lord."

"I do, for I've only just discovered how my heart is engaged, and tonight it would appear hers is similarly so. With me! Yet I cannot offer her what Lord Nash is offering her."

"Lord Nash? That is a surprise, my Lord."

"Yes, isn't it?"

Silverton looked up at the silence that greeted his ironic words. "Well, Briggs, aren't you going to advise me? You who have the advantage of at least three decades on me to confer the kind of wisdom my late Pater might have."

"I would never presume." Briggs sounded shocked. "But I do think the young lady who visited you earlier is very charming, and it is no surprise to hear you evince the sentiments you just have."

"So, what should I do? Offer my congratulations at their wedding and then resume my search for a wife?"

"You could...try and offer the young lady some other enticement if her heart is, as you've suggested, more engaged in these quarters, my Lord."

Since Lord Silverton couldn't offer Kitty marriage, she'd made it clear he offered *nothing* she wanted.

The reflection was excoriating but it didn't stop him being drawn back to the theater, and inviting into his box his friend, Lord

Ludbridge, and Lord Ludbridge's brother, Mr. Ralph Tunley, who arrived with Miss Hazlett. She was introduced as a distant cousin visiting from the provinces, though Silverton knew exactly who she was.

But Silverton had eyes only for Kitty. Leaning over the balcony, he watched, mesmerized and with a heart more sore than he believed it was capable of feeling, the woman who would soon become Lady Nash. She was like a breath of fresh air, her movements quick and artful, effortlessly inviting the complete subjugation of her audience. Little wonder the men adored her and the women envied her. While her pretty voice carried liltingly to the far corners of the theatre, his mind went over what might have been had she not been stained by her birth which, in his mother's eyes, precluded a union between them.

"Miss La Bijou has literally taken London by storm, has she not?" He hoped he didn't feel as lovestruck as he felt as he turned back to address his guests. In that split second, as the lamplight cast a ray across Miss Hazlett's sketch pad, he was checked by the astonishing likeness Miss Hazlett was rendering of the young woman on stage. When she looked up to find Silverton watching her, she tried to cover up the drawing with her hand, but he was too quick, saying in awed tones, "You have captured Miss La Bijou's liveliness as if you knew her intimately."

Miss Hazlett blushed. "You are very kind, sir, but there are grave deficiencies which obviously you cannot see." Nevertheless, she allowed him to take the sketch from her as he moved back to her chair at the rear of the box whereupon he held it up to the light so as to study it more closely. "And her necklace!" he exclaimed. "The detail is remarkable. There's the heart-shaped centerpiece surrounded by the cluster of diamonds. I'm told she wears this token of admiration gifted to by her husband-to-be on every possible occasion." The thought made him feel ill. He'd have been more than happy to have gifted her such tokens if he could have had her love and been allowed to look after her. "Can you really see so well from this distance?"

"Miss Hazlett has a remarkable eye for detail." Mr. Tunley sounded proud. "I'd forgotten just how clever she was. It's been too long since she visited us in London." Mr. Tunley looked indulgently at his so-called cousin and Silverton was struck by the feeling that he was surrounded by April and May and that he really was missing out. The tender smiles exchanged by the couple shared made it quite clear there were more than cousinly feelings afoot. He stared more closely at them. He could have sworn their fingers had been linked a moment before.

"Where did you say you hailed from, Miss Hazlett?"

"I'm governess to a young lady who lives in Oxford and who will be making her debut next year."

"A governess? When you could be making your name and fortune with your art?"

"I am a woman, my lord."

The way she said the words closed down the conversation but she might as well have added that participating in commerce would strip away her right to any pretentions towards respectability and that without respectability, she was nothing. No doubt it would be up to young Mr. Tunley to gather together sufficient funds to enable them to marry. That was their intention; Silverton would have to have been blind not to have seen the feeling that blazed between them. Caught in the crossfire, he only felt more bereft at what he'd allowed to have had taken from him. Yet, it was not as if he enjoyed free will. Indeed, if Silverton had not been born into a great and noble family he would have been in a position to follow his heart.

If he'd been a younger son, he would not have had the expectations that, as an eldest son, weighed upon his shoulders. If he recalled correctly, Mr. Tunley was a sixth son. Well, as Silverton was going to have to marry soon he hoped his children would be free to follow their inclinations when it came to marriage.

It was at this point that Lord Ludbridge seemed to see the sketch for the first time.

"Good Lord, she's wearing the ruby necklace!" He reached over to stab the paper before tracing the outline of the young woman's face. "May I...may I have it?" He seemed suddenly greatly agitated. "I would like to buy it from you, Miss Hazlett. Yes, indeed. You see, I'm looking for a necklace very similar to this one. You'd be doing me a great service."

A little bemused, Miss Hazlett tore off the page, and when the performance came to an end, Lord Ludbridge accompanied Silverton backstage while the others cited another engagement.

"And so you came to see me one last time." Kitty almost purred the words as she greeted him, yet there was recrimination there, too. Silverton kissed her fingertips and smiled past the stab of desire and pain. "You are so sweet, Lord Silverton." Her words were sugared and meaningless but Silverton fancied he saw hurt and disappointment behind her eyes. What could he say? That he would have married her if he'd been anyone other than a first son? "And I'm delighted to make Lord Ludbridge's acquaintance," she added, bobbing a curtsey.

"Perhaps you'd join us for supper," Silverton asked, wishing he didn't sound so hopeful. This might be the last time he'd have Kitty to himself—or without Nash—for just a couple of hours.

To his disappointment, she shook her head. "After I've changed I'm meeting Nash at Mistress Kate's for supper and dancing."

"But if you won't come out with me, I won't see you again before you and Lord Nash are married on Saturday."

"You sound so disappointed, Lord Silverton." She tapped him on the shoulder with her fan, before enveloping herself in an opera cape and donning a rakish feathered headdress and excusing herself with a nod. "Good evening, gentlemen.

"Lord Nash isn't going to escort you?"

Kitty shook her head as she turned in the doorway. "Sometimes I'm very late if Mr. Lazarus wants to rehearse parts of the play. But Madame Kate's is so close to the theater, and nobody bothers me along the way."

Silverton was shocked. "Surely you are mistaken for—"

"Oh, I give them short shrift. Don't worry, Lord Silverton. I walk through the Haymarket most nights, and nothing has ever happened."

"Well, I shall escort you tonight, Kitty. I insist."

Kitty smiled and even looked pleased, he was glad to note. She inclined her head. "I'll accept your offer, since I shall be wearing the very beautiful ruby necklace Nash gave me as a betrothal gift. Even though it won't be seen when I'm outdoors, I shall be glad of your protection." She patted her throat. "Look at the workmanship of that centerpiece ruby with the tiny clusters of diamonds all around it the heart-shaped ruby. Isn't it beautiful?"

"Who did you say gave you that necklace, Miss La Bijou?" Lord Ludbridge asked, and Kitty replied with pride and a pointed look at Silverton, "Lord Nash. He's very generous, don't you agree?"

"I say, are you feeling all right, Teddy?" Silverton asked. "Looking a bit green around the gills."

His friend reassured them he was perfectly fine before he excused himself as he was due to make an appearance at Lady Marks's Riverside Soiree, while Silverton was determined to make the most of the short time he had before Kitty met Lord Nash.

"Perhaps I could entice you to stop for a short while to share a drink with me, Kitty," he entreated. "In case you didn't hear me say it before, this might be the last time I see you before you are married, and there's something I'd like to ask you."

She stopped amid the milling crowds on a corner beneath a lamp above which flapped a sign for a tavern called *The Green Frog*. "That's far too enticing, Lord Silverton, so I'll have to decline. You can say what you need to say, here."

"Enticing? Is that what you said? Too enticing to spend time with me, yet you use that as a reason *not* to spend what I'd intended to be a very special moment together, Kitty?"

"Of course, my Lord. You want to persuade me not to marry Lord Nash, and perhaps you'll even kiss me, and I really shan't like that because the other night just reminded me how very much I like kissing you, and I can't be reminded of such things when I'm to marry Nash."

"How can you marry Lord Nash if you have feelings for me, Kitty?"

Kitty shrugged. "Perhaps, if you were courting Miss Bunting and hoping to make her your wife because she was a perfect candidate, you might still have preferred the idea of kissing me; yet obviously Miss Bunting offered what you felt you wanted and needed."

She started walking again, and Silverton had to lengthen his stride to keep up. The evening was thronged with people of all walks of life, the air crisp and cold and suddenly Silverton had never felt more alive, walking beside the incomparable Miss Kitty La Bijou.

"Kitty!" In a burst of feeling, he gripped her hand and swung her around to face him. "What you said was all but telling me you prefer me to Nash."

She put her head on one side. "I believe I intimated that I *did* prefer you to Nash." She sent him another of her engaging, beatific smiles. "But I like Nash very much, and Nash is making me an offer that will give me my heart's desire." She held out her hand and tapped her betrothal ring. "Marriage. Security. To a man who pleases me very much, and has the power to make me happy for the rest of my days."

"Please tell me you accept he's not the man foretold as your destiny by the gypsy fortune-teller?"

Kitty chuckled. "I was rather fanciful for rather a long time. No, I don't believe in that sort of thing anymore, though it was good fortune I did when I met Nash otherwise things would never have developed the way they have."

"Perhaps if you hadn't persisted with your fanciful beliefs for so long we would have been together, Kitty."

She shrugged. "Then I'd not be contemplating the happiest day of my life in three days' time."

"The happiest moment of *my* life was when you said you preferred me to Nash."

"Please let me go, Lord Silverton; people are staring."

Silverton dropped his arm, and Kitty carried on walking. "You don't seem to understand me, my Lord. The happiest day is destined to be the one where I gain what has been denied me from birth —respectability."

"Oh, Kitty, Kitty, we *could* be so happy together!" Silverton urged. "Forget Nash. Come and live with me. I'll make his generosity pale into insignificance compared with the...ruby and diamond necklaces, gowns, and carriages I'll shower upon you."

"As your mistress?" She shook her head. "Goodnight, Lord Silverton. Now, please leave. I am nearly at Mistress Kate's, and I do not want Nash to observe you following me."

CHAPTER 21

Surrounded by a throng of well-dressed revelers in the riverside tent, Araminta stared across the rippling water where a barge was anchored ready to deliver its colorful fireworks display later in the evening. She shivered. Not from the cool breeze that had sprung up, making this evening considerably colder than that fateful evening when Lord Ludbridge had proposed in the rotunda on the hill a few hundred yards away, but from anticipation of how she and Lord Ludbridge might come to a new understanding.

Debenham had been out all day—gaming, she had no doubt. Once, this would have made Araminta furious, but tonight it was marvelously convenient. Debenham hadn't inquired where she'd be, so it had been easy to slip away to Lady Marks's riverside entertainment and assume he'd not bother to follow. When various admiring gentlemen stopped to pay their respects, she'd pretended her husband was somewhere in the crowd.

She touched one of the colored lanterns which festooned the tent like a Persian Alhambra and wondered what might have delayed her darling Teddy. Her anticipation was at fever pitch, so when someone touched her shoulder and she discovered only Mr. Woking profering a choice of claret or Madeira, she bit back her irritation and chose the latter with ill grace. Draining her wine quickly, she immediately felt another bolstering draft would be very nice but Mr. Woking was staring at her with his usual bovine adoration. Well, that's how he usually looked at her but tonight she caught something else in his tone when he murmured, "All alone, Lady Debenham? Where is that reprobate uncle of mine when you need him, eh?"

Araminta sent him a narrowed look, as she tried to interpret whether he'd spoken mockingly or with genuine sympathy. Surely, despite his supposed disappointment when she'd reneged on her agreement to marry him the very night of Lady Marks's last entertainment, he didn't still harbor a grudge? She glanced about her, assessing the competition. Aside from a sprinkling of fresh-faced debutantes, there were few to rival Araminta in beauty, which gave her a surge of gratification, and she said airily, "I expect he'll arrive when he pleases. He does like to keep his eye on me, Mr. Woking. Who is that young lady staring at us? See, over in that corner."

Mr. Woking turned, squinted, then raised one eyebrow. "Miss Lucinda Martindale, Lord Beecham's ward. I didn't think she was officially 'out.'" He sent the young lady who was quite conspicuous with her bright, golden ringlets and her pretty, petite figure, a lavish bow, muttering under his breath. "I wonder who is chaperoning her. I believe she's gone through five governesses in the past two years. Miss Hazlett is no doubt having her work cut out."

"Did you say Miss Hazlett?" The name of Araminta's illegitimate half-sister amid this gathering of gentry was somehow shocking. "I thought she worked for the Lamonts. Or, rather, she did."

"That's right, but now she is Miss Martindale's governess. Speaking of the Lamonts, there's Miss Maria Lamont over there, which means her brother is about, and he owes me a pretty sum."

"Oh, you men and your love of gaming. I wish Debenham weren't so fond of it. Excuse me, Mr. Woking. Someone is beckoning to me."

Relieved to at last see the object of her desire, Araminta turned her back on the young man and hurried across to the doorway through which Lord Ludbridge had just entered, alone. His eyes lit up when he saw her, but though her own were dancing with invitation, Araminta put her fingers to her lips.

"At last, you have arrived, my dear Lord Ludbridge," she murmured, holding up her fan to shield her excitement from others. "I've been in a fever of anticipation to see you again."

"And I, you, Lady Debenham, for I have just come from the theatre and—well, it's the most extraordinary thing, but I've found your ruby necklace."

"You have?" Araminta's smile spread and her heart pounded as she imagined Lord Ludbridge, later this evening, holding up her hair from behind and fastening the catch over her naked throat during their forthcoming tryst. "Oh, Lord Ludbridge," she breathed, "you are my hero, and I intend to reward you. You have it with you?"

"Alas, I have not yet secured it, for it was being worn by a very beautiful actress, the much-celebrated Miss Kitty La Bijou, whom we both saw in *Romeo and Juliet* several months ago." He thrust out his hand, and she gasped to see the expertly rendered sketch which so clearly identified her necklace, though she noticed Miss La Bijou's head had been torn away—something she suddenly felt like doing with her own hands to the young lady, right at this moment. Her own throat suddenly was very dry and she felt light-headed with fear as she contemplated the possible ramifications. Miss La Bijou lodged with Mrs. Mobbs. Had she stolen Araminta's necklace? "Miss Kitty La Bijou? How is that possible?"

"Ah, Lady Debenham, Lord Ludbridge. I'm so glad you both have graced my entertainment with your presence." In a rustle of silk, their hostess sidled up to them. She smiled warmly at each, beckoning over a servant to refill their glasses. "I promise the fireworks will surpass even those of last time but, alas, I do not see Lord Debenham. Will he be attending?"

"I do hope so," Araminta lied smoothly. "He had other claims on his time, alas. An important parliamentary dinner." Her heart fluttered at the reminder of Lady Marks's last riverside extravaganza. Well, a lot of water had passed under the bridge and right now Araminta was just as desperate to be properly reunited with her darling Teddy as she had been then.

She was about to turn back to Lord Ludbridge in order to prettily request his gallant company up the hill, when, to her chagrin, his attention was claimed by a garrulous matron and her simpering charge who swept by in a blur of waving ostrich feathers.

Meanwhile, Lady Marks was similarly waylaid, and while Araminta could have been included in the discussion, she chose to absent herself momentarily so she could put her best-laid plans into action. Perhaps it was better that Lord Ludbridge not be seen in company with her during a walk. One during which she intended to lead him up the hill to the rotunda. Silently congratulating herself on her cleverness, she withdrew from her reticule the discreet note she'd written earlier that evening, and put out her hand to waylay a bewigged footman on his return from supplying a garrulous group with more champagne.

"I need you to give this to that gentleman over there," she said, handing the note to the waiter and pointing to Lord Ludbridge. "The tall, fair-haired gentleman beneath the gold lantern."

"The one standing beside the gentleman with whiskers, ma'am?"

"That is correct."

Assured that the recipient had been properly identified, and reassured that the nature of the note was cryptic enough that it would cause no damage if perchance it fell into the wrong hands, Araminta sent a final seductive glance in Lord Ludbridge's direction before leaving the tent for the welcoming fresh air.

She knew from before that it was not a long or onerous climb to reach the top of the hill where the enclosed rotunda perched with its magnificent river views.

Jane had again reported that access was easily gained; that the window seats were still lined with comfortable cushions, and that the door was unlocked. Now Araminta would simply avail herself of a hanging lantern, and take a short detour around the back of the entertainment in order to be hidden from general view as she made her ascent. Her evening slippers were made of silk so she removed them when she was out of sight, but the ground was soft, and it was no hardship to gain the sanctuary of her enclosed rotunda though she was breathless from the exertion by the time she hooked the lantern on the rafter by the entrance.

Soon she and Teddy would be as one—just as they should have been almost a year ago. Her hear skittered as she slipped inside to wait, hoping it wouldn't be long before Teddy could make his escape from the dreadful feathered ladies. Even though the note was cryptic, she'd made it quite plain where she wanted to meet, and the gleam in his eye had assured her that he was as desirous as she that they repeat their union of eight months before.

This time with a different conclusion.

The cool air from the river wafted beneath the now closed door and swirled around the room, making her even more anxious to feel Teddy's arms about her as she stood in the centre of the room. If she couldn't have Teddy as a husband, she was determined to enjoy him as a lover. Besides, he'd located the ruby diamond necklace, and soon he would retrieve it for her, perhaps returning it with the letter. He'd promised her both, after all, and she'd promised him his reward.

For a brief moment she considered delaying the seduction she had in mind until all her aims had been achieved, but since that would mean denying herself as much as Teddy, she thought she could allow a little latitude. The truth was—even despite the cool air—she was hot and hungry to feel his arms about her and to revel in the slickness of their naked skins as they writhed in mutual passion. Just thinking about it made her squirm, so that when she heard the soft crunch of footsteps upon the gravel just beyond the steps that led up to the portico, she was consumed by the most intense rush of desire she'd ever experienced.

Quickly, she arranged herself in an artfully seductive pose, half reclining upon the red-velvet upholstered banquette, one knee bent and her skirt rucked up, discreetly, but with a flash of stocking top and bare thigh above. She'd have liked to have removed her gown altogether and simply thrown herself into his arms, but Teddy was a man of restraint. His gentlemanly doctrine had held fast in the face of her womanly enticements the night he'd asked for her hand in marriage. Foolish, foolish man!

Well, she'd forgiven him now. And she needed him as much as she did then. Only this time, for herself. She put her hands to her heated cheeks, then to the rise and swell of her bosom, cupping her breasts and dipping her head in coquettish invitation as the door was slowly, tentatively opened.

Her breath caught in her throat, and she felt the rush of moisture between her legs and a whirl of mindless wantonness that left her giddy and dazed.

And then her head cleared, as if cold water had been poured over her. Horrified, she beheld the beak-nosed, oafish face of Mr. Woking, peering owlishly into the gloom.

"Mr. Woking!" Araminta shrieked as he stepped inside. He blinked as if caught by surprise, but closed the door behind him nevertheless.

"Get out this instant! What are you doing here?"

At her shrillness, he seemed to gather his wits, stepping across the stone floor, one hand extended and holding, Araminta now saw, a piece of parchment.

"Thief!" she cried, lunging forward to try to snatch the note she'd written to Teddy, but at the last moment, Mr. Woking put it away.

"Who is the thief?" He thrust forward his receding chin as he put his hands on his hips and looked pointedly from her face to her mid-region. "My uncle is the thief, though he does not know it. Yes, the thief of *my* baby!"

Araminta took a couple of shaky steps backward and shook her head. "Of course, it's not your baby," she muttered, her hands nevertheless fluttering to her stomach, as she thought of how the baby Mr. Woking claimed to have fathered had already been lodged in her belly for more than a month the night she seduced him. Not that he could ever know that. No one ever must. Especially not her husband.

"Does my uncle know that you and I had intimate relations the night before you eloped? And that's putting it delicately." He edged a little closer, his eyes pinpricks of spite. "Does he?"

"You are bosky, Mr. Woking. You don't know what you're talking about."

"I don't?" He gave a little hiccup, while Araminta tried to push away the awful memory of how she'd been forced to such extremes after she'd gained access to his townhouse, and of their grubby ten-second exchange of bodily fluids.

She closed her eyes and tried not to scream. No, she needed to be as clearheaded as she could, for Mr. Woking was not thinking like a rational human being. Certainly not like a gentleman, and the lascivious way his gaze raked her from head to toe was making her increasingly anxious.

"I don't know what I'm talking about, you say?" His breathing came fast and furious now. "You wanted me for your husband because of my prospects, and you thought you'd not win a viscount—my uncle, to be precise. You wanted to be Lady Debenham—didn't you—only my uncle wasn't interested, initially. So why did Debenham have to use trickery to win an acceptance of his so-called marriage offer?" He made a sweeping gesture along the banquette, picking up her reticule as he answered his own question. "I don't think he did. I think you saw your chance, and you threw yourself upon him in just the same way you did me, so when he came up with a counter-offer, you thought he was a better prospect than me, didn't you?" He gave an ugly laugh, and took an unsteady step toward her, fumbling with her reticule at the same time, loosening the drawstring and dipping his hand inside. "Pity you didn't factor in the death of two cousins that now give me greater precedence over my uncle, and surely a bitter irony for you since *surely* you can't prefer Debenham over me." He shrugged, his mouth an ugly trembling line as he looked at her the same time as he withdrew the contents of her reticule. "So what do you keep in here, my lovely Lady Debenham? Notes for all your lovers? Is there a token for me? And what is this?"

"Give it back. It's...nothing!" Araminta tried to snatch the small vial from his hand, but Mr. Woking pulled the stopper, laughing as the tiny Queen's Anne Lace seeds scattered about the room. "Fairy dust? Is this how you bewitch us men?" He tossed the glass bottle and her reticule back onto the banquette and his shoulders slumped, his voice breaking as he went on, "The truth is, Miss Partington, that I still prefer you over all other contenders. I pine for you. Day and night. Your image fills my dreams, and sometimes I wake, trembling with desire for a woman I can never have. A woman who tricked me after using me most shamefully. Now it seems the woman I love is still not satisfied." With a shuddering sigh, he withdrew her note from his waistcoat pocket where he'd shoved it a moment ago, and waved it in front of her face. "Well, now it's time for this woman I love to satisfy me just a little. I need her to do something for me. Something that will help ease my nightmares."

He put out his hand and touched the festooned sleeve of Araminta's evening dress. "You recoil? Do I disgust you so much?" His lips curled. "Take off your gown."

Araminta gasped. "How dare you, Mr. Woking? I will not."

"Take it off and I won't touch you."

"What?"

"Just do as I say. You can trust me as a man of honor."

"A man of honor does not ask an unwilling lady to remove her gown."

"A lady of honor does not flaunt her body and her wares and then run away without following through on her original intent. Go on! Take it off. Turn around and I'll undo the buttons at the back."

For a moment, Araminta considered fleeing except Mr. Woking was blocking the door and she knew he'd be too fast and probably tear her gown in the process. She was fearful but she was not terrified. Mr. Woking was pathetic; he was not a rapist and she doubted he would be violent.

Hoping she could take him at his word, Araminta turned her back, her skin crawling at the feel of his fingers fumbling with her buttons.

"Now take it off. Since I've given you my word of honor I won't touch you, you need to take it off yourself."

It was hard to control her breathing, she was so furious at this indignity. She swung round. "I will not!" she hissed.

"Then I will tell Debenham the truth about the night you threw yourself at me when I brought you to my townhouse. You wanted a husband and you'd had no success finding one. The season was winding down and you decided that having me as a husband would be better than having no husband at all." He waved his finger at her as he tried to focus through his bleary gaze. "The maids were listening at the key hole. They'll lend their testimony. So if you want me to remain close-lipped, do as I say and take off your dress."

Defeated, Araminta pulled her dress over her head and dropped it onto the floor, where it pooled into a puddle of silk. Turning, her expression blazing, she stamped her foot but was silent.

"Now your petticoat."

Araminta's mouth dropped open but, after a great show of reluctance, she did as he requested. Mr. Woking wanted to humiliate her. Well, let him have his sport. She was helpless, but while she would remove her gown, she would go no farther.

"Your stays, my lady? Go on. Unlace those. Do it slowly, so that I might see better. I want to gaze upon you as I do every night in my dreams. That's right. And now your chemise."

"What?" Revulsion crawled up her gullet. She swung round towards the door. Where was Teddy? Even if he hadn't received the note, surely she'd given him enough hints that this is where she'd be?

"Your chemise. I want to see your skin glow like alabaster in the lamplight. One glimpse will satisfy and in return I shall stay silent."

Araminta glared. Silence echoed around them. Ominous and close. There was no one to render her assistance.

"Take it off, Lady Debenham," he whispered. "That's if you want your secret to remain with me."

With trembling fingers, Araminta did as she was bid, thrusting out her chin in angry defiance as the last of her coverings, save her stockings, slithered to the ground.

"Exquisite." He clasped his hands together as if in supplication but his appreciation was no panacea for the fury she felt. "Now raise your arms above your head and turn around."

Mr. Woking advanced, his breath coming in short bursts, almost as if he were trying to hold back sobs. "Stop. Stay where you are. I want to savor this moment." Slowly he began to circle her, reaching out, almost trailing his hand over her skin, but not quite touching her. His eyes were glazed with rapture.

A bird startled in the eaves and Araminta jumped. Teddy? She wasn't sure if she wanted him to come and rescue her, or whether there would be too much to explain and it was best to get this over with and pretend it had never happened.

"Even after the birth of my child, you are every bit as beautiful as I remember. Dear Lord, Araminta, you truly are...exquisite." He blinked rapidly.

In the rays of moonlight that filtered through the diamond-paned windows, Araminta saw that he was crying. Horrified, she watched as he dropped to his knees, his arms encircling her as he buried his face in her belly and wept. "I loved you, Araminta. I'd have gone to the ends of the world and back to have made you mine. But you betrayed me. Betrayed me with my uncle who now calls himself the father of my child."

"It's...it's not your child."

He raised his tortured gaze to hers. "How do you know that? It is *impossible* to know that since you slept with me one night and my uncle the next and nine months later bore a child. But I was first, Araminta. *That* is what I base my belief upon. I was your first lover, and I should have been your husband." He pushed his head into the softness of her belly once more and inhaled deeply. "You smell so good, Araminta. God, you do not know what this restraint costs me."

He struggled to his feet, his arousal quite apparent and, gasping she covered her face with her hands as she turned away.

"There's no need to make your aversion quite so plain." He sounded wounded. "Though once it was different. Once I was the man you sought in the most unladylike fashion. And so it is time for me to leave you—" he moved in front of her, stooping to pick up her gown which he draped over his arm— "in a most unladylike fashion."

IN THE DEATHLY SILENCE AND BONE-CHILLING COLD, ARAMINTA LOOKED at the door but did not move. She was trapped, and she had no idea what to do. Yes, she was free to leave, but Mr. Woking had taken her ball gown, and a lady in chemise and petticoat—since he'd at least left her those— could go nowhere.

After a few minutes of frantic dashing from one side of the room to the other, turning over cushions in the hope something would yield inspiration as to how to extricate her from this nightmare, she collapsed onto the banquette, sobbing.

How could her husband's own nephew humiliate her so? One day, she would find a means to take her revenge, and she would take great pleasure in plotting the villain's downfall, but right now, Araminta was at the complete mercy of fate.

And that arrived in the form of more crunching footsteps preceding the arrival of another visitor.

Lord Ludbridge? She prepared to throw herself into his arms and beg his help, telling him she'd been the victim of a vagrant woman who'd threatened her and stolen her clothes.

He would believe her, understand her fright, and seek to comfort her.

And even if he'd abandoned her eight months ago, right now just when she needed him most, at least he was here *now*—her knight in shining armor, coming to her rescue.

The footsteps drew closer, the tap of leather upon the polished marble portico stairs sending Araminta's heart into freefall. Soon he would enfold her in his arms. She could drown in the sensation of finally being united in body and soul with the man she loved. Yes, it was a concern that the Queen Anne's Lace seeds that Mrs. Mobbs told her she must take to prevent conception were now scattered to the winds. Yet surely she could not be so unlucky that a child would result from the encounter she was anticipating so fervently when it was only six weeks after the birth of her child? Somehow she'd indicate her desire that he withdraw early before he spilled his seed. The idea of another pregnancy horrified her, even if it was a consequence of making love with the one true man she'd ever met.

The doorknob turned. She put her hand to her heart and drew in a shaking breath as slowly, on creaking hinges, the door opened. Teddy was coming to her at last and his love and kindness and belief in her would make up for all the trauma and horror she'd endured, now with Mr. Woking, and during all the months of her hateful marriage.

"What a sight for sore eyes," came a low growl, full of desire. "Well, well, you said you'd signal to me when the time was right, but I have to give you full marks, my darling, for being so creative."

It was too dim to make out from this distance who the speaker was, but the salacious tone did not belong to Teddy; she knew that much.

Araminta forced herself not to scream. "Debenham?"

"My good nephew gave me your note." He chuckled as he strode forward, already loosening his stock, his eyes gleaming, satyr-like. "I must say, he looked rather dark when he thrust it without a word into my hand as I passed him near the riverside tent. I asked him if he'd seen you. He said the note would explain everything."

Debenham stopped in the middle of the floor and looked her up and down with great appreciation. He resembled a raven with his black eyes glinting in the moonlight and his dark clothing worn with such sartorial elegance relieved only by the snowiest of white linen at his throat. "I thought you'd lost your appetite for bedroom sport, Araminta, but now I find you in a greater fever to have me than I'd expected so soon after your confinement." He chuckled again before repeating the words she'd written in her note: 'Meet me in the rotunda on top of the hill as soon as you get this. I am ready.' Well, there's nothing cryptic about that, is there? Couldn't have made it any plainer, my dear, and I am glad for it. I like a wife who knows what she wants and isn't ashamed to say it. Now, come to me."

He held out his arms and, forcing a smile, Araminta ran her sweating palms down her petticoat and advanced toward him.

"Ah, what a woman," Debenham murmured into her hair as he wrapped his arms about her. Holding her tightly, his exploring hands roamed over her flanks, her bosom, pressed against her mound. Such fondling clearly fueled his own arousal which Araminta could feel pressing into her belly.

Without a word, he bent and grasped the hem of her petticoat, whipping it upward and over her head. Nimbly, he unlaced her stays, and within seconds, her chemise joined the tumble of clothes upon the ground. For the second time that night, Araminta stood naked, feeling even more vulnerable than she had when Mr. Woking had sized her up like a fox his prey, though her aversion had a different motivation. She'd felt she could control Mr. Woking. With her husband, that was not the case.

Fortunately, Debenham had not noticed the absence of her ball gown. What had Mr. Woking done with it? Its light, flimsy fabric meant it could be rolled into mere nothingness. Had he tossed it away outside somewhere nearby or had he taken it with him?

She shook her head, closed her eyes and tried to banish the thought. She could not worry about that now. Her first concern must be pleasing her husband, and she would need to do that thoroughly to shore up his goodwill toward her in the hopes of averting any difficult questions when he left her.

Twining her arms about his neck, she pressed her naked body suggestively against his, then trailed one hand down his hard chest to massage his groin.

"Oh, I am more than ready, my husband," she purred, gyrating against his erection. "I do love an intelligent man. I wondered if you'd be clever enough to find me." She buried her head against his chest and inhaled the aroma of arrack, sweat, and leather while she allowed him access to her body. He was clearly enjoying the novelty of her nakedness, standing in a foreign location. His hands roamed over her body, his fingers twining themselves in the thatch of hair at the juncture of her legs. Araminta groaned softly. She must throw herself into this with all the enthusiasm of which she was capable. Debenham was her husband, and as he'd reminded her earlier, she was utterly reliant on him. This little episode might help ameliorate his mood if she remained unable to present him with the ruby necklace.

"I was surprised you entrusted such a wicked little note to my nephew," he murmured, tickling her ear with his tongue, "though, no doubt, taunting him was part of the pleasure for you, my dear girl. I know you too well." He chuckled as he pinched her nipple. "Taunting him with what he can never have. I'm surprised you're not concerned he might be peeping through the windows and watching us from the darkness?"

Araminta gave a low, throaty laugh. "And would that be so terrible? Surely you'd want to show him how a real man conducts maneuvers, Debenham darling."

To her surprise, Debenham burst out laughing. "You are full of surprises, Lady Debenham." He whisked her into his arms and strode across to the banquette where he laid her over the cushions before quickly divesting himself of his clothes.

"Tell me, is this one of the pleasures you've been so eager to taste, dear heart?" he asked when he was stark naked and his enormous member was thrust under her nose. "Ah yes." He closed his eyes and exhaled on a sigh of rapture as Araminta took him into her mouth. He was huge and eager as he rammed himself down her throat, but it occurred to her that she might just satisfy him this way rather than risk an unwanted pregnancy if his desire for rutting ran the full gamut.

He adjusted his position to give her deeper access, standing above her, while she lay on her back upon the banquette, pleasuring him, massaging his shaft, doing what she must to satisfy her husband in the hope he'd drain his seed other than inside her. His breath was coming deeper and more rapidly as his thrusting grew more urgent. Araminta felt no desire for similar satisfaction. She wanted only to urge him on to climax so she could escape. Or so he could leave, sated, and she could find a means of sneaking away in the darkness, possibly avoiding detection.

"And now for the grand finale!"

Unexpectedly he withdrew, fell upon her, prized her legs apart and plunged himself deep inside her, gasping in the throes of ecstatic ejaculation.

Horrified, Araminta stared above his shoulder, into the gloom of the room as Debenham had his fill of pleasure, before he went limp on top of her.

After a few minutes, he raised himself, his eyes gleaming. "That was good, wasn't it, my sweeting?" he growled. "Just what you've been waiting for with growing impatience?" He rolled onto his side and grinned. "Couldn't afford to arouse you too much and have your shrieking bring the rest of them away from the fireworks. I'll save that for round two later tonight, now that I've been reminded of how damned good you are in bed." At the sound of a loud bang outside, he sat up. "The fireworks have begun...for the rest of the party, that is, eh, my love?" he quipped.

Araminta hoped his good humor would last. She pressed her lips together in a smile and nodded as she rose, but drew back when he extended his hand with the invitation they join the rest of the party.

He looked about to press her when his attention was suddenly diverted.

"What's this?"

Araminta looked up and saw he held the sketch Teddy had given her earlier that evening and which Mr. Woking must have removed from her reticule.

His eyes widened. "Good God, that woman is wearing your ruby necklace." His brow furrowed as he turned to Araminta, silently demanding understanding.

"Debenham, I'm not sure what to do!" Fearfully, Araminta stabbed her finger in the direction of the picture. "You see, it's gone missing. I didn't know how to tell you, but I've put the word about, and now I've received this." She swallowed, truly afraid that Debenham would angrily consider Araminta was in the wrong or would not believe her. "It was stolen...several weeks ago...and now I've just received this together with a demand for money. No, not the full amount, because whoever did this knows I do not have that kind of money, and besides, it's too distinctive for them to sell it easily."

"Someone's blackmailing you?" His anger was more explosive than she'd expected and to her surprise, he gripped her shoulders and pulled her against him, as he repeated, "Someone dares to blackmail *Lady Debenham*? My wife?"

Araminta nodded. "Yes," she whispered, shuddering as she began to cry, this time for real. "I just didn't know how to tell you, Debenham. I thought I could get it back without you knowing, so you wouldn't be angry with me."

"Angry with you?" He held her at arm's length, his scowl fueling her terror, before he brought his mouth down on hers in a deep, almost satisfying kiss for the fact that it was clear his desire for her was much greater than his anger. "No, my love, my anger is reserved for whoever is behind this, and by God, they will be made to pay. No one steals from or blackmails a Debenham! Now, come my love, and let us return to the entertainment." He folded the sketch and put it in his pocket. "Don't you fret about unpleasant matters such as this. You can rest assured that I will take care of it." Once more, his eyes roamed over her body with salacious appreciation. "By God, Araminta, I'd forgotten how you could fire me up."

Araminta managed a more robust smile this time for his lack of direct anger towards her regarding the loss of her necklace was some solace. She prayed he'd not pry too closely and discover the reason behind it changing hands but at least Araminta knew into whose possession the necklace had fallen and that Teddy was on the case to get it back for her. "I knew I could depend upon you, my darling. I should have gone to you straight away." She sighed and stared wistfully out of the window. "What a wonderful sight it is, the stars and the fireworks. I want to stay here longer and reflect upon the pleasure we've just enjoyed. You go back if you wish, and I shall join you later."

Finally, she persuaded him to return without her, and to her relief, he left without argument.

As the door closed behind him, and in the wake of no uncomfortable questions regarding clothing—or the lack of it—Araminta lay back against the cushions now in disarray upon the red-velvet banquette. With a sigh of fear and despair, she wondered how she would get herself home and into the house with no questions asked.

But that was only part of her problems tonight.

How had Miss La Bijou come into possession of her necklace?

And what did she know of the circumstances regarding its departure from Lady Debenham's custody?

Would there be further desperately uncomfortable questions Araminta would be forced to answer before she could finally breathe freely again?

CHAPTER 22

*I*t was almost a relief to Araminta that her parents made an unexpected visit to London, visiting her the following day. She needed something to deflect Debenham, though, thank the Lord, she'd found her ballgrown thrust into a bush near the doorway to the rotunda. It was clean and undamaged so she'd managed to return to the riverside tent looking as elegant and unruffled as she had when she'd arrived. As Debenham had gone to her immediately, Araminta was glad she'd not caught sight of Lord Ludbridge amongst the guests in the tent. Today, she was sure, he'd be visiting Miss La Bijou to retrieve her necklace.

"Are you all right, Araminta dearest?" Lady Partington sent a concerned look in her daughter's direction as she raised her head from her embroidery. The weather was gray and dull today, and Lord and Lady Partington had settled themselves comfortably in her drawing room, as if they had no intention of leaving for a week. "Don't you think Araminta is looking peaky today?" She turned to her husband for consensus, and Araminta had to hold her tongue so as not to snap that it was unlikely Lord Partington would remember what his daughter looked like. He'd been absent so much of the time she was growing up, and only recently had she learned it was because he favored his 'other family.' With the maturity she'd gained since she'd been married, she felt a fool, now, for not having understood earlier the dark desires that drew her father away from his marital responsibilities.

Even when Araminta had returned to The Grange on her recent visit, he'd barely spent a night at home, and several times she'd seen him in a carriage with a rather plain, serious-faced, middle-aged woman whom Araminta presumed was his mistress—the solicitor's daughter he'd initially intended to marry.

Araminta put down the lid of the piano with a clatter and sighed, "Really, Mama; it's nothing!"

"Nothing? When you say it like that?" Her father put down his newspaper and regarded her closely. "Tell us what is troubling you, Araminta. Your mother is right. You've been as restless as a gypsy this whole morning. I'm sure it can't be that young William is cutting a tooth since you've not seen him in two days."

"Are you suggesting I lack a mother's concern?" Araminta sent him a challenging look. "Besides, how would you know how many times I've been to the nursery?"

"Now, now, Araminta, you don't talk back to your father like that," admonished her mother while her father added, warningly, "For someone who likes to be lavished with fine clothes and jewels, I hope you accord your husband greater respect than you just have your father."

"Debenham has hardly showered me with jewels and fine clothes," Araminta muttered.

"What about that exquisite ruby and diamond necklace he gave you on your wedding day?" her mother remarked. "I've never seen anything so exquisite but nor have I seen you wearing it, lately."

Araminta did not want to be reminded of that right now but her mother went on, "In fact, I saw that actress, Kitty La Bijou, wearing a piece very similar when I attended the theatre with Lady Wilson the other night. I wondered if she'd had it copied."

Araminta's mouth dropped open as her mind went over a suitable response. She noticed that her father's head had jerked up and that he was regarding the two of them with tense interest.

"Is that the truth, mama? Well, let me tell you something..." She drew in a breath ready to concoct something to preserve a necessary fiction. "Debenham took it to pay a gambling debt, though please don't reveal this. He told me it had been stolen, but I know the truth. Perhaps he gave it to Miss La Bijou." She looked suitably distressed, though that wasn't hard. In fact, she was sick with fear at what might transpire once the necklace was returned, as it soon must be. Her greatest hope was that Lord Ludbridge would meekly pay to get it back from that silly actress, though there was some solace in the fact she perceived Miss La Bijou was really quite kind and well-meaning. What Araminta feared most was that questions would be asked of Miss La Bijou if Debenham got to her first.

She pressed on with her version. "A pretty pass it is when a respectable and virtuous viscount's wife sees her hard-earned jewels worn by such common gutter fodder. Kitty La Bijou wearing Lady Debenham's wedding necklace *on stage*."

Araminta was surprised and buoyed up by her father's reaction. She'd not expected he'd be so sympathetic to her cause; in fact, he was looking virtually apoplectic on her account.

"Kitty La Bijou?" he now repeated.

"That's right. Perhaps you saw her in *Romeo and Juliet*. She's like a lovely piece of Dresden china with that golden hair, but she'll be raddled and washed-up by the time she's twenty-five."

Lady Partington sent a worried look at her husband, dropping her wooden frame in her lap after grazing her finger with her embroidery needle. "Are you all right, my dear?"

"Kitty La Bijou is...an actress?"

Araminta tilted her head. "I'm surprised you've not heard of her since she's so frequently lauded in the gossip sheets. She's very popular." Araminta sniffed. "But you don't read the gossip sheets, do you, Papa? And you rarely come to London. But, somehow, this Kitty La Bijou has come into possession of my necklace, and no doubt she intends to wear it when she weds Lord Nash on Saturday. She's taunting me. I think Debenham gave it to her."

"Kitty La Bijou is marrying Lord Nash on Saturday? My old friend, Monty's son?"

Araminta saw that her father had gone almost purple in the face. "Oh, so you know his family, do you? But, of course you do. So, how Lord Nash can be allowed to marry so unsuitably is quite beyond me. Really, I don't care who marries whom, but I do think it unconscionable that a guttersnipe should be allowed to get away with possessing the necklace that was given to *me*, and something is going to be done about it; I promise you." Araminta raised the lid of the piano and played a few crashing chords for emphasis. "Debenham has not treated me well, I'm afraid, Papa, but I earned that necklace, and I'm going to get it back."

Her father had risen but seemed unable to move. He stared at Araminta with an odd look in his eye. "You say that your ruby necklace, a Debenham family heirloom, has been taken from you without your consent and you accuse this...actress...Kitty La Bijou...of stealing it?"

"I'm not saying *she* stole it, necessarily," Araminta said, but with less conviction than before for she had the strangest sense that her father knew something she didn't. "Though even if Debenham gave it to her, that's almost the same."

"Indeed, I *had* heard rumors that the necklace had gone missing. Had been stolen, in fact," her father said, almost thoughtfully. "Though Debenham was the one looking for it. He belongs to my club, as you know. I heard he'd shown a few members the sketch. Enraged by the act, he was, and calling for blood and anyone to speak up if they knew details. I hadn't known this...actress was involved."

Araminta tried to control her trembling. She'd wanted only to defend herself to her parents in case whispers got about. But it seemed the word was all over town already. And Debenham was furious, determined to get to the bottom of the matter. Araminta regretted her loose mouth. What had she said? It was hard, sometimes, to keep track of so many lies.

She looked at her shoes; her toes curled into the ends as she fought to control her nerves, though, of course, her parents couldn't see that. She took a shaky breath. "Then why doesn't Debenham go straight to Miss La Bijou and demand that she return it?" She had to ask, outright, the question most troubling her. For if Miss La Bijou knew anything of the truth the night she'd helped Araminta, then Araminta's life was in jeopardy. Debenham might very well kill her if it all came out.

She cast her mind over the evening Miss Bijou had rendered Araminta help in that dingy dwelling that belonged to Mrs. Mobbs. Had she discovered that the baby she thought had been prevented from making its arrival too early had in fact been born that night, and then spirited away? Did she know that her landlady, Mrs. Mobbs, had found a replacement child six weeks later?

Araminta swallowed, her throat dry but her palms slick with sweat. Was Miss La Bijou somehow involved in a grand plan to blackmail Araminta, with the help of Mrs. Mobbs?

The more she plumbed the possibilities, the more terrified she became.

She'd not received any blackmail threat or demands. But why was the necklace gracing Miss La Bijou's neck, when the proceeds were for the upbringing of her child, and to hide the truth?

Her father was rocking on his heels, looking down at her, while her mother was looking, confused, at both of them.

"You ask why Debenham does not confront Miss La Bijou direct?" Her father said. "Because he does not know the woman in the sketch *is* Kitty...er...Miss La Bijou. No one does." He sent Araminta a piercing look. "The part of the sketch which identifies her was torn away." He cleared his throat. "But Debenham is angry. He believes your good name is at issue, as much as anything else, Araminta." He put his hands behind his back and began to pace, his head down. "Debenham does not know Miss La Bijou has your necklace but I fear she might have some reckoning to do once he finds out. I fear the girl might be in danger."

"Miss La Bijou...in danger? Well, it would serve her right if she stole it!"

Her father stopped before Araminta and shook his head slowly, his expression almost sorrowful. "You are my daughter and I will always see to your interests as best I can." He took a long breath, adding after a pause, "But it saddens me, when I consider my offspring, to know that you, who have been blessed with good breeding, beauty and...*so much*...do not appreciate your good fortune."

"I hardly consider it good fortune to have had my necklace stolen by an actress who might have received it from my own husband, for all I know," Araminta grumbled. She didn't like the look in her father's eye. He'd spared her little enough attention when she was a child growing up, she scarcely felt she deserved his opprobrium now.

"I do not think it Miss La Bijou's good fortune to be wearing a necklace that will invite a great deal of trouble upon her doorstep."

Araminta said nothing as she turned away. But her mind felt like it had been invaded by a swarm of bumblebees. Surely Teddy would get to Kitty La Bijou before Debenham discovered that she was the woman in the sketch he'd found in her reticule.

When she turned back to her father, she had plastered on a smile and her tone was placating as she said, "I'm sure all will be comfortably settled."

She was about to say more but her mother cut in. "Ruby necklaces aside, I'm sorry if you are not happy with Debenham, my darling, but perhaps you are fortunate in a way you will never fully understand. You have given him a son within nine months of your marriage. Whatever happens, you have done your duty and for that, alone, your husband will treasure you, even if he is not always kind to you. Is that not right, Humphrey?"

Araminta caught the meaningful look her parents shared. Even she was perceptive enough to interpret the plaintive lament hidden beneath her mother's seemingly innocuous words. Lady Partington had spent her entire marriage trying to provide her husband with an heir, and, in failing, she'd earned nothing but scorn.

The reminder was all the more reason for Araminta not to lose her nerve. Whatever happened, she must doggedly maintain the fiction that she had been the best and most dutiful of wives. She must do whatever she could to trade on what the world, and Debenham, believed: that she'd fulfilled his greatest requirement by producing for her husband a healthy son.

CHAPTER 23

$\mathcal{K}$itty held up her arms so Dorcas could slip the beautiful confection of cream net and silk over her head. It slithered sensuously over her curves, and she stared, smiling, at her reflection.

Outside, she could hear church bells ring and, when they ceased, the chirping of birds as sunlight suddenly filtered through the window, despite the weather having been so dreary of late.

This was the happiest day of her life.

Dorcas sighed, and Kitty clasped her hands and whispered, "I'm going to be married today, Dorcas. Can you believe it? Today, I shall become the wife of a future viscount."

Dorcas tweaked the folds of her gown, then adjusted one of the curls which clustered from Kitty's high crown. Kitty wished she would smile but instead she said, "Yer mama should be 'ere. Why do yer 'ave no family when Lord Nash 'as brought 'is sister an' 'is cousin?" Dorcas shook her head. "If I were gettin' married I'd want all me loved ones ter see me joy." Her expression clouded even more. "That ain't neva goin' ter 'appen, though."

"It will!" Kitty turned and gripped her friend's shoulders. "You *will* find some lovely man who truly appreciates your goodness and kind spirit. Have faith and it will happen." She dropped her hands and raised her eyes to the ceiling. "I had faith, even when in my heart I was deeply unsure about Nash, but see how it's all turned out?" She jumped up and did a twirl.

"What do yer mean, miss?"

Kitty, now pulling on her gloves in preparation, as Minnie had just put her head around the door to say that carriage was ready to take them to the church, looked up with a smile. "What did you ask me, Dorcas?"

"What do yer mean yer still 'ad faith when yer 'eart weren't engaged wiv Lord Nash? Were it more important ter be married, or more important that it were ter Lord Nash?"

"Why, of course I had to love Lord Nash to want to consider marrying him." Kitty paused as she fiddled with the tiny buttons of her left glove, her words halting. She didn't like the line Dorcas had taken. "Come now, Dorcas, you look lovely too. What a pity Lissa won't be there to do a lightning sketch for posterity. Of anyone in my family, I wish I could have invited her."

"'Cept Lord Nash said yer wasn't ter invite any of 'em, didn't 'e?"

"No need to say it in such an accusing way, Dorcas. I'm not cross that he's invited his sister and cousin, while I couldn't do the same. I understand the reasons. He can't afford to anger his grandfather when the old man is so ill, even if Nash is quite within his rights to wed. Remember, he's twenty-four. He attained his majority three years ago, and in fact, was nearly married when he was twenty-one except that he had what he now calls a lucky escape, which made him realize how important it was to choose a bride compatible and pleasing in every way." She smiled. "Like me."

She had to keep reminding herself just how lucky she was, for her heart beat nervously, and her hands felt clammy and shaking. She hadn't spent the night with Nash and had tossed and turned, slipping into a short and feverish sleep at dawn.

"Lord Nash is a very lucky man," Dorcas said softly as they sat together in the carriage, rocking gently over the cobblestones. "I 'ope 'e realizes that."

"I'm the lucky one," Kitty objected. "How many men of his station marry so low if they choose to marry for love?"

She didn't like the woebegone looks Dorcas kept sending her as they progressed in a deepening silence. It was hard not to snap at her, but Kitty wasn't going to sour the mood any further. Dorcas had been acting quite strange, lately. She'd kept asking after Lord Silverton, and whether Kitty had seen him again. She'd repeatedly tried to persuade Kitty to accompany her to his townhouse "to say goodbye" and looked so downcast at Kitty's refusal she'd wondered if Dorcas herself could be in love with him.

Organ music struck up on cue as Kitty and Dorcas arrived in the doorway of St Margaret's, and it was only now that she felt that instead of this being a figment of her childish imaginings, it really was her dream come true. This was the sound her own mother had heard, perhaps, more than twenty years ago when she progressed down the aisle on her father's arm, to marry her father, Lord Partington. But Lord Partington wasn't there. No bridegroom had been waiting for her poor mother.

Anxiously, Kitty peered into the dim recesses of the church, and her heart lurched with sudden relief to see Nash, in company with another gentleman, staring at the priest. A great sense of relief swept over her. So it was true. She *would* be married. Legally. Finally, a Miss Hazlett was going to get a ring on her finger, and not only enjoy the love of a good man, but respectability for herself and her children.

Nash turned when she was a few yards away, his expression full of love. He looked so handsome, his fine-featured face with its small scar below the eye relaxing into a smile of hope and adoration that made Kitty's belly cleave. She smiled back at him warmly, as she made her approach, turning slightly when she heard footsteps behind her. Another guest.

Perhaps someone from her family had learned of these nuptials and come to pay their respects. She swallowed, and her heart hitched a little as she turned to see it was Silverton. Her old friend, despite his feelings, had come to honor their union. Forcing aside her feelings for

Lord Silverton, she concentrated on the fact that Nash loved her. *And that he loved her enough to marry her.*

Silverton slipped into a pew on the right-hand side while Kitty continued her progress down the aisle.

When she drew level with Nash, he gazed down at her, gripping the tips of her fingers in a light reassurance. "You look beautiful," he whispered as the vicar began to intone the service, his strong voice filling the holy space with his solemn words.

And then Nash was saying his vows, Kitty glancing over her shoulder at the sound of more footsteps—louder, this time, for they muffled his words.

Her head reeled when she saw her father advancing but he wasn't smiling. Nervously she glanced at Nash, still murmuring "...take thee, Catherine Jane Hazlett, to be my wedded wife, to have and to hold from this day forward, for better for worse, for richer for poorer..."

So her father had come to see her in her finest hour? Surely he should be pleased that Nash was making an honest woman of her? Was his scowl self recrimination for the reminder that he'd not behaved as honorably towards her mother? Or was it anger that Kitty had run away and become the celebrated actress, Kitty La Bijou? It was impossible to know, with her father.

Nash was still speaking, binding himself to her for eternity"...in sickness and in health, to love and to cherish, till death us do part, according to God's holy ordinance; and thereto I plight thee my troth."

She realized her father hadn't slipped into a pew, and now his footsteps were joined by another pair. Not her mother's for these, too, belonged to a male the way they clattered with loud purpose into the church, interrupting proceedings as a voice rose above the vicar's: "That boy has no authority to wed before he's twenty-five, and is no gentleman if he's told the lady otherwise!"

The vicar stopped speaking; Nash swung his head around, crying out, "Father! How dare you?" while Kitty stared with horror at the young man next to her who threw up his hands as he defended himself.

Frozen, she stared at him, confused but with a creeping sense of dreadful disappointment permeating her very bones, it seemed.

"Not true, Father!" Angrily, Nash faced his father while Kitty's own barked, "I will not see my daughter tricked into a farce of a marriage, but nor would I see her marry above her station when it would be to the detriment of too many others."

"Father!" Kitty cried as devastation threatened to undo her a second time.

Lord Partington drew level and now he clapped his hand on her shoulder. "Don't take it amiss, my girl. It ain't that I don't love you any less than the others, and I'm aware that the wrong I did your mother has blighted your prospects."

It was a double blow. The two men who should have given her the greatest support had pulled any foundation for future happiness from beneath her feet. Finally, she thought she was about to achieve her greatest dream; a dream that her own father had denied her through his selfishness: respectability.

With a gasp, Kitty spun around, avoiding Nash's outstretched arm and his plea to believe him. Gathering up her train in a bundle, she pushed past her father who tried to grip her hand in passing, but she tugged herself free, picking up her skirts, running only faster as she heard the cries behind her to stop.

Stop? For what? For whom? Her father who had given her nothing except a lineage to be ashamed of? For Nash who claimed to love her but who had deceived her?

"Kitty, come back! Believe me—" Nash's voice was filled with agony. Or was it remorse?

Believe him? She could never believe anyone again. In passing, she glimpsed Lord Silverton's shocked expression as he, too, rose from the pew.

Kitty wasn't about to stop for anyone. She fled into the street, nearly slipping on the slick cobbles, righting herself and plunging beneath the hooves of a passing hackney. Regaining her footing once more, she hastily snatched up the part of her train that had fallen in the mud, and continued her mad dash along the pavement, jostling passersby who stared, stupidly, at the sight of a young woman in wedding finery, sobbing as she clutched her ruby necklace like some good luck talisman. Good luck? She hated the wretched thing. She'd like to rip it from her neck and hurl it into the street if it weren't for the fact it might have to sustain her through the empty, frightening years ahead when, as a lonely, unloved, unrespected woman, she had to find her own way in the world.

She realised that the carriage up ahead had slowed and as she drew level, the door opened, and a face peered out. "Miss, do yer need 'elp? Why, if it ain't Kitty La Bijou. Lawks, get in, girlie! Yer look like yers fleein' from the divil, yer do!"

Kitty could hear running footsteps behind her, gaining, and with a surge of effort, she gripped the woman's outstretched hand for the carriage had resumed its steady clip. For a few seconds, she sailed through the air as her feet left the ground.

Then she was dragged into the carriage, the door was slammed shut, and she was half lying across the seat, her eyes closed as she drew breath at last.

"Mrs. Mobbs!" she exclaimed when she blinked. "Good heavens! What are you doing here?"

"More to the point, what are yer doin' runnin' through the streets o' London in a weddin' dress, if me eyes don't deceive me, an' wearin' the finest ruby necklace I ever did see."

"Lord Nash gave it to me...the day he asked me to marry him." Her voice caught and, heart racing while she tried to catch her breath, she dropped her head to look at her hands, unadorned by his wedding ring and not likely to receive one, ever again.

"I know that, me dear."

Kitty jerked her head up. "You know it?"

Mrs. Mobbs nodded. "Yer've jest run away from the church, 'aven't yer? So yer learned the truth, eh?"

Kitty clung to the seat as the vehicle rounded a corner. "That Lord Nash was in no position to marry me?"

"Nah, that 'e bought yer pretty necklace from Maggie Montgomery fer a very reasonable sum." Mrs. Mobbs looked her up and down. "So yer didn't like the fact 'e still enjoys visitin' some o' the girls?" She shrugged. "Not that 'e's done it fer a very long time. Not since the night 'e bought the ruby necklace, couple o' weeks back. Said 'e were givin' up other women now he'd fallen right hard fer yer."

Mrs. Mobbs leaned across to pat Kitty's shoulder in a motherly fashion. "There, told yer the truth 'bout how 'e feels, so now yer can go back if yer wants. Always did 'ave a soft spot fer yer, girlie."

Kitty stared, feeling even worse after Mrs. Mobbs' supposedly bolstering speech. "He bought it from a...brothel?"

"Don't reckon Maggie likes her 'stablishment referred to in such terms," Mrs. Mobbs said, warningly. "Now, if yer don't want ter go back ter the church, yer can come wiv me, though if I were you, here's a word of advice. Take yersel' back to 'is Lordship for 'e can look after yer better than I can."

"I don't want to go back to his Lordship and I don't expect you to look after me."

The carriage had drawn to a halt down a side street, and Mrs. Mobbs was reaching down on the floor for what Kitty now saw was a tiny baby, wrapped in swaddling clothes and sleeping soundly.

"'Ere, yer can pick it up fer me," Mrs. Mobbs said, handing her the child then cupping Kitty's elbow as she lead her through a door. "It's a good little 'un, this 'un is. Borned of a poor scullery maid, she were, so Maggie Montgomery's goin' to find the bonny lad a nice spot in the country. I jest bin to fetch 'im. That's right, warm yerself by the fire."

It was only then, and the recognition of the wide-eyed scullery maid who was passing with a pail of water, that Kitty realized she was in Maggie Montomery's establishment. Horrified, she looked about her, still clutching the baby, which she thrust into Mrs. Mobbs' arms.

"Why have you taken me here? I must go!"

"I ain't taken yer anywhere. I jest gave yer a carriage ride to save yer from certain individuals yer were fleein' from an' I gave yer good warning yer should get back to Lord Nash if yer wanted to look after yersel'. No need ter accuse me o' sommat I ain't done," Mrs. Mobbs defended herself. "Ah, Maggie, look who I picked up. And it were more than jest the babe."

With her heart in her mouth, Kitty stared between the two women: Mrs. Mobbs, slatternly as ever with her greasy hair spilling out from her filthy mob cab, and her enormous breasts spilling out of the top of her print gown; and Mrs. Montgomery, magnificently upholstered, her icy gaze lit up with unusual warmth as she purred, "Kitty La Bijou. We meet once again. Your exploits are legendary, and you have caused me more than a little trouble lately with regard to a certain ruby necklace which I see you happily still have in your possession." She looked at Kitty's muddy slippers, the torn netting of her embroidered train, and her grubby gloves and made a sympathetic tutting noise.

"Goodness, that necklace has caused quite a stir, but enough of that. We'll discuss the matter, later. In the meantime, it's clear you need to rest, my poor girl. Follow me, and I shall find you a room… while we decide what to do with you."

CHAPTER 24

*I*t was thanks to Dorcas that Silverton had any idea of where to set his footsteps. Dorcas had been the fleetest of foot, initially, but then she'd been right behind Kitty, carrying her mistress's train.

Nevertheless, when Silverton reached the street corner where Dorcas was staring into the hazy distance, and they had long since left Lord Nash and his father and Kitty's father behind, the young maid turned to him with real fear in her eyes.

"That were Maggie Montgomery's carriage," she said with dismay. "I recognized the insignia. Faded now, though. She got it cheap from one o' 'er customers. When the door opened I saw the blue velvet upholstery, too. Miss Kitty's bin took by Maggie Montgomery."

Silverton was surprised but by no means fearful. "What would Maggie Montgomery want with Kitty? Well, at least we know where she's gone and they can hardly keep her a prisoner against her will, Dorcas." But the shaking of the little maid's shoulders reminded him of why she was so afraid. Dorcas knew all about Maggie Montgomery and the practices that propped up her evil empire.

Dorcas was now two steps ahead of him, hurrying up the street in pursuit of the carriage. "You got ter save 'er, m'lord!" she called over her shoulder. "You can't let 'em make her sign a contract."

Silverton followed her. Like Dorcas, he was obviously just as anxious as get to Kitty. He was also, of course, very sorry for Kitty, but he couldn't deny the fact that he was also rather pleased to be in a position to play knight errant.

Of course, marching up to Maggie and demanding Kitty's freedom —if it were a case of that through some arrangement he did not at this moment know anything about—would be perfectly easy for him whereas it was no wonder Dorcas was all but running. She had every right to fear Maggie Montgomery because she was poor and power-less. But Silverton was a man of consequence and means. "Rest assured I won't let them make Miss Kitty do anything she doesn't want to do, Dorcas." He sounded calm and in control but the truth was that the closer he came to Maggie Montgomery's the more his heart thundered.

What would Kitty be feeling when she saw him? Would her avowed feelings for Silverton override her pain and anguish in the wake of Nash's betrayal?

Dorcas swung round. "Believe me, m'Lord, Mrs. Montgomery can do you a great deal of harm." She fingered the fichu at her throat as she swallowed convulsively. "She certainly *would* if someone more powerful than you made it worth her while."

Silverton raised a brow as he drew level with Dorcas and offered her his arm for she was still breathless from the rapid pace.

"Someone more powerful? I'm afraid I don't know what you mean, Dorcas?"

Her lip trembled as she brushed away a flyaway strand of hair and there was moisture behind her eyes which he was certain wasn't from the glare of the weak sun that filtered through the clouds. "It was 'cos Lord Debenham wanted you in his clutches that I were given me free-dom," she explained, ending on a little sob. "May the Lord forgive me but I didn't know wot else ter do, not that I were given much choice."

He stopped and stared into her frightened little face but she turned her head away. Her mouth was set in a thin line, her shoulders hunched.

This was something he hadn't been expecting. Quelling his forboding, he said mildly, "Come Dorcas, you're being cryptic." Could she be suggesting Lord Debenham were somehow involved? Debenham was an old crony of his. The man had sought his aid many a time. He trusted Silverton. But Dorcas's words, though surely untrue, made him feel less confident than he had a moment before.

Dorcas began to hurry away once more and Silverton followed, his thoughts wildly disturbed. What could Debenham have to do with any of this? With Dorcas or with Kitty?

When Dorcas stumbled on a cobblestone just ahead of him, Silverton steadied her, forcing her to a stop and she turned, closing her eyes a moment as if struggling for courage. Clenching her hands, she thrust her chin up and said in a rush, "Me freedom were a condition of two things: keepin' an eye on Miss Kitty so she stayed safe from a certain client prepared to pay a lotta money to 'ave the favors of the celebrated Kitty La Bijou—and secretly deliverin' some letters into your bedchamber wot you once wrote to a lady you was fond of in the past."

"Lady Anstey." Silverton strove to keep the acid from his tone for he knew very well that Lady Ansey was in possession of some quite torrid correspondence from him during the early heady days of their brief and unwise liaison. A cloud of anger blurred his vision.

So Mrs. Montgomery wanted Kitty for her own ends while Debenham had learned of Silverton's affair and sought to use it to his advantage? "And why could not you deliver these letters directly into my hand?"

Dorcas shook her head. "I asked the same thing but Mrs. Montgomery said time would tell, only the letters had to be put there for when needed and that she'd find out if I told anyone. She said that if I wanted Miss Kitty to be safe I had to do as she said."

"So you *did* do as she asked?" He calculated the time. "That would have been just a few days ago…when you and Kitty came to visit me at my townhouse. Dorcas, do you understand—?"

She put up her hand to stop him interrupting. "I understand very well, m'Lord. I understand that it were Lord Debenham wot wanted the deed done about them letters but I didn't know wot else to do. I tried to persuade Miss Kitty to return again to your 'ouse so's I could explain, only she wouldn't. Then I thought I'd tell yer straight after today. Well, I'm tellin' yer now, ain't I?"

"You are, and I'm very glad for it. Thanks to you I'm well prepared for when Debenham launches his little game, if that's his intention." He glanced up. "But right now Kitty needs us."

They'd reached the railing of Maggie Montgomery's but now Dorcas stopped in her tracks as he was about to mount the stairs. "I ain't goin' near there. I can't, m'lord."

"Have no fear, Dorcas, I'm here with you. Kitty is probably drinking tea and in no danger at all."

Dorcas looked dubiously up the road. "An afta yer get 'er out? Where'll she go, m'lord? Where will *I* go?"

"Why, you'll come to me, of course. You'll both come to me. Kitty *always* comes to me when she needs help." The knowledge filled him with the greatest satisfaction. And happiness. Kitty needed his help. And she had nowhere to go but home to be with him.

Home to be with him. Where she belonged. She desired him as much—more—than she did Lord Nash. She'd admitted it numerous times; the only reason she'd chosen Nash was because he offered her marriage. Well, Silverton could offer her much more than Nash when it came to matters of the heart.

The excitement that coursed throughout his entire body made him feel quite lightheaded with joy, propelling him to the top of the stairs in the gloomy and foreboding building.

He was not surprised by the unctuous welcome he received when he was shown into Maggie Montgomery's sitting room while Dorcas hovered in the passage, refusing to go down to the kitchen.

"Lord Silverton, to what do I owe this pleasure?" she purred, waving him to her red velvet sofa while she poured them both a snifter of brandy.

He sank down into the plush cushions, smiling pleasantly as if he'd come to pay a social call. "I've come to fetch Kitty La Bijou." With a smile, he tossed back the shot, its welcome warmth feeding his anticipation. Soon he'd have Kitty all to himself. Forever and always. They were destined to be together. He'd felt it from the start. Unconsciously his lips turned up at the memory of her guile-less smile and he realised the warmth he felt was not from the brandy. How could he not have known it before? Of course he needed Kitty to feel whole. She made him conscious of all the good things in his life. She radiated happiness, which in turn fed into him like a wellspring, dissipating the onerous, unpleasant matters that often niggled at him. The only times he'd really felt entirely unbur-dened was when he was playing cribbage in front of the fire with Kitty.

Or kissing her.

"Miss La Bijou? And what would you want with such an attractive young lady, my Lord? An adornment I believe your wife-to-be might not reckon such a rare prize as you do? You are to be married before the summer, if I am correct."

Silverton met the challenge in her eye. Maggie Montgomery considered Kitty as much a prize as he did and she was not going to give her up easily.

Now was not the time to feel guilt over what he owed Miss Mandelton. His duty right now was to Kitty. Kitty needed him. And he needed her. Yes! She made him feel whole and he loved her.

He allowed that Miss Mandelton needed him, too. She needed a husband and their families were in accord that it was a suitable match. Silverton needed a wife of her social standing. A wife who would cause no scandal; who would be easily accepted into society. He had a duty to his parents, to his family name.

It's true that when he'd learned with shock and amazement in the church just now that Lord Partington was Kitty's father, he'd felt a brief surge of hope that something might be possible between Kitty and himself, but even Lord Partington had understood it was impos-sible for his own daughter, Kitty, a bastard, to marry a peer of the realm.

And Silverton must never allow matters of the heart to detract him from his duty towards the family line.

"Where *is* Miss La Bijou?" he asked, his tone sharper this time. The logistics of marriage aside, he'd do everything within his power to protect the young woman he loved above all others.

"Miss La Bijou?" Maggie repeated the name as she regarded him of the top of steepled fingers. "Ah yes, the young lady we were discussing. So you really have come here for her?"

"I saw her in your carriage so I know she's here." He put down his glass. "If you would kindly take me to her?"

She frowned, shifting in her chair, discreetly pushing back the squirrel's tail that supplemented her hair piece. At least, Silverton was pretty sure it was a squirrel's tail. "Lord Silverton, I must tell you that you are not the only one who wants Miss La Bijou. Lord Debenham is on his way, also. He is greatly desirous of interviewing Miss La Bijou over a minor matter that has caused more than a little trouble."

"Lord Debenham?" A stab of foreboding made his voice sharper than he'd intended. He should have quizzed Dorcas more thoroughly, he realised.

Mrs. Montgomery thrust out her bosom and ran the tip of her tongue over her top lip. "You see, it concerns a ruby necklace. A very valuable ruby necklace which, in fact, had been gifted to Lady Debenham though of course it belongs, officially, to Lord Debenham. As you would understand, it is worth a great deal of money. I have to add that Lord Nash acquired the necklace from these premises but only after I had already paid a great sum for it." She patted her false hair. "That is the truth of the matter. However, Lord Debenham maintains Miss La Bijou stole the valuable piece of jewellery from his wife. The fact is, Lady Debenham was dunned, and she begged me to fetch her a decent price for the necklace which is why it came into my hands. Naturally she cannot tell her husband which is perhaps why he's come to believe that Miss La Bijou stole it from Lady Debenham." Maggie Montgomery clicked her tongue then sighed deeply before adding in tones of great sympathy, "I can understand why you are so greatly disturbed, knowing what a fondness you have for Miss Bijou which is why I'm sure we can come to some arrangement that will ensure Miss Bijou does not have to endure the cold comfort of a gaol cell before a possible hanging."

"Neither you nor Debenham is in a position to make false claims or bargains! Lord Nash bought that necklace for Miss La Bijou therefore it is rightfully hers!" Silverton spluttered.

"I'm afraid, Lord Silverton, that you and Lord Nash might find that Lord Debenham has a compelling case." Maggie smiled her thin smile. "Unless I am amply compensated for the ruby necklace, Miss Bijou will go to the highest bidder."

"Preposterous!" Lord Silverton tried to rein in his anger as he thrust his body forward. If Maggie Montgomery had been a man he'd have put his hands around her turkey neck. "You are using Miss La Bijou as a pawn in a matter where she had already been deceived. We both known she is entirely innocent of the theft of this ridiculous bauble." The loathesome creature before him blurred as he breathed deeply. "Would you really increase Miss La Bijou's distress with the information that the man she believed was marrying her today bought her a stolen necklace bought from a... *brothel* and that, furthermore, she is being accused of stealing it!"

"Lord Silverton, it is not like you to be so coarse." Mrs. Montgomery's tone was low and as angry as Silverton's. Beneath the portrait of Lord Nelson she looked like an avenging Valkyrie. "Do you not understand that I shall be severely out of pocket if I simply hand over to you your young lady, still wearing the necklace." She put her head back and smiled, her confidence returning as she no doubt took in his anxiety to be reunited with Kitty. "No need to be so discomposed, Lord Silverton, when a simple payment is all that's required. If you can offer me what the necklace is worth then I'm sure Lord Debenham will not wish to trouble either you or Miss La Bijou further.

KITTY SAT HUNCHED MISERABLY ON THE WROUGHT-IRON DOUBLE BED

with its blue satin coverlet and comfortable cushions. A small fire lit the grate. It looked as if the room were awaiting guests.

But surely it had not been prepared for her?

She certainly did not want to be here. And she was suddenly very frightened. Mrs. Mobbs had claimed her necklace was stolen and then Mrs. Montgomery had said someone was on his way to fetch it before she'd ushered Kitty into the room and closed the door. *No*, she'd in fact pushed Kitty into the room and turned the key in the lock.

Kitty fingered the heavy stones and a sob tore at her throat though she'd not give voice to it. How could she be in the middle of such a nightmare?

The necklace had been Nash's engagement gift to her. She hated it now, but she was in no position to simply unclasp it and hand it over to whoever desired it—even if she never wanted to see it again and be reminded of Nash's faithlessness. The truth was, it might be the only item of value to sustain her if she were destined to be alone in the world.

She put her hands up to cover her face and tried not to cry. How could her life have spiraled downhill so quickly? Half an hour ago she was supposed to have married Lord Nash. Nash…the man for whom she'd compromised all her values in order to be his…plaything.

But he'd betrayed her. First with his cheating, then with his protestations of true love. And he'd bought this very ruby necklace here in this brothel in one of *several* transactions he'd made that night.

What a little fool she was.

She wondered if Maggie intended forcibly coercing her into becoming one of her girls? Terror skittered up her spine. No, it could not be possible.

But who was there for her in the wake of Nash's betrayal?

Immediately Lord Silverton's smile came to mind. Lord Silverton, she thought, suddenly awash with want. If anyone would save her, he would.

The bolstering thought flitted through her mind at the precise moment she heard heavy footsteps approaching then a hasty rapping on the door. Before she'd said anything, there was a fumbling of the key in the lock and the door was thrust open, and there Silverton stood, smiling and handsome, his arms outstretched as he advanced toward her.

Joy filled her heart.

He *had* come for her. He was here, just as he always was when she needed him. With a choking cry, she threw herself off the bed and into his embrace and his arms went about her, crushing her to his strong, athletic body.

"Oh, Silverton, I thought you'd never come!" she cried, which wasn't entirely true, but it was nice to be able to give vent to a heart-felt outpouring that expressed that her very desires and hopes had come true.

"How could I not when you needed me, Kitty?" he murmured while she reveled in his warmth and the wonderfully familiar smell of his cologne, woody and masculine, which sent tendrils of desire all the way through her.

She raised her head to look at him. "At first, I wished you hadn't come to the church because of how it made me feel here when I knew those feelings should be reserved for Nash," she admitted, "but now I'm so glad you did because, oh, I need some comfort right now."

He held her tightly, murmuring soothing endearments that made her want to curl into him and never let him go. "I will always be on hand to comfort you, Kitty, my love."

Strange how the offer of Silverton's comfort was more affecting than Nash's offer of enduring love. Somehow she knew Silverton could be depended upon whereas Nash...well, couldn't.

"You do know that I love you, Kitty?"

His words made her want to cry. Happily, she nodded, pushing slightly away so he could see it in her eyes. "I've always felt so...right... with you, Silverton. I should have trusted my feelings more." Impulsively, she twined her arms about his neck and pressed herself against him. "I wanted marriage more than anything, I'll admit it, but if you want the honest truth, I loved you more than I ever loved Nash. Even during the good times." She hiccupped on a small sob of pain as she recalled Nash's piratical smile and his habit of brushing aside all her objections when he desired something. It had made him seem so manly at the time. Now such reflections made him seem just self-absorbed and selfish. "I *wanted* to love Nash more because he offered me what you would not. But then he betrayed me," she added, sadly. "Not even just once though I should have learned my lesson the first time."

Silverton put his hands on Kitty's shoulders and tilted up her chin; and as Kitty gazed into his face with its kind blue-grey eyes that smoldered with passion, beneath which there was no dueling scar; and she admired, as she always did, the lovely springy waves of his hair that framed his handsome yet strongly made face, she knew she'd always been fated to kiss those sensitive lips and to lose herself in his mutual need.

"I will never betray you, Kitty," he promised, cradling her in his arms, then whisking her feet off the floor and placing her on the bed. "So will you be mine, Kitty?" He cupped her cheek, his expression heartbreakingly tender as he joined her on the bed and gently toyed with the top button of her gown. "I cannot offer you marriage but I can offer you my heart and my constancy and devotion. Forever."

Kitty held her breath and could hear only the beating of her own heart. And then the soft, reassuring timbre of his voice before his words made any semblance of sense and she realised that this was an offer she should not, could not, refuse.

"I've never lost my heart before, Kitty. And then, when I met you I suddenly realised the pain and emptiness of being unable to spend every moment of every day with you." He stroked her hair. "Not just the passionate moments but those mundane everyday ones where we'd talk about the weather and...how much orange rind we prefer in our marmalade." His familiar, wry smile clutched at her heart and she shifted closer to him, needing to hear the depth of his feelings.

He smiled sweetly. "That's what I want with you, Kitty. To spend every possible moment I can in your utterly delightful company, because you make me feel whole and you make me feel happy." His expression darkened and the hand that had been stroking her temples stilled. He hunched over her, his expression full of both pain and passion. "But you already know how I'm situated. You know of my duty to my family. My impending marriage to Miss Mandelton. Yet I want *you*, Kitty. Much more than I want to be respectably married to the right woman, I want *you*." He swallowed, his pain clearly not being eased by the admission. His body tensed. "And more than anything in the world I want you to want me as much. But that means you'd be saying yes to becoming my mistress. And that could threaten to tear your heart in two. Just as it could mine."

Kitty shook her head. She already knew of the sacrifices required to be united in love with the one man who satisfied all her needs. No more prompting or avowals of his love were necessary for already she felt close to exploding into a shower of passionate flames.

"Yes, I will become your mistress because I want *you* more than I've ever wanted anything!"

There could be no mistaking how much her ardor matched his for within seconds they were both naked and she was beneath him on that big, comfortable bed, his arms wrapped tightly around her as he blazed a trail of kisses the length of her throat, inciting her whole body to meet what he offered, with the same enthusiasm.

She arched her body, passion bubbling in her veins, and she was ready for him, every nerve ending heightened and ready to snap when his fingers found the slippery wetness between her legs that was testament to how much she wanted him. Their first coupling was destined to be passionate, incendiary and climactic. They had the rest of their lives for discovering their mutual wants and desires in a more leisurely fashion but for now there was just this one, urgent need for losing themselves in one another.

"Come inside me," she gasped, wrapping her legs around his waist, pulling him against her more tightly, aware their time was limited. She'd shatter in a moment but it would be in a mutual joining of their bodies."Now!"

"Kitty, I love you and I adore you," he whispered as he prepared to do as she asked. Sincerity blazed from his face. "I will be true to you, I swear it, until the day you die; and you will never have cause to regret..."

"Becoming your mistress," she supplied, impatiently now, not even flinching from the description because when her father condemned her from birth to being a bastard she should have known she could never become a respectable wife and mother. Silverton and his offer promised her best chance of happiness in life. She knew it with utter certainty.

"But I will love you as if you were my wife," he vowed with a smile of ecstasy as he slid into her; and Kitty had no doubt this was true this as he was caught up in the excitement of becoming one. An excitement she surely felt as keenly and deeply as he, raw primal pleasure sweeping away any residual disappointment she might have harbored at the fact she'd not achieved what Nash had so briefly seemed to offer.

What was a glittering wedding ring when Silverton's love was pure and true? A glittering wedding ring that was a sham, besides.

With a gasp, Kitty reached the pinnacle just before Silverton did, shattering with a cry of joy which signaled her lover's own climax.

Collapsing, truly satisfied, she basked in the tenderness of his embrace, soaking up the warmth and love he was offering her now and forever.

She'd always loved Silverton, she realized. Life was a journey of compromises, and she could be happy with the one she'd made, she thought, as she gazed into his adoring expression.

Still breathing heavily, he asked, "Did I tell you I love you, Miss Kitty La Bijou?" Resting on one elbow, he gazed down at her, tracing the outline of her mouth with his fingertip.

She nodded.

"And did I tell you I loved you from the time you decided the spelling pig at the Tower of London couldn't really spell?"

She nodded again. "That was about when I fell in love with you. Except I didn't know it at the time." Her heart hitched. She loved these playful sessions with Silverton. She'd shared many of them over the cribbage table and they'd been far more enjoyable than awaiting Nash, or following a session with Nash in the lover's bower he'd leased for her.

"And did you know that you wield such power over me that I could refuse you nothing?"

"You make me laugh, Lord Silverton."

"You make me happy, Kitty La Bijou."

She became serious. "You *do* make me happy, Lord Silverton. You always have."

"I *want* to make you happy, Kitty."

She was about to curl herself against him and suggest they do it all over again as another surge of love and desire flooded through her, when their banter was disturbed by a loud and insistent rapping at the door.

Silverton looked outraged as he jerked his head in the direction of the door and shouted to whoever was on the other side, "I thought the arrangement we had was understood!"

He glanced down at her and said for her edification, "Darling, there was a little disagreement over your necklace which I'm afraid you'll have to surrender. In order to placate Mrs. Montgomery and put an end to the matter, I've paid her a great deal more than it's worth but don't worry," he assured her, "you and I shall go shopping for a more than adequate replacement. However," he added in more clipped tones, "I said we would emerge from here *when we were ready*."

The rapping sounded again, and this time Nash's voice issued through the keyhole, loud and desperate. "Kitty, I need to explain! Please, listen to me! Are you in there?"

Silverton shook his head, disbelievingly, while Kitty sat up, shocked, covering herself with the coverlet as if Nash might bust in at any moment. Right now she hated him and she wanted him to know it.

"There's nothing you can say, Lord Nash," she said with as much dignity as she could manage. Then in an even louder voice, "You have betrayed me!"

"Kitty, I beg you, listen to me! You never gave me a chance to explain! Why, you ran off before I could say *anything* that would make you stay."

"There's nothing you *can* say that will make any difference, Lord

Nash." Indignantly, Kitty stared at the door, rising onto her knees as she wrapped her arms about Lord Silverton and kissed his right ear. She felt even more powerful when she saw the concern in his eyes. But he had no need to worry where Kitty's heart and allegiances now belonged.

Nash's tone became more pleading. "Kitty, please, I—"

"It's too late, Nash. I'm in here with Lord Silverton who has shown me how a true gentleman behaves—"

"Lord Silverton? What has he got to do with any of this? Besides, Lord Silverton isn't prepared to marry you. And I am! My father thought the marriage was not legal, but I went through every avenue with my solicitor, and he declared that the vows we were to say were indeed legally binding. I've now persuaded my father of the fact, and I'm here to persuade you. As my father will. Dorcas told me you'd been picked up by your old landlady and taken here, though Lord knows why."

Mrs. Montgomery's voice sounded in the passage, and then there was the sound of the key being turned in the lock, and the door was pushed open.

And there was barely any time for Kitty and Lord Silverton to hastily cover themselves, before Lord Nash's earnest, eager face was staring at them.

First with disbelief.

Then, shock and horror.

And finally anger and dismay.

Certainly, dismay was written all over Lord Silverton's face as Kitty looked between the two men...the one who would have married her after all, and the one...

She loved.

She swallowed, and tears welled up in her eyes. For both men.

"I'm sorry, Nash," she whispered.

He looked as if she'd whipped him across the face with a cat o' nine tails.

"I'm sorry, Kitty." It was Lord Silverton who was speaking, tenderly stroking the strands of flyaway hair from her forehead.

"Kitty? How could you?" Lord Nash asked brokenly. "We would have been married by now if…if you'd had faith in me."

Kitty dropped her eyes. Guilt scored her right through to the deepest recesses of her heart. Then she raised her head and whispered, "You deceived me once, Nash. With Jennie. And then you deceived me again…over the necklace. I thought this was just one more time. It's true; I should have had faith. I should have waited." She swallowed and gently stroked Lord Silverton's cheek as she found herself leaning unconsciously into him. Tenderness made her feel choked with emotion but quite sure of her mind. Especially when she saw how clearly the intensity of her feelings were reflected in Silverton's expression. He loved her truly, deeply. She had no doubt of it.

Sadly, she looked at Nash. "The truth is, that despite everything that's happened today; despite the fact that you have granted me more than I ever could have imagined would be mine, I *have* found my heart's desire. Yes, I thought I wanted marriage above all else." She tilted her head so that Lord Silverton could see the sincerity of her expression. Love, greater than she'd ever felt or even believed possible, flowered in her breast and her breath hitched in her throat as she opened her mouth to say the truest words she'd ever spoken. "But now I know that, above all, I wanted love." Almost tentatively she touched her finger to Silverton's lips and she thought she would cry with joy to see all her hopes for the future reflected in the eyes of the darling man before her. "And love is what I've found."

The End

WHAT HAPPENS NEXT...?

The Daughters of Sin series follows the intertwining lives and sibling rivalry of Lord Partington's two nobly born - and two illegitimate - daughters as they compete for love during several London Seasons.

With Hetty and Araminta both falling for men on opposing sides of a dastardly plot that is being investigated by Stephen Cranbourne, now a secret agent in the Foreign Office, there's lashings of skullduggery and intrigue bound up in the central romance.

And, just in case you're ever worried that someone doesn't get their happy ending, or just desserts – rest assured that they will do, either in their book, or by the end of the series.

What Readers are Saying About the Series:

"It's refreshing to read a Regency that doesn't remind me of others, and I found the heroine to be very relatable...I am a huge Regency fan, but there is no denying that the category is a little crowded. This was a nice change of pace... I also have a serious weak spot for twisty family dynamics." ~ **Amazon reader**

"Great characters and roller-coaster story with plot twists that surprised me at every turn. I could not believe how it ended but I loved it! ~ **Amazon reader**

Below is the order of the books:

Book 1: Her Gilded Prison
Book 2: Dangerous Gentlemen
Book 3: The Mysterious Governess Book 4: Beyond Rubies
Book 5: Lady Unveiled: The Cuckold Conspiracy

Here's a bit about them:

She was determined to secure the succession, he was in it for the pleasure. Falling in love was not part of the arrangement.
*** When dashing twenty-five-year-old Stephen Cranbourne arrives at the estate he will one day inherit, it's expected he will make a match with his beautiful second cousin, Araminta. But while proud, fiery Araminta and her shy, plain sister, Hetty, parade their very different charms before him, it's their mother, Sybil, a lonely and discarded wife, who evokes first his sympathy and then stokes his lustful fires.

Shy, plain Hetty was the wallflower beneath his notice...until a terrible mistake has one dangerous, delicious rake believing she's the "fair Cyprian" ordered for his pleasure. *** Shy, self-effacing Henrietta knows her place—in her dazzling older sister's shadow. She's a little brown peahen to Araminta's bird of paradise. But when Hetty mistakenly becomes embroiled in the Regency underworld, the innocent debutante finds herself shockingly compromised by the dashing, dangerous Sir Aubrey, the very gentleman her heart desires. And the man Araminta has in her cold, calculating sights. Branded an enemy of the Crown, bitter over the loss of his wife, Sir Aubrey wants only to lose himself in the warm, willing body of the young "prostitute" Hetty. As he tutors her in the art of lovemaking, Aubrey is pleased to find Hetty not only an ardent student, but a bright, witty and charming companion. Despite a spoiled Araminta plotting for a marriage offer and a powerful political enemy damaging his reputation, Aubrey may suffer the greatest betrayal at the hands of the little "concubine" who's managed to breach the stony exterior of his heart.

Lissa Hazlett lives life in the shadows. The beautiful, illegitimate daughter of Viscount Partington earns her living as an overworked governess while her vain and spoiled half sister, Araminta, enjoys London's social whirl as its most feted debutante. When Lissa's rare talent as a portraitist brings her unexpectedly into the bosom of society – and into the midst of a scandal involving Araminta and suspected English traitor Lord Debenham – she finds an unlikely ally: charming and besotted Ralph Tunley, Lord Debenham's underpaid, enterprising secretary.

Fame. Fortune. And finally a marriage proposal! Book 4 of the Daughters of Sin series introduces Miss Kitty La Bijou, celebrated London actress, mistress to handsome Lord Nash and the unacknowledged illegitimate daughter of Viscount Partington. Having escaped her humble beginnings, Kitty has found fame, fortune and love, but the respectability she craves eludes her. When she stumbles across Araminta, her legitimate half-sister, on the verge of giving birth just seven months after marrying dangerous Viscount Debenham, Kitty realises respectability is no guarantee of character or happiness. But helping Araminta has unwittingly embroiled Kitty in a scandalous deception involving a ruthless brothel madam, a priceless ruby necklace and the future heir to a dazzling fortune. And when Kitty finally receives an offer of marriage she must choose. Respectability or love?

Kitty has the love of the man of her dreams but as London's most acclaimed actress and a member of the demimondaine, she accepts she can never be kind and handsome Lord Silverton's lawful wedded wife. When Kitty comes to the aid of shy, accident-prone and kind-hearted Octavia Mandelton, her sense of justice leads to her making the most difficult decision of her life: Give up the man she loves for the sake of honour. For Octavia is still betrothed to Lord Silverton who'd rescued Kitty in dramatic circumstances only weeks before. Cast adrift, Kitty joins forces with her sister, Lissa, a talented artist posing as a governess in order to bring to justice a dangerous spy, villainous Lord Debenham. Complicating matters is the fact Debenham is married to their half-sister, vain and beautiful Araminta. However, Araminta has a dark secret which only Kitty knows and which she realizes she is duty-bound to expose if she's to achieve justice and win happiness for deserving Lissa and Lissa's enterprising sweetheart, Ralph Tunley, long-suffering secretary to Lord Debenham. All seems set for a happy ending when Kitty tumbles into mortal danger. A danger from which only a truly honorable man can save her. A man like Silverton who must now make the hardest choice of his life if he's to live with his conscience.

Alternatively:

Buy the first three books in the series

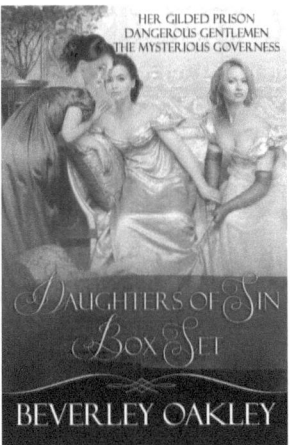

Or, buy the complete series as a Box set and save.

Four very different sisters compete for love during an exciting London season: a celebrated actress with a heart of gold, a shy yet daring wallflower, and the artistic, illegitimate daughter of a nobleman. Caught up in a high-stakes game of intrigue and deceit orchestrated by their sister, the ton's reigning beauty, each must play their part to bring a dangerous traitor to justice while finding a man deserving of their love and special talents.

THE SCANDALOUS MISS BRIGHTWELL SERIES

Book 1 Rake's Honour

Book 2 Rogue's Kiss

Book 3 Devil's Run

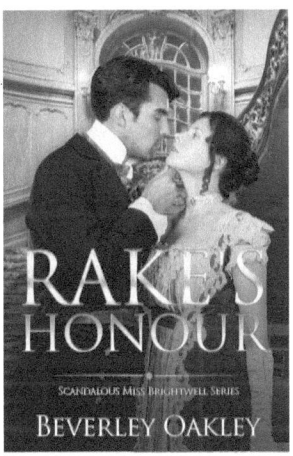

RAKE'S HONOUR (Book 1)

Beautiful, impoverished Fanny Brightwell has a few scores to settle—and a heart to win—before she can secure the title her ambitious mama demands.

Fanny is used to trading on her wits and Patrician beauty to ensure her family retains its tenuous hold on respectability. While her reprobate brother gambles away their fortune, and her feather-brained sister threatens to destroy the girls' collective reputation by succumbing to any lure cast her way, Fanny is regarded as the Brightwell family's saviour.

Pressured by her mother into accepting a marriage offer from lecherous Lord Slyther, a desperately unhappy Fanny is given one final opportunity to pull out of her nuptials—provided she secures an equally rich and titled suitor within two weeks. For if Fanny doesn't make a good match, she and her sister can look forward to a lifetime attending to Great Aunt Seraphina's chilblains.

During a single lapse of good judgment one evening while in masquerade as a fairy sprite, Fanny, discovers dashing rake, Viscount Fenton is just the man to satisfy the exacting criteria of both her mama and herself; a discovery which gives the lie to the refrain she's been told since infancy: that she has no heart.

But the discovery brings with it the painful realisation that her heart could just cost her her happiness.

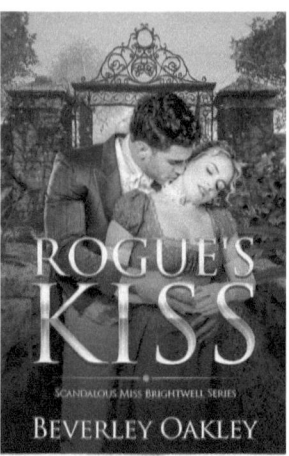

ROGUE'S KISS (Book 2)

Would a potential suitor be bolder if he were told the object of his desire had only six months to live?

Sweet, pretty Thea Brightwell's dull, quiet life with her crotchety aunt is about to be turned upside down by a visit to Bath.

A chance encounter in the spa town with wealthy, handsome Mr Grayling sets Thea's heart aflutter, but the fledgeling affair is quickly nipped in the bud by her aunt who has no intention of losing her unpaid nurse and companion.

Unbeknownst to penniless Thea, she has an unlikely champion in her well-meaning but 'not-too-bright' Cousin Bertram who has decided to play matchmaker.

If the lack of a dowry is the only impediment to Mr Grayling making an offer of marriage, Bertram reasons the gentleman would play a riskier hand if he were told that the damsel he covets were destined for her deathbed within six months?

Crotchety maiden aunts, love letters gone astray, and 'old flames' appearing from the woodwork lead to a most disconcerting outcome!

ROGUE'S KISS can be read as a stand-alone. It follows award-winning racy Regency romp RAKE'S HONOUR.

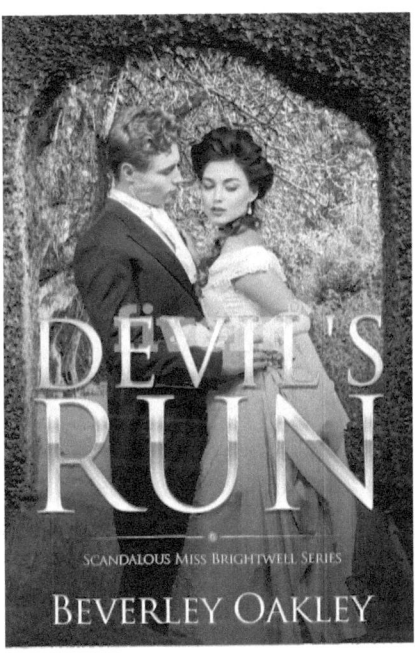

A rigged horserace and a marriage offer riding on the outcome. When Miss Eliza Montrose unexpectedly becomes legal owner of the horse tipped to win the East Anglia Cup, her future is finally in her hands – but at what cost?

George Bramley, nephew to the Earl of Quamby, will wager anything. Even his future bride.

Miss Eliza Montrose will accept any wager to be reunited with the child she was forced to relinquish after an indiscretion — even if it means marrying a man she does not love.

But with her heart suddenly engaged by handsome, charming Rufus Patmore who has just bought a horse from her betrothed, George Bramley, in whose household her son lives as a pauper child, the outcome of the wager is suddenly fraught with peril.

ABOUT THE AUTHOR

Beverley was seventeen when she bundled up her first 500+ page romance and sent it to a publisher. Rejection followed swiftly. Drowning one's heroine on the last page, she was informed, was not in line with the expectations of romance readers.

So Beverley became a journalist.

After a whirlwind romance with a handsome Norwegian bush pilot she met in Botswana's beautiful Okavango Delta, Beverley discovered what real romance was all about, saved her heroine from a watery grave in her next manuscript and published her first romance in 2009.

Since then, she's written more than fifteen sizzling historical romances laced with mystery and intrigue under the name Beverley Oakley.

She also writes psychological historical mysteries, and Colonial-Africa-set romantic suspense, as Beverley Eikli.

With an inspiring view of a Gothic nineteenth-century insane asylum across the road, Beverley lives north of Melbourne with her gorgeous husband, two lovely daughters and a rambunctious Rhodesian Ridgeback called Mombo, named after the safari lodge where she and her husband met.

You can read more at www.beverleyoakley.com

www.beverleyoakley.com
www.beverleyoakley.com
beverley.oakley@gmail.com